HARM
NOT THE
EARTH

HARM
NOT THE
EARTH

A Laurel Highlands Mystery

LIZ MILLIRON

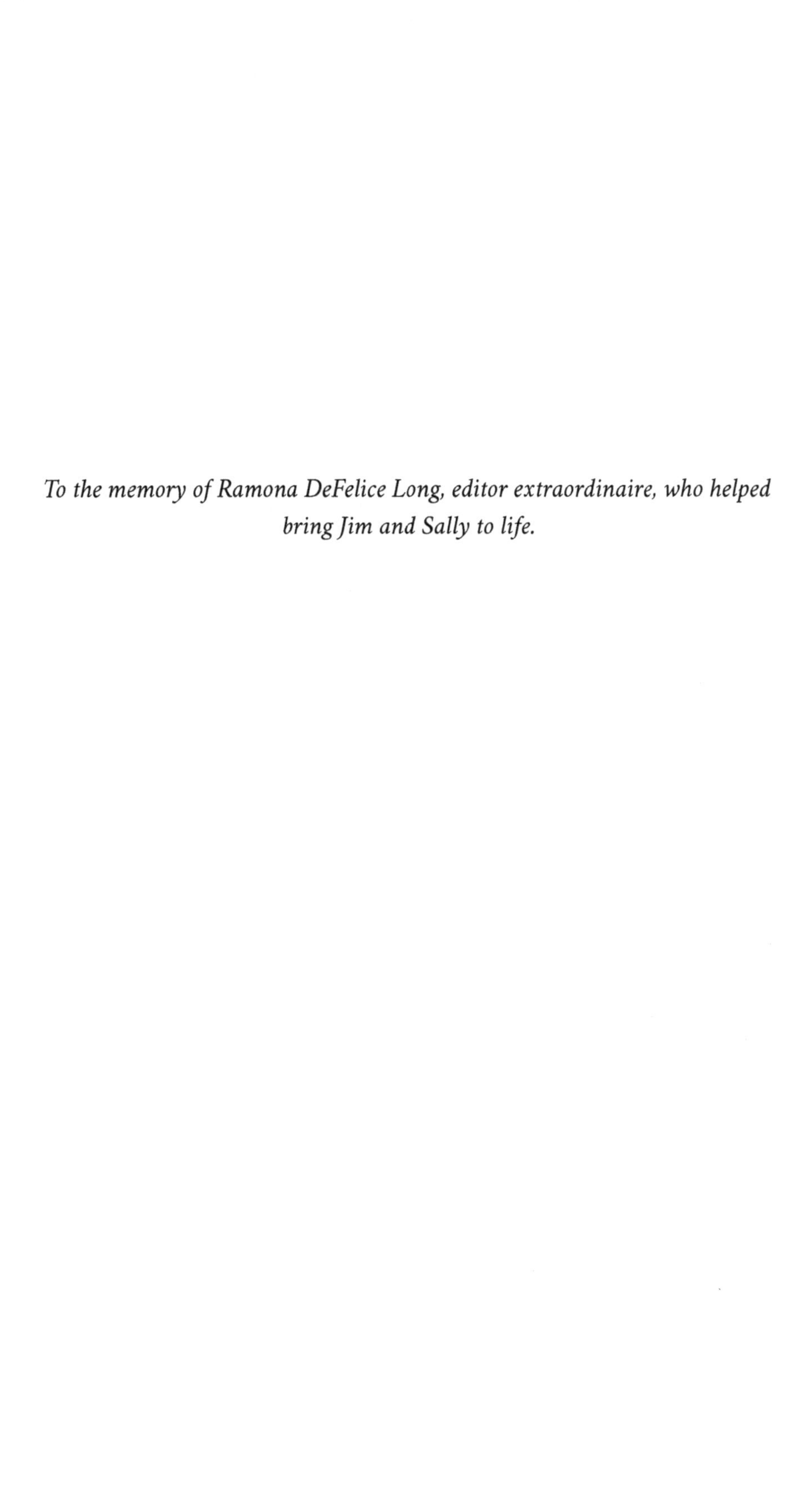

To the memory of Ramona DeFelice Long, editor extraordinaire, who helped bring Jim and Sally to life.

Praise for The Laurel Highlands Mystery Series

"Like fine wine, this series continues to get better with time, and you want to savor every sip. The prowess of the characters to do the right thing is evident in this well-written and executed mystery that immediately grabbed my attention. Two dead bodies, an accident or murder?, and an abused woman, how does she fit in?, set the tone for how well this story is being told. Both Jim and Sally looks for clues that will lead to the truth in this captivating drama where a web of deceit takes hold. The author does a great job in keeping me intrigued and in suspense as to how this will play out with each piece of the puzzle taking shape, that when completed will point to the person responsible. As usual, the visually descriptive narrative puts me in the middle of all the action with its engaging dialogue, the local setting, and a great cast of characters whose roles are pivotal in the telling of this tale. This is another great read in a terrific series. I look forward to the new adventures awaiting Duncan and Sally." - Dru Ann Love of Dru's Book Musings

For *Broken Trust*...

"State Trooper Jim Duncan and public defender Sally Castle make an irresistible crime-fighting duo in *Broken Trust*, the new mystery in Liz Milliron's Laurel Highlands series. Compelling; fast-paced; and filled with twists as Jim and Sally try to balance their jobs and their personal relationship while on the hunt for a killer in rustic Pennsylvania. Highly recommended." —R.G. Belsky, author of the Clare Carlson mystery series

Chapter One

Sally Castle leaned on the top railing of the footbridge that spanned the Casselman River and led to the business area of Confluence. The July sun pounded her head, making her grateful she wore oversized sunglasses and had remembered to load up on the sunscreen. Below her, the river surged brown and angry, whitecaps chasing each other on the surface, water lapping against the uppermost edge of the banks. Trees leaned at crazy angles and tickled the top of the river with low-hanging branches. "I don't think I've ever seen the water this high in July."

Jim Duncan moved to stand beside her and his shoulder brushed hers. "It's all the rain." He wrapped his arm around her shoulders and pulled her close.

Sally shivered, but not with cold. It had taken a year of dancing around each other, including surviving a fairly nasty reality check this past Memorial Day, when his job with the Pennsylvania State Police collided with hers as an assistant public defender in Fayette County. But she and Jim were finally an "item" as they said back in her high school days. Despite the fact she was well out of her teen years, his touch sent ripples of electricity down her skin. She leaned into him, enjoying the warmth of the closeness, even on the ninety-plus-degree summer day.

The river splashed at the bank, revealing a glimpse of bright pink. "What was that?" she asked as she straightened.

"What was what?"

Another flash of pink. "That." Sally pointed toward a spot a little upriver from the bridge. "I swear I saw something neon pink under that tree. The one right there, the big maple that looks like it might tip into the river."

Jim shaded his eyes. "I see it. The tree, not the pink. Could be a piece of debris from further upriver."

They walked back across the bridge to the footpath, where a man met them. He jerked his thumb toward the tree. "Hey, Jim. Glad I saw you. I think there's a problem."

"What?" Jim asked.

"I saw a bike early this morning. I recognized it as Lindy Hunter's and figured she was out on one of her photography jaunts. That was hours ago. Just came back through and the bike is still there."

"I don't see the problem."

"I can't find Lindy."

* * *

Duncan gave his keys to Sally and instructed her to go to his house, get his Jeep, and meet him by the gazebo in the middle of town. Then he double-timed it across the footbridge as he pushed the bike beside him. Once there, he spotted a group of adults gathered in front of the library and jogged over.

One of them, Tyler Yakanzyk, the owner of Confluence Cyclery, turned to greet him. "The man we wanted to see."

Duncan took in the somber faces of the group. "Does this have to do with Lindy Hunter?" It was serious, whatever it was. He'd seen more cheerful faces at a funeral home.

Yakanzyk glanced at the others. "She's missing. Left this morning to go bike riding and didn't come home for lunch. Where'd you find her bike?"

"I didn't. Someone else did and gave it to me. Could she have left it? I mean, kids miss meals all the time in the summer. Maybe she got distracted, lost track of time"

"Her mother said Lindy promised she'd be home. She's not the kind of kid to say one thing and do another. She's not responding to her cell phone, calls, or texts."

Duncan rubbed his chin. "Anyone call 911?"

"Not yet. Bob Hunter thinks we should look around ourselves first. He went out earlier, found nothing, and came back for help. Karen is at the house in case Lindy comes back."

Duncan rolled the pink bike over to Hunter, who stood off to the side, huddled with a few other guys looking at a map. "Hey, Bob. Lindy went out on her bike?"

"Yeah. She likes to go on the trails near the river. She's never pulled a stunt like this. She'll have some explaining to do when we find her."

A cold feeling settled on Duncan's shoulders. High water, abandoned bike, missing girl? Not a good combination. "Would she leave it behind?"

Hunter frowned. "No. She might lay it down or prop it against a tree while she was doing something, but she'd never walk away from it. She loves that bike." He looked at it. "What aren't you telling us, Jim?"

Duncan turned to Yakanzyk. "You should make that call to 911. Now."

Chapter Two

Sally pulled the Jeep into a parking space by the gazebo, Rizzo, Jim's Golden Retriever, in the passenger seat. A knot of people stood in front of the library, Jim in the middle. She got out, but hadn't taken two steps when Jim hurried over. "What's wrong?" she asked.

"Lindy Hunter is missing. Get in." He took the keys and slid behind the steering wheel. "You brought the doofus? Why?" He pushed Rizzo into the back seat to make room for Sally.

She got in and buckled her seat belt. "When I opened the door to the Jeep he leapt in. I figured it would be less of a hassle to bring him instead of fighting to get him back inside."

"You're right about that. Besides, he might be useful."

"Who's Lindy Hunter?"

"Local girl." Duncan spun the steering wheel and headed south, following the Casselman River. "She's ten or eleven, if I remember. Her dad, Bob, said she went out on her bike this morning and promised to be home by noon. She didn't come back and they can't get in touch with her."

Sally sobered. "The pink bike?"

"We've called the authorities and we're going to search in the meantime. Bob said she was biking down by the river. Budding photographer. She likes to take pictures of the flowers and grasses and stuff."

"Isn't that kind of dangerous with the water so high?" She pushed Rizzo, who'd stuck his head between the seats, into the back seat again.

"Yes. You've seen my backyard. Water gets high, soaks the ground…it gets slippery. If she climbed down the embankment to get a picture, she could have slid into the river. If she went in the water…Bob says she's a good swimmer, but with the current running this fast I don't want to think about it." Jim reached a small grassy area and parked. He reached in the back and handed Sally a leash. "Clip this on Rizzo."

Sally got out of the Jeep, got Rizzo, and put the leash on the wriggling dog. "He's not trained in search and rescue, is he?"

Jim removed a radio from the back of the Jeep. "No, but he might see or smell something that interests him and lead us in the right direction. Let's go that way." He pointed up the river.

They walked in silence for almost five minutes, listening to the sound of the rushing water, the birds, some buzzing cicadas, and Rizzo's snuffling as he joyfully explored the trail. Suddenly, Jim paused. "You hear that?"

Sally strained to listen. A faint, thin cry reached her ears. "I think so. It could be a voice calling for help. Sounds like it's coming from that clump of trees."

The two adults and the dog headed toward the trees. As they got closer, the sound intensified. It was definitely a child's voice, faded with fatigue and fear. Suddenly, Rizzo barked and ran to the river's edge, pulling Sally behind him.

A young girl floated in the water, clinging to a mass of tree limbs and wood jumbled together. Sally saw at once it was too far for the girl to crawl to the shore. As it was, every time she moved, the wood creaked and the pile threatened to disintegrate, which would send child and wood tumbling downriver. Sally took a step toward the edge, but scrambled backward as the dirt collapsed under her weight.

Jim grabbed her arm and pulled her back. "Careful! We don't need two victims."

Sally made sure of her footing, then cupped her hands around her mouth. "Lindy? Lindy! Over here, sweetie. Look over here."

The child turned her head, bedraggled blonde hair floating on the water. "Please help me! I can't hold on."

Jim scanned the ground. "There's no way I can swim out there. Current's too fast and the water's too high. And if I try to use that fallen wood to support me, I'll tear the whole thing to bits." He took a step toward the water. "Lindy, it's Mr. Duncan. Can you hear me?"

"Yeah."

"I know you're tired and you want to let go, but I need you to hang on for a couple more minutes, okay? I need some stuff from my Jeep and we'll get you out of there." He pulled the keys out of his pocket and handed them to Sally. "Here, go—"

"Get the Jeep and come back. Got it." She tugged the leash. "Come on, buddy. We gotta be the cavalry." She and the dog ran off, leaving Jim kneeling on the river bank, shouting encouragement to Lindy.

She didn't know what Jim wanted, but it must be something that could help. She ran to the grassy area where they'd left the SUV, jumped in, and drove to where they'd seen the child. "Now what?" she said when she parked.

Jim stood. "Back it up until I tell you to stop." He waved to Sally as she inched toward him, then held up his hand. "That's good. Turn it off and come here."

Sally got out, left Rizzo in the Jeep, and went around the back. "I assume you have a plan."

Jim turned, arms full of a length of nylon rope and a life vest. "I'm gonna tie the rope around this vest and toss it to Lindy. If she can grab it, we can pull her to shore. I need you to tie the other end around the trailer hitch of the Jeep. No granny knots."

She yanked the rope out of his hands. "Don't worry, Mr. Boy Scout. I know how to tie a knot." As Jim fastened one end to the life vest, she looped the other around the hitch, securing it with two half-hitch knots, trying to ignore the sobs of the girl behind her. "All set." She straightened and brushed her hands together.

Jim had finished with the life vest and inspected her work. "Nice." Then he picked his way to the edge of the river, staying on the firm ground. "Lindy. I'm going to throw this to you. When it's close, you need to grab it and hold on. Understand?"

Lindy looked over. "I don't think I can. I'm too scared."

"I know you are. But you can do this. I have faith in you," Jim said. His voice projected calm and confidence.

Sally knelt on the ground. "You got this, Lindy. We're going to help you, but you have to help us, too. You focus on me and the rope, and we'll get you home."

Lindy's pale face gleamed against the dark water, hair plastered to her cheek and forehead. "I'll try."

"Good girl." Sally looked over at Jim. "Go."

The first throw sailed over Lindy's head. The second landed at least four feet short. "Damn it," Jim said as he pulled the vest in for another attempt.

"She's tired, Jim." Sally looked at the girl. "Do you want me to try?"

"Give me one more shot, then yes." He exhaled then sent the vest flying. This time it landed on the jumble of wood, near Lindy's hand. "Grab the vest with your left hand," Jim said. "Then let go and grab it with your right."

"What if the rope breaks?" Lindy asked, voice weak and trembly.

"It won't." Jim grabbed the line and motioned for Sally to pick it up as well. "That's a good, strong knot and this is new rope. You hang on, and Ms. Castle and I will pull you ashore. On the count of three. One...two...three!"

Lindy scrabbled for the bright yellow floatation device. Water splashed and for a moment her head was lost to view as she was submerged in the river. After an agonizing amount of time, which was probably only a second, she surfaced, spitting water, but the vest was clutched to her chest.

"Pull." Jim and Sally pulled the rope in hand over hand. Lindy was a heavy weight on the end of the line, dragging against the current. It felt like forever, but the girl finally bumped up against the shore and lay there, sobbing.

"Sally, I'll hold the rope." Jim nodded toward Lindy. "Don't let go, but get down there and help her up. Carefully. I don't need both of you sliding back down."

Rope in hand, Sally crept to the water's edge, shoes squelching in the water-soaked ground. Once or twice her feet slipped and she heard Jim's muttered profanity, but each time she righted herself. As soon as she reached Lindy, she put her arm around the girl's thin, shaking shoulders and led her to safety.

Jim met them at the Jeep with a blanket, which he draped around Lindy and rubbed warmth into her arms. Rizzo pushed his way through the adults to lick Lindy's hands and arms. "I told you we'd get you back. You did a great job, Lindy. Your mom and dad will be proud of you."

Lindy sniffled. "I'm scared, Mr. Duncan."

Sally untied the rope, coiled it, and deposited the gear in the cargo area. Her sneakers were a mess, but she'd worry about them later, after they returned the frightened girl to her parents. She pulled another blanket out of the Jeep and handed it to Jim. "The other one is wet."

Jim took the replacement and exchanged it for the soaked one. Then he hugged Lindy and continued to rub her dry. "It's all over. You don't have to worry about it anymore."

She pulled away. "No, you don't understand." She wiped her face with the back of her hand. "I saw a man in the river. He wasn't moving. I think he's dead."

* * *

Duncan drove back to the main square. By tacit agreement, he and Sally didn't discuss Lindy's statement, although they had shared a quizzical look when they first heard it. A body? Maybe, but Duncan couldn't quite bring himself to believe it. The rain had been intense, but not *that* intense. In her panic, Lindy most likely saw a half-submerged log or battered tree that tricked her eyes. That's all.

Still, he wondered. The cop in him wanted to question Lindy right away. But firing questions at a child minutes after a traumatic experience would not be right. Better to let her calm down, let the recollection be clear. After all, the PSP had waited three days to question him after he shot someone. If it worked for adults, why not kids? After a night's sleep, she might decide she was wrong.

In the backseat, Rizzo followed his canine instincts, draped himself over the shaking, sodden young girl, and smothered her with affection.

Next to him, Sally called ahead to the bike shop, alerting those still in the square that Lindy Hunter was safe and on her way back to her parents.

The crowd had returned to the gazebo and Duncan spotted Bob Hunter and his wife, Karen, pacing in front of the municipal building.

"Lindy!" Karen bolted toward the Jeep as soon as Duncan parked and opened the door.

Lindy scrambled out of the back. "Mom! Dad!" She crashed into both parents and broke into tears.

Hunter clapped Duncan on the shoulder. "I can't thank you enough."

Duncan looked around for Rizzo, who'd jumped out after Lindy, but Sally already had him well in hand. "Don't mention it. This is the good part of my job." He pulled Hunter away from the others. "Hey, when we got her out, Lindy said she saw a body in the river. I'm pretty sure what she saw was a fallen log, but keep an eye on her, okay? I'm going to make some calls just in case. Let me know if she says anything else or if you think I can help."

Hunter nodded and returned to his family.

Sally pushed Rizzo into the Jeep, then closed the door. "You really think—"

"Shh. Not here. Let's go home." They waved and headed toward Duncan's house.

They pulled in and as soon as he opened the car door, Rizzo scrambled out and bolted to the back. Duncan and Sally followed. Once in the kitchen, Duncan poured a glass of merlot for Sally and opened a bottle of Edmund Fitzgerald stout for himself.

Sally accepted the glass and sat at the table. "Did she see a body or not?"

"You don't beat around the bush, do you?" Duncan leaned against the countertop and took a long pull from the beer. "Realistically? I doubt it. She was terrified and the mind will create all sorts of horrors when you're in that state. That's true for adults, never mind eleven-year-old kids."

"Except…"

Duncan stared into the middle distance and rolled the bottle between his hands. "I'd be remiss if I didn't check. See if any missing persons have been reported in this area or nearby. Maybe McAllister knows something." He grabbed his phone and called the young trooper, but almost immediately received a text response that she couldn't talk. He sent her a message to call him, then focused on Sally. "Would you do me a favor?"

She grinned and shook her head. "Yes, I'll check with my sources at the courthouse and see what I can find." She set her glass on the table, came over, and wrapped her arms around his waist. "You're a good egg, Jim Duncan. Did you know that?"

"So I've been told." He set aside the bottle and placed his hands on her hips.

She smiled, then sobered. "What happens if we do find a missing person?"

"We'll cross that bridge when we come to it. So tell me. Where'd you learn to tie such a good half-hitch?"

A coy look came into her eyes. "I figured if I was going to be hanging out with you a lot, it could come in handy." She let go of his waist, grabbed his hands, and pulled. "Come upstairs and I'll show you what else I've learned."

Chapter Three

The first thing Sally noticed when she pulled into Jim's driveway around six on Monday evening was a column of smoke rising from the backyard. The second thing was the tantalizing aroma that greeted her when she opened the door of her Toyota.

She followed her nose and found him standing over a charcoal grill, Rizzo at his feet. "Smells delicious. No wonder Rizzo didn't come and greet me." She gave Jim a quick kiss, then inspected the contents of the grill, a piece of salmon on a wood plank, and several vegetable kebobs.

He turned the skewers. "Cedar-planked salmon, grilled veggies, and inside is a loaf of fresh sourdough with butter."

Any other thoughts left her mind. "I'll go and set the table."

"You do that."

Rizzo didn't follow her indoors, not that she blamed him. She dropped her purse on the counter by the door and quickly set the table, first inhaling the scent of the fresh bread.

Jim came in a few minutes later, Rizzo hot on his heels. "Coming through, make a hole." He deposited the fish and vegetables on the table.

There was little conversation as Sally savored the delicate taste of the salmon and the perfection of the kebabs. She cut her third slice of bread and slathered it with butter. "And here I was going to suggest dinner at River's Edge."

He drained the beer from his glass. "I picked up the salmon today. Use it while it's fresh, right?"

"That doesn't look like your usual drink."

"It's not." He speared the last bit of salmon. "Stouts and porters are too heavy. This is a pilsner. Pairing beer isn't that different than pairing wine, you know."

She shrugged and turned her attention back to the food. Once done, they cleaned up, then went to sit in Jim's Adirondack chairs on the porch while Rizzo flopped on the floor in front of them. "Okay, before I fall into a food coma, did you find any missing persons reports locally?" she asked.

"Not a one." He drummed his fingers on the chair's arm. "I even checked the areas upriver in case the body floated downstream. You?"

"Nothing. You must be right. Lindy didn't see what she thought." Sally glanced at him. "Why don't you have a swing out here?"

"I'd have to fix the ceiling and beams first. They aren't strong enough to hold the weight."

Sally looked up, then turned her head. "Who's coming down the street? He looks like he has a purpose."

"Bob Hunter." Jim got up and went to the porch steps to meet his neighbor. "Bob, something wrong?"

Hunter reached Jim's yard and stopped. "You said if I needed anything to talk to you. Well, I'm talking to you."

"Sure, what's going on? Come on up."

"It's Lindy." Bob came to the stairs and ran a hand through his already messy hair. "The nightmares last night, God…Jim I've never seen her like that. She swears she saw a dead man in that river. I hoped you could come talk to her, either help her get it out of her system or check things out if she sounds legit to you."

Jim glanced back at Sally.

She stood. "Do you want me to put Rizzo inside or get his leash?"

"The latter," Jim told her. "Petting animals helps folks relax, especially kids."

They walked the short distance to the Hunter residence, a small, plain box-like house on Yough Street. Bob's wife sat with Lindy in the living room. No longer wet and shivering, Lindy retained her pale, terrorized look.

"Sally, I don't think you've been introduced to my wife, Karen." Bob waved at the woman. "Lindy, look who's here. Rizzo."

Sally let go of the leash, letting the Golden Retriever go straight to Lindy and snuffle her shirt. Lindy giggled in response.

"That's the first laugh I've heard from her in twenty-four hours," Bob said in an undertone.

Jim crossed the living room to kneel in front of the child. "Hey, Lindy. Your dad said you had a rough night."

She looked up, blue-gray eyes huge above pale purple smudges. "They don't believe me, Mr. Duncan. But I saw him. A dead man. I'm not a little kid. I know the difference between a person and a log."

Jim shot a look at Sally. "Why don't you tell me about it?"

Lindy took a deep breath. "It wasn't long after I fell in. See, I'd gone over to the Casselman on my bike. I was gonna take some pictures 'cause I thought the water might wash up some interesting stuff. I got too close to the edge. I guess the dirt was too wet and I slid." She paused.

"Go on," Jim said.

"I tried to remember what Dad said to do if I ever fell in, but the water was real fast. This thing floated by me and I reached out, thinking it was a log. But it was a man. I pushed away from him and he kinda rolled over. His face was all blue and puffy."

Probably from being in the water so long, Sally thought. A question came to mind, but she bit her lip. This was Jim's show. The parents wouldn't appreciate their girl being bombarded with questions from a stranger.

"Do you remember what he was wearing?" Jim asked.

Lindy frowned. "A plaid shirt, I remember that, dark. Brown pants. I didn't see his feet."

"Did he have a tie that you saw?"

"No," she drew out the word, "but I don't *think* he had one."

"What did he look like? I mean, could you tell his skin or hair color?"

"He was white, I think. He had red hair."

"Okay." Jim rubbed her arm. "Can you show me where you fell in? Or point to it if I give you a map?"

Lindy nodded.

Sally watched the entire interaction without speaking. This is what made Jim so good at his job. He focused all his attention on Lindy and kept his voice calm, soothing, yet not condescending. He met her at her eye level instead of towering over her. At that moment, Lindy had to feel important, that her issue was the single most important thing Jim would take care of that day. Sally knew that's how she'd feel if she were in the young girl's shoes.

"Do you know how to read a topographic map, Lindy?" Jim asked.

"Yeah. Dad taught me how. I use one to mark all the good places for pictures and stuff."

Jim looked up. "Do you have one?"

Bob Hunter nodded.

"Would you get it, please?" Bob fetched a map of the area and Jim spread it in front of Lindy. "Where'd you see this man?"

Lindy studied it for a moment. "Well, I fell in here." She touched a spot. "I'd only drifted for a few minutes maybe before he passed me, so here maybe? I'm not sure." She pointed to another spot.

"That's great, Lindy. Good job." Jim handed the paper back to Lindy's dad.

"You believe me, don't you Mr. Duncan? You gotta believe me. I'm not lying."

Jim knelt again. "I believe you and I'm going to look to see what I can find. You want me to tell your Mom and Dad when I finish?"

"Yes, please." Lindy gave a tiny smile. "Thanks, Mr. Duncan."

Jim stood, met Sally's gaze, and jerked his head in the direction of the front door, indicating she should follow. She tugged Rizzo's leash, smiled at Karen Hunter, then left. The men stood in the front yard, Bob Hunter clearly worried, Jim's expression neutral, yet compassionate. "Confluence being in Somerset County, it's technically not my investigation, but Sally and I will take Rizzo down and poke around. Based on where Lindy says she saw this body, I think I know where it would end up, even if she's a little off in her description of the place, which she may well be."

Bob glanced at Sally. "I hate to waste your time."

"You're not wasting our time, Mr. Hunter," Sally said. "If it'll set Lindy's mind at ease, it's worth it. And if she did see a body, finding it might put someone else at peace, too."

Bob's answering smile looked grim. "You mean whoever's missing him, if anyone."

Sally shared a look with Jim. "Well," she said, "not to put too fine a point on it, but yes."

Chapter Four

Back in the Jeep, Duncan glanced at the dashboard. Eight o'clock. At least an hour of sunlight remained, which meant there was plenty of time to check the river. If he went immediately. No reason to delay.

Sally settled beside him and fastened her seatbelt. "Do you believe her? Lindy?"

"Don't you?"

Sally considered a moment. "Yes. She's a good witness. No hysterics, no confusion when she tells her story. A day later she still says she saw a body and, considering her age, her recollection is very detailed. She's compelling and credible. I've deposed adult witnesses who didn't come across as well."

"I agree. I can take you back to the house if you'd like." He put the Jeep in gear. "But Doofus and I are headed to the river to look around. I don't have enough to justify calling out a search team, but this is my town. I can poke around if I want to."

"I'm going. You really think Rizzo will find anything?"

"He has a curious nose and a knack for finding interesting, smelly objects. What's more interesting and smelly than a dead body?"

Minutes later, he parked in the same grassy area near where they'd pulled Lindy Hunter out of the water. After consulting a topo map he had in the Jeep, he took hold of Rizzo's leash, and the three of them walked downriver. "Based on the water level, what I know of the Casselman's current, and Lindy's account, we're looking at a fairly small search area." He shook Rizzo's lead as the dog headed for a pile of garbage, pulling him back on task.

Sally walked beside him, staying well away from the water. "You think it caught on something downstream from where we found Lindy?"

"Yes. Otherwise, we'd have seen the corpse when we pulled her out." He whistled and tugged Rizzo away from a pile of rotting vegetation. "Come on, you. That's not what we're looking for."

They walked for several minutes. Rizzo found a ton of stinky things that excited his canine senses. Swampy water, dead fish, garbage, even a half-rotted squirrel carcass. But no human remains. Duncan was about to call off the search for the day when Rizzo became intensely excited about a jumbled mass of sticks, garbage, and debris stuck on a spur of the embankment. No amount of tugging would deter him. Duncan gave up and headed for the target area.

"I'll stay here and hold Rizzo," Sally said. "If it's a secondary crime scene, no use two of us mucking things up."

These were the moments when he truly appreciated Sally's knowledge of criminal law. He picked his way toward the pile of wood, placing his feet carefully to avoid slipping and ending up in the water. He didn't have gloves, so he picked up a stick to prod the area, cursing his lack of foresight.

"See anything?" Sally called to him.

"Not yet. Hold on." Abandoning the stick, Duncan pushed aside some of the soggy wood, valiantly attempting not to destroy what evidence there might be. He caught sight of a pale blob.

Sally tied the leash to a sturdy tree and picked her way over. "Did you find something? What is it?"

"I don't know." He pushed aside some more garbage. He spotted a long, tan slab. A leg in khaki pants, ending in a foot still wearing a quality hiking boot. Plaid shirt, liberally streaked with mud. The pale smudge was the hand, protruding from the shirtsleeve. "Your phone have service?"

"Yeah, why?"

Duncan let the wood, leaves, and trash fall back into place. "We need to call the state police. And a coroner."

* * *

After Duncan made all the appropriate phone calls, he sent Sally back to his house with Rizzo while he guarded the scene. Techs swarmed the river bank area, the deputy coroner worked over the corpse, and a state police trooper went into Confluence to interview Lindy Hunter and her family.

It was a familiar situation, but at the same time it wasn't. The trooper working the scene was not Aislyn McAllister or Alan Porter or any of the familiar faces from the Uniontown barracks. Corporal Henry Travers out of Somerset was competent and brusque, and extended Duncan some professional courtesy, but little else. As soon as Travers introduced himself, Duncan remembered him. Amber Alert, a young boy gone missing from his Fayette County home who turned up with his step-father in a Somerset County gas station. The boy had insisted he didn't want to go with the step-father. The man said the child was exaggerating. Travers had sided with the adult, Duncan with the kid. When all was said and done, Duncan's faith in the child had been rewarded. Back then, it hadn't been *Corporal* Travers. Duncan wondered if Travers remembered that incident.

The deputy coroner was not Tom Burns, with his usual mordant humor, but a middle-aged woman who answered every one of Duncan's questions with a waspish "We won't know until the autopsy." At least that was her answer until she simply stopped responding. Instinct led him to pull out his phone, zoom in, and snap his own picture of the dead man. The pale, bloated, bearded face looked familiar and unfamiliar at the same time. Before Duncan could take another picture, the deputy coroner stepped around the body, impeding his view.

Out of the corner of his eye, Duncan caught sight of Travers, returning from his interview with Lindy Hunter. "Learn anything?"

"What a waste of time." Travers hooked his thumbs in his duty belt and stared at the deputy coroner, now zipping the body and a sample of surrounding water and debris into a body bag. "The girl is useless."

Duncan bristled. "She's a kid. She's not useless. In fact, when I talked to her earlier, she seemed pretty put together."

"You have low expectations for a child witness. Same as always."

Guess he does remember. Duncan made a note to follow up with the Hunters later. "What did she say?"

Travers shrugged. "Not much more than what you told me. I pressed her for confirmation and that's when she started stuttering, suddenly wasn't sure of things, maybe she didn't see what she thought she did, yada, yada." He waved a hand. "You know how it goes."

"Were her parents there?"

"Yeah, her dad."

"You were calm and understanding, of course. Adjusted your questioning to suit her age?"

Travers turned. "I questioned a witness, like I have about a million times. You may live in this town, Trooper First Class Duncan, but I do know how to do my job." The way Travers stressed Duncan's rank made it plain he didn't want help. Especially not from a man he'd opposed in the past and been proved wrong.

Duncan thought about mentioning the victim seemed familiar, but decided to stay silent. He wasn't sure and speculation wouldn't help Travers's attitude. Especially if it turned out to be a wild goose chase.

Travers hmph-ed and called to the deputy coroner, who jockeyed the heavily laden body bag onto a gurney. "Miriam. Immediate observations?"

She instructed two techs to wheel the gurney to the waiting coroner's van and, peeling off her surgical gloves, walked over to the troopers. "As I keep saying, we won't know anything until we perform a full autopsy. However. I suspect, from the condition of the body, he's been in the water for a while, maybe as long as twenty-four hours or even longer. The skin of his fingers is wrinkled and I expect to find the same on his feet. The water is cool, which would slow decomp, but the various river scavengers have had a start on him. I saw no signs of violence, no stab or gunshot wounds. No petechial hemorrhaging that would indicate strangulation, no ligature marks. No defensive wounds. Beyond that, I'm not prepared to say anything." She shot Duncan a disapproving stare.

"Can I see the victim?" Duncan asked. It would at least put his suspicions to rest.

Miriam scowled. "You should have said something earlier. I'm not opening that body bag now and risking the water sample running out of it."

"Did he have ID?" Travers asked.

"None," the woman said. "No wallet, no keys, no spare change. No wedding band. A John Doe." She sniffed. "You want anything else, we'll probably get to the autopsy tomorrow."

Travers took off his hat and wiped sweat from his forehead. "I'll catch up with you on that." The woman walked off and he turned to Duncan. "For all we know, the dead guy was fishing for smallmouth, slipped, and drowned."

Duncan thought back to the body and his observations of the clothes. "He wore good boots, khakis, and a button-down. No hip waders, no fishing vest. None of the gear I'd expect to see. Besides, the water is way too high to fish safely."

"How would you know?"

Duncan fixed his compatriot with a calm stare. "I fish."

Travers's face reddened a bit and he coughed. "Could be some city guy who doesn't know his ass from his elbow when it comes to fishing."

Duncan inclined his head. "Possible."

"It's a hell of a weekend for pulling victims out of the Casselman, I'll tell you that much."

"Another dead body?"

"Not dead, but not in good shape." Travers settled his hat. "We found a guy Saturday a mile or so outside of Rockwood. Who knows how long he was in the river. Took him to Somerset Hospital. At least that one had ID, Carl Ritchie of Markleton."

"He say anything?"

"Nah, he was unconscious when they found him. As of this morning, there hasn't been any change in his condition." Travers studied the whitecaps that lapped at the edge of the embankment and tickled overhanging tree limbs "Water level looks high down here, too. Damn rain."

"Been a record-setting month, that's for sure." Carl Ritchie. Duncan knew that name. From where? "Downstream or upstream from Rockwood?"

"Down."

"You need anything else?"

"No. If I have any questions, I'll be in touch. Uniontown barracks you said?"

"Yes. If you can't reach me, talk to Lieutenant Dan Nicols. He'll be able to find me anywhere. Good luck." Duncan hiked back toward Confluence. Sally had taken the Jeep, but one of the things he liked about his town was how easily he could walk to any destination.

John Doe might be a clueless city-boy fisherman, down for the day, and had a horrible stroke of bad luck. But Duncan's sixth sense, honed by nearly fourteen years of service, said otherwise.

Chapter Five

Tuesday morning, Sally sat in her basement office at the Fayette County Courthouse and listened to the slow roll of thunder. The day brought a return of the torrential storms that had hammered the region for the last couple of weeks. Hopefully it wouldn't bring another body. Jim told her about Carl Ritchie, the man found near Rockwood, and she agreed with his assessment. Two men found in the Casselman in the same week was too much of a coincidence to ignore.

She had some free time that morning, so she searched for any information on Ritchie. Forty years old and a resident of Somerset, he worked at a lumber mill and volunteered with the Casselman Water Preservation Society. He'd been with the CWPS for years, his work cited in several outdoors-related articles in local media as "instrumental" in the upswing in smallmouth bass fishing associated with the cleanup efforts along the river. She paused at a photo of Ritchie with two other men, posing near a bend of water and a newly cleaned portion of the Casselman. According to the caption, the second man's name was Mike Brower, another long-time volunteer at the CWPS. She hadn't gotten a close look at the face of the corpse they'd found, and prolonged exposure to water could distort a person's features, but she swore there was a resemblance.

Then she noticed the third man in the picture. Jim. But he hadn't indicated he'd known either victim. The date on the story was from three years ago. Who knew how many people he'd encountered since then and if he'd only met them this once, it was hardly surprising he hadn't recognized them. The picture might jog his memory. She sent a link to the story to her phone so she could show him later.

She glanced at the clock. Crap. Five minutes to make it up to Judge Rankin's chambers for a plea bargain hearing. She chugged the last of her coffee, swept her papers into her briefcase, and headed for the elevator.

Once she got off the elevator, she quick-stepped toward her destination when a familiar voice stopped her in her tracks.

"Sally Castle, I've been looking for you. Long time no see."

Sally turned to see a short, vivacious redhead. The demure pencil skirt and white blouse covering her curvy frame were model business attire, but the twinkle in her brown eyes was pure mischief. "Kim? Good grief, it's been what, ten years?"

"At least that." Kimberly Dunphy set down her dark brown briefcase and gave Sally an enthusiastic hug.

"How'd you find me? I know, stupid question." Sally and Kim had been law school classmates, both focusing on criminal law. After graduation, they lost touch. Sally headed for the Allegheny County District Attorney's office and Kim took off for parts unknown.

"It wasn't hard. The DA's office in Allegheny County said you'd come down here and from that point it was easy-peasy. Everybody in this courthouse seems to know you and have a story." Kim laughed. "Come on, I'll buy you breakfast and we can catch up."

Sally glanced at her watch. "I'd love to. But I'm due in chambers in, like, two minutes and Judge Rankin will roast me if I'm late."

"Okay, lunch. I'm not going to take no for an answer. You know me."

Sally did, in fact, know her old classmate. Kim's reputation for getting what she wanted was legendary in law school. It couldn't have changed much in the intervening years. "Lunch is good. Either meet me in the foyer on the main floor at noon or meet me at a place called Dex's. It's not far from here."

"Dex's, noon. I'll be there. Ta." Kim walked away, then turned. "Oh, Sally. Bring an open mind. Because I have a proposition for you that I know you'll want to say yes to as soon as you have the scoop." She sashayed toward the elevator and punched the button.

Sally stood transfixed. What the hell did that mean? She glanced at her watch. Shit. Judge Rankin was going to kill her.

***

Duncan detoured from his Tuesday morning patrol duties to head into Uniontown. Confluence wasn't in the Uniontown barracks response area, but part of being the "local cop" was taking care of things that happened in the town. John Doe might as well have washed up in Duncan's backyard. That and he couldn't shake the feeling that he should recognize the bearded face. Unfortunately, he didn't know anybody in the Somerset County coroner's office, which might make getting information tricky if the deputy coroner from the scene was any indication. But Duncan knew someone who might give him a hand with that.

Once inside the Fayette County coroner's office, he headed toward the noise of a saw and a babble of voices. He breathed in the faint scent of burning bone and he stopped outside the autopsy area. Deputy Coroner Tom Burns set aside the saw and popped the skull cap off the body of a flabby male corpse. As the pathologist extracted the brain, Burns caught sight of Duncan. Burns shrugged, pointed with his chin, then nodded to the wall. The message was clear: I'm busy. Go wait in my office.

Duncan obliged, sat at Burns's desk, and flipped through the pages of a comic magazine while he waited.

Perhaps thirty minutes later, Burns appeared in the doorway. "Get your feet off my desk and unhand my reading material." He took the magazine back, set it on a pile, and examined the desktop for dirt.

Duncan stood and moved aside. "Really? Is that how you greet a friend?"

Burns sat and swept microscopic debris from the desktop. "You should know better. This is my personal workspace. I've told you before, I have standards and those include cleanliness and organization at my desk."

"I've seen you with your feet in the same place."

"Yes, but they're mine," Burns replied in a lofty tone. "Now. How can I be of service?"

Duncan ran down the discovery of the John Doe. "I've used up all the time I had waiting for you, but I'm interested in the autopsy results."

Burns reached for a pile of folders. "I don't recall any potential drowning victims coming through here."

"It wouldn't have. Everything would have been handled through the Somerset County coroner."

Burns lifted his eyebrows. "So call them."

"The barracks in Somerset handled the call. Strictly speaking, I'm a bystander on this one."

If possible, Burns raised his eyebrows higher. "Why would you think I can help you?"

Duncan leaned on a filing cabinet and grinned. "Why not? Don't all you coroners and medical examiners talk to each other? Like a fraternity or something?"

"There is a Pennsylvania Coroners Association and, yes, we do get together. Educational events and whatnot." Burns leaned back and his chair squeaked. "Did you get the name of the deputy coroner at the scene?"

"Miriam something. She didn't talk much."

Burns's eyes took on a resigned look. "Middle-aged, graying brown hair, no makeup, medium height, about twenty pounds overweight?"

"Uh, yeah, that sounds about right."

Burns winced. "I'm afraid I won't be of much help, sorry." At Duncan's unspoken question, Burns continued. "Miriam Goldman. We met at the last educational seminar. She wasn't impressed with my level of decorum and intimated she was glad I worked in a different county, so she only had to see me a couple times a year."

"Aw, hell, Burns."

"Hey, how was I to know the lady had no sense of humor?"

"You're impossible."

"Yeah, Ace tells me that all the time." Burns sat up and pulled out a book, some kind of directory by the look of it. "All is not lost. Let me see what I can do."

"Thanks." Duncan clapped the younger man on the shoulder.

"Yeah, well, it's gonna cost you."

"Cost me what?"

Burns flipped another couple of pages in the directory. "I don't know. But it will."

Chapter Six

Shortly before noon, Sally gathered up her purse and umbrella. On her way out, she stopped at Doris's desk. "Hey, would you do me a favor?"

The secretary looked up. "That depends on what the favor is."

"I need a listing of all missing persons reports for Fayette and Somerset counties for, let's say, the last week."

"Why on earth would you need that?"

Sally told Doris about the body found in Confluence on Monday. "I'd like to put a name with a face."

Doris gave her a knowing smile. "You or your beau?"

Sally shrugged. "Both, I guess." She headed for the door, then stopped. "Oh, and if the name Mike Brower comes up, highlight it, please? Thanks, Doris." She left without waiting for a response.

Outside, it had stopped raining, so she decided to tempt fate and walk to Dex's. Once inside, it wasn't hard to spot Kim's red hair. She'd snagged a table for two and was studying the menu, a glass of white wine in front of her. Sally threaded her way through the crowd and pulled out the chair opposite her old classmate. "I see you didn't have any trouble finding the place." She sat, caught the attention of a passing waitress, and asked for a glass of water. "Have you been waiting long?"

"Long enough to salivate over half the options on the lunch menu." Kim raised her eyebrows as the waitress returned with Sally's drink. "Water? What did you do with Sally Castle? I thought you were a red wine girl."

"Not when I'm on the county's clock." Well, most of the time.

"Funny you should say that because it touches directly on what I wanted to talk to you about." Kim returned her attention to the menu. "But first, what's your favorite at this place?"

"Depending on my mood, I tend to go with either the bacon cheeseburger or the Pittsburgh salad with grilled chicken. I have it on very good authority the Reuben sandwich is excellent." Sally's gaze flicked over the lunch menu. What did being on the county's time have to do with anything? She knew better than to ask Kim, whose knack for dramatic flair meant she wouldn't say anything until she was good and ready.

The women studied their menus for a couple of minutes, the only conversation a brief debate on the dietary merits of lean meats. The waitress returned. "What the hell." Kim tossed aside the menu. "I'll have the Reuben with a side of sweet potato fries."

"I'm going to go out of my norm and have a Cuban with the house chips, please." Sally handed the menu to the waitress, who scribbled their orders and left. "All right. Let's skip the social niceties. Why the sudden urge to see me? Our next class reunion isn't for two years and you haven't been burning up my phone lines."

Kim sipped her wine and appeared to dodge the question. "How's work?"

Sally sighed, not bothering to hide it. "Work's great. I like my boss, I'm doing meaningful stuff, I get along with my coworkers and colleagues at the district attorney's office."

"Public defense is a step down from prosecution, you have to admit. I was sure you'd be DA in Allegheny County one day. Your ability to argue a case was something to watch."

"It's only a step down if you look at it that way." Sally unwrapped her silverware and laid the napkin in her lap. "True, it's not as glamorous as prosecution. And yes, there does tend to be a revolving door of clients, at least sometimes it seems that way. But if you're looking to fulfill the spirit of the law, as well as the letter, it can be great. Some of the people I represent, well, they might be guilty, but there's satisfaction in knowing you protected their legal rights and made sure they got a fair shake instead of a bum deal."

Kim studied her over the edge of the wineglass. "Pay's not great, though, right?"

"There's more to job satisfaction than a fat paycheck."

The sandwiches arrived and Kim was silent while the waitress laid down the plates. When they were alone again, Kim said, "What if you could have both? Job satisfaction and the paycheck?" She took a bite of the Reuben. "You weren't kidding. This is good."

Kim was obviously hinting around something and Sally's gut instinct knew what. But she also had no intention of giving Kim the satisfaction of hearing a plea for information. Instead, Sally focused on her sandwich and the chips, which were the perfect blend of grease, salt, and crispness. "Glad you like it."

After a couple of minutes, Kim's desire to be questioned apparently lost out to her need to spill her news. "What would you say if I told you I intend to open a practice here, specializing in criminal law defense?"

"In Uniontown?"

"It's a thinner field. I establish my credibility here and relocate. Or open another office, if things are really good."

Sally patted her mouth with her napkin. "I'd say go for it and wish you the best of luck. What prompts this move? I thought you had the inside track to become partner with a firm up in Pittsburgh."

"Yeah, so did I." Kim stabbed her fork through a couple of fries. "Until they passed me over for a guy. I billed twice as many hours as he did and my acquittal rate was loads better than his. But he's engaged to the senior partner's daughter and has a stellar golf handicap. You know how it goes."

"Ouch." No matter how far women had come in the legal field, the old boys' network was alive and well. "So you decided to strike out on your own."

"You got it." Kim finished the first half of her sandwich, wiped her hands, and pushed aside her plate. "Except I figure I'll have a better shot of making this work with a partner. That's where you come in."

Sally's instincts had not been wrong. But she decided to play innocent. A little deceptive, maybe, it was but the only way to get Kim to give the full picture. "What do you mean? I have a job and I told you, I like it."

Kim blew out a breath. "Stop with the air-head act, it doesn't suit you. I want you to join me, isn't it obvious?" She counted out the points of her argument. "You were tops in our class when it came to mock trial. You can argue the pants off anybody. You've got a passion for law like no one I've ever seen. You aced the bar exam. You've got a head for the business side of running a practice. Shall I go on?"

"No, I've got it. But what's the upside for me?"

"The upside?" Kim's jaw dropped slightly. "Uh, numero uno, more money. Yeah, I hear you, money's not *the* most important thing, but it is *an* important thing. I know what an assistant public defender makes. Second, I know the kind of clients that come through your office and I know some of them are people you'd rather not represent."

Immediately, the name Ethan Haverton and the case from last May that almost ruined things between Sally and Jim sprang to her mind. Did Kim know about him, a case that deserved the term *fiasco* if ever one did?

"You go into private practice with me, you get to choose your clients. You want to keep representing folks who can't afford high-priced attorneys? That's fine with me. More than fine. But at least you don't have to accept the case of every sleazeball who wanders through your door. And hey, every once in a while, one of them may be able to actually, you know, pay their court fees." Kim sat back. "I really don't see any downsides. It's not like I'm asking you to relocate to New York City or Los Angeles, or defend mob hit men. You get to stay right here, do the job you say you love, get a better class of client, and a heftier fee. It's a no brainer."

"It's also a crap ton of work."

"You don't already work that way?"

"My current job allows me to work what I consider a reasonable amount of hours and have a social life. Starting our own practice will take eighty hours a week minimum. You know that."

Kim grinned. "Since when did you have a social life?"

Sally knew her cheeks were red. "If you must know, I'm seeing someone. True, his schedule is as crazy as mine, so he'd completely understand working overtime. But I think he'd be unhappy if I always said no, I've gotta work and I don't want that."

"Ooo, you've got a guy? What's he like in bed?" Kim leaned forward and propped her chin on her fist.

Sally waved her off. "My point is, yes, the things you list are strong benefits, but I've got a solid deal where I am, I make enough to live the life I want to, and really, I don't wind up defending too many sleaze balls, as you call them. So thanks, but no thanks."

Kim shook her head. "You can't give me a decision before you think about it. Talk it over with this guy of yours. I think once you get over the knee-jerk reaction, you'll see it differently." She looked around the room. "Now, how about some dessert?"

Chapter Seven

While Duncan went about his normal patrol duties, he racked his brain for names of troopers he might know in the Somerset barracks. He'd done a stint there immediately after leaving the academy. But most of the folks he knew had moved on or retired. There was nothing left but to hope Corporal Travers would open up to a fellow trooper, even if that person was from a different service area.

Immediately after first shift, Duncan confirmed Travers was on duty. Then he set out on the hour-long drive to Somerset. The day wasn't so nice that he wanted to spend an extra two hours in his Jeep, half of it on the Turnpike. He debated taking the longer, yet more scenic, route, but ultimately decided in favor of speed.

Travers was seated at a desk reviewing what Duncan assumed were zone assignments for his shift. He cleared his throat. "Excuse me, Corporal Travers?"

Travers looked up. "Duncan, right? From Uniontown? You're the guy who found the Casselman victim in Confluence."

Jackass. Pretending to forget Duncan's name was beyond petty. "That's me. I was wondering—"

"Thank you for your help that day. Quite a stroke of luck, having an experienced trooper on the scene to secure things." Travers looked back at his sheet of assignments.

Duncan wondered if he'd get the chance to complete a sentence. "You're welcome. Anything I can do to help. That leads me to why I'm here."

Travers pulled his attention away again, a curious expression on his face.

"Oh?"

"It's about the John Doe. What can you tell me about him?"

"Trooper, you've already done your job and done it damn well. For which I'm grateful. But as far as you're concerned, the matter is closed."

Duncan pulled over a chair and sat. He wasn't going to stand there, hat in hand, like a rookie fresh out of the academy. "I didn't get a good look that day, but I can't shake the feeling I've seen the victim before."

Travers tapped his pen on the desk. "You've seen him? Where? Why didn't you give me his name?"

"I told you, I didn't get a good look so I don't have a name to give. All I have is a gut feeling."

Travers waved his hand. "It probably just seems that way. Amazing how all drowning victims look the same after they've been in the water for a while."

"Then he definitely drowned?"

"The investigation is ongoing and I'm not at liberty to discuss autopsy results. If you remember anything definitive, or if anyone in Confluence has information, call me." Travers stood and moved toward a half-empty coffee pot. He grabbed a mug, two packets of artificial sweetener, and a mini container of creamer.

The statement had a definite air of dismissal, but Duncan followed and pressed ahead. "It's been two days. You must have done the autopsy by now. What were the results?"

"A full statement on the incident is in today's paper." Travers stirred his coffee. "I think there are extra copies out at the desk. I understand something like this, especially in a town as small as Confluence, is unnerving. People have no reason to be alarmed about an accidental drowning death. Take a few on your way out and pass them around."

Duncan repressed a sigh of frustration. "I'm confused. First you tell me you can't say anything, but then you keep calling this a drowning and accidental at that. Which is it?"

"The investigation is ongoing. Read the statement in the paper. I have nothing further to say." Travers pushed past Duncan on the way back to his desk.

Duncan understood not wanting to say too much to a member of the press. But this was ridiculous. "Look, I'm not some damned reporter. I'm a member of the PSP, same as you. Who was at the scene of a deceased man. If we're dealing with an accidental death, tell me and I'll get out of your hair. What you've said, or more accurately *not* said, leads me to think the circumstances around this man's death are suspicious. I'd like to help."

"It's out of your area."

"Come on. Those lines aren't exact around here, you know that. Somerset County cuts right through Confluence. For all we know, his head was in Fayette and his feet were in the next county."

Travers set down his mug and wheeled about to face Duncan. He drew himself up to his full height, about two inches shorter than Duncan, and put his hands on his duty belt. "I'm telling you that assistance, while appreciated, is not needed. Things are under control. Unless you have further business to discuss with me, I have a shift to run."

Duncan recognized the stance. He'd used it himself with recalcitrant witnesses to demonstrate command presence. Travers used it now to put Duncan in his place as a mere trooper first class. He fought to maintain a professional expression but seethed inside. Travers had been wrong all those years ago. He was going to use a tiny difference in rank to lord it over Duncan now? "If I think of anything, I'll be in touch."

Travers sat. "You do that."

Duncan left. So much for playing by the rules. He knew John Doe, he felt it in his bones. But from where?

* * *

Before leaving Somerset, Duncan decided to swing by the hospital. Carl Ritchie, the man pulled out of the river near Rockwood, might be conscious and more talkative than Travers. Duncan had grabbed a copy of the *Daily American*, the local paper, before he left the barracks, but the statement in the story proved even less helpful than the conversation with Travers as it offered no real information beyond what Duncan already knew.

He obtained Ritchie's room number from the information desk and headed up. He encountered no difficulties with the hospital staff, probably because he was still in uniform. His conscience squirmed a little at what could be interpreted as deceit, but after all, he wasn't responsible for people's assumptions.

Ritchie was unconscious, a monitor clipped to his finger. A machine beeped next to him, keeping track of his heart rate. Duncan stood in the door and stared. Two men found floating in the same river. Two separate accidents? No way. Two men in the same accident? Maybe. Or it was something more sinister. Only Carl Ritchie could say and it looked like that might take a while.

A voice broke through Duncan's thoughts. "Excuse me, Trooper? Can I help you with something?"

He turned to see a fresh-faced nurse in cheerful blue and white scrubs standing next to him. "I hoped to be able to talk to Mr. Ritchie."

The nurse gave a rueful smile. "As you can see, he isn't up to it right now."

"Has he said anything?"

"Not a word." She tilted her head. "I haven't seen you here before."

"I'm new to the investigation." Duncan glanced at her name tag. Loretta Smith. "Actually, I was at the scene of another incident on the same river. Only in that one, the victim was deceased. I wanted to talk to Mr. Ritchie and see if there was a connection."

The young nurse shook her head. "I'm sorry. I wish I could help you out."

"Maybe you can. What are the extent of his injuries?"

Smith hesitated a minute before answering. "Lots of abrasions. There was some water in his lungs. If he hadn't been pulled out when he was, I'd be willing to bet he would have drowned. But the worst is a contusion to the skull, which caused a serious concussion."

"Bad enough he could die?"

"Perhaps, but there are so many possible complications. We're sure he was in the water for an extended period of time." She waved her hand at the room. "He might recover, but so much could still go wrong."

Duncan handed her his card. "If he regains consciousness, would you call me? It's very important. We don't know how or why this other man died, or even who he is. Mr. Ritchie may hold the answers. John Doe's family deserves to know what happened and if foul play is suspected, of course we want to investigate fully."

Smith took the card, giving it a cursory glance before sticking it in her pocket. "Of course, Trooper."

"Thank you." Duncan touched his hat and left. He wasn't too concerned about his barracks commander finding out he'd been there. The lieutenant was pretty tolerant. Which was good, because Duncan felt positive Travers wouldn't be happy about the hospital visit. At all.

Chapter Eight

Sally set a freshly tossed salad on the table at the same time Rizzo dashed to the back door, barking a welcome. Jim must be home. Sally heard him tussle with the dog. It was easy to imagine Rizzo's joyous and physical greeting from the barks and thumps that issued from the back door.

Three months ago, dinner would have been Chinese takeout eaten in the living room. Now she was preparing spaghetti Bolognese, waiting for Jim to come home so she could tell him about Kim's job offer.

And to tell him he knew a dead man.

Moments later, Jim entered, pushing the dog in front of him. "Let me in, Doofus," he said. He leaned over to kiss Sally.

Of course, three months ago she wouldn't have been having dinner with Jim on a regular basis. Before she answered, she took off his campaign hat and kissed him back, hard. "You're late. Did something happen?" Hopefully, another dead body hadn't washed up somewhere on a river bank.

"I had to run out to Somerset. You find any missing person reports?"

"None for Carl Ritchie and none for anyone who matched John Doe. No one missed them, at least no one inclined to file a report. Sorry." She kissed him again, this time gentler and slower. "Did I ever tell you I'm a sucker for a man in uniform?"

He chuckled and pulled back. "This man in uniform has to get this twenty-pound weight off before his back gives out. Hold that thought."

She gazed at his backside as he walked away. Damn. Three months ago, she didn't have that on a regular basis, either. "Need any help?"

He threw a look over his shoulder and winked. "I'll be fine. Don't want dinner to burn."

While he went upstairs, Sally put the finishing touches on the spaghetti sauce simmering on the stove, and drained the pasta.

They sat and Sally buttered a slice of bread as she contemplated the man across from her. "What's out in Somerset?"

Jim told her about his meeting with Travers and the stop at Somerset Hospital. "I have to hope the same nurse is on duty when Ritchie wakes up and that she calls me."

"If Ritchie wakes up."

"Well, yes." He helped himself to seconds.

Next to them on the floor, Rizzo waited patiently, head on his paws. The dog had been trained not to beg at the table, but Sally knew his sharp canine nose wouldn't miss the tiniest bit of the meat-filled sauce if it hit the floor.

"What I don't understand is why Travers was so rude," she said.

"We met years ago on an Amber Alert. Witness statements conflicted, we sided with different people. I turned out to be right, he was wrong. He never got over it." Jim shrugged.

No wonder the two troopers didn't get along. The last person Jim would want to work alongside was a man with an oversized ego. "Oh, that reminds me. I didn't find any missing persons reports, but I did find something else." She jumped up and fetched her phone from her purse. "The second victim, Carl Ritchie."

"What about him?"

"I found a picture." She showed Jim the photo. "You're in it. You know both of them."

"I am?" Jim pinched and zoomed in on the picture. "Son of a bitch, I did know him. It's coming back. Carl Ritchie and Mike Brower, the guys from the preservation society. Mike's the Casselman victim. Shit."

"What were you doing with them?" She watched his face his look of confusion gave way to concern.

"It was a spring cleanup project on the river. This was a few years ago. They were looking for local volunteers, so I spent a couple weekends clearing debris, picking up trash, that sort of thing. I talked mostly with Mike, this picture might be the only time I met Carl. They fish smallmouth a lot and I'm more of a fan of going out on the gorge, but we traded stories and tips. Good guys. Looks like I need to find out what the CWPS has been up to."

"I can do that for you. I've got some time tomorrow." She considered a moment as Jim nodded his thanks. "If they spend that much time on the river, then it could have been two accidents, as weird as that feels."

Jim handed back the phone. "No way. Mike was experienced and I gotta assume Carl was, too. Smart and capable. They'd have been able to handle anything on the water except a major problem. Something's wrong."

Sally played with the phone, mind churning. Jim was convinced, that was clear. She could also tell from his expression and his body language he was upset. She didn't know Brower and Ritchie from Adam, but if Jim thought there was more to the story than two-men-fall-in-the-river-and-one-dies that was good enough for her. "Do you think Travers is playing games with you or is he inept?"

"When I worked with him, he wasn't incompetent. A bit of an ego, definitely. One that got bruised pretty bad."

"Okay, but now you have information."

"Except I already talked to him this morning. If I'd known all this earlier, it would be different."

The heat of embarrassment crept up Sally's neck. "I'm sorry, I should have gotten in touch as soon as I found the picture."

"Hell, Sally. I'm not blaming you. The order things happened in is inconvenient, that's all." He leaned over and kissed her.

Sally gave his hand a squeeze. "Thanks for that. Could Tom Burns tell you how long Mike had been in the water? If he can, you might be able to extrapolate something or show you the autopsy photos. Then you could tell Travers you know the victims, give some hard information, and move things forward."

"Because showing him up a second time would definitely improve his attitude." Jim rolled a bit of bread between his fingers. "Burns might, if he was in on the autopsy."

"He's not?"

"Nope. The Somerset County Coroner's Office is in charge. Burns is looking into it for me, though. Maybe he'll get lucky. Meanwhile, I'll have to suck it up and give talking to Travers another shot." Jim popped the bread into his mouth. "I have a question for you." He paused. "I've been toying with the idea of applying for a position with the Criminal Investigation division. Greaves planted the idea in my head last spring and I keep coming back to it. What do you think?"

"You mean being a full-time investigator, like a detective? That'd be different."

"Yes, it would. You don't like the idea."

"That's not it at all." Sally couldn't imagine him out of PSP gray, but she also knew investigative work was his strong suit. Would such a shift mean more regular hours for him? If it did, would the hours she'd spend in a private practice be worse? "I think you'd be good at it. When would you start?"

He grinned. "There'd have to be an opening first, preferably in my current troop so I can stay local."

On one hand, she was glad to hear him say that because it meant she could stay put. On the other, a move to another county would be the perfect response to Kim and one she could hardly argue with.

"Anyway, that was my day. What about yours?"

"Tell you later, after you eat your dinner."

They finished the meal in comfortable silence, the sound of summer cicadas and warblers clear through the screen door. As soon as they stood, Rizzo leapt to his feet. Sally reached down and rubbed his ears. "Sorry, buddy. This is all bad for you."

From the look Rizzo gave her, he obviously didn't care.

Kitchen cleaned up, they headed for the front porch, Jim holding a bottle of his favorite Edmund Fitzgerald porter and her with a glass of merlot.

"Have you given any thought to that swing?" Sally said as she sat in her Adirondack chair.

Jim dropped into the other chair and greeted one of his neighbors who passed by walking a tiny dog. "It would be a pain in the ass. I told you, I'd have to redo the entire porch roof." He grumbled, but his voice betrayed his lack of annoyance. "Are you gonna tell me about your day or is that information off limits according to the rules?"

After last May's disastrous communications failure, they'd set some restrictions around what could be discussed and what couldn't. "No, it isn't." She ran a finger around the rim of her glass. "I got a job offer."

He paused, bottle at his lips. "Oh? From who?"

"Old law school classmate. She's starting a private practice for criminal law defense and she wants me to be her partner."

He lowered the bottle. "You interested?"

"No...yes...maybe." She hastened to take a drink. "Private practice has benefits, no doubt. More money, more ability to choose my clients so I don't get stuck defending people like Ethan Haverton."

Jim said nothing, but he didn't have to. The disgusted look on his face said it all. He remembered that case, too.

"I don't particularly care about the money and yes, it would be nice to be able to be a bit more selective on the client front. But..."

"But what?"

She downed a gulp of wine. "It's a lot of work. I could easily find myself working ten or twelve hour days. Maybe even longer." She held up the glass, letting the sun make tiny rainbows through it, determined not to look at Jim, not to let him see the indecision on her face. Deep down, Sally knew she could do a lot of good as a private practice attorney. She could finally help the people they had to turn away from public defense for what Sally considered absurd reasons. She'd probably even enjoy working with Kim, even though the other woman was more than a little brash. Sally knew Kim's pushy attitude covered a good heart and dogged determination.

But her position with the Public Defender was safe. She would never run out of clients, she was helping people, and most importantly, the workload was manageable so it didn't threaten the relationship she was building with Jim.

His voice broke into her thoughts. "You aren't sure you want to do that."

"Do you blame me?"

"Hell, no. I've worked twelve hours straight or more when shit hits the fan. It sucks. That lifestyle cost me a wife."

The words came out before Sally could stop them. "I don't want it to cost me you." Her voice sounded small to her ears.

Jim set his bottle on the porch floor, twisted so he faced her, and brushed the hair off her forehead. "This friend give you a deadline?"

"No, but I can tell she wants a decision fast and she wants it to be a yes." She looked into his hazel eyes, which were full of understanding.

"I can't tell you what to do. I will say this. You merely working a shitload of hours will not cause me to run for the hills." He kissed her hand. "Take your time. Think about it. Do not let yourself be bullied into an answer. It's your life and your career."

She thought he'd never look sexier than when he was in uniform or a well-fitting suit. She was wrong. She bit her lip and giggled. "When have I ever let someone tell me what to do?"

"Never that I know of." He shook his head. "At least this decision won't place you in mortal peril. I hope."

Chapter Nine

As soon as roll call ended Wednesday morning, Duncan hit the road for patrol, but not before cornering McAllister, who was coming off an overnight shift. "I need a favor."

"Sure thing, Boss."

"I need background checks on Carl Ritchie and Mike Brower. Basic information only."

"And you can't do this…why?"

"Let's just say I don't want to draw too much attention to myself. Can you do it?"

"Sure. You're only keeping me from sleep."

Aw, hell. "Forget it. I'll figure something out."

She laughed. "I'm teasing, Boss. This won't take much time. Should I call you?"

"Please." He left and started his patrol. A half-hour later, he'd gone through a fast-food drive-through for a breakfast sandwich when his phone buzzed. McAllister. "Whatcha got?"

"Nothing exciting, that's for sure. Carl Ritchie, age forty. Lived in Markleton, over in Somerset County. Never married. Both parents deceased. Aside from a twelve-year-old misdemeanor conviction for disturbing the peace during an environmental rally in Harrisburg, his record is clean. He worked full-time as a loan manager for a bank in Somerset and co-founded the Casselman Water Preservation Society five years ago. He received no income from the non-profit organization."

"What about Brower?"

"Also a fat lot of nothing," she said. "Mike Brower, age forty-five. His residence is listed as Rockwood. His marital status shows as divorced. He works as a human resources specialist for a lumber company in Rockwood and has been with Ritchie from the beginning at CWPS. Like his partner, none of his income comes from the environmental group. I've got contact information for his ex-wife, who lives in Pittsburgh, and his parents, who are in Altoona. You want it?"

"Yes, please. Text it to me." Little wonder no missing persons reports had popped. He'd limited his search to Fayette and Somerset counties. Anybody who would file a report lived in other counties, and if Brower had a girlfriend or other friends, they either hadn't been suspicious or he wasn't gone long enough to worry them. "I owe you one."

"Uh, Boss? You owe me a lot. Fortunately, I stopped keeping score quite a while ago. Anything else?"

"Nope, that's it. Thanks." He shoved the rest of the sandwich in his mouth. Then he placed a phone call to Somerset Hospital. There was no change in Carl Ritchie's condition.

As he swung out of the parking lot, he prioritized his tasks. He needed to find out more about Mike Brower. And that meant a trip to Altoona.

* * *

Wednesday morning, Sally reviewed her schedule in her head. Nothing major on the docket for awhile. "Hey, Doris."

The office secretary came to Sally's office. "You called?"

"I left some stuff on your desk yesterday to be filed and I need some copies made before my one o'clock meeting with Judge Slattery. I'm barricading myself in my office. I'll be out for lunch."

"Got it." Doris took a step.

"Hey. One more thing."

Doris stopped and turned.

"If a woman named Kim Dunphy calls or comes looking for me, I'm out. You don't know where I am or when I'll be back."

"Is she a client?"

"No, a former classmate."

"Why don't you want to see her?"

"Long story, but she wants something from me and I don't want to give it. You'll cover for me, right?" Sally asked, but she knew the answer. Doris would defend "her" attorneys until the day they put her six feet under.

As expected, the older woman nodded. "I have no idea where you are."

Sally flashed a smile. "Has anyone told you you're worth your weight in gold?"

"I'd be rich if that were true." Doris left and closed the office door.

Sally took a hit of her coffee. Then she jiggled the mouse to wake up her computer, logged in, and launched a browser.

Jim was positive the accidents had been anything but. That raised the question of why someone would have it out for both victims. What did Brower and Ritchie have in common? The Casselman Water Preservation Society. Time to learn a little more about the environmental group.

The organization's website was functional, but not fancy. One of the first things Sally noticed was CWPS had a post office box and an email, but no phone numbers and no physical address. The PO Box was in Rockwood, the same town where Ritchie had been found. The email address was a generic webmail service.

Sally clicked around the site. The mission of the CWPS was to raise awareness of the natural resources of the area and engage in conservation activities throughout the Casselman watershed. They sponsored a number of activities throughout the year, some devoted to cleanup, some to fishing, some to whitewater rafting. A watchdog organization, they had no authority to enforce regulations on local businesses, but through monitoring and reporting were able to do enough that they were credited with helping in the resurgence of the watershed. Beautiful pictures decorated every page of the site. Someone had quite the eye for photography.

A knock at the door interrupted her. "I'm busy," she said.

Tanelsa Parson, her colleague and erstwhile partner in crime, opened the door, ever the picture of legal professionalism, today in a navy-blue pencil skirt with a ruffled, pinstriped shirt, and a matching blazer. While the three-inch stiletto heels didn't have the signature red soles of Louboutins, they most assuredly featured some high-end designer's name somewhere. When your wife worked as a fashion industry buyer, it tended to elevate the quality of your wardrobe. "Good morning to you too." she said. "What's got your panties in a twist?"

"I told you, I'm busy." Sally clicked through her search results.

"With what?"

Knowing the quickest way to satisfy Tanelsa's curiosity and send her away, Sally went with the truth. "How familiar are you with an organization called the Casselman Water Preservation Society?" Besides, Tanelsa might be helpful.

"Not at all. Should I be?"

"Probably not, but I figured I'd ask." Sally scanned the article. "Come look at this."

Tanelsa came to the desk. "What is it?"

"According to the story, they've been very active in bringing about a lot of improvements along the Casselman River. Look at these pictures, specifically these two guys. What do you think?"

"The activity makes sense, given the organization's name." Tanelsa squinted. "This shot, from a few years ago, they look all buddy-buddy. Is that your boyfriend?"

"Yeah, he volunteered with the group. Now look at this one."

Tanelsa took a moment. "It's a posed shot, but still outdoors. They should be more relaxed. They're standing a fraction too far away from each other, like when you're supposed to look like the other person's friend, but you secretly can't stand him."

"Exactly."

Tanelsa put the picture on the desk. "This is all fascinating, of course, but why would you care about them? New client?"

"No." Sally brought her up to speed on the victim found in Confluence, as well as her and Jim's speculation as to the identity. "Your observation confirms what I saw. Something happened that created some space between the two victims. My question is, what?"

Tanelsa groaned. "Sally, don't you have enough real work to keep you busy? The last time we decided to go off the reservation was interesting, but a little too exciting for my blood."

"As you've observed, Jim knows both men, particularly Mike Brower. So far, the party line is this is an accident. Jim is positive that's not the case. Because of his connection, he wants to know what's going on. And if it's important to him, it's important to me."

"Of course it is."

Sally clicked over to another article. "Look at this."

Tanelsa read over Sally's shoulder. "They've been involved in getting the Pennsylvania Department of Environmental Protection and the EPA to investigate and fine local companies? Some no-name do-gooder organization can do that?"

"Small, but mighty, apparently." Sally clicked print on the article.

"What are you gonna do with that?"

"Give it to Jim." Sally got up, scooted around her co-worker, and went to the printer. "The trooper who responded to the Casselman scene is parroting the standard the-investigation-is-ongoing line, but says it's probably an unfortunate coincidence both men had accidents along the river."

Tanelsa, who had followed, snorted. "Coincidence my ass."

"Yeah, that's what Jim said." Sally picked up the printout. "If CWPS was rattling cages and threatening to get companies in legal trouble, I'd say that was motive to shut them up. Wouldn't you?"

Chapter Ten

Duncan's phone buzzed halfway through his Wednesday morning patrol. The text was from Tom Burns and unusually short. "Meet me." He didn't specify a place or time, so Duncan took that to mean he should go the Fayette County coroner's office as soon as possible.

When Duncan arrived at the yellow-brick building on West Peter Street in Uniontown, Burns crouched in front of a cabinet in the exam area, restocking supplies.

"You rang?" Duncan asked from the doorway.

Burns pointed. "Toss me those boxes of gloves."

Duncan looked down, grabbed the two boxes and lobbed them underhand across the room. "I hope you didn't text me to get help with your maintenance chores."

"No, but you gotta admit, you're kind of handy with that." Burns placed the boxes in the cabinet, stood, and moved to the next one.

"Burns, I'm on the clock." Duncan repressed the urge to sigh. "If you have some information for me, spill it."

"Wait a second, Mr. Impatient." Burns counted and reorganized the contents of the second cabinet. "There, all done. Follow me." He led Duncan to a small office where the desk betrayed evidence of breakfast and an open can of energy drink.

"If you got more sleep, or had a cup of coffee, you wouldn't need that stuff," Duncan said and pointed.

Burns drained the tiny can. "I was at an accident scene with multiple fatalities late last night. Took until after midnight to finish. Coffee isn't going to cut it." He rubbed his face, then sifted through the papers on the desktop. "Ah, here it is. Don't say I never gave you anything." He handed over a single sheet.

"What's this?" Duncan skimmed the sheet.

"Summary of the report on your Confluence victim." Burns dropped into his chair and propped his feet on the desktop. "My notes, really. Miriam is not my biggest fan. But she's also pissed off a few people in her own office, so I was able to play on that to get the scoop. There was water in the victim's lungs and he aspirated sand and mud. But the key finding is the hemorrhaging into the mastoid air sinuses." He tapped the side of his head, behind his ear. "Those are right here. Without that, you don't have a drowning."

Not very suspicious. "So he drowned and the coroner ruled it an accident?" Maybe Travers was right and it was a bad week for river incidents.

"I didn't say that." Burns pointed with a pen. "They also found evidence of a subdural bleed."

Duncan looked up. "He was hit on the head." Maybe an accident, but maybe not.

"Or something hit him on the head." Burns jabbed the pen in the air. "One option is he hit his head on something, fell in the water, and drowned before the bleed could kill him."

"Or he was assaulted, went in the river as a result, and then drowned. Or he was dumped in."

Burns tapped his nose. "It's almost like you do this for a living. But yes. That's why everything is undetermined and they want the police to look further."

"Very funny." Duncan went back and scanned the page of Burns's notes. Shame his friend couldn't get the whole report, but this was more than he expected. "They make an ID yet?"

"Yes. The victim is Michael Edward Brower of Rockwood."

Duncan was not surprised, but it was always good to get the official word. He tossed the paper back on Burns's desk. "Thanks."

"I'll add it to your tab." Burns sat up and shelved the report. "Now what?"

"I need to find out why two experienced outdoorsmen ended up in the Casselman, one of them dead."

"You don't buy the accident line?"

"Not hardly."

* * *

Sally had dashed off an email to CWPS before she headed out the door for her late-morning court appearance. She didn't receive an automatic bounce-back or out-of-office response, which was a good sign. She held two pictures side by side, one from an early feature on the environmental group and one from a couple months ago. In the first, Ritchie and Brower stood with arms slung around each other's shoulders, wide smiles on their faces. In the second, the two men merely stood side by side, not touching, both with stiff posture and the cardboard smiles of a publicity shot. What had happened to change the relationship? With any luck, somebody other than the two victims monitored the email account and she could dig out the story.

When court adjourned at noon, she checked her phone. One call, from a Somerset area code number, and one voice mail. She tapped to listen.

"Ms. Castle? This is Tara Jennings with Casselman Water Protection. I saw your email. I'd like to talk to you. It's about Carl and Mike. Give me a call at this number. Thanks."

As Sally walked back to her office, she dialed the number. "Hello, is this Tara? Sally Castle, returning your call."

"Oh, hi. I'm kinda busy right now, but I want to talk to you. Can we meet later?"

"Where?"

"I'm at Ohiopyle State Park, right in the town for the time being."

Sally swiftly checked the calendar on her phone. "I'm free at three. It'll take me some time to get to the park. Will you still be there at four?"

Crowd and outdoor noise filtered over the line. Whatever Tara was doing, she was not alone. "I can be. Look for a woman with a camera wearing a blue shirt. I'll be near the visitors' center. See you then."

Sally clicked off. It was a vague description, but Tara must have thought it was enough to go on. As Sally mulled over what the woman, who sounded fairly young, thought was so important, a voice broke through her thoughts.

"Sally. You're avoiding me."

Sally jerked her head up. "Kim. I haven't been avoiding you. I've been busy."

Kim stood a few paces away, arms crossed and foot tapping, but there was a grin on her face. "Liar. I've visited your office twice and the dragon lady at the front desk keeps telling me you aren't there."

And yet here you are. "Her name is Doris and she's one of our office secretaries. She's only doing her job." Sally hung a sharp right and headed down the stairs.

A click of heels told her Kim followed. "Whatever. How about lunch?"

"Not today, I have stuff to do." Sally pushed through the door to the public defender's office and stopped at Doris's desk to flip through some mail. Thankfully, the office appeared empty.

"Busy, busy, you're always busy." Kim scoffed. "Seems to me you'd say yes if only to get away from the slave driver you call a boss."

Bryan Gerrity, the public defender, appeared from his office. "Who's a slave driver? Oh, Sally, it's you. Got a moment?" He held his glasses in his hand, the tone of his voice making it clear his question wasn't really a request.

While she felt a well of gratitude for the intervention, she wondered if he'd found out about her not-quite-related-to-business internet search and was less than impressed. "Sure, Bryan." She turned to Kim. "Like I said, busy."

Kim tutted. "You can't avoid me forever, Sal. Ta." She sashayed out of the office.

As soon as the door clicked shut, Sally dropped the mail and leaned forward until her forehead rested on the divider between desks and door.

"Who, pray tell, was that and why is she calling me names?" Bryan asked, a note of amusement in his voice.

Sally straightened. "Kim Dunphy, an old friend of mine from law school. Clearly, she doesn't know you." She swept up her mail. "Thanks for the save."

"No problem."

"Am I in trouble?"

"What would make you think that?"

"Your no-nonsense tone of voice and posture, for starters"

"No, you're not in trouble. I heard the conversation and figured you could use a hand." Bryan regarded her. "Let me guess. She wants you to give up the glamorous life of public defense for private practice."

"How'd you know?" Not for the first time, Sally wondered if Bryan was psychic.

He shrugged. "She looks like a that kind of lawyer. She's trying to talk to you. Her body language screams she wants something. Not hard to put the story together. What are you going to tell her?"

"I haven't made up my mind. Hand to God, Bryan, that's the truth. Yes, she wants me to jump ship, but I'm not so sure I want to jump."

"A lot more money in private practice. Freedom to choose your clients. I can see the attraction."

"Maybe, but those benefits come with a price."

Bryan put on his glasses and walked over to her. "Sally, I won't lie and tell you I wouldn't miss you. You're a hell of an attorney and you've done a lot of good for this office."

"I've also gotten in a spot of trouble a time or two."

He chucked her on the shoulder. "Maybe. I'd still hate to lose you. But you have to do what's right for you. If you need advice, I'm here. I promise I will keep my bias in check."

Sally bit her lip. "Thanks, Bry."

He gave her a faux salute and headed back to his office.

Sally checked the clock. Twelve-fifteen. She mentally reviewed her afternoon. If she ate lunch at her desk and worked without interruption, she could scoot out a bit early to meet Tara Jennings at Ohiopyle. She pushed Kim and her offer to the back burner. Time to think about that later.

Chapter Eleven

Duncan spent a good part of his shift alternating regular patrol duty with attempting to find the last person who had talked to Mike Brower. Now that there was a positive ID, he could call people. Most of them were slightly confused as to why yet another state police trooper was asking questions but willing to talk.

"We didn't get worried," said a fellow employee at the lumber company where Brower worked. "He wasn't due back until next Monday. He often takes off into the woods during these summer vacations and we don't hear from him."

"When was the last time you talked to or saw him?"

The man paused. "Friday, lunchtime. I heard him yell good-bye to someone in the yard."

"You're sure it was him?"

"Well, the guy yelled back, 'see you in a week, Mike,' so yeah, pretty sure."

That was as specific as things got. What had happened in the intervening days? Ritchie, Brower's partner at CWPS, remained his best bet for information. Unfortunately, Ritchie stubbornly stayed unconscious.

It was almost three, near the end of his shift, when his phone rang. Unknown number, but he recognize a Somerset exchange. "This is Trooper Duncan."

"Trooper, yes, this is Loretta Smith. I'm a nurse at Somerset Hospital, we spoke the other day."

"I remember. How can I help you?"

"You wanted to know when Carl Ritchie regained consciousness."

Hallelujah. "I'm on my way. I'll be there in an hour or so."

"Don't bother."

"Why?"

"Carl Ritchie isn't awake. He's dead. It happened last night. I'm sorry, I know you wanted to talk to him."

Damn it. "Did he say anything before he died?"

"Not anything we could understand. He was rather delirious." Smith paused. "Except for one brief moment."

"What did he say?"

"Only three words that we could make out. Water, Ryan, Mike."

Duncan thanked her and hung up. Two of the three words made sense. Water probably referred to the Casselman. Mike was clearly Mike Brower. But who the hell was Ryan?

* * *

Sally left work around three and drove to Ohiopyle State Park. She wove her way through traffic and around the town, finally squeezing her Camry into a spot on a side street. Even on an afternoon in the middle of the week, the tourist town was hopping, almost certainly due to the bright blue sky and blazing July sun. In the distance, she could see the water of the Youghiogheny still rode high, Ohiopyle Falls little more than a bump. But plenty of bikers and rollerbladers thronged through the streets and the riverside trail. Dozens of people would be at Cucumber Falls, the natural waterslides at Meadow Run, or hiking in the woods. It was that kind of day.

She had been smart enough to leave her suit jacket in the car but hadn't had enough time to change out of her court clothes. Her heels, pale blue blouse and pinstriped skirt were wildly out of place among the crowd of tank tops, T-shirts, and shorts. Oh well.

Once she reached the grassy area near the river, she said the hell with it and took off her shoes. Barefoot, she made her way over to the visitors' center and overlook. Children romped through the grass, engaged in some form of tag, while parents sat nearby. Sally smiled. Someday, maybe. Neither she nor Jim were in their twenties anymore, but they'd only been on firm relationship ground for a few months. It was probably best not to hurry into family life.

As she drew near the center, she could hear the rush of the water as it swept by. She was no expert, but it looked exceptionally rough, too rough for the kayakers who normally thronged the river. She leaned on the railing, entranced by the rolling whitewater. Those who enjoyed high-adventure rafting were probably in seventh heaven. A crowd of Black-Eyed Susans bounced their heads and a slight breeze ruffled the leaves of the trees. Momentarily diverted from her mission, she wished Jim were there. Maybe if the weather stayed nice, they could come back this weekend. Take a few trips down those water slides.

The sight of a young woman with a camera, including a telephoto lens, brought Sally back to her task. The woman wore a faded blue tank top with "Try the Casselman" written in peeling white script on the back over a pair of short-short cutoffs and sport sandals. Her dark hair was styled in a pixie cut, vivid blue streaks standing out in the sun. If that was Tara, why hadn't she told Sally to look for the woman with blue hair? Much more noticeable than a blue shirt.

Sally wandered over, shoes in hand. "Excuse me, are you Tara Jennings?"

The woman didn't turn around and continued to peer through her lens, snapping picture after picture. "Who wants to know?"

"I'm Sally Castle. You called me and we arranged to meet, remember?"

The woman lowered her camera and turned around. Her deep blue eyes were lined with black kohl eyeliner, the lashes impossibly dark and thick. Alabaster skin said she wore a ton of SPF 50 sunscreen. "Oh, sorry. Yeah, I'm Tara. Pleased to meet you." She went back to her photography.

Sally waited for Tara to continue the conversation, but when it seemed that wouldn't happen, spoke. "You said you wanted to meet to talk about CWPS. If this is a bad time, we can do this later." *On a day when I don't have to leave work early and can enjoy the park afterward.*

Tara snapped a few more pictures, then screwed on a lens cap and hung the camera around her neck. "No. I wanted to finish up my shots is all. We can talk now."

"You're a photographer. Professional?"

"Yes, I freelance. That's what I do for CWPS. Mostly for their website and promotional materials."

"This is the Yough, though."

"Yeah, but it's one ecosystem, isn't it? Besides, the pictures I'm taking today are for another client."

"Oh. Did you do anything other than pictures? For example, did you work in their office?"

"They don't have one." Tara ran a hand through her hair. "Let's sit over here. The sun's pretty hot. It doesn't bother me, but I can't imagine that blouse and skirt are too comfy right about now." She led the way over to a dark green bench underneath the shade of some trees. "I looked you up when I saw your email. You're a criminal defense attorney."

"I am."

"Are you representing Mike?"

The question took Sally's breath away for a moment. "Why would you think that?" she asked, in an attempt to buy time.

"Carl is in the hospital. When I saw the news story, and how the cops aren't saying whether it was an accident, I called Mike. He isn't answering his phone."

Sally waited.

"Carl and Mike, they had a huge, blow-out fight. They've been sniping at each other for a while. But this…I swear they were going to beat each other to a pulp."

Two men, badly beaten. "Do you know what it was about?"

"I'm not sure." Tara worried the cuticle on her thumb. "The big project lately has been dust pollution and the effects on the Casselman, specifically the smallmouth bass population."

"Yes, I read something online about that. Wasn't CWPS pretty involved in raising awareness and getting the state environmental officials involved? I thought conditions had improved."

Tara bobbed her head, setting the blue-streaked hair swinging. "Yeah. But

Mike took some readings recently and said levels were creeping up again. He wanted to sound the alarm before it got real bad."

"Carl disagreed?"

"That's it, I don't know." Tara picked away the torn cuticle and started on her other one. "But they definitely disagreed. Carl told Mike, 'you can't file that, it's illegal' or something. I think he was going to alert the DEP."

"Then what?"

Tara swallowed. "Mike said, 'you do that you son-of-a-bitch and I swear I'll kill you.'"

"When did you hear this?"

"Uh, last Thursday maybe? I was meeting them for dinner to discuss photos for a new awareness campaign. I got to the restaurant and the guys were already at the table, arguing. I heard them when I got close."

"Once they realized you'd heard them, did they say anything?"

"They both brushed it off, said it was nothing. They were blowing off steam, you know? But then I heard about Carl, and, well, I started wondering. And Mike is missing."

Sally reviewed the information. Tara obviously had not heard about Mike. "I'm sorry to tell you, but Mike is dead."

"What? How?"

"He drowned in the Casselman over the weekend."

"No friggin' way. Mike not only knew how to swim, he was a certified river guide. He wouldn't have been on the water in a boat without a life jacket."

Sally hadn't examined the body closely, but she had not seen a jacket on Mike Brower. Plus, Jim had not told her that a boat had been recovered at either scene or along the river. She rolled the information from Tara around in her head. Mike had information he intended to act on. Carl not only disagreed, he thought the action would cross the line. Had the disagreement turned physical? Were they truly looking at a case of a fistfight turned bad? "Have you told anyone else?"

"No. I mean, until you emailed, I didn't think about it. Even with Carl, that might have been an accident, you know? He loved being on the river, so having an accident isn't a stretch, even when you're skilled. And Mike said he'd be off for a week and out of touch."

"Perfectly understandable."

"But you think I need to talk to someone, like the cops?"

"Let me look into it a bit more. But depending on what I find, yes, I have a friend in the state police who would be very interested in talking to you."

* * *

As Sally prepared to leave Ohiopyle, her phone sounded the tone associated with a text from Jim. *Dex's at five-thirty? Been a hell of a day.* It was four o'clock. It would be tight, but she should have just enough time to stop at her apartment and change into something slightly more comfortable. She replied she might be a few minutes late, but she'd be there as soon as possible.

After she'd swapped her court attire for jeans and a soft cotton v-neck tee, she drove to the restaurant. She walked through the door at Dex's only a few minutes after the agreed-upon time, prepared to snag a table and order drinks for the both of them. Jim was already there, sitting at his preferred corner booth. In front of him was a rocks glass with a splash of whiskey. Since his drink of choice was dark beer, she knew immediately the day had been more than just rough.

When she approached the table, he stood to kiss her. "I ordered you a glass of merlot," he said, as they both sat.

"Thanks." She studied his face. It hadn't looked this haggard since his friend Lonnie had been killed. Maybe not even then. "No beer? You did have a bad day. What happened?"

He downed the rest of his drink. "Carl Ritchie is dead."

"No, when?"

"Last night."

"Did he ever wake up and say anything?"

"Briefly. The nurse who called said he mostly mumbled. They could only make out three words. Water, Ryan, and Mike." Jim pushed his empty glass aside. "Let's order." A few minutes later, they'd given the waitress their orders, Jim asking for his usual Reuben with an Edmund Fitzgerald and Sally choosing a grilled chicken sandwich with fries.

After the waitress left, Sally continued the conversation. "Water and Mike I get. The Casselman and Mike Brower. Who is Ryan?"

"No freaking clue."

"Did you tell Corporal Travers?"

"No. I'm sure the hospital staff notified him. He finds out they called me and he'll lose his shit."

"That puts my afternoon in a different light." She told him about her meeting with Tara Jennings. "I didn't think the two were getting along, even before I talked to Tara. I've been looking at stories online. Everybody was chummy in that shot with you in it, but as time went by the two must have disagreed over something. From the pictures, it looks to me as though they didn't want to be in each other's company." She paused. "Is it possible they had a knock-down fight, ended up in the river, and Brower drowned?"

"Of course it's possible. But I wouldn't call that murder. That's a fight that went bad. Incredibly bad, considering they both died, just not at the same time."

Sally paused. "But that doesn't explain who Ryan is."

"No, it does not. He could be a bystander, another person involved, someone who tried to break things up. Lots of options." He ran his finger over the bottle. "This Tara you met with. She said she heard them argue, but not exactly what they were fighting about?"

"I told you. Mike wanted to file something with somebody, and Carl said it was illegal. Or she thinks that's what he said."

They sat in silence until the food arrived. Sally took a bite of her sandwich. She chewed, swallowed, then said, "Are we blowing this out of proportion?"

Jim squirted ketchup on his fries. "What do you mean?"

"Only that our past history makes us pretty cynical. What's the likelihood that this is exactly what Travers thinks it is? A river tragedy."

"It's pretty convenient, if that's the case." He bit off a hunk of Reuben with uncharacteristic ferocity. His bad mood must have made him hungry. Or he skipped lunch.

"That's my point. Neither of us like convenient explanations. But this is the Laurel Highlands we're talking about. Not New York City. Hell, it's not even Pittsburgh." She pointed a fry at him. "Not every death is a murder. In fact, I'd say most of them aren't. Despite our experiences."

"Okay, fine. You're right. I may be conditioned by past events." He sighed and frowned at the sandwich in his hands. "I knew both Mike and Carl. Not well, but they were good guys. Fellow fishermen. They were trying to make the Laurel Highlands a better place. I don't like their deaths being dismissed as accidents."

She studied his face, dissatisfaction etched in every little crease. "I understand. I don't like it as an explanation either. I'll ask again. Do you think Travers is incompetent? If that's the case you should go to Nicols."

"No, I think he's lazy. That's unfortunate, but not really dereliction of duty. Besides, they'll have called in Somerset Criminal Investigation by now. Nicols has always given me a little leeway, but calling CI is standard procedure." He glanced up. "It's out of my hands. The hell with it. I'm going to leave it alone."

She paused a moment, then picked up her sandwich. "You're a damn poor liar, Jim Duncan."

Chapter Twelve

Duncan rose early on Thursday morning and decided to clear his head with a run around town. Fog lay thick on the river and swirled through the streets in wispy tendrils. Overhead, geese honked as they winged their way to their destination. The humidity in the air promised another scorcher of a day, but the sky, a brilliant blue dotted with only the barest trace of clouds, held no hint of the recent rains. He could hear the rush of water over the thud of his footfalls. The entire environment, combined with the steadiness of his pace, helped him think.

Duncan had serious doubts about the whole "two men fight and fall in the river" theory, but if he'd learned anything, it was Corporal Travers didn't want help. Most likely he didn't need it, either. Just because he took issue with the Somerset corporal's approach to his work didn't mean the man was incompetent. CI would be involved by now, so the whole issue truly was out of his hands.

But if the information Travers handed over was incomplete or drew the wrong picture, would the CI trooper have enough information to reach a good conclusion? When he got home last night, he reviewed the few times he'd worked with CWPS. Brower and Ritchie had been enthusiastic about their work. Knowledgeable, friendly. They'd shared beers after a long day of cleanup along the river. Maybe they hadn't been close buddies and it had been a while since Duncan had seen them, but dismissing their deaths as accidents? No, that wasn't right. And it didn't explain the unknown Ryan.

Sally was right about one thing, though. Solving three murders over the course of six months had given him a jaundiced view of unexpected and unexplained deaths. The fact that two men might be the victim of nothing more than unfortunate circumstances left a bad taste in his mouth and he was honest enough to admit it. God, it was like he had become addicted to the chase or something, totally unwilling to accept a simpler explanation. He thought about his friend Nate Greaves's question from this spring, during the investigation into Lonnie Butler's death. "Why haven't you ever applied to join Criminal Investigation?"

Why hadn't he? True, he liked patrol, liked being out on the road, talking to people. Not wearing a suit and sitting in an office. On the other hand, he liked figuring out the puzzle. Patrol troopers handled the first encounter and Nicols had always allowed Duncan a bit more freedom in how he spent his shift time. In Criminal Investigation, the State Police detective's job was to solve puzzles. Who, what, where, when, why, and how. Yes, patrol still held appeal, but maybe it was time for something new.

A voice broke through his thoughts. "Jim. How's it going?" Bob Hunter stood at the edge of his property.

Duncan slowed and stopped. "Hey, Bob. How's Lindy?"

Hunter's smile, tight and sad, told the whole story. "She's getting by. The accident, falling in the water and being afraid she'd drown, is tough enough. Throw a dead body on top of it and, well, she's struggling. But she's a strong kid. She'll get through it." Hunter paused. "Is there any more information about the body Lindy saw, the one in the Casselman?"

"Not really. At least not that they're telling me. They're still investigating." He thought a moment. "Hey, do you still have Lindy's camera or did she lose it? And did it survive the water?"

"We have it. She had a special strap for carrying it so it wouldn't fall off if she fell. And we got the shock-proof, water-proof case for it, so it should work."

"Should. You haven't tried it?"

"No. She hasn't wanted to touch it, or take pictures, since that day. Karen put it somewhere for safekeeping." Hunter's forehead creased. "Why?"

"Turns out I knew the guy who died, Mike Brower. The scuttlebutt is this will go down as an accident."

"Let me guess. You aren't convinced."

"No." Duncan scrubbed a hand through his sweat-damp hair. "No one from the Somerset barracks asked for the camera or the photos?"

Hunter shook his head. "Nope."

"Mind if I take a look? Maybe Lindy took a picture of something important and she didn't realize it."

"Sure thing. I'll dig out the camera and run the memory card over to you."

* * *

Thursday morning, Sally planned her day as she parked in the Fayette County courthouse parking lot, entered the building, and made her way to the stairs leading to the public defender's office. No court appearances today, no meetings. Yesterday, she'd sat in front of Jim and questioned why he was unwilling to accept an accidental death explanation. The truth was, that explanation left her unhappy as well. But her counterargument had been sound. Not every death in the Laurel Highlands was murder.

But if Jim's intuition said otherwise, there was probably more to it. She didn't know Mike Brower or Carl Ritchie, had no skin in the game when it came to investigating their deaths. Except that it was important to Jim. That was enough for her.

Before she could get to the stairs, she was distracted by the sight of Kim Dunphy chatting with the county sheriff's deputies who manned the front entrance metal detectors. "Kim, what the hell are you doing here?" she asked.

Kim laughed at a joke from one of the deputies, then said goodbye, and strolled over to Sally. "You keep dodging my calls, so I figured I'd show up early. Catch you before you got to work."

"For God's sake, Kim." Sally shot a look around the massive lobby. The deputies had returned to discussing the Pittsburgh sports scene and paid her no attention. She jerked her head in the direction of the district attorney's office, went to the corner, and whirled to face her classmate. "This is definitely not cool. You cannot come to my current workplace and ask if I'm going to quit and join your new law firm."

"Hey, it's not like I was going to bust into your office and start shouting." Kim winked. "But while we're here, you give any more thought to the offer?"

"I rolled it around."

"Lawyer-speak for I dismissed it completely. I told you Sally, it's a knee-jerk response and not your style."

"You think what you like. My answer is no." Sally paused and nodded to a woman from the county commissioner's office who passed by. "I'm happy with my current position. Plus, I don't think our styles would mesh. You're a little…assertive for my taste."

"I'm assertive. Uh, okay. Like you can't be the same." Kim waved off any response. "Be that as it may, let me ask you this. How many deadbeats are on the docket today?"

"Comments like that aren't going to win me over."

Kim held up her hands. "I apologize. It was a cheap shot. But honestly, think about your last six clients. Can you, with a straight face, tell me this is what you saw yourself doing when you were in law school? Is this truly where you want to be?"

No, it wasn't where Sally had seen herself. But she hadn't lied when she said she was happy. "I know these people aren't your idea of perfect clients. That doesn't matter. I'm doing important work."

"I'm sure you are. But you could be doing the same work for more money."

Sally looked at Kim's face, recognizing the same determination she often felt herself. "For the last time. I appreciate the offer. But I'm not interested. Good luck in finding someone. If a name comes to me and I think it's a good fit, I'll let you know." She turned and moved toward the stairs.

Kim's voice made her pause. "I'm not going away until I get the answer I want, Sally. You should know that."

Sally descended the stairs to her basement office. Yes, she did know. Kim was feisty, smart, and tenacious. All good qualities for a defense attorney. Not so great for those who opposed her, in or out of court. Sally juggled her briefcase, purse, and coffee cup, searching for her keys. She lost her grip on the travel mug and it crashed to the ground. The lid burst off and hot coffee splashed the floor. "Oh, for f—"

"Now, now, language," Tanelsa said as she appeared on the stairway. "Relax, we have paper towels. Hold on a sec." She opened the door and fetched the roll of towels. "I'll even help."

"Nah, I've got it." Sally deposited her things on Doris's desk, ripped off a handful of paper, and crouched to mop up the spreading brown puddle.

Ignoring her protests, Tanelsa bent down with her own wad. "Not a great start to the day. What's got you so aggravated at eight in the morning?"

"Oh…it's nothing."

"Right. Anything to do with the redhead upstairs?"

"You saw her?"

"Hard to miss. She's flamboyant in a very professional way. I bet she's hell in the courtroom."

"How can you tell she's a lawyer?" Sally tossed the soggy paper in the trash, retrieved her belongings, and went to her tiny office.

Tanelsa followed her. "She's got that look. Friend of yours?"

"Old classmate." Sally sorted through the message slips on her desk. Nothing earthshaking.

Tanelsa studied her. "Let me guess. She's trying to get you to jump ship and you aren't jumping."

"What makes you say that?"

Tanelsa shrugged, barely creasing her light summer blouse. "She's a lawyer. You say she's a former classmate, so probably criminal law. You're out of sorts, which means she's asked you to do something you don't want to do. I'll go so far as to say you've already told her no and she won't leave it alone. How close am I?"

"It's a good thing you and I are on the same side. Am I so easy to read?"

"Only to people who know you, like Jim and I."

Sally tossed aside the message slips. "Kim, that's her name, is starting a law firm and she wants me to join as her partner."

"You've been invited in on the ground floor of a firm? As a full partner? Why wouldn't you jump at that?"

"I won't deny it's tempting. But I've got a good gig here and good things happening elsewhere in my life." Tanelsa smirked, but Sally drove on. "Building a new firm takes a lot of effort and I don't feel like working all those hours."

"What does Jim say?"

"He told me to do what would make me happy and he wasn't going to abandon me over a crazy work day."

"Then what's your problem?"

"I don't…look, can we not talk about this before I'm properly caffeinated?" Sally pushed past her friend and headed for the communal coffee maker. She popped in a pod of her favorite blend and waited for the coffee to brew. The rich smell relaxed her.

As soon as it was Tanelsa's turn, she grabbed a mug and a pod of the same coffee. "In all seriousness, I'd be very glad if you stuck around. But Sally, you should give this offer some serious thought. You don't get this kind of opportunity every day and I doubt your friend is going to ask twice."

"Oh, that's where you're wrong." Sally blew on the top of her mug. "Kim's more stubborn than I am. She's already asked at least that many times. And she'll keep asking until she gets the answer she wants."

Chapter Thirteen

Duncan returned from his run, shed his sweaty clothes, and turned on the shower, making the water as hot as he could stand it. The steam would clear his head and help him think.

Burns told him an official ID had been made. The Casselman John Doe was Mike Brower. Which meant they'd have questioned Brower's parents and any co-workers. Problem was the only person he knew associated with the investigation, Travers, wouldn't share the results of that without pressure from above. Lieutenant Nicols was likely to be sympathetic to Duncan's intuition, but he wouldn't butt into an investigation in another county for that.

He thought of the two victims as he'd known them a couple of years ago. Yes, it could be two freak accidents or even one freak accident that claimed the lives of both men. If that was the case, why hadn't news broken about it by now? Both bodies had shown signs of severe beating. Duncan didn't know of any industrial facilities on the river that would do that. He'd read Burns's notes. The injuries were too extensive to be caused by rocks in the riverbed.

Then there was the name, Ryan. Who was he?

Duncan toweled himself dry. The least he could do was find this Ryan and ask some questions. If the information indicated accidental death, he'd back off. If not, well, he'd try once again to talk to Travers or find out who in the Somerset County CI division was leading the charge and go to him.

Ritchie was a dead end. No family, no wife to talk to. He could go to the bank where Ritchie worked, question co-workers. Same with Brower.

However, Duncan preferred to start closer to home. That meant a trip to Altoona. The Browers would probably wonder why a stranger wanted to know about their son, but Duncan would handle that when he got there.

Before Duncan left Confluence, he sent Sally a brief text letting her know he'd be out of pocket for most of the day. Then he called Brower's parents, identified himself as a friend of their son's, and asked if they'd be willing to talk. The bewilderment and grief in Brower Senior's voice were clear, but he agreed. Anything to find out what happened.

* * *

With a history as a railroad town, and a current economy fighting to recover after the industrial decline, Altoona was a city of working-class homes. The Brower residence was no exception, a sturdy, mid-century brick structure fronted by a pristine lawn, neatly trimmed hedges, and colorful flowers. Duncan parked his Jeep on the street and approached the front door.

The man who answered appeared to be a healthier and more vibrant, albeit older, version of the Casselman victim. There was a little more gray in his hair and he had the florid features of a man who liked his beer but was likely the same height and build. His dark blue eyes shone with an intelligent light, but purple smudges underneath betrayed a lack of sleep. "May I help you?"

"Yes, sir. Jim Duncan, I called you earlier."

"Of course, come in." He closed the door. "You said you're a friend of Mike's?"

Duncan followed the elder Brower into the front living room. "Not a very close friend, unfortunately. I volunteered with his organization a couple times some years back. When two guys love fishing, it creates a bond."

"You fish? You ever join Mike to go after smallmouth?"

"No, I'm usually down on the Youghiogheny or on the Gorge looking for trout. But to a certain extent, fishing is fishing. Mike was very passionate about restoring and protecting the Laurel Highlands."

Mike's father took a ragged breath. "That he was."

A woman with gray hair, brown eyes, and a Mrs. Santa Claus figure sat on a plaid tweed couch, surrounded by pamphlets from a funeral home. "Who's this, Harold?" she asked. Tired, bloodshot eyes in a drawn, pale face said she also had not slept well lately.

"Jim Duncan, ma'am." Duncan took a quick inventory of the room. Retired working class, he decided. Enough money to live comfortably in Altoona, but put them somewhere else and they'd be on a tight budget.

Mrs. Brower gave a tired smile. "Sir, ma'am, what are you military?"

"I'm with the Pennsylvania State Police, stationed in Fayette County."

Harold frowned. "You said you were a friend of Mike's. We've already talked to the police."

"I was. I also happen to work for the PSP. I'm not associated with the official investigation into your son's death."

"Then why are you here? Is something wrong?"

"Please, Mr. Duncan. Sit down," Mrs. Brower said, gathering up the pamphlets. "We may be mourning, but we can act like civilized people. Would you like a cup of coffee?" She pulled a tissue from the cuff of her sleeve and dabbed her eyes.

"No, ma'am, I don't want to trouble you."

She stood and pasted a smile on her worn face. "See here, young man. If you're going to come into our house for coffee and a talk, enough with this sir and ma'am nonsense. I'm Gladys, that's Harold. Would you like cream or sugar?"

"No m…thank you. Black is fine."

Gladys patted him on the shoulder. "Hold on a minute." She trudged out of the room.

Harold turned to Duncan. "Mike is our only son. She's trying to be normal, but she's devastated."

"I understand. You said you were willing to talk, but if you've changed your mind, that's okay."

"No. We want to know what happened. Mike spent hundreds of hours on that river."

Gladys returned with a tray and three mugs of coffee. "My boy didn't die in an accident." She might be holding back tears, but her voice was fierce. "No more than that other man, the one he worked with. I don't care what they said."

Duncan took his mug and sat. "Carl Ritchie?"

"Yes, him." Gladys looked at her worn tissue and fumbled with a box for another one. "Mike was a Boy Scout, he made Eagle. He's been an outdoorsman for most of his life. We only met Carl a couple of times, but he was the same." Tears coursed down her cheeks and she dropped the box of tissues.

Duncan pulled out his handkerchief and handed it to her. "Tell me about Mike. As I told your husband, I didn't know him well, but he struck me as very passionate."

Gladys accepted the handkerchief and dried her eyes. "He was. Always has been. His Eagle Scout project was restoring a local recreation area. Camping, hiking, fishing, boating…he loved it all. If he could have quit his job and made money from his conservation efforts, he would have."

"Did he work alone?" Duncan asked. He took his phone out of his pocket and opened the Notes app.

Harold answered. "For a few years, yes. Then he met Carl. It was a match made in heaven. Both of 'em lived for the outdoors."

"They were close?"

"For a while. I got the impression things had become a little strained between them."

Duncan thought of the newspaper picture. "Do you know why?"

Gladys answered. "Mike could be difficult. He was a very outgoing boy, social to an extreme. As long as people agreed with him, he could be the life of the party. But when you didn't, well, I often told him growing up he needed to learn to disagree politely. I'm not sure he ever learned that trick." She sniffed and dabbed her eyes again. "But as is so often the case with people like that, he never stayed mad long. You'd fight with him and five minutes later he would act like it never happened. It was impossible for him to hold a grudge."

Except maybe this time he'd not gotten past the arguing stage. "Do you know anything about Carl?"

Harold shook his head. "The times we met him, we never talked about anything personal. It was always about the organization."

Damn. "Did Mike mention arguing with anybody recently, maybe in relation to CWPS?"

Harold thought a second. "Not especially. At least not that he named. He often criticized people and companies for not appreciating the resources in the area, especially companies in the Laurel Highlands. Given his personality, he probably got in lots of heated discussions. Although…"

"Yes?"

Harold looked at his wife. "There was one that stood out, wasn't there? Something to do with the fish."

Gladys frowned. "Yes. A mining company of sorts. Mike was worried about the smallmouth bass. He'd worked so hard to improve conditions on the river and this company jeopardized that. In fact, that was the trip he said he would be taking when he called last week, to check things out."

Duncan leaned forward. "Do you know how they were a threat?"

She played with the handkerchief. "No, I'm sorry. I regret that I sometimes tuned him out when he went on rants. I didn't understand half of what he would say, so I threw in a lot of uh-huhs and yeses. When he was in full sail he never noticed." She turned to her husband. "Do you know?"

Harold rubbed his chin. "It was a mining company. Dust pollution? Yes, that was it. I remember because I always thought dust was an air quality issue, not water."

A mining company capable of introducing dust into the Casselman. There couldn't be many of those around. Duncan moved on. "When did you last speak to him?"

"Last Wednesday, dinnertime."

Duncan made a note of that. "What about work? Did he mention anything on that front?"

Harold shifted position on the couch. "Very rarely. Mike worked for a lumber company. I think he did something related to personnel. Other than occasionally saying a nine-to-five job was a pain in the ass and he'd rather be on the river, he rarely mentioned work."

"Any friends you know of?"

"None that were so special he talked about them."

Mike Brower sounded like a semi-loner who loved nature. Duncan thought briefly about his own interaction with the man. They'd never discussed anything except the projects they'd worked on. "On a personal level, did Mike have a girlfriend?"

"He did hint he was in a relationship a couple of months ago," Gladys said, "but said things were complicated. I gathered she was married and considering a divorce."

"Was this someone from CWPS?" Duncan asked as he made another note.

"He didn't say. I figured he'd tell me when he was ready."

It sounded like Mike didn't tell his parents a lot of things. "One last question. Did Mike ever mention anyone named Ryan?"

"Not that I recall." Gladys smoothed out the handkerchief, folded it, and handed it back. "You're asking a lot of questions, Jim. Questions we've already answered. May I ask why?"

"Your son was an acquaintance, but I did enjoy his company and I supported the CWPS mission. I want to get the facts straight in my mind and make sure I don't miss anything. I owe him that much."

Gladys paled and gripped her husband's arm. "Do you think he might have been killed by someone?"

"That's what I'm trying to find out."

Chapter Fourteen

Later that morning, fresh cup of coffee in hand and her immediate responsibilities dealt with, Sally closed the door to her office. Jim's text earlier had worried her a bit. Why was he driving to Altoona to meet the Browers? She hadn't been kidding when they talked yesterday. Not every death in the area was murder. However, as soon as she'd shown that picture to Jim, she'd known how events would go from there. No matter how lightly he knew the victims, he wouldn't let the investigation go. If he wanted answers and if Travers wouldn't give them, Jim would go looking his own.

Did she want to get involved this time? She didn't know Carl Ritchie or Mike Brower from Adam, as the saying went. Who was she kidding? Jim's problems were hers now. Since this was a case being handled by a different troop in a different county, he wouldn't be able to spend much patrol time asking questions. If the both of them pooled their resources, perhaps they could get an answer before Travers knew what was going on.

If Jim had gone off to ask questions of Brower's parents, the logical thing would be for her to find out more about Ritchie. She ran a quick check. Carl was single, forty, and lived in Markleton. His modest income came from a job as a bank manager. There were no past convictions on his record and he had a good credit score. His car, several years old, was paid for.

That wasn't helpful. She needed to talk to some people, his co-workers or the landlord. Markleton was an hour away. She could make time to go this afternoon, but having a cover story would be helpful.

At that moment, Tanelsa appeared. "What are you scheming?"

"Who said I was scheming? Why do you always jump to the worst conclusion?"

Tanelsa crossed her arms. "You've got that look on your face, the one that means you're trying to justify something to yourself."

No sense hiding it. Tanelsa was too good at reading body language. She'd spot a lie in a heartbeat. "I'm thinking of going to Markleton this afternoon. I need to find out more about a man named Carl Ritchie."

"Who the hell is he?"

"He's one of the guys from the picture I showed you, the one with Jim in it."

"The Casselman group?"

"That's the one." Sally downed some coffee, which had gone almost cold. "On the surface, the deaths are being written off as accidental."

Tanelsa nodded. "And Jim is dissatisfied with that explanation. Two guys from the same group dead within a week? Hell, I wouldn't be satisfied either."

"Especially as Jim said both are experienced outdoorsmen and it would take a major accident to injure both like this."

"Let me guess. He hasn't heard about any accidents of that nature."

"You got it." Sally shuffled some papers on her desk, tidying up.

Tanelsa continued to study her. "Okay, I get why he's looking into this. What're they to you?"

Of course, Tanelsa would ask the hard question. "By themselves, not much. Aside from the fact I know Jim well enough that if he has suspicions, I do, too. But mostly it's concern for Jim."

"Why?"

Sally told her friend about Travers. "I'm not sure how much trouble this jerk can make. But if I help Jim out, and we can get an answer, or at least actionable information, quickly, maybe Jim can avoid Travers's ire. Or the consequences. I'm pretty sure Travers being pissed is a foregone conclusion at this point."

"Weak, Sally. Very weak."

Sally dropped some folders in a drawer and slammed it shut. "You're married. Tell me, if Lisa wanted your help with something, and you could give it, wouldn't you? Especially if it might keep her out of trouble?"

"Of course."

"Same with Jim and me. We aren't married, but if I can help him I will."

Tanelsa spread her hands. "You got me. So what's your first step?"

"I have to go to Markleton."

*　*　*

After leaving the Browers, Duncan consulted the Maps app on his phone for directions to the lumber yard where Mike Brower had worked. He'd resisted the smartphone revolution for a long time, but damn if the thing didn't come in handy.

The lumber yard was big. Stacks of cut boards towered under cover, protected from the rain, while industrial-sized saws ripped some into smaller boards and others worked at turning logs into finished product. A man in a hardhat expertly drove a forklift to move piles of wood across the yard, adding the roar of a diesel engine to the intense buzzing. Duncan snagged a passing employee. "Excuse me, I'm looking for the main office."

The man removed a pair of foam ear protectors. "Sorry, I can't hear you."

"The main office," Duncan shouted. "Where is it?"

The worker pointed at a faded blue building off in the corner of the yard. "Over there. Not sure you'll find anyone with time to talk. Management's been kinda short-handed lately with Brower gone."

"That wouldn't be Mike Brower, would it?"

"Yup. Got the word this morning that he was dead. Some kind of accident on the river, I think."

Duncan bristled. Travers might say "the investigation continued," but he was clearly giving people the impression Brower's death was a mishap. "Did you know Mike well?"

The guy shook his head. "Nah, I only started a couple weeks ago. I mean, he processed my paperwork, but that's about it."

"Is there someone here who knew him better?"

"Uh, try the office. Look, I gotta get back to work." The worker hurried away.

Duncan strode over to the office, taking in details of the yard as he went. While activity was everywhere, it was organized, not a chaotic mess. Everybody wore the appropriate protective gear. Sawdust lay everywhere, but Duncan didn't spot any visible safety hazards, none caused by carelessness anyway.

The volume inside the office was a bit lower than outside, but not by much. Duncan still had to raise his voice. "Excuse me. I'm looking for someone who knew Mike Brower."

A middle-aged man with a beer belly, thinning hair, and a harassed expression stood at the desk. He looked at Duncan. "Who's asking?"

"My name is Jim Duncan. I'm with the State Police and I knew Brower. I worked with his environmental group a few years ago."

"Brower's not here any longer. Died over the weekend, accident on the Casselman." He went back to shuffling papers.

"So I heard, mister...?"

"Tanner, Jack Tanner. I'm the manager of the yard. Now having to manage and do human resources, until I find Mike's replacement." Tanner set down the papers and ran a hand over his head. "I've already talked to the police."

"I understand. As I said, I volunteered with Brower. I have a few questions of my own, if you wouldn't mind answering them. Probably nothing the police haven't asked."

"Then why are you here? Can't you get the information from them?"

"It's kinda complicated." Duncan paused. "I knew Brower, I liked his organization and I respected him as an environmentalist and fisherman. I don't want to see anything fall through the cracks."

"Respected him?" Tanner snorted. "Your mistake there."

Duncan's interest perked up. "Why do you say that?"

"He was an arrogant son of a bitch. Oh, he did his job well. Never had a problem with him. But occasionally he'd make himself a pain in the ass. We're a lumber company. We cut trees. We do it responsibly. We even plant new ones, one sapling for every mature tree we cut. That was Brower's idea.

He still kept threatening to call people to make sure we weren't raping the land, as he called it. Destroying the natural beauty of the Laurel Highlands."

"What people?"

"No freaking idea. We've got so many licenses and permits, undergo so many yearly inspections, I have no clue who else he could call. Occasionally he'd go off on rants about all the sawdust, how the wind could carry it, pollute the land, the water. Especially the water. Dust pollution, he called it."

"Did he talk about anything else?"

"You name it. Too much sugar and the evils of processed food. How people need to get off their phones and on their feet. And politics? Don't get him started."

"He had opinions."

"About the only thing he didn't have something to say about was professional sports, and by that, I mean real sports like hockey or football. Not bass fishing." Tanner snorted. "I suppose that environmental group of his did some good, but man, he could be a a real asshole."

"He was difficult to work with, then?"

"That's just it." Tanner sank into a swivel chair lightly coated with dust. "When he focused on his job, he was great. Every employee's records were kept up to date, organized to a fault. New employees were brought in quickly and when folks left the processing was handled smoothly. It was only when he went off the rails that he irritated others."

"Did he do that recently?"

Tanner thought. "Right before he left on vacation. He was planning some river expedition. One of the guys made a crack about the river, Brower got angry, they traded words and it almost came to blows. Insane."

"Who was the other guy?"

"Ben Mankel, one of our best forklift operators."

Duncan gazed out the window. "Is he here?"

"It's his day off."

Duncan transferred his attention back to Tanner. "Don't suppose you could see your way clear to giving me his phone number and address, could you?"

Again, he ran his hand over his head, making the few strands of hair almost stand straight up. "You're with the state police you say?"

"I am." Duncan showed his badge.

"So if I say no, you'll look up Ben on your own?"

"Most likely." Duncan cracked a grin.

Tanner sighed, reached for a pen and paper, and then pulled up a record on the dust-covered computer. He scribbled and handed it to Duncan. "Here," he said. "Address and phone number." He squinted. "You're right, pretty much what the police already asked. You said you knew Brower. You not on board with the accident explanation?"

Duncan took the sheet. "Let's say I'm covering all the bases."

Chapter Fifteen

Sally took the afternoon off and drove to Markleton. The drive took a little less than an hour and Sally arrived at Laurel Highlands Trust, the bank where Carl Ritchie worked, at slightly past one-thirty in the afternoon. LHT was one of those small, independent banks, probably pretty popular with locals.

Inside, however, there were few patrons. A couple of old ladies at the tellers, no one with the lone advisor, who got up and moved toward Sally. He was an older man in a dark brown suit, white shirt, and a conservative necktie appropriate for his profession. "Good afternoon and welcome to Laurel Highlands Trust. Can I help you?"

Sally shifted her purse. "Maybe. I'm looking for someone who knew Carl Ritchie."

"Carl is, unfortunately, not here."

"I'm aware of that." Her gaze flicked to his lapel, but he didn't wear a name tag. "I'm sorry, your name is?"

"John Snyder. I'm the bank manager."

Not Ryan. "Isn't it unusual for a manager to be working the floor?"

"Given Carl's death, we're a little short-handed." He flashed a rueful smile. "Would you like to sit down Miss...?"

"Castle, Sally Castle." She shook John's hand. "I have a few questions about Carl. Maybe you can help me."

His age-spotted forehead creased. "Questions? I don't understand."

"I think it would be better if we talked in private."

Snyder maintained his puzzled expression, but led her to a small office in the back. He closed the door and waved toward two plain wooden chairs that matched the mahogany desk. "Please, sit. Coffee, tea, water?"

"I'm good, thanks." The chair was rock hard. LHT must not be successful enough for its manager to go in for plush executive furniture.

"You said you had questions about Carl. What's this about?" Snyder took the desk chair and sat back.

"There is some concern Mr. Ritchie's death may not have been accidental. Were you aware that his partner at the Casselman Water Protection Society also died recently?"

"No, I didn't know that. Brower was his name, right?"

"Yes, Mike Brower. His body washed up near Confluence."

"Is that why Carl's death is suspicious?"

"Yes. Two men, experienced outdoorsmen, from the same organization in allegedly fatal accidents within days of each other. It seems too coincidental to be true."

"Understandable." John steepled his fingers. "The police have already been by to ask questions about Carl. I don't see what your purpose is here, Miss Castle. Are you with the state police?"

"No, I work for the Fayette County Public Defender. I have questions and I'm following up on my own."

"I see." John paused, maybe thinking why on earth a Fayette County lawyer would be involved in investigating two deaths in Somerset County. "How do you think I can help you?"

"For starters, I understand Mr. Ritchie was a loan manager. Was he the only one?"

"Yes, we're a small bank. Carl handled the vast majority of our consumer loans. If things got particularly busy, I'd step in, but that was rare."

"Was he good at his job, a reliable employee?"

"Oh yes. As I said, it was unusual for me to have to help. He had a gift for talking to the public, helping them find exactly what they needed. I would not have hesitated to leave management of the bank in his hands, if the situation required it."

"Did he get along with all of your other employees?"

John shifted in his chair. "As far as I knew. He was always respectful toward the single women who work here. I don't believe he was close to our one other male teller, but they seemed friendly when I saw them interact. He flattered the older women, but they seemed to like it."

"Flirting?"

"Oh, nothing like that." John grinned. "The women, Betty and Carol, are older than Carl and widowed. He treated them well, paid a lot of compliments, that sort of thing. When a woman gets older, she tends to fade into the background. Carl made sure Carol and Betty were noticed. It's probably a situation a young, pretty woman like yourself is not familiar with."

Not personally, but Sally had seen enough of her mother's older friends overlooked. Even Doris, despite the fact she sat at the front of the office, was occasionally ignored in favor of the other, younger secretary. "The male teller, what's his name?"

"Evan Tadwell. He's, oh, in his mid-thirties. I suspect the only reason he's in Markleton is because he's looking after his elderly mother. He never misses the opportunity to let us know what a backwater this is."

"Is there anybody at the bank named Ryan?"

"No, why?"

"I'm curious." Sally bit her lip before continuing. "What about the public? Did he ever fight or argue with any of them?"

"Nothing that ever went beyond what I'd consider professional." At Sally's inquiring look, John continued. "We can't afford to take on the risky loans that bigger banks give. Sometimes Carl had to tell people no, and some of those people weren't happy. But if you're asking if Carl ever came to blows with a customer, or got in a really significant argument, the answer is no. He was a good man who did his job well and got along with people."

And yet he wound up in the Casselman River, the victim of a beating. "Did you ever meet his partner, Mike Brower?"

"A few times. CWPS had an account here. Mike would come in to talk things over with Carl."

"A big account?"

John's answering smile was thin. "I'm not at liberty to discuss exact amounts without a warrant or court order. But no, I do not believe the amount of money was outrageous."

Rebuked, Sally plowed on. "The two men were friendly, as far as you can tell?"

"Mostly, except…"

"Except what?"

John looked like he was weighing his words before he spoke. "Mike was in here, oh, a week ago. Maybe more like two. I thought it was routine business at the teller, but Carl leapt up to talk to him. Mike didn't sound like he wanted to talk. He said something like 'We've already discussed this and my mind is made up. The stakes are too high.'"

Interesting. "What did Mr. Ritchie say?"

"Let me think." John's gaze focused on the wall behind Sally. "That the reputation of CWPS was also at stake and this wasn't the way to go about things. But Mike shook him off."

"Was that all?" Maybe that was the source of the contention between the two men.

"No." John focused on Sally again. "As Mike was leaving, Carl asked if he'd broken it off with her yet."

"Her? Her who?"

"Carl didn't say a name. But you mentioned the name Ryan, earlier. Didn't you?"

"Yes."

John folded his hands on the desk. "As I said, there's no one who works here with that name. But now that I think on it, I swear Carl told Mike that he'd better break it off before Ryan found out and killed him."

* * *

From the bank, Sally drove over to Carl's home, a duplex in a more residential part of town. Clean and quiet, but nothing fancy. A couple of older cars and trucks were parked along the street. At his address, a middle-aged man supervised the removal of furniture and personal items. "No, no, Put that by the curb. And be careful. Someone may want it."

Sally skirted the men, who manhandled a large chest of drawers to the edge of the street. "Excuse me. I'm looking for the landlord."

"You found him." The man wiped a high forehead exposed by a receding hairline. "Paul Gostwick. You looking to rent? I'm full up, but this unit'll be ready in a week or two." He surveyed Sally. "Though honestly, you don't look like you belong in this neighborhood."

She held out her court credentials. "No, not renting. I'm interested in information about the man who used to live here, Carl Ritchie."

Paul took the credentials, studied them a moment, and handed them back. "Uh, okay, but I don't see what a lawyer from Fayette County wants with Carl. He get into some kind of trouble before he died?"

"No. I'm assisting with the investigation into his death." She put the ID away. That had a nice, generic tone.

Paul clearly remained puzzled. "He died in a river accident. Least that's what I gathered."

"They're still investigating." She cast a look at the furniture and boxes on the grass. "You're cleaning out his apartment? Who for?"

"For myself." Paul indicated the other men should continue and stepped away. "Carl ain't got family, no wife. No friends interested in taking his stuff. I gotta empty this unit so I can rent it again. If that sounds callous, well, I'm a business man."

"I understand." The furniture was plain and well worn. The boxes contained unadorned plates that would easily transfer from microwave to table. The glassware might have been picked up at a discount store. All stuff suited to an older bachelor. "What do you plan to do with it?"

"Goodwill, Salvation Army. Stuff no one will take will go to the curb for the pickers." Paul wiped his face again. "Is that what you wanted to know?"

"Not exactly." She faced him. "Tell me, what kind of tenant was Mr. Ritchie?"

"The perfect kind. Quiet, never made a fuss, always paid his rent on time. Wish they were all like that."

"You never had any problems with him them? Odd visitors, arguments?"

"Nope, not anything serious enough to get involved or call the cops."

Sally held out a picture of Mike Brower. "You ever see this man visit?"

"Oh yeah. Mike. He and Carl did some environmental thing together. Always going out in the woods or along the river." Paul leaned aside to shout at the workers. "Careful of that lamp, that's decent stuff. You break it, you'll clean up the mess."

Sally glanced over her shoulder. "So they got along as far as you can tell. Mr. Ritchie and Mr. Brower. Mike."

"I suppose." Paul shrugged. "I mean, sometimes they argued, but hell. Friends argue all the time, don't they? Everything's not always sunshine and roses."

"Had you heard them argue recently?"

"Lady, you're killing me. The cops already asked all this shit."

She flashed a smile. "Humor me? Please?"

He sighed. "Carl was out of sorts about something in the last week. About what, I don't know. I was taking out trash one night when he got home and he was talking to himself. How some guy didn't know what he was doing, nothing was worth this kind of risk, and the ends didn't justify the means."

That might go along with what John Snyder at the bank said. "Did you get a name?"

"No, Carl only used 'he', no names. But whatever it is, it musta been serious."

"How can you tell?"

"I said hello and he ignored me." Paul shook his head. "Not like Carl at all, he always said hi, asked how I was doing. He was polite that way. My wife, she has fibromyalgia and Carl always asked after her."

If Carl's partner was up to something, that would definitely be distracting. "What about other visitors? Women?"

Paul laughed. "Carl didn't date much. Not that he was gay, mind you, he simply didn't date."

"I see. Visitors?"

He screwed up his face. "There was a guy, a month or so ago. Nice suit, clearly had some money. I was going out and the guy was leaving. He wanted Carl to talk to *him*, some third guy I guess, make him see reason. Carl said he'd try, but he, this third guy, was pretty stubborn."

"But it was a friendly conversation?"

"Yeah, seemed to be." Paul looked over at the workers, who had continued to haul the contents of the apartment out. "We about done?"

"Almost. Did Mr. Ritchie ever have a visitor named Ryan, or did you ever hear him use that name?"

"Ryan?" He frowned. "No. Doesn't ring any bells. Sorry." He checked the workers again. "Anything else?"

"No, thanks for your time." Sally meandered back to her car, lost in thought. It seemed to her that Mike wanted to do something and Carl disagreed. Not a minor disagreement, either. And another player had entered the picture, the man in the suit. Ryan remained a mystery.

She climbed into her car. God, and Jim thought he might like to do this full time?

Chapter Sixteen

When Sally arrived at Jim's house that evening, he met her at the door wearing what looked suspiciously like fishing gear. "Are you going somewhere?"

"Brower's parents mentioned he said he was going to do a survey of a section of the Casselman. Thought I'd go take a look."

Sally hesitated. "That's why you went to Altoona?"

"To talk to the family, yes. They definitely don't believe their son's death was accidental."

"Is that what Travers told them?"

"It might not have been Travers, but yeah, that's the story. I also don't see any indications of a serious investigation. As far as I can tell, Travers is taking the easy way out."

Sally bit her lip, then said, "Jim…are you sure you want to do this? Travers does not seem like an understanding guy. This one could get you in real trouble."

Jim spun his keys on his finger. "I don't want to crash into someone else's investigation. I don't. On the other hand, I'm not going to stand by and let someone write this off as an accident without due diligence. Obviously, the Somerset Coroner isn't satisfied either, or else he would have issued a finding of accidental death." He paused. "Mike's parents also said he had a married girlfriend."

"With a jealous husband?"

"I don't know. I have to find her first."

She sighed. Dog with a bone, same as always. "Let me get the hiking boots and clothes out of my trunk."

"You keep hiking gear in your trunk?"

"Ever since I started dating you I do."

On the way to the river, she brought him up to speed on what she'd learned about Ritchie. "I found nothing that makes me suspect someone had it out for either man."

Jim shot her a sideways look. "What happened to leave it alone? What's good for the goose is good for the gander, and all that."

"Yeah, except I guess a part of me knew you wouldn't be satisfied with a half-assed investigation. If I can help you out, I will." She studied the lush green trees as they rolled along. "Based on my conversations earlier, we need to add two more figures to the party. Ryan and this unknown suited guy."

"Except you said the guy in the suit seemed friendly."

"To Carl, yes. From what I learned by talking to the landlord, there was a definite disagreement with Mike. It's still possible, at least in my mind, that Mike was the target and Carl was collateral damage, so to speak."

"I'll grant you that." He drummed on the steering wheel. "Sounds to me like Ryan is related to the unknown girlfriend somehow. Husband maybe."

Sally flashed a grin and continued to look out the window. "Where exactly are we going and what are we going to do once we get there?"

He concentrated on driving as he left the main road and headed onto a half dirt-half gravel track. "Mike's parents said he talked about dust pollution that could affect the fish and he liked fishing for smallmouth bass. While they didn't know the exact spot, I know where fishing for smallmouth has gotten pretty popular. I want to check out the scene, see if it results in any new leads."

"Are you thinking it's the potential murder scene?"

"As far as I'm concerned, the whole river, or at least the part in Somerset County, is the scene until I can narrow it down."

It took maybe thirty minutes to reach their destination, a picturesque river bend where the water of the Casselman would have splashed over the rocks, if it had been lower, and the sunlight dappled the water. Trees lined both sides of the river. The water levels had receded enough that at least half a dozen men stood in it holding fishing poles. Sally got out and shut the door of the Jeep. "What a beautiful spot. What are we looking for?"

Jim followed. "I don't know." He looked up and down the river. "Nice day. Nice crowd for a weeknight." He trudged over to the nearest fisherman. "Hey there, how's the luck today?"

The man flicked his pole and shook his head. "Mediocre."

"That's why they call it fishing, not catching, right?"

The fisherman laughed. "Oh, there's plenty of fish. They aren't taking the bait. If fish were more intelligent I'd say they were giving us the middle fin and trying to make our lives harder."

"Isn't that the way?" Jim crouched to scoop up a handful of water and let it run out. Next to him, the guy took a step and slipped. Jim reached out to grab an arm and keep him from falling in the water.

"Thanks." The fisherman wound up his line, then cast again. "Man, I hope that guy is able to make his plans reality. The footing here really sucks."

Jim scooped another handful of water, again let it run out, and stood. "What guy?"

"Some guy with money from up in Pittsburgh, liked to fish." The man cast again and called to another fisherman. "Hey, Frank, what was that guy's name, the one with all the fancy plans?"

Frank thought a moment. "Whitney, Xavier Whitney. Sounds like a guy with money to spend, don't it? Hey, something wrong with the water? You seem awfully interested."

"Nope," Jim said. "Looks perfect to me. No wonder the fish like to call this spot home."

Sally looked from Frank to the first fisherman. "What were the plans, Mr…what was your name again?"

"Don Reich." He cast again. "Whitney was gonna revamp this spot. Clean up the road, provide better access to the river, even put in a fancy composting toilet for us to use. He's retired, loves fishing, loves the Laurel Highlands, and said he wanted to bring more people down to see what a jewel we got here. In a responsible fashion, of course. That's why the toilets.

I'd sure like a clean place to take a leak, but I don't know as I'd like all the people that come with it."

"Unless that jerk drove him off," Frank added. "I told you, Don. More people mean the game commission might release more fish. And city folk who think this is a lark won't stick around. In the end, we'd benefit."

"What jerk?" Jim asked.

Don made another cast. "Guys from whaddaya call it, that river environmental group."

"Casselman Water Preservation Society?" Sally asked, shooting a look at Jim.

"Yeah, that's it." Don turned his head and spit. "Actually, the one guy seemed interested. It was the other one. Ranting and raving about how things like that always sounded great, until the dozers showed up, and the asphalt got poured."

Frank broke in. "Hell, Whitney wasn't gonna pour any asphalt. Everything he talked about was sustainable development. Gravel, native stone, and the like. All he was gonna do was cut back the bushes, use natural wood to build some lookout points, make some secure spots you could stand on and cast. I've been fishing this river since I was a boy. The knees aren't what they used to be. I'd love easier access and a nice flat place to stand on. Loudmouth wouldn't hear of it."

Jim studied the river, then turned to Don. "Loudmouth got a name?"

"I'm sure he does, but I didn't get it." Don wheeled in his line. "Frank, you ever get the name of that jag-off who raised holy hell over the fishing access plans?"

Frank twitched his line. "No. Arrogant cuss. Shoot. They do cleanup projects and the like down at Ohiopyle all the time. Why not here?"

"Because we want to keep this fishing spot to ourselves, you nitwit," Don retorted. "We don't want any damn tourists scaring away the fish."

Jim took a couple of steps toward the water.

Sally took up the questions. "What about anything else? You ever have troubles with other people around here? Maybe businesses affecting the fish or anything?"

Frank changed lures on his hook and made another cast. "Nope. They've done a real good job cleaning up the water. I haven't seen this many fish in a dog's age. Loudmouth came here a couple times, though. Last time was, oh, a week ago? Took some water samples all the time muttering about stone and water quality. Look, I'm all for preserving the environment, but this nut job, he went too far if you ask me. Nature's meant to be enjoyed, not looked at on picture postcards and all that shit."

Jim came back. "I'm with you there. Do me a favor." He handed Frank a business card. "If Loudmouth comes back, or you hear of any other problems, would you mind calling me? Either number, day or night."

Frank studied the card. "State police? Somebody get killed?"

Jim glanced at Sally. "Honestly? I don't know."

Chapter Seventeen

Duncan left Friday morning roll-call engaged in a friendly debate with McAllister. "Twenty bucks says the Steelers don't finish better than ten and six this upcoming season," he said, holding out his hand.

She grasped it. "You're on. Fool, prepare to be parted from your money."

Lieutenant Dan Nicols appeared and pointed at Duncan. "You, my office, now." He turned without waiting for a response.

McAllister gave a low whistle. "What did you do to get called to see the principal?"

"I have a suspicion," Duncan said. "Catch you later." He followed Nicols into his office. "Sir?"

Nicols didn't look up. "Close the door. Sit."

Duncan followed orders and waited.

Nicols fixed his trooper with a hard stare and folded his hands on the top of his desk. "Got a call from the barracks commander in Somerset yesterday. Have you been interfering in an investigation being run by Corporal Henry Travers?"

Oh boy. Duncan chose his words carefully. "I have not interfered with Corporal Travers's investigation."

"But you did go to Somerset."

"Yes, sir. I had information regarding the victim found in the Casselman River over the weekend in Confluence and believed it necessary to share that information with Corporal Travers."

"You also drove to Altoona to see the victim's family."

Duncan inwardly winced. "Yes, sir."

"And you stopped at the hospital to see another man, Carl Ritchie."

Nicols's cool tone made Duncan's mind writhe, but he kept his composure. "Yes, sir."

Nicols didn't budge. "Thank you for being honest, although I didn't expect anything less. You don't consider this interference?"

"No, sir. I in no way impeded Corporal Travers in his investigation. I immediately informed Corporal Travers of everything I learned. I did not prevent anyone from contacting him and I was very clear that he was the primary investigator."

Nicols leaned back. "Why did you do all this?"

"Turns out I knew both victims. I volunteered with their environmental organization."

"I see. That doesn't explain why you continue to be involved."

The concern in Duncan's mind quieted as he realized Nicols wasn't going to come down on him too hard. If he was, he'd have done it already. "I'm not satisfied with an accidental death explanation and that's the direction Travers appears to be going. The Somerset County coroner hasn't issued a finding, so he's not satisfied either. I knew both Carl Ritchie and Mike Brower. Not well, but enough to know it'd have to be a hell of an accident, one that made the news."

"And nothing has."

"Precisely. I wouldn't want to see any death fluffed off, but these? I worked alongside these guys, shared a beer or three with them. I think their group, the CWPS, does good work. They deserve a full investigation, and if I have to make sure it happens, well, so be it. But I have been careful not to get in Corporal Travers's way."

"I see." Nicols rearranged some papers on his desk. "Do you believe Travers is incompetent?"

Duncan paused. "No, sir. I have no reason to believe he's derelict in his duty, either. I do, however, think he is…overlooking a possible connection between the two victims. They'd argued recently, pretty intensely. Yesterday, I learned both men had an altercation with a man from Pittsburgh over expansion of fishing access. And Brower may have had a married girlfriend whose husband was, shall we say, less than thrilled to find out his wife had strayed."

A ghost of a grin flitted across Nicols's face. "No wonder you're not satisfied. I wouldn't be either. You say you've passed all this to Travers. You do know that they've probably gotten someone from Troop A's Criminal Investigation division involved by this point?"

"Yes, sir. But that person hasn't been in touch. Travers is my main point of contact. I haven't had the opportunity to inform him of what I learned yesterday about the fishing access issue." He took a breath. "Between you and me, I think both incidents deserve attention. However, I am aware this is not my investigation and if you tell me to leave it alone, I will."

It was Nicols's turn to pause. "All right. Here's the deal." Nicols leaned forward, a knowing look in his dark eyes. "I'll talk to the Somerset commander again, let him know we've spoken, and I believe you've raised valid concerns. In the meantime, ask your questions, but stay the hell out of their way and your work for this troop better not suffer. Sound fair?"

"Yes, sir." Duncan half stood. "If that's all—"

"No, it's not."

He dropped back into the chair.

Nicols pulled out a paper with the PSP logo at the top. "This year is a promotion cycle."

"Yes, sir, I am aware of that."

"Corporal Vanderbilt is retiring in September."

"I know that, too. We're already planning his retirement send-off."

"There will be a corporal opening at this barracks." Nicols raised an eyebrow.

Duncan figured he knew where his lieutenant was going, but continued to play dumb. "Sir?"

Nicols's smile was knowing. "I want you to apply for promotion."

"I've never been a climb-the-ladder guy, you know that."

"Cut the crap." Nicols sobered. "You should have been promoted years ago, but we haven't had a corporal's slot here in Uniontown. I've been selfishly glad you've stayed. Why? Because you're a damn fine trooper. One of my best and I didn't want to lose you."

"I appreciate the sentiment."

"Except now it's time. I want you to put your name in."

Duncan weighed his commander's words. "Sir, corporals are administrative. I like action."

"Oh, bullshit." Nicols pushed over the paper. "Yes, you'd add some shift patrol administration to your job. Running roll call, doing zone assignments, writing evaluations. You'd still be patrolling, you know that." The light came back into Nicols's eyes.

Duncan thought of McAllister's reaction if she heard he'd passed on this promotion cycle. She'd be pissed as hell. He picked up the paper, the official announcement of the written promotion exam. "I'll think about it, sir."

"You do that." Nicols spoke as though it was a foregone conclusion his trooper would test. "Now get out there and do your job."

Duncan folded the paper. "Yes, sir."

* * *

Mid-morning Friday, Sally got a second cup of coffee. Back in her office, she made a couple of phone calls and typed up a counter-proposal for a plea agreement to be submitted on Monday. Those tasks complete, she pulled out a fresh sheet of paper, divided it into columns, and started writing. Carl Ritchie. No criminal history. He was there when Xavier Whitney made his pitch for improved river access. Was he the more reasonable man or was he Loudmouth? This fight with his partner, the one where Brower threatened him, what had it been about? Tara, the CWPS photographer, didn't know, but someone had to.

Mike Brower. He also had no criminal history. His parents described him as passionate about the environment, but he had a bit of a temper. Especially when crossed. She had the same question regarding Whitney's proposal. Was Mike Loudmouth? Only one man knew for sure. *Find Xavier Whitney* Sally wrote on her paper. Maybe Whitney even knew why Mike and Carl fought, especially if it was related to the river access project.

A quick search revealed a couple of Xavier Whitneys. *Seriously?* Sally thought. *More than one person has that name?* However, only one of the men lived in Pittsburgh and had the right background. That trip would require some planning. It wasn't a dead end, but on hold for now.

But there were two other avenues of possibility with Brower. He'd gone to the Casselman to look for pollution, something about dust and stone. Not being a conservationist, Sally had no idea what that meant but she wrote it down. What businesses involving stone were in the area that could produce water pollution?

Mike's parents mentioned a married girlfriend. Did she have a jealous husband named Ryan? Carl had told Mike that Ryan would not be happy if he found out what was going on with "her," and Mike needed to break it off. From what Sally knew of Mike's injuries, they'd be consistent with a fight. It didn't explain Carl, though, unless he'd intervened on behalf of his friend and gotten clocked for his troubles. *Find the girlfriend,* Sally wrote.

She sat back and looked at the paper. It was a big to-do list, not in terms of number of items, but scope. Bigger than she had time for at work. She stood and went to Bryan Gerrity's office. She knocked on the doorframe. "Hey Bryan," she said as her boss looked up. "Remember that day off you offered me last week, the one I turned down?"

The public defender paused in the act of writing and looked up. "Yeah, you said you were too busy."

"Can I take it today?"

"Why?"

"I have some things to take care of. I don't have anything on my calendar that can't wait until Monday. I could squeeze these other things in, but it would be more appropriate if I didn't do them on the county's time."

The sunlight reflected off Bryan's glasses, making them opaque and obscuring his eyes. "Things. What kind of things?"

"Nothing important. It's not related to work." *Not my work.* Sally held her hand behind her and crossed her fingers.

Bryan twiddled his pen. "Anything I should know about?"

"Nope. It doesn't concern you or this office in the slightest."

He stared at her and Sally wished she could see his eyes clearly. Finally, he said, "Fine. Don't get into trouble."

"I won't. Thanks, Bry." She went back to her office and grabbed her purse. Who first, Whitney or the girlfriend? Whitney was in Pittsburgh. The girlfriend was probably closer to home. If she truly was married, Mike would want to keep the relationship on the q-t, but it would be great fodder for office gossip at CWPS. Sally pulled out her cell phone and dialed Tara's number.

* * *

Duncan folded the promotion announcement as he headed back to the bullpen, thoughts distracted. He hadn't quite lied to Nicols, but he had exaggerated. Of course, he'd thought about making corporal. But once he'd become eligible, advancing in rank meant leaving Uniontown, since the barracks didn't need another corporal. Staying in this location meant more to him than the stripe. Over the years, he thought about it less and thus hadn't put Vandy's retirement and the fact that it was a promotion year together.

Until Nicols handed him the announcement.

Then there was the whole Criminal Investigation route. If he applied for a position there, it'd be a lateral transfer, not a promotion. But it would mean leaving the Uniontown barracks. Promotion wouldn't. Decisions, decisions. So much simpler if he stayed a patrol trooper.

McAllister's voice jolted him out of his thoughts. "What did the big guy want? You in trouble?"

Duncan shook his head. "No, not really. He told me not to interfere with Travers."

"You're giving up?"

Duncan lifted an eyebrow. "I didn't say that. Nicols agreed with me, something is up. He told me I could keep asking questions, but not to get in the way. I guess a lot depends on your definition of interference."

McAllister cracked a grin. "Good, because I have something for you." Then she noticed the paper in Duncan's hand. "What's that?"

"Nothing."

She snatched it away and read. "It's a promotion year? Boss, are you gonna be promoted to corporal?"

Annoyed at himself for not tossing the letter before anyone saw it, Duncan grabbed it back. "Okay, you're still in your first year, but I know you know that's not how it works."

"But you're thinking about it." She tailed him as he continued on to sign out a patrol car.

"Maybe." He took the keys, and strode to the parking lot.

McAllister persisted. "Oh come on, Boss. You'd be great at it. Vanderbilt's retiring. Doesn't that mean we need a new corporal? Why risk getting a stranger and someone who doesn't understand how things work around here?"

Duncan didn't reply and looked for the patrol car, hoping McAllister would give up and leave. He should have known better.

"You don't live that far from the barracks. Sure Somerset County, but still the Laurel Highlands. You've spent what, twelve years of your almost fourteen in Uniontown? You know the quirks, you know the weirdos. The strange shit that happens in Fayette-nam doesn't faze you. Plus, it would put you on equal footing with guys like our own Corporal Sheffield and this Corporal Travers, which you definitely should be. I can't see—"

"McAllister." He whirled to face her. "I said I might be thinking about it. That's enough. Now, you said you had some information for me?"

She blinked. "Yeah. So, this guy they pulled out of the Casselman."

"Mike Brower."

"Him. And the dead guy from Somerset, Carl Ritchie. They ran this environmental group, right?"

"The Casselman Water Preservation Society."

"That's it." McAllister removed a photocopy from her pocket, what looked like a news story. "Have you ever heard of Laurel Mountain Quarrying?"

Duncan spun his keys on his finger. Where was she going with this?

"Doesn't ring a bell."

"They are, as the name would indicate, a quarrying company here in the Laurel Highlands. When I heard about CWPS, it rang a bell. This story is why." She held out the paper. "The company CEO, a woman named Caroline Longchamp, had a run-in with Brower at a rally. Turns out quarrying makes a lot of dust pollution. Brower, and I assume Ritchie, were not happy with that."

Duncan read the story and handed it back. "Okay, but why would they care? According to this, Laurel Mountain isn't near the Casselman."

"But there is a stream near the facility. And that stream feeds right into the Casselman River."

Chapter Eighteen

Back in Ohiopyle, Sally stood under a tree, scanning the scene. It was another glorious day, the first day of the weekend, and, judging by the crowds, a lot of people were playing hooky from work so they could enjoy the outside attractions. All around her, people toted canoes or kayaks, zipped by on bikes, or meandered down to the observation point to watch the river. The water level had finally receded enough to allow river-based activities to resume. All the while, Sally scanned for a sight of blue hair.

Tara Jennings had agreed to meet Sally again, this time for lunch. Reluctantly agreed? Sally wouldn't quite go that far, but for a woman who claimed she'd heard one man threaten another, she hadn't been filled with enthusiasm for another meeting. Why?

Maybe you're interrupting her plans. Stop suspecting everyone. Sally continued her search of the crowd, but no woman with blue-streaked hair appeared.

Tara's voice sounded from behind her. "Afternoon, Ms. Castle."

Sally pivoted. "Hello. I was expecting to see you down by the water."

Tara shrugged. "I got some shots earlier, before the crowds showed up. Too many people now, although I did shoot some candids for another gig. The sandwich shop okay?"

"Sure." Sally followed the younger woman into Ohiopyle Bakery and Sandwich Shoppe. They didn't speak much while waiting in line and Sally studied the board. Tara ordered a vegetarian option with hummus, while Sally opted for roasted turkey. In a reasonable amount of time, considering the crowd, they had their food.

"Why don't we sit on the patio?" Tara asked, gesturing at the filled tables. "Enjoy the sun and get some Vitamin D."

"Works for me." Sally followed her outside and snagged a table as it was vacated. They unwrapped their sandwiches. Sally's plan was to let Tara eat a bit and get comfortable first. A person with a happy tummy might be more likely to talk.

Tara pre-empted that plan. "What did you want to talk about?" She licked a bit of hummus from her finger and took a bite, all the while watching Sally from wary eyes.

"When we first talked, you said Mike had threatened Carl. When exactly did that happen, do you remember?"

"I don't know. I told you, they've been at it for a while."

"But the last argument, where Mike made his threat. When was that? Think."

Tara's face pinched in thought. "Wednesday, no Thursday. Not yesterday, a week ago. I was supposed to meet them for breakfast. Mike was taking a weekend trip along the Casselman and he wanted to give me an assignment. I showed up and they were at it. Mike shouted, made his threat, and stormed out without saying anything to me."

"What did Carl say?"

"He brushed it off, said not to worry about it. Mike was being Mike. He'd get testy sometimes, especially when people challenged him." She fell silent a moment then said, "Then he did it? Mike killed Carl? But then what happened to Mike? The state police talked to me yesterday, wanted to know if I knew where Mike had been."

"Did they tell you about the dead man found in the Casselman down near Confluence?"

"Yeah, they said they'd ID'd him as Mike. That's why they wanted to know when I'd last seen him."

"Did Corporal Travers say Mike and Carl definitely were in a physical fight?"

"They aren't sure yet." Tara took another bite, chewed, and swallowed. "I didn't talk to any Travers. It was some woman in a suit. I didn't know the state police wore regular clothes."

Jim had mentioned the involvement of Troop A's Criminal Investigation division. This woman must be from there. Hopefully, she would be more open to Jim's opinions than Travers had been. Sally focused on Tara. "Mike may have had a girlfriend at CWPS. Do you know anything about that?"

Tara's eyes narrowed. "Why are you asking?"

Damn it. Sally had hoped Tara wouldn't pose that question. Not having bothered to come up with a story, Sally opted for a vague version of the truth. "A friend of mine is concerned that the police might not pursue the matter hard enough. They might write off both deaths as accidents. I'm helping him out. Did Mike have a girlfriend?"

Tara considered the words as she slowly chewed. Then she took a drink from her bottled water. "He did. Well, I'm pretty sure he did. They didn't talk about it much, obviously."

"Why not?"

"Because Angela is married." Tara's tone implied the unsaid "duh."

Sally wiped her fingers on her napkin. The roasted Italian garlic bread was amazing. "If they didn't talk about it, how do you know? Or more accurately, why did you suspect?"

"Little things." Tara toyed with the second half of her sandwich. "Mike went off on a day trip and came back with a bouquet of wildflowers he'd picked. Gave them to Angie. They joked more than normal co-workers. Like everything had a hidden meaning. She was always touching him, they held lots of whispered conversations, stuff like that. Mike didn't think much of Angie's husband. More than once he said Angie deserved someone better." Tara picked up her sandwich. "You know how you get the feeling that two people are getting it on?"

Sally nodded.

"You couldn't look at Mike and Angie together without knowing, or at least strongly suspecting, that they were sleeping together."

Sally finished her sandwich and opened her bag of chips. "Did Angie's husband know?"

Tara's words came slowly. "I'm not sure. Maybe. If he did, Mike was heading for a huge pile of shit."

"Why do you say that?"

"I saw Ryan a couple times. He works out, like, a lot, or at least he did. He's mean as hell and he's jealous, I could tell that right off. If anybody is capable of beating someone to a pulp, he is."

The girlfriend's husband *was* Ryan. "You mentioned this to the police, right?"

"Sure did." Tara took another bite of her sandwich and wiped hummus from her fingers. "A guy with stripes on his sleeve. He wrote it down, but honestly, it was tough to tell if he was interested or not. Cops. They never want to give away anything."

Sally made an absent-minded noise in response and continued to eat. A beating from a jealous husband didn't make any sense in the case of Carl Ritchie, but it explained Mike Brower's injuries to a tee.

* * *

Laurel Mountain Quarrying. Duncan hadn't stopped thinking about them since talking to McAllister. The newspaper story had been pretty light on details, simply reporting that higher levels of dust had been found in water samples of the Casselman and a small tributary. The stream did indeed flow by the company's major site. CWPS claimed Laurel Mountain was at fault. The company CEO, Caroline Longchamp, denied it, citing passing grades by the Pennsylvania Department of Environmental Protection and the EPA. A protest, a picket line, really, headed by Mike descended on the quarry site. Words were exchanged, heated words. Some punches thrown. State police out of the Somerset station had broken things up, everyone sent home with a stern warning.

The lush summer landscape of Fayette County rolled by as Duncan made his patrol east on route 40, intending to swing toward Ohiopyle State Park and eventually through the state game lands. It was another beautiful summer day. A cruise through Ohiopyle so people would see a police presence, hopefully keep the crowds in check, wouldn't go amiss.

Too bad he couldn't spend some time at the computer searching for information on Laurel Mountain, but considering Nicols had issued his heads-up this morning, it wouldn't be a wise move. Better stick to patrol and do the research when he wasn't supposed to be keeping law and order.

Except didn't he have a computer in his pocket? That's what McAllister kept saying, referring to the smartphone Duncan still used mostly to make calls and send and receive texts. Although his protégé had found a neat little app that he could use the check the water levels of his favorite boating and fishing spots. He turned off route 40 onto Ohiopyle Road, pulled into a parking lot, and took the phone from his pocket. Unlocking it, he tapped the little icon for the web browser and typed "Laurel Mountain Quarrying" into the search.

The search engine returned a bunch of links, mostly to the company's website and other business-related sites for the Laurel Highlands. He typed the name again, this time adding CWPS.

A different list of links came back. There was the news article McAllister showed him, plus a couple from other sources. An article in the Uniontown *Herald* about the dust level increase in the Casselman, referencing the proximity of any sources for the pollution, which included Laurel Mountain. But according to this, the dust had been abated. Duncan checked the by-line. The article, written by Dominic St. Andrew, was dated two years ago.

An op-ed written by…Mike Brower.

Duncan tapped the link to open the article. The website was some naturalist one and seemed not limited to Pennsylvania locations. The pages looked to be a collection of editorials from many different writers. It was possible the site accepted material from anyone who could type. Duncan navigated through a couple of other articles. They contained varying levels of editing, grammar, and coherence, but the theme was clear. Big companies were ruining the natural beauty of America.

He went back to Mike's piece on Laurel Mountain. His writing was a higher caliber than some others, but that merely made his message sharper. He didn't pull any punches, either. Laurel Mountain might contribute to the local economy, but at what cost? Caroline Longchamp was named as a "money-grubbing bitch out to rape the southwestern Pennsylvania landscape for the profit of a few, including herself." Ouch. Duncan wondered if Longchamp had seen this. If so, what had she thought?

The patrol car didn't have a printer, but no matter. Duncan closed the browser and slipped the phone back into his pocket. He could find the article on a full-size computer and print a copy later. Handy little tool, the smartphone. He'd never admit it to McAllister.

Before he could pull out and continue on his way, the phone rang. Duncan took it out again and checked the caller ID. "Yeah, Burns?"

"Where are you?"

"Sitting in the parking lot of First National Bank on Chalk Hill-Ohiopyle Road. Why?"

"How soon can you meet me at Dex's?"

"I could probably be there in fifteen to twenty minutes, maybe less."

"Good. I'll see you then. You're buying." Burns ended the call without another word of explanation.

Chapter Nineteen

As promised, Duncan walked into Dex's right about when he said he would. He scanned the room and noted Burns sitting in the back corner booth, the one Duncan and Sally usually shared when they ate together. Removing his hat, Duncan wove his way through the tables filled with lunchtime diners, some of whom glanced at the uniformed officer in their midst, and slid into the booth. "How'd you know I like this one?"

"I didn't." Burns sipped from his glass, which was filled with dark liquid. "It was the only free table and the back corner means we may not be noticed. Although your uniform killed that. At least you took off that ridiculous headgear."

Burns not wanting to be noticed? "Why the cloak and dagger?"

"This is why." Burns slid a folder across the table.

Duncan took it. "What is it?"

"The full autopsy report for Mike Brower."

"How'd you get this?"

Burns sipped again. "Remember the notes I had? That was from a buddy of mine in Somerset County."

"You said." Duncan flipped through the contents of the report.

A waitress came by and asked if he wanted anything.

"No food today, thanks. I don't have time. But I will take a Coke."

"I have time and I'm starved," said Burns. "Bacon cheeseburger, extra cheese, and fries, if you please. Put it on his bill."

Duncan said nothing, but the waitress snickered as she jotted down the order, took the menu, and left.

Burns continued the conversation. "My buddy did not assist on the Brower autopsy, that was Miriam. But when I started asking questions, he became curious so he pulled that." He pointed at the folder. "I suggest you read it."

"I will, if you stop talking." Duncan read the data and the corresponding notes from the Somerset County coroner. Evidence of the subdural bleed, the water in the lungs, the ruptured sinuses, and his resulting undetermined finding. "It all looks pretty much like you said."

"Now look at the pictures."

Duncan was not squeamish. He'd worked too many accident scenes and attended too many autopsies. But the glaring photos, the antiseptic lighting, and the stainless steel and white background of the shots combined to create a sense of indecency. The naked human body, sliced open like a high school science project, should not be viewed this way. "Is that the bleed?" he pointed at a shot of the brain.

Burns nodded.

"Looks pretty bad to me."

"It is." Burns flipped to another shot. "In my opinion, this one occurred well before Brower went in the water and it's likely he'd have been semi-conscious, maybe unconscious, by the time he went in."

"If I understand you right, he didn't hit his head, then fall in the water soon after."

"No. Also, look at the heels of his boots."

Duncan flipped to pictures of the clothing. The heels were scuffed, the rear outer edge more so than the rest. "Someone dragged him."

"Yup." Burns drank the remainder of his soda and signaled for a refill. Once the waitress left, he continued. "My buddy agrees. Brower hit his head—"

"Or was hit."

Burns inclined his head. "Maybe he laid on the ground for a bit. Then someone, or a group of someones, dragged him off, most likely near the river. There are bits of gravel embedded in the rubber of the boot heel."

"Then our actor, or actors, tossed him in the river. But he was still breathing because he aspirated water."

"Exactly." The waitress appeared with Burns's food and the drinks, asked if they needed anything else, and left again when they demurred. "Clinically, you can't tell what happened when and that's probably why the coroner ruled the way he did. Autopsy is a negative process. We can only say what didn't happen. That leaves some possibilities."

Duncan closed the folder and slid it back. "What do you think?"

"Based on that report?" Burns nodded toward the folder. "I think the coroner is being very, very cautious. Me, I'd rule it homicide. Dead men don't bleed, not even in the brain. If he'd drowned soon after being hit, I don't think the bleed would be that extensive."

"Plus the scuffed boot heels."

"Right. I'd be willing to bet my last bottle of 18-year old Glenfiddich single malt this guy was murdered."

"You sound pretty confident." Duncan drew his finger down the condensation on his glass. "May I ask how that report made it from your buddy's hands to yours?"

"You may, but I wouldn't tell you. The less you know the better." Burns gave a conspiratorial wink.

"Fair deal. What do I owe you? I know it's something."

"Oh you do indeed. A bottle of 18-year old Glenfiddich ought to cover it."

Yowza. Duncan was mostly a beer drinker, but he liked whiskey enough to know that bottle wasn't cheap. He pulled out his wallet. "I don't have that much on me."

"Don't worry." Burns drained his glass. "I'll wait for you to get it."

"The money?"

"The bottle." Burns sat back. "Because the one I was willing to bet? That's what the report cost me."

* * *

Armed with a name, Angela Stewart, Sally left the sandwich shop and went back to her car. She cursed herself for not having her laptop and mobile hotspot with her. Then again, when she'd left home this morning, she didn't know she'd need them.

Tara said the Stewarts lived in the Laurel Highlands, but she wasn't sure where. Close enough that Angela could regularly volunteer with CWPS, but that didn't give Sally the name of a town, or even whether it was Fayette or Somerset County. A quick search on her phone didn't yield any results. The names were far too common to turn up reliably accurate hits.

She didn't want to drag Tanelsa into things, but she wasn't going to drive back to Uniontown to do the search, either. She dialed. "Hey, I need a favor."

"What else is new?" Tanelsa said, her grin evident in her light tone of voice.

"I need an address for a Ryan and Angela Stewart. Problem is, I can't give you much more than the fact that they live in the Laurel Highlands and Angela is a volunteer with CWPS. Oh, and apparently her husband is the jealous type who works out, or worked out, a lot."

"You sure do know how to give clear, easy tasks." Tanelsa sighed. "Give me some time and I'll see what I can find."

Sally thanked Tanelsa and hung up. Instead of waiting in a hot, stuffy car, she wandered back to the grassy area beside the Youghiogheny River and Ohiopyle Falls. She dropped onto a shaded bench and stared at the whitecaps dancing on the water. One more reason to wonder if Brower had been killed, aside from arguing with his friend and the conflict with Xavier Whitney. Dallying with another man's wife.

Her phone gave off the text tone associated with Jim. *Burns said Brower murdered. Catch you up later.* On the one hand, it was good Jim knew for certain. On the other, if he didn't think Travers was investigating thoroughly, this new knowledge wasn't going to deter Jim. He'd want to know how someone, especially someone he knew, was killed. He'd definitely want to know who did it.

She texted back, *Okay, watch your step. Dinner my place?* She added a smiley emoticon and sent it off. His agreement arrived moments later.

With that settled, she returned to studying the water. While Jim would undoubtedly find out about Angela and Xavier Whitney, if he had a head start it couldn't hurt. She'd stick to her plan. Now if only Tanelsa would call back.

Just as Sally figured she'd given her friend an impossible task, her phone rang. "Tanelsa. Did you find her?"

"The next time you ask for a favor, make it something simple, like, water my office plants." Tanelsa grumbled, but the words lacked the overtone of true irritation.

"I will, as soon as you buy me one."

"I found multiple Angela and Ryan Stewarts, but only one set is married to each other. Ryan, 50, and Angela, 45. I figure that has to be your pair."

"Where do they live?"

"Home address is in Fort Hill, Somerset County." Tanelsa read it off. "It looks like Angela works in Ohiopyle as a waitress at one of the local restaurants, at a place called Mulligan's."

"Do either of them have a criminal record?"

The click of computer keys came over the line. "Nothing for Angela. An assortment of minor crap for Ryan. Most recently, he has an arrest for beating up a guy at a bar. No charges were pressed. He said the guy got handsy with his wife and he clocked him."

Jealous and mean as shit. "Thanks, Tanelsa."

"You gonna tell me what this is about?"

"Later. First round's on me. Thanks again." Sally ended the call. How lucky that she was in Ohiopyle. Now to see if Angela was at work. Sally stood and snagged the attention of a nearby cyclist checking his bike chain. "Excuse me, have you heard of a place called Mulligan's here in town?"

The guy pointed. "Over there. If you want more than a burger and ice cream, though, you might want to try somewhere else."

"Thanks." Sally strolled in the direction indicated. Mulligan's was on the small side, maybe six tables inside and another three on the sidewalk. The hand-lettered slate sandwich board said the daily special was a grilled onion cheeseburger and fries, and the ice cream flavor of the day was pistachio. Inside, the bright yellow walls were covered with pictures of local flora and fauna, the Yough prominently featured in most of them. A tattooed man worked the grill, while a woman who looked too young to be Angela moved from table to table, taking orders and delivering plates of food. Sally waited until she finished at her current table before capturing her attention and asked anyway. "Excuse me, are you Angela Stewart?"

The young woman shook her head. "Angie's on her lunch break. Who're you?"

Sally gave her name. "I think Angela and I have a common acquaintance who recently died. I want to make sure she knows."

The girl didn't speak for a moment, then said. "Check by the river. That's where she usually goes. She's wearing a t-shirt same as mine." The waitress wore a bright turquoise shirt with Mulligan's written across it in yellow script.

Sally thanked her and left the cramped dining space. The shirt was not a subtle piece of clothing. Sally scanned the crowd. A middle-aged woman in a bright blue tee. Couldn't be too hard, right?

There, under an old oak with spreading limbs. The woman sat cross-legged on the grass, hands idly tearing bits from the sandwich she held, rolling the bread and tossing it to a few ducks that had gathered nearby. Sally approached. "Pardon me, Angela Stewart?"

The woman looked up. "Who wants to know?"

"Sally Castle, Fayette county public defender's office." Sally looked from the woman to the ducks, and back. "You shouldn't feed them bread. It's not good for them."

Up close, Angela did not look 45. Her short brown hair held no gray and her skin was smooth, with only faint crow's feet at her eyes. She wore no makeup other than a touch of mascara and some lip gloss. She was tan, but not overly so, and didn't have the weathered look of someone who spent a lot of time outdoors. But her brown eyes were haunted. The eyes of a woman with a lot on her mind and most of it trouble.

"I don't need a lawyer," Angela said.

"I never said you did," Sally replied. "You're Angela, then?"

"That's me. What do you want?"

"I want to talk to you about Mike Brower."

Angela looked away. "I don't know Mike Brower."

"Really?" Sally crossed her arms, moving slightly into cross-examination mode. "He runs the Casselman Water Preservation Society. I understood you volunteer there."

Angela kept her gaze on the ducks, who wandered away in search of more food. "Not anymore. I quit."

"Because of Mr. Brower?"

No answer.

"Did you know Mr. Brower is dead? His body was found in the Casselman near Confluence a few days ago."

Still no answer.

"People have told me you and Mr. Brower were involved. Is that true?"

Angela scrambled up. "I told you. I don't know Mike Brower. I don't know Carl Ritchie. I don't volunteer with CWPS anymore. Now excuse me, I have to get back to work." She fled back toward Mulligan's.

Sally watched her go.

Who said anything about Carl Ritchie?

Chapter Twenty

Sally took her time walking back from the river overlook. Angela was spooked, no doubt. The way she'd dropped Carl Ritchie's name, the deaths were connected. At least that's what she believed. Claiming she didn't know either victim was unbelievable in the extreme. CWPS wasn't that big of an organization. How could she not know them?

The sound of shouting pulled Sally out of her thoughts. Ahead of her, in front of Mulligan's, two people were engaged in an argument. Well, one person yelled while the other practically cowered in front of him, silent.

Angela.

Sally halted and studied the man. Taller than Angela by several inches, he was heavily muscled, but starting to get paunchy around the middle. His hair was cropped close, skin weather-beaten. Several faded tattoos decorated his muscular upper arms under a grease-streaked T-shirt. Carpenter-style jeans were cinched around his waist, under a stomach that was losing the fight against age. *Looks like Ryan needs to add to his ab workout*, Sally thought.

Sally took a couple steps closer. Neither Angela nor the man noticed her.

"I asked you who the hell you were talkin' to? I come down here to have a burger and you're off somewhere? With who?" He inched closer to Angela, drops of spittle catching the sun.

Angela pulled into herself even further. "I was looking at the river, Ryan. Swear to God, that was all."

So this was Ryan. Sally scrutinized him. Going to seed, yes, but still more than capable of administering a beating. Not a very genial personality, either.

"I told you this morning, I was stopping for lunch and I expected you to be here. Are you deaf and dumb, as well as stupid?"

"I took a break is all. I get one in the middle of the shift, you know that. I wasn't doing anything."

"I saw you talkin' to a woman. Who is she? She tryin' to get you to leave? You think you'll be able to take care of yourself on your pissant waitressing salary, you dumb bitch?"

"It was nothing like that," Angela said. Her entire posture screamed she was afraid and her voice was weak with fear. "She had some questions about CWPS, that's all. Nothing to do with you and me, hon."

Ryan laughed, an ugly sound. "That wife-stealer Brower? You know something about that. What?" He clenched his left fist and held it in from of Angela.

"I don't know anything." Angela's whimper was that of a small child, waiting for the blow to fall.

Enough of this shit. Sally stepped forward. "Ryan Stewart?"

He didn't take his eyes off his wife. "Who the hell are you?"

"The woman your wife was talking to."

He dropped his fist and turned to glare at Sally. "About what?"

"What she said, about CWPS. I'd heard she was a volunteer. Past tense. Angela confirmed it. End of conversation. Now back off."

He sneered. "Or what?"

"Or I'll call the police. I have a state trooper on speed dial." Sally lifted her chin. Of course, Jim could be anywhere in the county, so no guarantee he'd get there quickly, but Ryan Stewart didn't need to know that.

The man stepped back. "So what? This is my wife. We got a right to have a conversation anywhere we want."

Angela's gaze darted between them, a mouse caught by an overlarge cat.

Sally stood her ground. "What I heard was hardly a conversation. It was a screaming match, very one-sided if you ask me. And if you ask any of these other dozen people." She waved her hand to indicate the diners seated outside Mulligan's, as well as the passers-by. "I'm glad to see you, though. Saves me the time of finding you."

Ryan spat on the ground. "What for?"

"Did you know Mike Brower or Carl Ritchie?"

"Ritchie? Nah. But Brower? That wife-stealing prick? Oh yeah. I knew him." He spat again.

A man in a grease-stained apron came out of the restaurant. "I'm gonna have to insist you either leave, Mr. Stewart, or calm down. You're disturbing my customers."

"I'm leaving." He reached out, grabbed Angela's wrist, and pulled her forward sharply so she staggered. "Get your ass in the truck. Your shift is over."

The owner of Mulligan's took a step. "Actually, Angie has another four hours—"

"Her shift is over, asshole." Ryan glared at his wife. "I said get in the damn truck!"

Angela scampered to a faded red pickup and got into the passenger side.

Ryan followed, gunned the truck's engine, and roared off, laying on the horn to scatter some tourists with bikes crossing the street.

"I hope Angie is okay," the owner said as he watched the truck drive off.

Sally looked at him. "Does he do that often?"

"Pull her away from work?" The owner faced her and shook his head. "That I've never seen him do. But Angie's come in with enough stories for me to know the man has serious issues." He went back inside.

Sally looked off in the direction the truck had taken. Anger, jealousy, and a violent streak. Not a good combination at all.

* * *

Duncan showed up at Sally's at five. He'd had time to change into civvies and pick up the takeout Sally had ordered from their favorite Thai place. He knocked and let himself in. "Dinner delivery service is here."

She peered around the corner from the dining room. "Excellent. I'm famished."

"Pad Thai and green chicken curry, as ordered. I also got some extra spring rolls." He went to the dining room, where he deposited the takeout bag on the table and gave Sally a kiss on the lips.

She smiled and kissed him again. "You are a prince among men, did you know that Trooper First Class Duncan?"

"I try." While Sally fetched plates, he removed the takeout containers and chopsticks from the bag. "How'd your day go?"

"You first." She came in balancing a glass, a bottle of Edmund Fitzgerald, and a bottle opener on two plates.

Duncan grabbed the beer and the opener before they fell. "As I texted, it's not official, but if Tom Burns was in charge it would be. Mike Brower was murdered."

"Damn." She returned to the kitchen.

Duncan heard the slap of her hand against the counter. Why was she so upset about Brower? He followed her. "Something bothering you?"

She sighed, then turned and faced him. "To be honest, I was hoping this one would turn out to be a double accident."

He had raised the bottle halfway to his mouth but stopped. "Why?"

"Because…Corporal Travers. I don't want you getting in trouble. Nicols usually protects your ass, but if Travers goes to his lieutenant and makes a complaint, Nicols will pretty much have to do something and that could mean real problems for you."

"Too late." He took a swig from the beer.

"Oh, no, what happened?"

He told her about the meeting with Nicols, including the lieutenant's desire that Duncan put himself in the running for corporal. "Nicols agrees that the whole thing needs closer investigation, though."

"Are you going to do it?"

"The investigation?"

She slapped his arm with a towel. "No, silly. Promotion."

"Let's eat before it gets cold." He returned to the dining room and dished out the food. It was touching that everyone was so invested in his career, but also a bit uncomfortable. Okay, Sally he could understand and she was the one person who had a right to know. "To answer your question, I don't know. Nicols is right and I should have done it a few years ago. But I didn't. At this point, I'd probably be the oldest corporal in the Pennsylvania State Police."

"But?"

"I told you I was thinking about a transfer to CI. Now, I'm kinda torn between the two. Then again, I'm happy with where I am and maybe I don't need to change anything."

Sally held her chopsticks above her plate of noodles. "Like me with Kim."

"Exactly."

She twirled up some food. "You'd be good at it, I can tell you that."

He dug into his curry. "Thanks. McAllister shares your sentiment."

"Have you heard from someone in Somerset CI yet?"

"No. Either they haven't assigned anyone or that person hasn't gotten around to me. I can't think why not. After all, I recovered Mike's body. Don't know what they're doing."

"Another inept trooper?"

"Travers isn't inept, he's lazy. Likes the path of least resistance. However, you don't get to CI if that's your attitude. No, either they haven't assigned an investigator or there is a very good reason that person hasn't contacted me yet. After all he, or she, would have my statement from the initial scene when Travers did his interviews. That might be enough, or at least enough for now."

"Wouldn't a CI trooper do his own interviews?"

"Not necessarily." Duncan took a drink. "The patrol trooper usually handles the initial scene. Whether or not the trooper from CI follows up after those first statements is a matter of discretion."

They ate in silence for a while. Then Sally said, "Burns says Mike Brower was murdered. What does the Somerset coroner say?"

"Undetermined, which is why they haven't closed the case. Burns has seen the coroner's report and thinks the guy is being conservative." He told her about the extent of Brower's subdural bleed and the scuffed boots.

Sally twiddled her chopsticks. "You believe Burns over the coroner?"

"Don't kid yourself. There are only two reasons Tom Burns is a deputy coroner and not running the show in Fayette County. He doesn't have the experience needed to convince the electorate and he doesn't want the job. He's sharp, skilled, and if he says murder, well, that's good enough for me."

"Then I suppose I should tell you about my afternoon. Mike Brower almost certainly had a girlfriend. She's married, and her husband is the jealous type." She filled him in on her conversation with Tara and her afternoon in Ohiopyle.

"I wonder why Angela denied knowing him. I mean, she mentioned Carl and you didn't even ask about him. Pretty clear she's lying."

"If her husband is as jealous as we hear, and I think he is, maybe she knows Mike is dead and is afraid her loving spouse kicked the crap out of him. From what little I saw, I think he's abusing her."

"That explains why she'd deny knowing Mike, but not why she brought up Carl."

"No, it doesn't." Sally rested her chin on her fist. "If Mike knew about the abuse, would he confront Ryan? Could that be what happened?"

"From what I know of Mike, I think it's highly likely that he'd not only confront him, but urge Angela to pack up and leave."

"Which wouldn't make Ryan very happy."

"No, it wouldn't." Duncan took another mouthful.

Sally poked her food with her chopsticks. "It's also possible she knows, or suspects, who would have gone after both men and she's looking to protect herself."

"It's an idea. I want to look into Caroline Longchamp and Laurel Mountain Quarrying. The company has been brought up as a potential dust polluter and Mike published what is basically a screed about her online. Can't have made her happy."

"I found the guy from the fishing access deal, Xavier Whitney." She got up and fetched a piece of paper from her briefcase. "He lives in Pittsburgh," she said as she pushed the paper in front of Duncan. "Retired, big outdoorsman. He's next on my list of people to talk to."

"He can tell us who Loudmouth was that day, Mike or Carl. But I don't want you going to see him without me, got it?" He put his hands around

Sally's waist.

She wrapped her arms around his neck. "As long as you promise me one thing."

"Be careful?"

"No. I know you'll do that." Her face sobered and her green eyes turned thoughtful. "I want you to seriously think about this promotion business. I don't care if you go for it, but please give it careful thought."

"I will." He pulled her down and kissed her. "If you do the same with Kim."

Chapter Twenty-One

Sally woke up on Saturday, and spent an extra moment in bed, thinking. Before leaving, Jim had reminded her again not to meet Xavier Whitney on her own. But that didn't mean she couldn't do as much research as possible and be ready to meet him later when Jim's shift ended.

She slid out of bed, grabbed her robe, and headed for the kitchen. After she made her morning coffee and ate a breakfast of fruit, yogurt, and granola, she fetched her laptop from her office.

Within half an hour, she had a reasonable bio of Whitney. He'd lived in Pittsburgh all his life, and retired early, at 55, from a successful career running his own housing development business, which allowed him to indulge his passion for the outdoors. Five years later, he'd racked up a number of accomplishments, including winning several smallmouth bass events on the Casselman. In an article on one of them, he talked about how happy he was at the resurgence of the smallmouth population and the general health of the river system, but said access for sportsmen had lagged. As a former developer, he was positioned to do something about that.

"Oh, I bet you were, and I'm sure it was going to line your pocket somehow," Sally murmured as she wrote down the Pittsburgh address and phone number she found. She closed the laptop and reached for her phone.

A young-sounding woman answered. "Hello?"

"Yes, hi. I'm looking for Xavier Whitney. He owned Whitney Development. Is this the right number?" Sally crossed her fingers.

"Who's calling?" The young woman's voice turned wary.

"My name is Sally Castle." A flash of insight told her not to identify herself as a lawyer. "I live in the Laurel Highlands and I heard Mr. Whitney was very excited about some projects down here. I'd like to speak with him about them. Are you his daughter?"

"He's, uh, not h—I mean, not available right now."

The young woman sounded sheepish, and Sally was sure the girl was about to say Whitney wasn't home. Definitely the right number and the girl was almost certainly his daughter. "That's fine. Would you take a message and get it to him?"

"Yeah, sure." The young woman's voice brightened. "Let me get a pen."

Sally couldn't say she disapproved, since she'd gotten in too many tight spots herself from being too trusting. The memory of the last one still woke her up at night. Besides, by the time the message found the intended audience, Jim might be off work. Sally had promised not to meet with Whitney. She'd never promised not to contact him.

"Go ahead," the girl said.

Sally gave her name and cell phone number, stressing it was not an emergency and Whitney shouldn't rush. Then she thanked Whitney's daughter and hung up. Hopefully, the girl was as responsible as she sounded and Whitney would get the message.

* * *

Duncan couldn't remember the last time Saturday morning had been this busy.

He'd responded to three domestic complaints, all fueled by too much alcohol. Then there was an emergency in Ohiopyle, an accident involving two cars, a bicycle, and a pedestrian. Fortunately, no serious injuries although plenty of foul tempers. Especially when questioning revealed the cyclist had been the one at fault and it had cost him his fancy,$3,000-dollar cycle. He rounded out the morning by issuing a handful of traffic citations, most of them to out-of-towners who didn't understand the difference between driving in the city and driving the area's rural roadways.

Things finally quieted down around one and he took the opportunity to grab a late lunch. With luck, the excitement was over for the day. Sally texted him about leaving a message with Whitney. If the man called back, Duncan didn't want anything to delay the end of his shift. Sally acted a lot more carefully these days, but he still wouldn't put it past her to go meet with a respected businessman on her own if she thought it was necessary.

He took the opportunity to review the information he'd printed off yesterday about Caroline Longchamp and Laurel Mountain Quarrying. The company address was in Rockwood, a small town in Somerset County near the Casselman, but the facility itself was a couple miles from the river. They specialized in harvesting the sandstone that was so prevalent in the area, with a little bit of limestone thrown in for good measure. The company website had a whole page devoted to their environmental policy and Duncan clearly saw a medium-sized stream in many of the pictures. Ten to one, that was the Casselman tributary McAllister had spoken of.

The picture of Caroline Longchamp on the "About Us" web page was slightly intimidating. According to her bio, her grandfather had started Laurel Mountain. When Caroline inherited the company, it had been on the brink of insolvency. Through a series of hard business decisions, sharp deals, and a dose of pure determination, she'd rebuilt it into a profitable organization. The steely blue eyes in the tanned face said this woman didn't tolerate nonsense and steamrolled anyone who got in her way. Fifty-five, she'd let her hair go to a natural silver. No vanity and clinging to an image of youth for her. Duncan noted the hard set of her mouth, even though she smiled in the picture, and the crow's feet at her eyes. This was the face of a woman in a predominantly male field who didn't take shit from anyone.

Longchamp didn't have a criminal record of any kind. During her tenure, Laurel Mountain had received several warnings from the PADEP, but nothing had come of them. Duncan recognized her home address, Flanagan Road, off Mae West Road and not far from Confluence. Perfect. She lived in Fayette County. The only thing that would make it more perfect is if he could keep the patrol car and head home to meet Sally after the interview. Except he wasn't working tomorrow, so he'd have to suck up the hour drive and back.

He decided to run the risk that Longchamp wasn't at home and didn't call ahead. When he pulled into the sweeping driveway of the large, rambling farmhouse-style home, a black Land Rover was parked in front. He ran the plate. The vehicle belonged to Longchamp.

As he got out of the patrol car, Longchamp appeared from behind the house, clad in jeans and a faded plaid shirt with the sleeves rolled up. She held a garden hose with a spray head in one hand and a basket of gardening tools in the other. Judging from the faded, droopy look of the front flower bed, she intended to provide some much-needed TLC to the garden. He touched his hat. "Ms. Longchamp?"

She turned. "Yes?"

"Trooper Jim Duncan, Pennsylvania State Police. Do you have a moment?"

She put her gardening supplies down and her hands on her hips. A slightly aggressive posture. "What about?"

"I'm looking into the death of Mike Brower. I wanted to ask you a few questions."

Her body stiffened, the aggression ratcheting up. "I've already talked to a trooper and I have nothing more to say."

"I understand. But—"

"No, I don't think you do. It's my day off, my flowers need tending, and I have work to do so listen carefully. I've already given my statement. Mike Brower might have had the best interests of the Laurel Highlands environment at heart, but he was a rabble-rouser, rude, arrogant, and unwilling to listen to anyone whose opinion differed from his. I did not like him. I'm sorry to hear he's dead, but I can't help you. Now if you'll excuse me, this flower bed won't take care of itself. Good day." She knelt and attacked the weeds, clearly done with the conversation.

Chapter Twenty-Two

Sally's cell phone rang as she was making lunch. She didn't recognize the number, but it had a Pittsburgh area code. Playing a hunch, she answered. "Sally Castle speaking."

"Ms. Castle. Or is it Mrs. Castle? This is Xavier Whitney."

"It's miz, but please, call me Sally." Oh, if only everyone was this easy to find.

"Sally. I understand from Bella you're looking for me. That's my youngest daughter. She told me you called this morning."

"I did. I wanted to talk to you about your vision for the Laurel Highlands, especially fishing access along the Casselman. I'm very interested." *For reasons you don't want to know.*

"And I'd love to talk to you about them. Turns out I'm down there now. The cell phone coverage in this area isn't always reliable, though."

Sally's heart skipped. "That's fine, I'm actually located in Uniontown, so not all that far away."

"Thought from the phone number you might be. Would you like to meet?"

"Absolutely, but I have a few things to do early this afternoon. Would it be possible to meet you in Confluence at a place called the Lucky Dog Cafe around four?"

"I know Confluence and the Lucky Dog well. I'd be pleased to."

"I'd like to bring a friend with me, too. He's a very avid fisherman."

"Of course."

After making arrangements and hanging up, Sally indulged herself in a few moments of congratulatory relaxation. Then she grabbed her phone and texted Jim. *Found Whitney. Meeting at the Lucky Dog at four today. Don't dress up.*

A minute or so later her phone chimed his text tone. *10-4. You work fast, Counselor.*

She stretched. She'd do a bit of yoga, clean up the apartment a bit, and head for Jim's instead of meeting him at the Lucky Dog. Somehow, she didn't think he would be at all surprised to find her waiting when he got home.

* * *

Duncan squinted to make out the two figures standing in his front yard. His neighbor, Marge, and Sally. Of course, she was already there. At least she'd waited, although since the meeting was in a public space, where she was pretty well known, he was slightly less worried things would get out of hand. Slightly. The women moved aside as he pulled in and parked his Jeep. Sally opened her mouth as he got out. "Yes, I know," he said. "Give me five minutes. You know it doesn't take more than ten to walk to the Lucky Dog. And that's if we stroll."

She stuck out her tongue and went back to talking to Marge.

As promised, five minutes later Duncan and Sally walked out of the cluster of houses where he lived and headed toward Robert Brown Road. He grasped her hand. "What were you and Marge talking about?" Like he couldn't guess.

"You."

"What about me?" The pace he'd set was brisk, but Sally had no problem keeping up.

"How much happier and relaxed you've been these past couple months." She squeezed his hand. "We were wondering why that was."

Women.

They walked in comfortable silence until they reached Robert Brown Road, stopped and waited for a couple of cars. As soon as the traffic passed, they jogged across. In the parking lot of the Lucky Dog, Duncan halted and faced Sally. "Whitney. He's a housing developer?"

"Retired." Sally glanced at the yellow building. A dusty, but relatively new, Mercedes SUV stood in the lot. "Married, lives in Pittsburgh, three daughters, one at home. He loves the outdoors, especially the improvements the Casselman has seen in recent years. He wants to build out new fishing access."

"Got it. And I'm not in uniform because we don't want to scare him off?"

"That's it."

They headed for the restaurant. All the tables were filled, but a lone man occupied one set for three. Duncan judged him to be on the taller side, maybe a few inches shorter than his own six-three. The man looked like he ate well, his bald head gleaming in the overhead lights. His skin resembled old leather. "Mr. Whitney?" Duncan called as he and Sally made their way across the room.

Whitney stood. "In the flesh, all two-hundred pounds of it." He clasped Duncan's hand and then Sally's. His grip was firm, brisk. A businessman's handshake. "You must be Sally Castle and friend."

"We are," Sally said. She sat and the men followed. She grabbed one of the paper menus from the napkin holder. "Jim Duncan, Xavier Whitney. Seems you two share an interest in fishing. But let's order our food first."

"I won't argue with that," Xavier said with a chuckle.

They gave their orders to Tracey, the Lucky Dog's waitress, and studied each other without saying a word. Finally, a slow smile spread across Whitney's face. "So how are you two involved in the legal profession?"

Duncan blinked. "Come again?" He glanced at Sally, who quickly covered her surprise, but Whitney's statement had thrown her. Duncan surmised that she'd not told Whitney about being a lawyer, or about Duncan being a cop.

Tracey delivered their drinks, said the food would be right out, and moved away.

Whitney removed the paper from a straw. "The last time I was scrutinized this closely, I was in front of a Pittsburgh Housing Authority representative and two police officers while I explained all the perfectly plausible reasons a framed house could collapse and injure a man, none of which were my fault." He sipped. "If you two aren't involved in the law somehow, dinner is on me. Good tea." He sipped again.

So much for subterfuge. "I'm a trooper with the Pennsylvania State Police and Sally is an assistant public defender for Fayette County," Duncan said and twisted the top off his beer.

Whitney's keen gaze fixed on them. "This have to do with the two dead men from CWPS?"

Sally flushed. "Yes and no. We understand, Jim and I, that you have a project in mind involving the Casselman River."

"Fishing access areas, yes." Xavier sat back as Tracey set a bacon, lettuce, and tomato sandwich on naan in front of him. "My God that looks amazing."

Duncan opted for a burger with bacon and goat cheese, something Sally had made him try and he found surprisingly delicious. "As a fisherman myself, I can appreciate that. Smallmouth is popular along the Casselman, although I prefer trout on the Yough."

Xavier pointed half a sandwich at him. "Exactly. You get it. So many of the locals I talk to, they all want to keep things hush-hush. Hoard the best spots."

Duncan picked up his burger. "Fishermen are notoriously secretive. If you fish, you know that. We don't want people crashing our party."

Whitney shook his head. "I do understand. However, this is a beautiful area. All of the Laurel Highlands are. People want to enjoy it, but to do that, you have to make it accessible. You, Trooper, are obviously a man who is in shape. I appreciate that in a law enforcement officer. But folks like me, who persist in carrying a few more pounds than the doctor wants them to, can't go climbing through thickets and down embankments."

Sally, who had chosen the mahi-mahi fish tacos, reached for a napkin. "You said access, Mr. Whitney. What does that mean?"

"Please, call me Xavier." He wiped his fingers. "I'll tell you what it doesn't mean. Bulldozing wildlife and square acres of asphalt parking lots. That would defeat the purpose. No, there are a couple areas along the river I've marked. My plan is to put in gravel lots for maybe six to twelve cars. I'd add some wood shelters with bathrooms."

Sally picked up another taco. "Sounds reasonable."

"I want to clear a trail down to the water, with gravel paths and wooden handrails," Whitney continued. "Then clear out a small area so folks who need free space can set up, but those who want to wade into the water can do so. They've done amazing things with the Great Allegheny Passage and other trails up at Ohiopyle. I want to bring the same for fisherman along the Casselman. My granddaddy taught me to fish lo these many moons ago. My own grandsons are getting to the age where they can hold a pole and I want them to have the same memories."

Duncan listened while he ate. Whitney's plans sounded reasonable to him. He'd harbored doubts about the ability of a city businessman to understand and respect the beauty of the area instead of exploiting it, but Whitney seemed to get it. "I'm for anything that brings people back to nature without destroying it. But I understand some don't feel the same."

A glower settled on Whitney's cheerful face. "You're talking about the men from CWPS. The one wasn't so bad. But the other? You'd have thought I was proposing to raze the entire riverbank."

Duncan glanced at Sally. "We heard about that. Can you put a name to each man?"

Whitney polished off the first half of his sandwich, took a drink of iced tea, and picked up the other half. "Carl Ritchie was the more reasonable one. He at least wanted to hear the plans, look at the drawings. But Mike Brower? He didn't want to listen to a word. Then he flat out accused me of raping the land for personal profit."

Sally forked up some of the black beans that accompanied her meal. "Sounds harsh. Besides, where's the profit? Are you charging for this access?"

"That it was." Whitney took another bite. "I'll tell you plain, it didn't sit well with me. I'm an outdoorsman, but I'm also a business man. I know when my plans are sound. And I'm not going to charge folks a penny, which made it doubly insulting."

"He didn't believe you, I take it?"

"Nope. Seemed to think I was covering up some kind of income from the project. I didn't appreciate his attitude. He said he'd go to court to keep me from moving forward."

Duncan set down his burger. "What did you say to that?"

Whitney fixed him with a stare that remained friendly, but carried a hint of steel. "He'd regret it. He'd lose the suit, his shirt, and maybe a lot more."

Duncan lifted an eyebrow.

"I know what you're thinking, Trooper. Sounds pretty bad, doesn't it, considering both men are now dead. But if you're thinking it's a bit too coincidental for both incidents to be accidents, I'm not your guy. I was in Pittsburgh, in a meeting about bids on a new upscale apartment complex, acting as a consultant. There are about six people who will verify that." He took another bite. "You know, this sandwich is damn good. I think dinner's on me after all."

Chapter Twenty-Three

Sally watched as Whitney's Mercedes left the parking lot of the Lucky Dog. Then she turned to Jim. "What do you think?"

He stood there, a faint frown on his face, spinning his keyring on his finger. "I think I want ice cream. Let's go."

Sally followed Jim across a bridge and lagged behind as he strode up the hill. They cut through a little park of recreational trailers and through a gate in the fence to reach the soft serve shop. They said nothing while they walked. Sally's thoughts ran in circles and she was sure Jim's did as well.

At Outflow, Sally ordered a vanilla with sprinkles, while Jim opted for a twist of chocolate and vanilla. He paid and they struck out for his place.

It was so hot, the dessert melted faster than Sally could eat it. "What did you think of Whitney's story?" she asked, then chased a drip with her tongue.

Jim paused, attacking his own cone so quickly the ice cream barely had time to melt and run. "It's fine as far as it goes." He handed her a napkin.

She used it to blot melted vanilla from her wrist. How did he do it? His ice cream always disappeared before he started to wear it. "What do you mean by that?"

Jim paused, continuing to reduce the size of his cone. "I believe he's a housing developer. I believe he likes to fish and he wants to develop the area so more people have access to the Casselman. I believe he's a sharp businessman who meant exactly what he told Brower about going to court."

"What don't you believe?"

"I don't entirely buy his alibi."

"Why not?"

Jim turned so he was walking backward and could look in her face. "I don't doubt the fact he probably had some meeting in Pittsburgh about fancy apartments, but why use that as his alibi? Why something on a specific date?"

Sally frowned at her cone. After a moment, she realized why Jim was suspicious. "Because how would he know when Ritchie and Brower died?"

"We didn't mention anything about a time of death. Either he read something in the paper and is extrapolating or—"

"He knows when they went into the river because he's the one who pushed them in the drink, to use a very outdated expression." She crunched a bit of her cone. Since Jim was incapable of strolling at a leisurely pace, they'd already reached Dewy Street, more than halfway to his house. His ice cream was gone and Sally munched the remaining bit of hers. Her wrist was a sticky mess, something Rizzo would undoubtedly take care of once he saw her. She looked up. "Isn't that Bob Hunter?"

Lindy's father half-jogged toward them. "Hey there. Jim, I was going to your place. I found Lindy's pictures from that day." He held out a compact digital camera.

"Thanks, but you could have printed them."

Bob shrugged. "I thought having the original images would be helpful. That way you can zoom in on anything you see. Can't do that on a print. But what I can't find is the cord that connects the camera to a computer. As soon as Lindy cleans her room and finds it, I'll have her bring it over."

Sally took the camera and flipped open the door on the side so she could remove the memory card. "Good, it's a standard card. This is all we need. I have a card reader, so we won't have to fuss about finding a cable."

"I won't tell her that. I'll never get her to clean up her room." Bob chuckled. "I'm not sure those are gonna be helpful, though. I looked through them. It's mostly water and close-ups of plants. A few of guys fishing the river. I didn't see anything I considered interesting."

"Thanks, Bob." Jim shook his friend's hand. "You never know what is really important. I'll copy the photos and get the memory card back to you as soon as I can."

"No problem. Let me know if I can do anything else for you." Bob took the camera and walked back to his house.

Jim and Sally walked the rest of the way in silence. Once inside Jim's house, Sally rubbed Rizzo behind the ears while Jim poured a glass of merlot and opened a bottle of beer. As Sally expected, the Golden Retriever homed right in on the scent of ice cream on her skin. His big, pink tongue removed the residue all right, but didn't do much for the stickiness. Sally washed her hands, while Jim set the wineglass on the table. "You don't happen to have that card-reader thing on you, do you?"

Sally took the wineglass and headed for the front porch. "No. I'll bring it tomorrow. You're off, right?"

"I was going to suggest we could spend a day on the boat out on the reservoir, but maybe we can look at pictures and then go out." He dropped into his Adirondack chair.

Sally followed suit, dusting hers first. "I didn't hear anything this afternoon that would make me take Whitney off the suspect list. Sure, he might be confident of winning in court, but now he won't have to pay for what he wants. What about Caroline Longchamp?"

Jim told her about his brief meeting with the CEO of Laurel Mountain Quarrying. "Just because she chucked me out doesn't mean she's guilty."

"But it does nothing to make me want to cross her off as a suspect, either," Sally said. She sipped her wine. "Same thing with Angela Stewart. Maybe Tara was wrong, maybe Angela wasn't carrying on with Mike Brower."

"But a refusal to talk could mean she was and she doesn't want anyone to know." Jim took a pull from his beer. "Does Stewart's husband have a record?"

"Nothing serious," Sally said. Rizzo laid his head in her lap and she obligingly scratched behind his ears. "A few misdemeanors, bar fight kind of things. But the reason was always the same. Someone came on to his wife, or made what Ryan thought was a suggestive comment, or he thought Angela and the other guy were flirting. He sounds exactly like what Tara told me. A jealous guy with anger issues."

"Where does he work?"

"I didn't get that far. I looked for a criminal record, but I can look some more next week."

Jim set the bottle down so he could tick off items on his fingers. "To recap, we have a jealous husband, a company that possibly ran afoul of CWPS and that Brower wrote a scathing blog post on, and a developer who wants to build out and argued with Brower in public. That it?"

Sally spread her hands. "So far. Where does that leave us?"

Jim shrugged and checked the level of the beer remaining in the bottle. "Damned if I know."

Chapter Twenty-Four

Sunday morning, Duncan stood on his front porch, coffee in hand. As soon as the fog burned off, the deep blue sky promised another beautiful day. Overhead, he heard the mournful honk of geese as they winged their way to their destination. He inhaled, the damp, slightly fishy smell of the water combining with the richness of the dark roast coffee. *It doesn't get much better than this.*

But when Sally appeared beside him, it did. She rubbed her eyes, her hair tousled from sleep. A mumble that might be "good morning" came from her lips.

He'd assume it had been. "Good morning. Coffee's in the kitchen."

She shuffled off.

He shook his head. Until she'd started regularly spending Saturday night with him, he'd never realized she wasn't a morning person. Smart and funny, yes, but not before her morning caffeine.

She reappeared, steaming mug in hand, eyes moderately clearer. "How long have you been up?"

He glanced at his watch. "Since about five-thirty, so two hours. Long enough to go for a run and stop to buy you a cinnamon roll for breakfast."

"I love you."

He laughed. "I know we said we'd look at those pictures and go out on the boat, but I was thinking. You up to seeing if Angela Stewart is working today? Won't matter if she isn't. It'll be a nice day to spend in Ohiopyle. Hike down to Cucumber Falls, Great Gorge, or Meadow Run. If you bring your bathing suit, we can do the natural waterslides."

"I don't have my suit. It's at home." She went back inside and reappeared a moment later, cinnamon roll in hand. The color had returned to her cheeks. "Other than that, it's a great plan. When do you want to leave?"

"How soon can you get cleaned up?"

Her eyebrows drew together. "What's the rush? Mulligan's is a burger joint. I bet they don't open until noon."

"I thought we could bike in." He focused on his mug. Sally never passed up an opportunity to go out with him on his boat, but she wasn't quite the outdoors fan he was.

"To Ohiopyle?"

"It's only ten miles."

She threw him a dirty look. "I don't have a bike."

"You can use Marge's. She hasn't used it in a while, so I bought it from her for you to use. Oiled up the chain and pumped up the tires, too."

"How many miles did you say it was?"

"Ten…or so."

"You must be joking."

He emptied his mug. "If you're not up to it…" It was throwing down a gauntlet of sorts and Duncan knew it. Sally would never back down from a challenge.

"Are you implying I can't do it?" she retorted.

Knew she couldn't resist. "Wouldn't dream of it."

She closed her eyes and seemed to be counting. "Can I at least finish my breakfast and shower?"

"Absolutely."

She trudged inside, muttering under her breath.

By nine o'clock they were on their way. Duncan had briefly thought about bringing Rizzo, but they were on bikes and the pace would be too much. That and twenty miles round trip, plus all the walking in Ohiopyle, was too far for the dog. Duncan left him with Marge's kids, who promised to take good care of him, including a long walk along the river. By the joyful barks and game of chase that had been going on when Duncan left, he didn't think Rizzo minded being left behind.

* * *

A second cup of coffee and a hot shower had done wonders for Sally's mood. "I don't think I've been on a bike since I was a teenager," she said as they pedaled along.

"I try to do this a few times a summer. It's a good day-long walk, too. Leave home early, lunch in Ohiopyle, rest, good dinner that night. You work up an appetite." He noticed they had slowed a little as Sally unsuccessfully tried to hide a growing discomfort. Maybe he shouldn't have goaded her into doing this.

"For an outdoor fitness nut like you, sure. I'll pass." She shifted a little on her seat. "You're going to feed me well after all this, Jim Duncan. And I'm going to figure out some way you're going to make it up to me."

"You're not having fun?"

"That has nothing to do with it. But my butt is killing me." She freed her water bottle from its cage to take a drink. "Why the change of plans?"

He knew this question would come. He unfastened his own bottle. "A few reasons. By the time you drive home, get the card reader and cable, and drive back, it'll be almost noon. Half the day would be gone. It's a beautiful and much better spent outdoors than in a car. The patter about spending the day at Ohiopyle was true."

"And?"

"Day like today, Ohiopyle is going to be packed with visitors, a lot of them on bikes. We'll blend in." As long as Sally could still walk and he didn't wind up carrying her.

She thought about that. "Angela hopefully won't notice us until it's too late to bolt."

"You got it."

"I have to admit, it might work."

"For being a good sport, we'll leave in time to clean up when we get home and I'll take you to River's Edge for dinner."

"You're on." She suddenly picked up the pace and whizzed past him.

He sped up to match her. Maybe she was in better shape than she let on.

They did not keep up the racing speed into Ohiopyle and arrived late morning, not too winded and more importantly, not soaked in sweat. As predicted, the tiny town already seethed with tourists, some on bikes, some on foot. They rode past Mulligan's, which, as Sally predicted, did not open for another hour.

"What do we do with the bikes?" Sally asked.

"There's a place to chain them up," Duncan said. "Follow me."

After he watched Sally limp along after they left the bikes, Duncan ditched his original plan to hike down to Cucumber Falls. Instead, they killed time by wandering down to the overlook by Ohiopyle Falls.

Sally didn't say anything, but she immediately took a seat on one of the benches. "Any chance we could convince Angela to meet us right here? I suddenly don't feel a whole lot like moving."

"Do I need to go home, get the Jeep, and come back for you?"

She closed her eyes, felt her quads, and winced. "I'll get back to you on that."

Duncan's stomach was more than ready for lunch when they made their way back to Mulligan's, Sally's gait slowed by a limp she didn't even try to hide.

"I'm sorry. I thought you were in better shape or I never would have suggested biking. When we get back to Confluence, I have muscle cream at home that'll help."

She glared at him. "Who said I wasn't in shape?"

"I didn't mean that. I only meant for a twenty-mile bike ride—"

"I'm fine. And you're going to buy me a big-ass cheeseburger for lunch." She tossed her head, but the hitch in her walk marred what was certainly supposed to be a haughty stride.

"Yes, ma'am."

They arrived at Mulligan's and Sally ordered a bacon cheeseburger with a side of fries. "I'll take a mushroom Swiss, fries are fine," Duncan said to the young woman at the register. After he paid, he asked Sally, "You see her?"

"She's here." Sally turned so Angela wouldn't catch sight of her. "I'd say let's eat in that corner table, but it's too stinking hot. She's taking care of outside tables, too. Let's see if we can grab one on the patio."

Duncan took the plastic tag with their number. They filled their drinks at the fountain and went outside. A trio of young men had stood up to leave, and Sally snagged the table and practically fell onto the bench while Duncan fetched napkins to wipe it down.

Mulligan's thrived on fast service, so the food arrived in no time. "Enjoy your lunch," Angela said as she put down the plates. "If you need anything—" Recognition dawned in her eyes. "God, what are you doing here again?"

Sally smiled. "Having lunch. Angela, this is my friend, Jim. He has some questions for you."

Duncan held out his hand.

Angela didn't take it. Instead, she gripped her serving tray tighter. "I answered your questions. Why the hell do I need to answer his?"

"Because he's with the state police," Sally replied as she put ketchup on her burger.

Angela's grip on the tray became white-knuckled.

Damn it, Sally. What have I told you? But he held back the words. Keeping his voice low and soothing, he said, "Hi, Angela. You're not in trouble. I'm not looking to get your husband in a bind, either." Of course, if Ryan Stewart got himself in a mess, that was another matter. "I know you volunteer at CWPS. I have a few questions about Mike Brower. Answer them and we'll be on our way."

She paused. "I…can't."

"Why not?" Thank God, Sally focused on her lunch with laser-like intensity, apparently content to let him do the talking.

Angela huffed a laugh. "I'm working and this place is a madhouse. Also," she ran her tongue over her lips, "I'm scared. You don't know Ryan. He has a horrible temper. He finds out I was talking to you and he'll flip."

"The first objection is easy. Can you take a break?"

"I have one coming in about twenty minutes."

"You do that. It'll give us time to finish eating. Then meet us down by the river. It'll look like three friends chatting, no flirting at all. Between the crowd and the water, no one will hear what we talk about and Ryan doesn't need to know. Fair enough?"

Angela hesitated, then her grip on the tray relaxed. "Fine. I'll see you down there." She hurried off.

Duncan turned to Sally. "How many times have I told you not to do that?"

"A few." She was honest enough to admit it at least. "I felt she needed the shock. She shut me down so fast, I figured she wouldn't talk unless she was more scared of you than of her husband."

The approach had merit, but it rankled. "I don't like being used as a threat, Sally."

"I'm sorry, we should have agreed on the tactics, you're right. But you're not the threat. Your badge is. Now eat, or we'll miss our meeting."

The burgers were good and would have been better if they hadn't tried to set a land-speed record in eating. But they did, tossed their trash, and strolled to the edge of the water. A week of no rain had the water level down, but the whitecaps and the noise said it was still fast. Duncan picked a spot and watched the river, while Sally kept an eye out for Angela.

About the time he thought Angela had blown them off, Sally elbowed him. "Here she comes."

A minute later, Angela made it to the fence. "Are you…are you sure Ryan won't find out?"

"Sure? No. But look at the water and relax while you're talking. I'm not in uniform, no one is paying attention to us."

She took a ragged breath. "Okay."

"You volunteered with CWPS. You knew Mike Brower and Carl Ritchie. Were you and Brower having an affair?"

"Yes." Angela drew out the word. "Mike was…funny. Warm, you know? He paid attention to me in a way Ryan hasn't for years. It started out as joking, but, well, you know." She blushed.

Duncan had heard variations on this story dozens of times over the years. "Did Ryan know?"

"I think… He…I came home from a CWPS event after dinner one night. I was supposed to be home earlier. I swear, it was the event that ran long, nothing between Mike and me. But Ryan was furious. He pounded on the china cabinet, broke half the dishes in it. He said I'd better quit CWPS if I knew what was good for me. He knew I was carrying on with a wussy tree hugger, as Ryan called Mike. Ryan said I was his wife, and he wouldn't stand for being embarrassed in his own house."

Sally broke into the conversation. "Does Ryan do that often? Threaten you?"

Angela shrugged. "It's my fault, really. Ryan's been good to me and I'm… secretly seeing another guy."

Sally glanced at Jim. "It is not your fault."

Tears leaked from Angela's eyes. "Yeah, it is. I was a high-school dropout with no skills when I started dating Ryan. He didn't care and took me in when nobody else would. Never minded that all I could do was minimum wage work. He said it was his job to take care of me and that's what he was gonna do." She dashed a hand at her eyes. "It's only that Ryan, well, it hasn't been much fun lately. Mike was fun and I needed that. Still, I should be more grateful. I can't imagine trying to live on my own."

Duncan had responded to enough domestics to know Angela's story was all too common. But he also recognized the fierce light in Sally's eyes. If it were up to her, Ryan Stewart would be cooling his heels in jail before the sun went down. Being a jackass didn't make a guy a murderer, though.

Angela pulled a crumpled napkin from her pocket and wiped her nose. "Anyway. Mike came to the house shortly after that and tried to talk Ryan into letting me stay at CWPS because Mike knew how much I enjoyed it. I mean, the actual work, aside from the personal stuff."

"When was this?"

"A week ago Friday. I'm not sure what time. Mike said he would be in the field all weekend. I hadn't left for work yet, so maybe nine or ten in the morning?"

"How did Ryan react?" Duncan asked.

"Pretty much how you think he did." Angela studied her hands. "I've heard him swear a lot, but that was the worst. He finished up by telling Mike to get the hell out of the house or Nathan'd call the cops and have him arrested for trespassing. I told Mike maybe we better not see each other again, but he brushed it off. Typical Mike."

"Did Ryan say anything to you?"

Angela didn't speak for a moment, and when she lifted her gaze to meet Duncan's her eyes weren't just filled with tears. They were wide with fear. "Ryan said…if I didn't leave CWPS and break it off with Mike, Ryan would find him and beat him to a bloody pulp."

* * *

Sally didn't say much after they left Angela. In fact, she spoke little for the rest of the time they were in Ohiopyle. Her thoughts were so focused on Angela and her domestic situation, that even the pain in her legs faded as she and Jim biked their way back to Confluence. She declined to take Jim up on his offer of dinner out, preferring to stay home. She moved like an automaton through dinner. There had to be something Sally could do to help the other woman. Except if Angela wouldn't file charges or leave, whatever aid Sally could tender wouldn't be legal. That realization led back to wondering how she could convince Angela to ditch her loser husband, which seemed hopeless. The very definition of an infinite loop.

After dinner, they sat on Jim's front porch watching the gathering dusk and a sky bathed in fire. He nudged her with his knee. "Want to tell me what's been eating you all afternoon? Don't tell me nothing because I have a pretty good idea of what it is."

"My legs are sore. All that damn biking." They were, too. Once Sally had stopped moving, the complaint her muscles had been murmuring rose to a scream. She didn't need a rub-down with pain cream. She needed a bath in it. What the hell had she been thinking, agreeing to all that riding? Her pride wouldn't have suffered that much had she declined.

Jim shifted closer. "That's not it. If it were nothing more than leg cramps, you'd be bitching up a storm. And I'd deserve it, after the way I practically dared you to complete the ride."

"Nice of you to acknowledge that. I'm still thinking up the appropriate payback." She leaned into him and he put his arm around her shoulders.

CHAPTER TWENTY-FOUR

"Okay, but that's not what's really bothering you."

She paused then sighed. "Angela Stewart."

Jim squeezed her shoulders. "I figured that was it."

"Even if that stupid husband of hers is innocent of murder, she's being abused, Jim. We ought to be able to do something about it."

"Like what?"

"I don't know."

He sighed. "The system doesn't work that way."

"The system sucks."

He drew her in and kissed the top of her head. "Yes, it does. But it's what the two of us have chosen to work in."

She deflated a little, grateful for the strong arm around her. "I know. It's frustrating. I guess I can talk to her again, maybe convince her to leave and file a personal restraining order. She can go back to school, get a GED, maybe get vocational training."

"Oh, I think we can do more than that."

She straightened and looked into his face. What was he going to do, pull a stakeout of the Stewart home?

"Angela said enough that Ryan Stewart is a strong suspect for the murder of Mike Brower. I intend to pass that information on and make sure it's investigated. If I, or someone else, find evidence of spousal abuse in the process, well, too bad for Mr. Stewart."

"But that'll put her in more trouble. If Ryan finds out Angela ratted him out, he's going to be more than pissed and he'll take it out on her."

"I'll leave her out of it. Say it's an anonymous source.

Sally kissed his cheek. "You're a good egg, Jim Duncan."

"I try."

She sobered. "What about Carl Ritchie? Are you writing him off as an accident?"

Jim's face hardened. "Oh hell no. I see three possibilities. He had a fight with Brower over something, killed him, and injured himself so badly in the process he wound up dead. Or, he got in the way when Stewart came after Brower and wound up collateral damage."

"That explains the names. But what about the word water?"

"That makes me think the motive had something to do with the work at CWPS."

"Because that's where both victims worked and it could be related to their work on the Casselman." She drummed her fingers on the porch floor. "What's the third option?"

"Brower and Ritchie were killed for different reasons, which means we're looking for two actors."

"It's the more complicated scenario. I know how you feel about those."

He squeezed her shoulders. "Yes. But we learned in the Trafford affair last fall things can get complicated."

True. "What are you going to do?"

"First, dig a little deeper into Laurel Mountain and Xavier Whitney, respectively. It bothers me that Whitney offered an alibi for an event without an associated date."

She stood. "I've got a little free time on Monday. I'll look and see if there's any incidents between all our players that resulted in charges being filed. I'll admit to an ulterior motive to wanting to find something on Stewart."

"Don't let your righteous anger cloud your judgment." Jim followed her to her car and opened the door.

"I promise. I won't." From the look on his face, Sally was sure he didn't completely believe her.

Chapter Twenty-Five

Monday morning, Duncan left first shift roll call with a mental list. A fool, or an inexperienced investigator, would follow all the leads at once. Duncan was neither. Sally would find out what she could about CWPS and Ryan Stewart. That left him with LMQ and Whitney.

What Duncan needed was a more precise time of death. Whitney's comment that he had an alibi, at least for Brower's murder, troubled him. Did the developer know when Brower went into the water or was his claim to have an alibi a shot in the dark? Only one way to find out.

Duncan parked in front of the coroner's office in Uniontown. He'd called ahead to make sure Burns was in and not busy with an autopsy. Based on the information he'd received, Burns would be free for about thirty minutes by the time Duncan arrived. The conversation shouldn't take long.

A pounding noise and swearing drew Duncan's attention. He followed it to a hallway, where he found Burns alternately banging on a snack machine and reaching up inside in an attempt to snag a bag of chips that dangled from the spiral dispenser, and cursing the vending machine gods. Duncan leaned on the wall. "If you break it, I'll have to charge you with destruction of public property. That machine is owned by the county."

Burns grumbled and stood. "Well, then the county owes me a buck fifty for those chips." He examined his wrist and rubbed his arm. "What can I do for you?"

"Does reaching in ever work for you, or do you wind up hurting yourself and looking foolish?"

"Sometimes. Now what…do…you…want? I have an autopsy in twenty-five minutes. Thus my need for some mid-morning carbs." Burns returned to his office.

Duncan followed. "I need a better time of death on Mike Brower."

"No can do, my friend." Burns rifled through drawers.

"You can't even tell me how long he was in the water?"

"Nope." Burns unearthed a bag of peanuts from a bottom drawer and ripped them open. "The water will totally mess with time of death, you know that. It's July, so the river should be warmer, but the water is high, which means it's cooler and all of it makes determining rate of cooling for body temperature practically useless."

"What about damage to the body tissue from fish or something eating it?"

"The fauna in the Casselman aren't really carnivorous. Sure, there's some damage, but not enough to mean anything. I can tell you the corpse was pretty bloated, so it'd been more than fifteen minutes."

"I don't need sarcasm."

"Sorry. Bottom line, I can't give you the level of precision you're looking for." Burns poured the rest of the peanuts into his mouth and headed for the autopsy area to prepare.

Duncan rubbed his face and once again followed. "Fine. Did the report indicate anything that might be useful in determining what happened before Brower went into the water? Throw me a bone here, Burns. Anything."

The younger man paused. "One thing, and it may not mean much."

"I'll take it."

"Remember I told you about the subdural? There were rock fragments in the wound on the cranium. Sandstone. It was in some abrasions on his forearms and under his fingernails, too. Now, like I said, it might not mean anything. Sandstone isn't exactly uncommon in Somerset County."

"That's what LMQ deals with."

"It also makes up the majority of the bedrock in that area. If Brower fell, hit his head, scrabbled while in the water, it's perfectly probable he'd have sandstone fragments on his corpse."

"But you think he was murdered. So it also means he could have been killed in an area with a lot of exposed sandstone. Or killed with something that had stone residue."

"Correct." Burns laid out tools for the autopsy. "That doesn't implicate anyone at Laurel Mountain Quarrying. Remember—"

"I know. There's lots of sandstone in Somerset County." Duncan thought a moment. "Thanks, Burns. I still owe you that bottle of Glenfidditch."

"Believe me, I haven't forgotten."

Duncan left the coroner's office and sat in his patrol car. The information about the sandstone led him to think Brower had died near Laurel Mountain Quarrying or somewhere along the Casselman where there was significant exposed rock. The vagueness in the science meant time of death would have to be determined the old-fashioned way. He knew the end of the window when Brower was fished out of the Casselman. Determining the start would be more time-consuming.

He had to find out the last time Brower was last seen alive.

* * *

Sally adjusted the cushion she'd brought from home and closed her eyes as her butt complained. The good thing about her work is she didn't have to walk much, so she was able to spare her aching legs. The bad thing was she had to sit at a desk, which didn't make her glutes happy.

Damnit. The next time Jim proposes "a nice bike ride" I'll tell him exactly where he can put that bike.

Moving gingerly, she disposed of her morning casework, then checked the clock. There was half an hour before she needed to be in her next meeting, which meant she had about twenty free minutes. Her afternoon was booked. Should she start with Stewart or CWPS? It wasn't a hard call, especially when she remembered the look of fear in Angela Stewart's eyes.

As she expected, the financial check on Ryan Stewart produced more than a single sheet of paper. She retrieved the printouts, cursing as she hobbled back to her office. Tanelsa was bent over the desk, scribbling a note. "I thought you'd left already." Her forehead creased in puzzlement. "What's wrong with you? You're moving like an old lady."

"My pride kicked me in the ass yesterday."

"Excuse me?"

"I biked twenty miles round trip from Confluence to Ohiopyle. I haven't ridden a bike that much since I was a teenager."

Tanelsa whistled. "Damn. And you're walking today? That's quite an accomplishment." The grin that appeared should have been fined, it was so smug. "Let me guess. You didn't want to tell your man that you weren't up to it."

"Can we not discuss my lapses in judgment? What can I do for you?" Sally lowered herself onto the cushioned seat with care.

"It's not a big deal, a question about an upcoming case." She nodded at the sheaf of paper in Sally's hand. "What's that?"

"Nothing." She tried to twitch the stack away from Tanelsa's gaze before she saw anything.

It didn't work. "Isn't Ryan Stewart the guy you asked me to find?"

"I told you, don't worry about it."

"Uh huh. Because you run checks on random people all the time." Tanelsa crossed her arms and struck a pose.

"It's nothing important."

"Sally, please." The look she shot Sally was worthy of a schoolteacher.

Knowing that her colleague wouldn't back down and not willing to waste time arguing, Sally gave in. Besides, Tanelsa might have fresh insights since she was an outsider. "Turns out Mike Brower, he's the guy Jim and I found in the Casselman, was murdered. At least according to a friend of mine."

"Why should you trust this friend?"

"He's a deputy coroner who has a medical degree from the University of Pittsburgh. I think he knows what he's talking about."

Tanelsa blinked. "What does Ryan Stewart have to do with this Brower guy?"

"His wife, Angela, was having an affair with the victim. We, Jim and I, interviewed her this weekend. I learned enough from her that I want to know more about him."

"Let me see."

As Sally read each sheet, she passed it to Tanelsa. It didn't take long to form a picture of Ryan Stewart. A loud-mouthed bully who'd worked out so much in his youth that his biceps took most of the oxygen required by his brain. In addition to the information previously supplied, there was a litany of complaints from various neighbors over the years. When the police arrived, Angela always denied any problems. The couple had bounced from one low-rent residence to another over the last five years. Their bank balance was low. Credit card debt was high. Ryan's truck was paid for, but it was over ten years old. It looked like a failure to pay rent for several months in a row always preceded a move. Both Angela and Ryan had credit scores well below the national average.

Sally's eye was drawn to Stewart's employer. Laurel Mountain Quarrying. She sucked in her breath.

"What is it?" Tanelsa asked. "Besides the fact this guy seems like a real peach."

"He works for the same company that CWPS was protesting against. Another dead man, Carl Ritchie, also worked for CWPS." She told Tanelsa about Ritchie.

"You didn't notice this before?"

"I only checked Stewart's criminal record."

"Both of the CWPS guys are dead? Fishy. Think Stewart beat them up?"

"I'm not sure and I don't have time to pursue it at this moment. See you later." She tucked Stewart's background check into a drawer. Anticipating the pain, she sucked in her breath, grabbed her briefcase and files, and left.

No more bike rides. Ever.

* * *

The midday sun blazed down on the patrol car parked on the side of Walnut Hill Road and the dusty red Dodge Dart parked in front of it. Duncan handed over the ticket he'd just issued. "Information about where to send payment is there. If you choose to dispute the charge, information on how to do that is on the other side." He touched the brim of his campaign hat. "Drive safely and I hope you have a better day."

The motorist, a young man in his late twenties according to his license, grumbled an epithet and snatched the thin slip of paper. At least he waited until Duncan was back at his patrol car before pulling away. Slowly.

He rubbed his eyes. What had he been doing before the young hothead had ripped past him on the two-lane road doing eighty? An act that always stunned him. Yet it happened, and more frequently than people might think. Perhaps the drivers were going too fast to recognize the car they'd buzzed was a PSP-marked Ford Interceptor.

Back on task. He'd been puzzling out Mike Brower's and Carl Ritchie's last days. A task that was infinitely more interesting than issuing a traffic citation to a disgruntled motorist. He'd been vacillating between promotion and applying to Criminal Investigation. It would be so much easier if he could put in for promotion, then apply to CI. But things didn't work that way. He could try for promotion then apply to CI in a couple years if an opening at that rank became available. Or he could make the move to CI, then do the promotion later, again if a position was open. But not both at the same time.

Maybe the Brower-Ritchie case was the universe's way of telling him which way to go career-wise.

He pulled out his notepad. The close of the time-of-death window for Mike was clear. A week ago Monday, when his body was recovered from the Casselman. Actually, Duncan could safely say Sunday, which was when Lindy Hunter had reported seeing it. According to Travers, Carl had also been rescued on that Sunday. For the purposes of this exercise, it didn't matter that Carl hadn't died for another couple of days. Duncan was interested in when the two men could have gone into the water, not necessarily when death had occurred.

According to his notes, Harold Brower had talked to his son Thursday evening around six. Then Angela, the CWPS volunteer and Mike's girlfriend, said she saw him mid-morning on Friday.

Sally's source, the photographer. What was her name? Tara Jennings.

Had she told Sally exactly when she'd heard Mike and Carl argue? He took out his phone and sent Sally a text. *When did Tara J last see Brower?*

He didn't expect an immediate answer, so he went back to his timeline. Ritchie, what about him? Aside from the three intelligible words he'd muttered—Mike, Ryan, water—he hadn't given the medical personnel any information before he died and there weren't even the minor clues there had been with Mike.

Or were there?

Ritchie had died at Somerset Hospital, but that didn't mean there hadn't been an autopsy. He'd owe Burns two bottles of that damn whiskey if he asked for another favor, but it might come to that.

His phone pinged with a text alert. Sally. *Saw Ritchie and Brower argue the Thursday before Brower found.*

He texted back his thanks and prepared to put the phone away when it pinged again.

BTW, RS works for LMQ.

It took him a moment to puzzle out the message. Ryan Stewart worked for Laurel Mountain Quarrying. That was interesting. Especially if LMQ and CWPS and been engaged in some confrontation that might lead to trouble for the quarrying company. CWPS was only a volunteer organization, but if they raised a big enough stink and had the data to back it up, the state and federal environmental agencies could get involved.

What had the nurse at the hospital said about Carl? Abrasions, contusion to the skull, some water in the lungs, and a concussion. They thought he'd been in the water for a while. Same type of injuries on Mike.

Travers said they'd found Ritchie on Sunday. Thursday to Sunday definitely qualified as a while, but somehow Duncan doubted it was that long. Maybe that nurse at Somerset Hospital would still be friendly and answer a few questions.

Chapter Twenty-Six

Around noon, Sally reluctantly returned to her office, a chicken salad wrap and a bottle of water in hand. The day was so glorious, it was a shame not to eat on the little bench in front of the courthouse. Besides, the warm sun felt good on her aching body. But from Jim's texts, it sounded like he was trying to narrow a time-of-death window for the two victims. Sally's research into CWPS could help with that, so lunch at her desk it was. As she sat down, she heard steps at her door and she looked up.

Tanelsa stood in the doorway, purse in hand. "I was going to ask you out to lunch, but it looks like you've got it covered. Work-work or more on your project?"

"The project. I'm not going to get much time this afternoon and I need to find out more about this environmental group. Remember STOP and Southland Mining?"

"Hell yes." Tanelsa rubbed her forehead. "I'm not likely to forget something that put me in the hospital. Is this more of the same?"

"Different players, but maybe. Environmental groups put people's backs up. I'm trying to find out if the Casselman Water Protection Society was as irksome to Laurel Mountain Quarrying about water as STOP was to Southland."

"How many of these groups do you have down here?"

"More than you might imagine. People, especially long-time residents, can get touchy on both sides. Like fracking a while back. On the one hand, people were sitting on something that could actually be valuable. On the other, concerns about the environmental impact."

"I can imagine." Tanelsa adjusted her purse. "Do you need some help? You're gimping along like a lady from an old-age home, but I guess you'd be sitting. Unless that hurts, too."

"Believe me, it does." An extra pair of eyes would be good, but she didn't want to intrude on Tanelsa's time. Or put her in a situation where she'd get injured again. Sally had finally gotten to the point where Tanelsa's wife, Lisa, didn't refer to Sally as "the woman who put Tanelsa in the hospital." She had no desire to go back to that moniker. "It's okay. I don't want—"

"You're not going to get me in trouble." Tanelsa smirked and dropped her bag on the visitor's chair. "I do that fine on my own. Move over."

"What about your lunch?"

"I can grab something after we finish. My next appointment isn't until two. Move over."

Sally pulled her keyboard and computer monitor to a place where they could both see it and opened a web browser. "Last time we learned CWPS was started about five years ago. What we're looking for now is any history of actual confrontations involving the group, including anything that might help narrow the window on time of death for Mike Brower."

"Can't the coroner do that?"

Sally entered text in the search bar. "I guess not. Science is powerful, but sometimes you gotta go old school."

Tanelsa hitched her chair closer. "Are we only interested in incidents involving Laurel Mountain?"

"Anyone, I guess, because it would establish a pattern. But especially Laurel Mountain."

For a while, they searched in near silence, the only words exchanged when Tanelsa directed Sally to click somewhere. CWPS looked to be much less confrontational in its methods. No targeting of individual companies, no rotating rogues' galleries on its websites. Lots of pictures. A few mentions of the group at local events designed to raise awareness or promote the natural landscape of the Laurel Highlands. But nothing that was dated in a way that might indicate when Mike Brower or Carl Ritchie had been attacked.

"What's that story, right in the middle?" Tanelsa asked.

Sally clicked the link. "Looks like their study of the smallmouth bass population. See, here's the original water study that showed the dust levels. Blah, blah, blah, continual monitoring, dropping levels, rise in the fish population. I'd say this is their keynote achievement."

"Did they say where the dust came from?"

"Uh…blah, blah, blah, dust, fish, blah, water…here it is. 'Particulate matter may come from many sources. One of the worst offenders in this area is Laurel Mountain Quarrying. While the quarry itself is not on the Casselman, pollution of a tributary creek is surely the cause of the rise in local levels and will impact smallmouth bass populations.'"

"Very scientific sounding."

"But listen to this. 'CWPS has provided our findings to the Pennsylvania Department of Environmental Protection, as well as EPA offices in Pittsburgh. It is our wish, and our belief, that these agencies will take immediate steps to remediate the situation, up to and including the shuttering of Laurel Mountain Quarrying offices.'"

Tanelsa sat back. "They weren't asking too much, were they?"

Sally continued to read, but those few sentences were the meat of the article. "This couldn't have made people at LMQ happy."

"Not to mention all the people employed there. Why do so many environmental groups jump to 'shut it all down' before they, you know, look for other options? LMQ closes and it removes a source of pollution. It also removes a source of tax revenue for the county and employment for county residents. In an area that isn't exactly overflowing with high-paying jobs."

"Hmm." Sally closed the article and continued to skim. "Well, we know they weren't best buddies. What we want to know now is whether it went beyond words." She opened a news piece. "CWPS did a picket a few weeks ago, but aside from some shouting, nada. It's too long ago to directly relate to the two deaths last week."

Tanelsa leaned forward again. "Change your search. Try Brower, LMQ, CWPS, criminal, or something like that."

Sally obliged. "Here we go. A couple of members, yes, including Mike Brower, were arrested for criminal trespass during protests that shut down quarry operations. Words were exchanged between Brower and the foreman, there was some pushing and shoving." She pointed at the date on the story. "The incident occurred less than two weeks ago."

"There it is. Blows exchanged. Brower got into a fistfight with an LMQ employee. The two were pulled apart, Brower by his pal Ritchie. So they were both there. It's not the fight that resulted in the deaths, but who knows? Bad blood could have spilled over, especially if CWPS threatened to shut down the company at the same event."

Sally got up and stretched. Her lunch hour was nearly gone and she needed to use the facilities. She'd run out of time for this particular search session. "Does it say who the Laurel Mountain employee is?"

"Indeed it does." Tanelsa printed the article and stood. "Your buddy, Ryan Stewart."

* * *

Duncan waited until after his Monday shift to revisit Somerset Hospital. A quick call confirmed Loretta Smith was working, same floor where Carl had been cared for until his death. Duncan wasn't entirely sure why he waited so long. Perhaps so he could point to a full shift's worth of paperwork as proof that he wasn't usurping Travers's investigation. This was his project, done on private time.

Once at the hospital, he locked his duty weapon in the Jeep's lockbox, then checked in as required and headed straight for Ritchie's former floor. Sure enough, Loretta Smith stood at the nurses' station, making notes on a laptop computer on a rolling cart. He walked up. "Excuse me. Ms. Smith? Do you remember me?"

She looked up and frowned. "You're the trooper who was here wanting to speak to Carl Ritchie when he was unconscious. I called you after he died."

"That's me."

"I'm not sure what more you want. Well, actually I do. You want to know

153

how he ended up in that river. I don't think I can help you." Smith's forehead puckered. "That corporal told me you might come back. The one who seems to be in charge."

"Corporal Travers." Damn.

"That's him. He didn't outright say so, but I got the feeling he doesn't think much of you."

Duncan repressed a sigh. "I'm not surprised. He and I…we're colleagues, but we don't work out of the same barracks."

She considered his words. "He told me you might come sniffing around, asking questions. He said you had no business here and not to talk to you."

This time, Duncan couldn't hold back the exhale. "Well, thanks anyway. Have a good afternoon." He touched the brim of his hat and headed for the elevator.

Smith's voice made him stop. "That's it? You aren't going to try and convince me of what a nice guy you are and how this Corporal Travers is out of line?"

Duncan turned. "No, ma'am."

"Then why are you here?"

He thought a moment. "I knew Mr. Ritchie, did I tell you that? He wasn't a close friend, but he was a good guy. I volunteered with his environmental group a couple of times. I have my own questions and I'm looking for answers." He once again gave her a little salute as a way of saying goodbye and resumed his walk to the elevator.

Smith's voice brought him to another stop. "Ask."

He pivoted to face her. "Excuse me?"

"I said go ahead and ask your questions."

Duncan briefly wondered why she'd changed her mind, but decided not to look a gift horse in the mouth. "The day I visited, that first day, you said Mr. Ritchie had numerous injuries including some abrasions. I wanted to know if they found any stone fragments in those wounds."

"Yes. He had pieces under his skin, embedded in the wounds. Not very big, but they were there. Like he'd fallen or maybe even been dragged over it."

CHAPTER TWENTY-SIX

"You're sure?"

"Positive."

Duncan took a step toward her. "Do you know if it was sandstone?"

"I have no clue."

It was too much to ask for. "What about the head wound? You said severe contusion and a concussion. I'm assuming the skin was broken as a result."

Smith nodded. "Yep, stone was there too. We didn't keep that since it was the same stuff."

A thought occurred to him. "The water in his lungs. Did anyone analyze it?"

"Not here at the hospital. Since he was brought in via ambulance, I doubt the emergency personnel stopped to collect the water. They probably cleared his lungs and drove him in."

Not surprising, but unfortunate. An analysis of the water might have helped pinpoint a crime scene. "I believe he was pulled out of the river near Markleton. At least that's what Travers told me. Anything notable about his clothes?"

Smith tilted her head as if she was thinking. "He had lots of, I guess it's not seaweed, not in a river. But green viney things. Vegetation. It was caught in his clothes, snagged in buttons…almost like he'd been thrown in a patch of it and flailed around."

"You don't know what kind of vegetation?"

"Nope."

Damn. "Don't suppose you kept any of the stuff?"

"He came in as an accident victim. No reason to keep it because we didn't think it was evidence."

"Can you describe it?"

"Sure." She took a piece of paper and sketched. "This is what the green stuff looked like. Long, thin leaves. I thought it was maybe some kind of cattail because it looked like something that grows near water." Smith handed over the sheet. "The stone was brown, rough. Not slate or granite, I'd have recognized that. Not river rock, my mom has those in her garden at home. My kid recently did a project on sediment rock, it kinda looked like that."

It wasn't much, but at least he had a sketch and a description, which was more than he had when he started. One of his fishing buddies, Grant Carpenter, worked with the Western Pennsylvania Conservancy. Maybe he could help out. "Thank you very much. I appreciate the information." Duncan paused. "Mind telling me why you talked to me?"

Smith grinned. "Two, well, three reasons. I'm a sucker for a puzzle. You seem like a guy who hates unanswered questions, unsolved puzzles. So do I. Also, everybody was really quick to dismiss this as an accidental death."

"Everyone except you, I take it. Why?"

She shrugged. "I don't know. A feeling. You know that tickle in your gut that says all is not what it seems to be? That."

"I'm very familiar with it." He lifted an eyebrow. "You said three reasons. What's the third?"

Smith's grin turned a little wicked. "Has anyone ever told you you've got a great ass?"

* * *

Sally stopped at the kitchen doorway, cutting board and a fresh loaf of bread in her hands, to stare at Jim. "She said what?" Jim did have a great ass, but that was beside the point. Another woman had no right to come out and say it.

He kept putting down silverware as if nothing had happened. "It wasn't anything you haven't said, or thought, before." He looked up with a devilish grin on his face and a twinkle in his hazel eyes.

She stalked into the dining room and thumped down the bread, a little harder than necessary. "I hope you told her you were off-limits." She crossed her arms. A random comment by a nurse he'd met twice shouldn't raise her hackles, but it did.

He finished with the silverware, came around the table, and enfolded her in his arms. "Relax, Counselor. I told her my girlfriend agreed with her." He kissed her forehead. "Now who's being jealous?"

The timer beeped and Sally pulled away. "The chicken!" She hurried back to the kitchen, grabbed two oven mitts, and removed the bird from the oven. Perfectly browned and crisped. She transferred it to a platter, got the carving knife, and returned to the dining room.

After letting it rest, Jim carved while Sally served sides and cut the bread. Then they sat down. "Smells amazing," he said. "I only got roast chicken on Sundays growing up."

She laid a napkin across her lap. "Tell me about your day and I'll tell you about mine."

Jim recapped his findings, in between mouthfuls. "Now I'm back to wondering if they fought and fell in the water."

Sally tore apart a second slice of bread. "The plant they found on Carl. It wasn't on Mike."

"No."

"Which means they went in the water at different locations, right?"

He barely paused. "Or none of it got caught in Mike's clothes. The common denominator is the stone. Burns confirmed Mike had sandstone on his body."

"But the nurse couldn't identify the stone they found on Carl."

"No, she gave me a description, as well as a sketch of the plant though. I need to talk to my buddy at the Conservancy. He might be able to ID the leaves and the stone. Which might lead to the crime scene for both men." He looked up. "What about you?"

"CWPS had it in for Laurel Mountain Quarrying." She told him about the article, including the fact that Stewart and Mike had tangled. "That lets Angela off the hook. Now you can tell Stewart you found out about the fight from the news."

"True." Jim paused. "Did CWPS forward that data to the environmental agencies?"

"I don't know. I ran out of time to look into it today, but I might be able to scrape out some additional time tomorrow." She poked at the chicken on her plate. "I think it kind of points to Stewart as the culprit."

Jim laid down his knife and fork. "Haven't we been down this road? The one where you decide who the guilty party is before all the facts are in?"

She hung her head. He was talking about the murder of Colin Rafferty. She'd never forget the circumstances around her colleague's death or live down her part in how it all ended. Regaining her confidence, she continued. "What's your theory then?"

He resumed eating. "I don't have one, yet. Could be Stewart and Mike fought, nothing else. I still have to rule out Xavier Whitney."

"Who could be an overzealous businessman from Pittsburgh who wanted to complete a project."

"Yes. And it's still possible Carl and Mike fought and no one else is involved."

"Why are you so reluctant to finger Stewart?"

"I'm not reluctant, I don't have enough evidence. Why are you so gung-ho?"

Sally took a drink of her wine. "Not only is he an abuser, he works for the company that was on the outs with the victim's advocacy group. I think that's enough reason."

Jim reached over and clasped her clenched fist. "Sally, I mean this in the kindest way possible. Don't make this mistake again. I promise I will continue to investigate Stewart. If he's a murderer, we'll nail him. If he's abusing his wife, we'll get him for that, too. But not on the evidence we have."

Sally opened her mouth to retort but stopped. Jim was right. She'd been down that road and it led to disaster. "Promise me."

He lifted her hand and kissed it. "Promise."

Mollified, Sally relaxed. Then a thought struck her. "What about that camera Bob Hunter gave you? Have you looked at Lindy's pictures?"

Jim slapped the table. "Shit, I forgot. I put it on a mental list of things to do, and it completely slipped my mind."

"That's the problem with mental lists." Sally laid down her fork. "Let me see the card."

Jim got up and fetched it.

Sally turned it over in her hands. "You're in luck. I think I have a reader at home that will allow us to download the pictures. I'll take this home and check."

Jim took the card back and kissed her cheek. "Thanks." He set the card on the countertop and returned to the table. "That's that. Things are gonna come together, I can feel it."

Chapter Twenty-Seven

Tuesday morning, Duncan rose and called Grant at the Western Pennsylvania Conservancy. A nature nut in high school, Grant had gone on to the perfect job for him, tramping around and helping protect the flora and fauna of southwestern Pennsylvania. If anyone could provide information about the unknown plant and stone, Grant could.

He didn't answer, so Duncan left a message and went on his morning run. He'd crossed the bridge near River's Edge, over the Youghiogheny, coming back from the Allegheny Passage, and turned onto his street when his phone rang. He glanced at the caller ID. "Hey, Grant, long time no speak."

"Jim. How's the fishing on the Middle Yough these days?"

"If you don't know, you need to get down there and find out for yourself. I figured your job had you intimately familiar with about every aspect of the area."

Grant laughed. "Almost. Your message said you needed some information?"

"I'm looking to ID a plant and some stone. I have a rough sketch of the former and a decent description of the latter. It's for a case."

"I figured." Grant paused. "I'm over in Lower Turkeyfoot this morning. Any chance you can meet me?"

Duncan checked his watch. It was only nine and it wouldn't take long to get there. "Sure. I don't work until three this afternoon. Where should I meet you?"

Grant gave him a location. "You still driving a Jeep?"

"You know me. Dark blue."

"I'll be on the lookout. See you in an hour or so."

Duncan thought about showering, then decided to hold off. If Grant had him hiking through the underbrush or along the water, he'd need another one before he went on duty. He fed Rizzo, made sure his water bowl was full, and headed out.

Grant was waiting when Duncan arrived. Nearly as tall as he was, Grant had the muscular build and weathered face of someone who worked outdoors. He grasped Duncan's hand in a firm shake. "I thought you were still with the state cops. Don't they make you shave?"

"I'll do it later."

"What's this mysterious plant?"

"This." Duncan held out the sketch. "Not great, but it's all I've got. Witness said it had long, green leaves and shallow roots. She thought it was some kind of cattail or another water plant."

Grant took the paper and studied it a minute. "Where did they find this again?"

"Tangled in the clothing of a victim pulled from the Casselman. That's another reason my witness thinks it was a water plant."

"Looks a little like northeastern bulrush."

"What's that?"

"Come this way." Grant let him toward the river. In the marshy ground close to the water, slender green stems sprouted from the ground. Grouped in clumps, some of the stems were adorned with firework-burst shaped brown clusters that looked as though they had scales, from which tiny flowers peeked out. "The northeastern bulrush. Latin name *scirpus ancistrochaetus*. There are only a little over one hundred populations of them, many in decline, putting them in vulnerable status."

"How many locations along the Casselman?"

"Several. They like the wetlands, anywhere there's variable water depth. Around here, they like the sinkholes that form in sandstone."

"That leads me to my next question." Duncan ran a hand over the plant's leaves, then straightened. "The victim had bits of stone embedded in some abrasions on his body. Brownish, with sediment in it. Not granite or quartz or anything hard."

Grant considered the words. "Sounds like sandstone. If the plant is the bulrush, that would make sense. The two go together."

"We have another victim. This guy was found in the Casselman. No plant material, but sandstone fragments."

"You think they're connected?"

"It's possible." He pointed at the bulrush. "Can I take a picture of that?"

"As long as you don't pull it out of the ground, sure."

Duncan snapped a couple photos with his phone. He'd circle back to Somerset Hospital and see if Nurse Loretta Smith could make a positive ID. He stood. "Thanks, Grant. I appreciate you taking the time to talk to me."

Grant nodded. "As long as I can help out, I'm glad to do it."

"One more thing. I suppose these sinkholes are all over the place. Anyplace in particular I can look? I mean, doesn't most of Somerset County rest on sandstone? I'd like to narrow my search area down a bit."

"Yes, but remember. The bulrush likes water and your victims turned up in the river. Come over to my car." Grant led the way back to his mud-spattered Range Rover and opened the back. "I will assume you are familiar with a topographic map."

"Very familiar."

Grant spread it out. "Northeastern bulrush is found throughout the watershed. But I can think of only a few places where you'd find a sandstone sinkhole close enough to the river that I'd expect to see the stone fragments and the plant matter." He pointed at the map. "Here, a few miles upriver." He shifted the map and indicated two more spots. "Here, outside Fort Hill, and another spot a mile or so downstream from there."

Jim traced the river. "The one guy was pulled out downstream from Rockwood, so I don't have to go much beyond that. Anyplace around there?"

"Sure." Grant flipped the map. "Right here." He tapped a spot not that far from Rockwood.

And very near the headquarters for Laurel Mountain Quarrying.

* * *

Tuesday morning, Sally set herself the task of finding out everything there was to know about Ryan Stewart. She had his criminal background and limited financial information. There had to be more. He may or may not have been a murderer. But she was dead certain he had committed spousal abuse and she intended to prove it.

In between cases, she dug up every shred of information the legal system had about him. In addition to the information she already knew from her prior searches, she learned he'd been born in Somerset County. Public records, which included an assortment of minor complaints and associated information, indicated he had gone through all the usual shenanigans, both barely legal and definitely-not-so-legal, that typified a young man's life in the Laurel Highlands and then some. He had a juvenile criminal record, sealed of course, to go along with all the misdemeanors and citations he'd received as an adult. Sally read between the lines. Ryan Stewart had been a wild child.

She studied an old mug shot. In it, Stewart was twenty-three, chiseled jaw, shock of black hair, and even in the black and white photograph, his eyes held a challenging gleam that dared the onlooker to a fight. His plaid shirt sleeves were ripped off, exposing muscled biceps. The right one had a tattoo, "Born to be Wild" in script around what could have been the image of a Harley Davidson motorcycle and a rose. He hadn't graduated from high school, didn't even go back to get his GED. A far cry from the man who was starting to lose the battle against the onset of middle age. This Ryan was hot, tough, and sexy.

If a young girl was into bad boys, Ryan Stewart fit the bill.

Tanelsa walked by and stopped at the door. "That's quite the expression on your face. What are you doing?"

"Looking at the background of a guy who probably beats his wife." Sally kept her attention focused on her reading material. She willed Tanelsa to walk on and not inquire further. Sally wasn't in the mood to hear about all the very good reasons she should keep her mind on her own work.

No such luck. "Are you talking about Ryan Stewart?" Tanelsa came into the office. "Why do you still have that on your plate?"

"I didn't tell you the whole story. I met his wife, Angela, over the weekend."

"The one having an affair with the murdered man."

"Jim and I went to Ohiopyle, and we stopped for lunch at the place where she works." All true, even if it did leave out some details. "Remember the reports of arguing at their house? We got to talking with her and it definitely sounded like an abusive situation, even though Angela has never filed a complaint and didn't say anything to us. At least not in so many words."

"I know exactly what you're talking about. Dirtbag." Tanelsa rounded the desk.

"Angela seems like a nice woman in a bad situation. I thought I'd do a little digging and see if I could help her out."

"Always the Good Samaritan, aren't you?" Tanelsa looked through the material to date. "He was a looker as a young guy, I'll give you that. If that's your type. Somehow, I don't think you were ever attracted to the bad boy, though. I mean, look at you now."

"No, I wasn't. Well, not seriously. I admired from afar and wished I was daring enough to date that kind of guy. That was me as a teenager. I got older and realized I was better off sticking with nice guys who had good jobs."

Tanelsa finished skimming the printed background. "Is this all of it?"

"No." Sally tapped her computer screen. "Ryan and Angela married when he was in his mid-twenties. Without an education, it looks like he bounced from low-paying job to low-paying job."

"The stress of not keeping a job would contribute to anger at home, fueling abuse. Does his wife work?"

"Yes, but she mentioned she doesn't have the background to do more than food service. I didn't ask how long she'd worked at the burger shack she's at currently."

"But if she kept any sort of job, while he played occupational roulette, that would also make him feel small, which wouldn't help." Tanelsa finished reading from the computer screen. "What makes you think he's beating on her?"

"Instinct. The way she carries herself. Even if he doesn't hit her, you know there's verbal and emotional abuse that's just as bad."

"True." Tanelsa fixed her with a stare. "What else is going on? We find out this guy works at LMQ, was involved in a fight with the first dead guy, what was his name, Mike Brower? Now you believe he beats his wife. You looking for a backdoor?"

"Not precisely. I told Jim about all this." Sally waved her hand at the material. "If Angela keeps telling the cops that nothing is wrong, there's nothing he can do. I thought while Jim worked on the Laurel Mountain-CWPS angle, I'd go this route."

"Figuring that if either of you discovered anything juicy in one charge, it might help the other."

"You are too smart for this job, you know that? Maybe I should introduce you to Kim Dunphy."

"I don't know her that well, but I doubt we'd get along professionally for any length of time." Tanelsa lifted a perfectly shaped eyebrow. "What's your next step?"

"They live in Markleton. That's not too far away. I'm busy until two, but after that I'm free. I thought I'd drive over and see what the neighbors have to say about Mr. and Mrs. Stewart." She looked up. "Don't suppose you want to come with me?"

Tanelsa snorted. "Do you even have to ask?"

Chapter Twenty-Eight

Duncan got home around eleven. He could drive to Pittsburgh and research Whitney, but he wouldn't have a lot of time to get back so he wasn't late for three o'clock roll call. Or he could do some digging here and be armed with real information when he went to see the developer. If he had to. He decided that forewarned was forearmed. He'd get ready for his shift, go in early, and find out what the system had on Xavier Whitney.

But after getting to the barracks and searching the official records, the answer turned out to be precious little outside of what Duncan already knew. Whitney had been a successful housing developer in the city with a fondness for the outdoors, specifically the Laurel Highlands. His record was clean, no financial trouble on his part or his company's, no complaints filed with any agency that oversaw building and construction. No OSHA violations, no evidence of bad financials. Every official paper looked perfect, all the i's dotted and t's crossed.

"Hey, Boss." McAllister wandered through the bullpen. "You look…what's that word you use instead of cranky?"

"Not now, McAllister."

She paused by his desk. "Whatcha doing?"

"I figured I'd come in early, get the official story on Xavier Whitney."

"Who's he?"

"A retired housing developer with big plans for increased river access along the Casselman. He argued with our victims, specifically Brower."

McAllister perched on a nearby desk. "We have multiple victims now?

Since when?"

"Officially, we don't. But I'm suspicious." He told her about the sandstone connection and the northeastern bulrush fragments in Ritchie's clothes. "That's something else I need to do, but I'm on duty in a couple of hours. I want to look at that site by Laurel Mountain headquarters in Rockwood."

"Huh. Brower was last seen Monday morning. Ritchie is still an open question, is that it?"

"Pretty much. If I can pin down the supposed crime scene, maybe I can refine the last-seen time for Brower and get one for Ritchie."

"Logical." She shook her head, setting her blond curls bouncing. "I'm off tomorrow. Maybe Tommy-boy and I can give you an assist."

He half-smiled. "Oh, yes. Burns will be thrilled if you tell him your idea of fun is a tramp through the underbrush. 'Cause he's a real nature guy."

"He'll do it if I pitch it right." She winked. "Anyway, what'd you find on Whitney?"

Duncan waved at the computer. "Nothing. He looks like what he says he is."

"You research his supposed alibi?"

"There was a meeting and he was there. I have it from the host, the receptionist for the host, and the head of the company who ran the meeting. This is background."

"And?"

"I told you, zero. I may have found the only honest housing developer in the world, or at least in southwestern Pennsylvania."

"Bullshit." McAllister dragged over a chair and pushed Duncan so he moved. "You're not looking at the right stuff. I'm not surprised his public record is clean. But I don't think there's such a thing as an honest housing developer."

"And you call me a cynic."

She scowled. "When I was in high school, my best friend's dad was an independent contractor. If I told you the number of times he was underbid by guys like Whitney, then called in to fix all the shitty work, we'd be here until Friday." Her fingers danced over the keys. "None of that is going to show up in official records, but it's out there. You need to know where to look."

Duncan was willing to believe her. McAllister's computer skills far outstripped his and her technological know-how went much further. He waited. "What are you looking at?"

"Some of it's consumer review sites. Plus there are forums where those in the construction industry get together and bitch."

"Chat rooms?"

"Sort of. Ah ha. Here you go." She turned the screen. "You want inside dirt on Whitney? Ask and ye shall receive."

Duncan slid over. He scrolled through screen after screen of complaints, reports of low-quality work, and professional bullying. All words until… "There." He tapped the screen.

McAllister leaned in to look. "Where?"

"That guy. Ben's Contracting, Inc. He said he had a line on some work in downtown Pittsburgh until Whitney moved in on him." Duncan scribbled the contractor's name. He'd look up contact information in a moment.

"What makes this guy so special?" McAllister asked.

Duncan stood and stretched. "The cast on his right arm."

"Lots of guys break their arms in construction. It's a dangerous job."

"I'm betting not all of them get broken arms when they're bullied into retracting bids. Which is exactly what Mr. Ben's Contracting claims."

* * *

Duncan glanced at his watch. An hour had passed while he researched with McAllister and it was now slightly after one. He placed a call to Ben's Contracting. By a stroke of luck Ben Norwich, the guy who'd accused Whitney of strong-arm tactics, was working a job in Connellsville. If Duncan didn't waste time, he'd make it there and back, and not be late for roll call.

The work site in Connellsville turned out to be a larger building that, if the signage was right, had a future as apartments for the elderly. Not quite full assisted living, but not totally independent either. After asking some workers, Duncan was directed to a man standing off to the side. The tank top emblazoned with the company logo showed off the biceps of a person who did manual labor for a living. He wore a red hard hat as he studied blueprints on a table. His right forearm was encased in a white cast decorated with the logos of Pittsburgh sports teams.

Duncan strolled over. "Ben Norwich?"

The man didn't take his attention from his blueprints. "That's me. Who wants to know?"

"Trooper Jim Duncan of the Pennsylvania State Police."

Norwich jerked around. "That asshole! This is my job. Mine. And I'm not the one who started the damn fight. He did. Asshole breaks my arm then has the balls to call the cops on me?"

"Whoa, slow down." Duncan held out his hands. "I'm not here for anything except talk and no one sent me."

Norwich's face, a mix of suntan and red, didn't relax.

"Let me guess. The asshole is Xavier Whitney."

The contractor stayed silent.

"Here's the deal. I don't give a damn about whatever went on between you two. Well, not in that I'm looking to jack you up on charges. I want some background on Whitney. It's in relation to another investigation. He looks lily-white on paper, but I've yet to meet a guy in his business who doesn't have a few skeletons in the closet." Duncan pointed at the cast. "If he's responsible for that, as you claim, well, it looks like I'm right. But if you don't want to talk about it, that's fine." He half turned.

Norwich's voice stopped him "Wait."

When Duncan faced him again, some of the red had receded. The suntan, which looked to be almost permanent, had already taken its toll on Norwich's complexion, which made it hard to judge his age. Given that he owned his own company, he was probably somewhere in his mid-forties. This was a man who worked hard and probably relaxed hard, but he showed no signs of a beer gut or other indications of the party life. "Yes?"

"Xavier Whitney, world class dick." Norwich spat. "Runs a construction company and I don't think he ever sets foot on a site, except for a publicity stunt."

"I thought he was retired?"

"Technically, yes." Norwich threw a look over his shoulder at his crew. "He doesn't have a son, so his nephew runs the business. Three Rivers Development. They specialize in housing, high-end housing. But old Xavier keeps his fingers in. Can't walk away entirely."

"Tell me about the fight." Ben Norwich's body looked like someone who worked out, the physique of a much younger man. Of someone who'd have no problem beating a couple guys up. If the victim had been Xavier Whitney, Duncan would entertain Norwich as a suspect, but Duncan couldn't think of a single reason the contractor would take out any aggression on a couple of environmentalists.

Maybe if the environmentalists stood in the way of a high-paying job, but Duncan's intuition steered him away from that scenario.

Norwich waved at a pile of sheetrock. "Let's sit. There's a bit of shade over there." He led the way and perched on the pile of boards. "It was over a project, of course. Up in Pittsburgh. Small, high-end apartment complex plus a couple of shops. Wasn't going in downtown, but over on the East Side, all that new development." He rubbed his nose. "Anyway, we both put in a bid. Three Rivers was lower, but the site owner decided to go with me."

"Do you know why?"

"Because Whitney shorts his bids by doing crap work." Norwich's gaze was contemptuous. "Oh, it seems okay. But the materials are a shade less quality than mine, he cuts little corners in the execution, then covers it up with shiny paper and fixtures. There's a couple times I've been called in to repair work destroyed by water damage that never should have occurred, stuff like that."

"He doesn't have to fix his own mistakes?"

"He does…sometimes. Other times he claims it's an act of God, outside his responsibility. Often the fix is as shoddy as the original. Anyway." He spat again.

"The job."

"Whitney and his goon, who he calls his executive assistant, came to my office. Said I was going to withdraw my bid. Not using those words, but that's the drift. I refused. I won the job fair and square, and that's the contracting game. I made to leave my office and the goon grabs my arm. Twists it. Whitney said again that maybe I've realized I've taken on more than I can handle, and I should reconsider. I said no, the goon twists some more, and snap! Broken ulna."

"You didn't call the police?"

"I did. Whitney admitted to the conversation, but said I stormed out, his guy grabbed me to prevent it, and the broken arm was an accident. My word against his."

"The doctors couldn't tell from the break?"

Norwich shrugged. "They said it could've happened either way. Definitely a spiral fracture, but could have been a twist, could have been me jerking my arm. I knew then I was screwed."

"You abandoned the job?"

"I was out of the picture, but I didn't need my guys getting harassed. There's plenty of work. I let him have his little victory. Not sure why he wanted it so much." Norwich laughed. "Yes, I do. It's right on Center, visible to all the people driving up Fifth, gets his name out there, good publicity. No matter. When it's done, I'll probably have to go fix it." Someone over at the site called his name. "That all you need? I gotta get back to work."

"Thanks for taking the time." Duncan watched as the contractor headed back to his site. Genial little Xavier Whitney thought a job was worth fighting for because it'd get his name in front of all the people flocking to an up-and-coming neighborhood.

What would he do to win a job that would associate him with making access to the Casselman better for potentially thousands of Laurel Highlands tourists?

Chapter Twenty-Nine

Sally and Tanelsa wrapped up their work, then headed to Markleton, a small town in Somerset County, around two-thirty. The persistent rains had moved out of the area, leaving behind a deep blue sky with nary a cloud to be seen. Sally studied the water level as they drove over the Casselman and into Confluence. It had receded, but the river retained a touch of the angry brown roiling that had marked it earlier in the week. Another good storm and it would be right back to the near-flood level.

"Confluence," Tanelsa said. "Isn't that where your guy lives?"

"Jim lives down at the triangle end, over there." Sally waved.

"So what comes together?"

Sally shot her colleague a quizzical glance.

"Con-flu-ence." Tanelsa drew out the word. "The town must have gotten its name somehow."

"Oh. The Casselman and Laurel Hill Creek join the Youghiogheny. That's the part of town where Jim's house is. You and Lisa should come over some day. There's some nice river trails and a bike trail that leads into Ohiopyle." Sally's quads ached at the memory.

"We aren't much on hiking or biking."

"Not all of it is intense. River's Edge Cafe is a nice place to eat in the summer. Or Jim's yard backs right against the river. He's good on the grill. But he's got a Golden Retriever, so if you or Lisa don't like dogs, that's out. Rizzo isn't…dainty in his affection."

"Nah, dogs are cool." Tanelsa studied the scenery as town quickly gave way to farmland. "Speaking of your guy, didn't you promise him to stay out of this?"

"No. He promised to look into Stewart."

"Then why are you going out there?"

Sally squirmed. "Because he's one guy with a lot of things to do. If I can give him some information to use when he looks into Stewart, he'll be better off." It was a justification and Sally knew impatience and anger over Ryan's treatment of his wife were really her motivation.

From Tanelsa's expression, she knew it too. "If you say so."

When they reached Markleton, Sally drove to the Stewarts' address. The house, a duplex, showed its age, with late eighties architecture and faded siding. But it was neat. The yard had been mowed and someone had planted flowers in a small front garden, bright-pink petunias that had taken a pummeling in the recent rain, but were gamely making a comeback. An older, brown Chevy Silverado pickup was parked on one side. The other graveled driveway, splotched with green from the many weeds, stood empty.

Tanelsa got out, slipped on a pair of sunglasses, and slammed her door. "Which one is Stewarts'?"

"The empty side." Sally climbed the porch stairs, the paint peeled away in spots and the underlying wood gray and dry. Someone had removed the flakes to make it less shabby, but it hadn't worked. Instinctively, Sally knew Angela had done it, just as she must have planted the flowers. From what she'd read online about Ryan, Sally doubted he was much of a handyman or into gardening.

Wind chimes hung in the heavy, humid afternoon air, emitting an occasional jangle. Sally knocked on the door. A small, hand-lettered sign announced "NO SALESPEOPLE OR RELIGION." No problem. Sally was neither. She knocked again.

"I don't think anybody is home," Tanelsa said as she examined the mailbox. "Today's delivery is still here. Some junk, but it looks like a number of past due bills, too."

Sally climbed down the stairs and examined the front of the house. The windows were streaky. Not with dirt, but like someone tried to wash them and hadn't done a very good job. Angela's work again? Probably. Sally went up to the door of the other unit and knocked.

After a minute, a woman with straggly brown hair caught up in a ponytail, wearing a faded plaid shirt and nothing else, and with huge purple shadows under her eyes answered the door. She puffed on a cigarette. "Didn't you see the sign?" she asked. "Applies to here, too."

Sally hoped the woman was wearing shorts that were covered by the overlarge shirt. "I'm not a saleswoman or peddling religion." She introduced herself and Tanelsa.

The woman puffed her cigarette. "He finally went and did it, huh?"

"Did what?" Sally asked.

"Beat her so bad she called a lawyer. I been telling her for ages she needed to ditch him."

Tanelsa strolled over to the Stewarts' side of the duplex while Sally continued the conversation with the neighbor. "Do things get out of hand often, missus...?"

"Call me Debbie." The neighbor snorted. "Often? Only if you define every other day as often. I'd hear him yellin' and swearin' something fierce. Every morning, usually before he went to work. I'd hear him while I was watching my shows. Right old son of a bitch. One of those guys who was a looker in his youth and who didn't accept middle-age very well."

"He didn't?" Sally glanced over at Tanelsa, who was now reading some mail that had fallen out of the Stewarts's box. "Hey, tampering with the mail is a federal offense," she said to her colleague.

Undeterred, Tanelsa kept reading. "It's on the floor. I'm not touching it."

Sally rolled her eyes and turned back to the neighbor. "Go on. You were saying Ryan had a hard time with aging?"

"Oh yeah. Angela showed me their wedding picture once. Hard abs, black hair, and that tattoo looked mighty fine. Now he's got a thinning hairline and, as much as he works out, a beer gut. If he spent as much time on his stomach as his biceps, maybe he'd still be okay. But he'd also have to stop downing a case of Iron City every weekend." Debbie drew again on the cigarette.

"Did he hit her or was it mostly verbal? Did you or Angela ever call the police?"

"I mostly heard him screaming and some shattering plates. But I'm positive he hit her. She's a good looking woman, but she never wore anything that showed skin." Debbie puffed. "I called the cops oh, three or four times when he got real nasty. Don't know if she ever did. But they always went away empty-handed. She'd say how it was her fault, he was tired after a long shift, she shoulda known better. The usual shit a woman spews when her man is a loser, but she can't bear to part with him."

Sally knew it all too well. "I gather they're both at work now. Do you know when they'll be home?"

Debbie lit another cigarette from the old one, then flicked the butt into a puddle. "They usually get here around five, maybe closer to six. Loser that he is, at least he's got a job up the quarry."

"Thanks." Sally went back to the Stewarts duplex. She knocked and gestured at the mail. "Anything interesting?"

"Nope." Tanelsa stuffed it back in the box. "Junk mail and a shitload of overdue bills. Ryan Stewart may have a job, but either they simply don't pay anything or he's spending the money before Angela can take care of the house."

"Probably the latter." Despite Debbie's statement, Sally knocked again. "Mr. Stewart, are you home? My name is Sally Castle, I know your wife, Angela. I'd like to talk to you."

Nothing.

Tanelsa shrugged. "Drunk and passed out?"

"Maybe." She checked. Debbie still stood on her porch, attention glued to the scene playing out before her. "You said Mr. Stewart usually left for work early in the morning. Did you see or hear him today?" Sally asked.

Debbie exhaled, sending up a cloud of gray smoke. "Come to think of it, I didn't hear anything from either of them. The house was shut up tight yesterday evening, too."

"Maybe they went away somewhere for the night."

Debbie laughed. "Not likely. He didn't spend money if he didn't have to. At least not on Angie. Is a car there?"

"What kind of car?"

"Red Ford pickup with a dented rear fender."

Sally gestured to Tanelsa, who looked around the corner. She returned and shook her head. Sally turned to Debbie. "It's not there."

"Huh. Then I don't know what's going on."

Sally's skin prickled, a sensation very out of touch with the hot day. She reached toward the knob.

Debbie's voice stopped her. "You can't go in there without a warrant. I'll call the cops."

"I'm checking on the well-being of the resident," Sally said, the response automatic. Jim would do the same. He'd also take care not to leave fingerprints. She searched her pocket for something.

Tanelsa handed her a cloth from her purse. "I use this to clean my sunglass lenses. It ought to work."

Sally grasped the cloth and tried the door handle. It opened with ease. "Mr. Stewart?" she called, sticking her head in the doorway. "Are you here?" A rank smell assaulted her nostrils. Heavy and coppery, tinged with the faintest trace of rotting meat. She stepped through the door. Even from the living room, with its faded overstuffed furniture and threadbare carpet, she could hear and see the flies buzzing in the kitchen. She fought back the urge to retch.

"God, what is that smell?" Tanelsa gagged and covered her mouth.

"I think I know." Sally inched toward the kitchen, careful not to touch anything. She stopped at the doorway. A large man with muscled arms lay face down, the back of his thinning black hair matted with blood. A sticky red pool encircled his head, flies drawn to the feast laid out for them. The black edge of a tattoo was visible on his bicep, the front wheel of a motorcycle.

Tanelsa spoke from behind her. "Oh God above is that him?"

"Yup." Sally again choked back her desire to vomit. "Ryan Stewart."

* * *

Sally paced the scraggly front yard and chewed a fingernail. She could already see how this was going to play out for Angela and it wasn't good.

Tanelsa sat on the hood of Sally's Camry and rolled a bottle of water behind her neck. "You're awfully calm for a woman who discovered a dead guy. This a common thing for you?"

Sally's mind flashed to another dead body, face down on his desk, surrounded by a pool of blood. Colin. What a nightmare, and in more ways than one. She shivered. "Only once."

"You get that blasé after one?"

"No, I'm thinking." After Tanelsa had rushed, retching, from the kitchen, Sally had taken a deep breath and viewed Ryan Stewart with as much dispassion as she could muster. Somebody had done a number on him, the blows going well beyond what was needed to cause death. The killer had wanted to make a thorough job of it.

Or had been very, very angry.

A slightly familiar voice sounded behind her. "Ms…Castle?"

She turned to see Corporal Travers heading her way. Couldn't she have caught a little break and have someone else respond? "Yes."

He halted. "You again."

"Me again." She tried to smile.

Travers made no such attempt. "What the…what are you doing in Markleton?"

"We," she waved toward Tanelsa, "came to talk to him about a legal matter."

His scowl deepened. "Michael Brower? Helping out your…friend?"

"No." She dropped the smile. "It was a separate situation." Stewart might be involved in the Brower homicide, but Angela's abuse was not.

He pulled out his notepad. "When did you arrive?"

"About two o'clock, maybe closer to two-thirty. I knocked on the door and did not receive a response. Mr. Stewart's neighbor came out and we talked."

"About?"

"About how I believe Mr. Stewart is abusing his wife."

Travers blinked but recovered. "How did you wind up in the apartment?"

Tanelsa didn't look like she was up to answering anything, so Sally continued. "The neighbor, Debbie, she didn't give a last name, said she believed she heard his truck engine earlier, that he might have come home from work already. When I checked the driveway, though, there was no truck. But I wanted to make sure. I went over to the apartment and knocked again. I tried the handle because I was concerned. If Mr. Stewart was indeed home, I wanted to know he was okay before I left." She delivered the last line with nonchalance, as though it was perfectly normal for an attorney from another county to check on a relative stranger. She hoped Travers wouldn't ask about who would have driven away the truck if Ryan was at home.

Travers's expression said he didn't completely buy it, but he let the comment pass. "And then?"

"Upon entering the apartment, I was drawn to the kitchen by the smell and the presence of flies. That's when we saw Mr. Stewart. I stayed long enough to ascertain that he was dead, left, and called 911."

Travers eyed her with suspicion. "And this had nothing to do with Mike Brower?"

She lifted her chin. "Nothing at all."

The corporal scribbled something. "It won't work and your boy is going to get himself in a shitload of trouble, you know that, right?"

"I haven't the faintest idea what you're talking about."

Travers took a step closer and dropped his voice. "You tell Trooper First Class Duncan that he's out of line. I'll have his ass in a sling over this." He stepped back. "Mr. Stewart's wife, where is she?"

Sally wanted to snap that she had no idea, but she forced herself to be civil. "She works at Mulligan's in Ohiopyle. I assume she's there."

"And if she's not?"

"Then I don't know."

"Don't know or won't tell me? If Stewart came home, someone drove his truck away."

Before she could respond, a woman in a dark blue suit came over. "Problem, Corporal?"

"No." Travers took a step back. "This is Ms. Sally Castle. She found the victim."

The suited woman came over and extended her hand. "Trooper Ilene Foster, Criminal Investigation, Troop A."

Sally shook her hand. "Pleased to meet you. Well, not under these circumstances, but…"

Trooper Foster chuckled. "I understand." She held out her hand for Travers's notebook. "I'll take it from here, Corporal. Why don't you go interview Mr. Stewart's neighbor? Do you need more paper?"

"No, I have a spare in my patrol car." Travers thrust out the notebook and stalked back toward the duplex.

Sally held her breath. Who was this new person? Would she be easy to deal with or cut from the same cloth as Travers? "Criminal Investigation? I mean, this is obviously a homicide, is that why you were called in?"

"You know how the PSP works, huh?"

"I have a friend who is a trooper stationed in Uniontown."

"Ah, Fayette-nam. I did two years there when I first graduated from the academy. Lovely area, crazy crime."

"Yes." She recognized the small-talk as an attempt to put her at ease and determined she wouldn't let it work.

"You seem to be familiar with Corporal Travers."

"We met at another scene, a drowning victim in Confluence along the Casselman River."

Ilene Foster busied herself reading the notes. "Yes, Michael Brower. That one landed on my plate as well. That's where I've heard your name before. I was going to get in touch with you for some follow-up questions."

"Oh?"

"Yes, things are hopping over in our area. We're a man down, too, which is why I haven't been in touch yet. I'm now in charge of the Brower investigation. Him and Carl Ritchie. You probably don't know about that one."

Oh, thank God. "Actually, I do." At Ilene's inquisitive glance, she offered a slight smile. "That friend I mentioned, he told me."

"Your friend wouldn't happen to be Trooper Jim Duncan, would he? His name has come up a couple of times and he's on my list of people to speak to."

"I'm sure he'll be happy to assist," Sally said. Dropping her voice, she muttered, "More than happy."

Ilene continued to read. "I'm glad to hear it. I hope Trooper Duncan can fill in a few things for me." She looked up and smiled. She gestured at Tanelsa. "Would you please give me your name, ma'am?"

Tanelsa uncapped her water bottle. "Tanelsa Parson. I'm with her." She nodded at Sally and took a drink.

Ilene returned her attention to Sally. "Tell me what happened."

Sally repeated what she'd told Travers.

The other woman gave Sally a calculating look. "The fact that Mr. Stewart's name has come up in the investigation of Mike Brower's homicide has nothing to do with you being here?"

Sally sensed any attempt to play coy with this woman would not only fail but possibly make an antagonist out of someone who might otherwise be helpful. "I know Mr. Stewart works, I'm sorry worked, for Laurel Mountain Quarrying and there is a possible connection to Mr. Brower and Mr. Ritchie, but honestly my primary motivation in coming here was the welfare of Angela Stewart." She wouldn't get an answer to the question, but she asked anyway. "Any idea when he died?"

"If you're friends with Trooper Duncan, you know that I not only can't tell you at this stage, I wouldn't." Ilene paused. "You're sure Mrs. Stewart's being abused?"

"Pretty sure. I work public defense now, but I started in Allegheny County in prosecution. I've seen enough abused women to recognize the warning signs."

Ilene closed the notebook. "Did you speak to Mrs. Stewart this morning?"

"No, she wasn't home when we arrived."

"And the truck that the neighbor, Debbie, mentioned, it wasn't here?"

"No."

"Could Mrs. Stewart have taken it?"

Sally considered that. It was dangerous ground. "Possibly. I mean, she does work in Ohiopyle and that's not walking distance from here. She has to get to work somehow. On the other hand, I believe she goes in earlier and her husband wouldn't have been at home. From what I've seen, I don't think Mr. Stewart would be willing to let her drive his vehicle. I didn't see a car when we spoke to her. "

Ilene's smile faded. "I thought you didn't see her today?"

Damn her mouth. Despite Sally's resolve not to relax, Ilene had gotten around her defenses. "That's true. Jim and I took a bike ride to Ohiopyle over the weekend. We stopped for lunch and happened to see Angela. That's how I know she works in Ohiopyle."

"I see." The easy grin returned. "What was the name of the restaurant?"

"Mulligan's. They do burgers and ice cream."

"Then I'll find Mrs. Stewart at work?"

"I don't see why you wouldn't." Sally shot her a quizzical glance. "Is there something you aren't telling me, Trooper?"

The grin turned mischievous. "If there was, I wouldn't be likely to say anything to you, would I?"

Chapter Thirty

Duncan pulled into the barracks parking lot in plenty of time for second-shift roll call. He locked his Jeep and headed toward the building. Two troopers stood outside in conversation. As he neared them, he could tell one of them was Corporal Gary Sheffield of the Uniontown barracks, nicknamed "Golden Gary," based on his ability to fall into a pile of shit and find a gold mine. The other was Corporal Henry Travers.

Duncan's step slowed a bit, but he had to get to roll call. He squared his shoulders and prepared to run the gauntlet.

"There he is, Travers," called out Sheffield, his voice a bit louder than it needed to be. "You can take a crack at him. But he's Nicols's favorite boy, so don't expect anything to change. Maybe the fact that you're from another barracks will help, though."

Travers shifted his stance so he blocked the door. "Good afternoon, Trooper First Class Duncan."

Again, the slight emphasis on rank. "Good afternoon."

"Where have you been?"

"Running some errands."

"What kind of errands?"

Duncan gazed right into the higher-ranked trooper's eyes. "With all due respect, I don't think my personal business is your concern. My shift doesn't start for another five minutes. Until then, what I do is my own affair."

Travers dropped the false geniality. "Not when it interferes with my investigation."

"I'm not interfering. You are free to conduct whatever lines of inquiry you feel are appropriate." He paused. "I am curious, though."

"About what?"

He shot a look at Sheffield, who ought to have had popcorn in his hands based on the expression of glee at the sight of Duncan being dressed down, however mildly. "Normal procedure is to hand over these kinds of things to Criminal Investigation, so this isn't your investigation either. You must be collecting the last bits of information before you do that. Or you're following instructions. Otherwise I'd be talking to someone else."

Travers's face took on an ugly cast. "What are you implying?"

"Nothing." Duncan kept his voice mild.

Travers took a step forward. His intent was obviously to intimidate, but since he stood a good two inches shorter and was several pounds lighter than his opponent, the attempt failed. "Look, Duncan," he snarled. "I see what you're doing, and it won't work."

"What am I doing?"

"You think solving this homicide will put a shine on your résumé. Let me tell you something. The promotion board doesn't care about your rule-breaking, however successful. In fact, they're likely to be the furthest thing from impressed."

"I've told you before. I knew Mike Brower. Turns out I knew Carl Ritchie, too. They were good guys, so naturally I'm curious about the resolution of things. My only intention is to see justice served. The promotion board doesn't figure into it at all."

Travers's lip curled. "Still cocky, I see. Like with that kid all those years ago. That won't help either."

Duncan maintained a stone-cold expression, or at least he hoped so. "It's only cocky if you aren't right."

The other man blanched.

Score, Duncan thought. "Excuse me, Corporal. I'm going to be late for roll call."

* * *

Duncan walked into the barracks, stopped, shut his eyes, and collected himself. He would not allow the run-in with the Somerset corporal to ruin his attitude. But damn, maybe Sally was right. Being a corporal himself wouldn't stop Travers from being an asshole. But it would get rid of a reason for him to treat Duncan like a pissant lower-ranked officer.

Pinsky, the desk trooper, shook his head in sympathy. "I saw those two waiting for you. Heard them talking before you got here. What a couple of arrogant dicks. Shitty start to a shift, brother."

"Don't you know it." Duncan's attention was snared by the approach of the barracks commander, Lieutenant Dan Nicols. "Duncan, you have a visitor in conference two. Been waiting for you. You're excused from roll call."

"Does Corporal Sheffield know or should I duck out and tell him?"

"I'll do it. You deal with your visitor."

Duncan might have imagined it, but there seemed to be a look of satisfaction on Nicols's face. He never showed it publicly, but perhaps Golden Gary wasn't his favorite trooper, either.

Duncan went to conference room two. Seated inside was a woman in a dark blue suit, slacks pressed and creased to perfection. Her dark blue jacket was unbuttoned to show a crisp white shirt. She wrote on a pad, her short dark-brown hair behind her ear, showing off a simple diamond stud. The pen was a cheap Bic, the notepad top-flip, much like Duncan's own. Cop, he decided, not lawyer.

He entered the room. "You wanted to see me?"

The woman stood and held out her hand. "Trooper Ilene Foster, Criminal Investigation out of Troop A, Somerset." She tilted her head. "Are you the infamous Jim Duncan? I expected you to be at least ten feet tall and breathe fire." Her dark brown eyes crinkled at the edge.

Duncan relaxed a smidge. "I'm only eight feet and I do all my fire breathing before breakfast." He pulled out a chair and sat. "How can I help you, Trooper Foster?"

"Call me Ilene." She sat again and looked at her notes. "I've recently taken over the investigation into the deaths of Michael Brower and Carl Ritchie."

She lifted her head to face him. "You're familiar with both men?"

"Yes. I helped recover Brower's body after he was found by a young girl in Confluence. It turns out I knew both victims. I helped out with their organization a couple of times."

"Did you tell that to Travers in your initial statement?"

Duncan hesitated. Foster seemed more amiable than Travers, but it was never good form to throw a fellow trooper under the bus. "I mentioned that Brower looked sort of familiar at the scene, but the deputy coroner had already finished with the body and I was unable to confirm at that time. As soon as I realized I knew both victims, I passed that information to Corporal Travers."

"What did he say about that?"

"He thanked me for the information. Nothing else."

"Hmm." Foster sat back. "I apologize for the fact it's taken me so long to follow up with you personally."

"Quite all right. As you're here now, however, I assume you need something from me."

Foster's answering laugh was dry. "I do. I've reviewed Corporal Travers's notes from the Brower scene and there are some…gaps. I wanted to talk to you, see if you could fill them in."

It was hard to read Foster's cool stare, but her words led Duncan to take a gamble. "I'll be honest with you. I'm not entirely satisfied with the explanations to date. From my vantage point, everybody seems mighty keen to write these deaths off as accidents."

"You aren't in agreement?"

"No. I didn't know either man well, but well enough to know it is unlikely they'd fall victim to an accident without significant contributing factors. Those factors aren't present. Something's up. Travers didn't want to hear my thoughts on the matter, so I decided to do a little poking around on my own."

Foster flipped to a fresh sheet of paper. "Tell me what you know."

Duncan talked. All about the tension between Carl and Mike, presence of the plant and sandstone, the conflict between CWPS and Laurel Mountain

Quarrying, Xavier Whitney's role, Caroline Longchamp's refusal to talk, and the run-in between Mike and Ryan Stewart. "Friend of mine says the bulrush likes sandstone sinkholes, one of which isn't that far from LMQ. Brower's shoe heels were worn, as though he'd been dragged after he was beaten."

"What did Ritchie say before he died? Water, Mike, Ryan?" Foster tapped the pen against her lips.

"Correct. So far I haven't come across an explanation that makes sense. At this point, I'm not willing to shut my mind to any possibility."

She nodded. "What do you think happened?"

"Somebody beat the crap out of Mike and Carl, then threw them in the river. Mike drowned, Carl died in Somerset Hospital, but it damn sure wasn't an accident. I think there's a third party here somewhere. It's too pat if the two friends got into a fight and both happened to die."

Foster assessed him. "They were right. You are smart."

"They?"

"You have a reputation, Duncan. I know Nate Greaves."

That explained a lot. Greaves was the one who had suggested Duncan apply for a position in Criminal Investigation. "I hope whatever you've heard is good. All I want is to make sure we get the right answer and I'm happy to help in any way I can."

"I'm glad to hear it. I happen to agree with your assessment. And there's one other fact you don't know yet."

"What's that?"

Foster looked him in the eye. "Ryan Stewart was found dead this morning. Definitely murder. Someone bashed his skull in with a marble-based hunting trophy. We found it in the trash."

Duncan said nothing.

"His wife is missing."

"Angela?"

"Yes. I called her employer on the way over here. She didn't show up to work. Her boss doesn't know where she'd go. Doesn't look good."

"He was probably abusing her. Did anyone tell you that?"

"Yes, that's why I said it doesn't look good."

Duncan weighed the new information. "No, it doesn't."

"I see two possibilities. One is that Angela Stewart finally snapped and beat her husband to death. The other is Stewart was somehow involved with Brower and Ritchie, and the same person killed him."

"Or Stewart knew too much about who killed the others and was silenced."

"Also possible. Do you think the wife is capable of murder?"

"Anyone can kill if pushed too hard. Angela is certainly physically strong enough, especially if she used something as heavy as marble." Duncan thought back to meeting Angela in Ohiopyle that day. "I don't know if she's emotionally strong enough, though. When I spoke to her, she was as scared as a rabbit under the gaze of a hawk. She might have snapped, but I think you would have found her over the body, covered in blood and in shock. She's that type."

"I see." Foster reviewed her notes. "Then your suspect pool comes down to this Whitney, someone associated with LMQ who may be acting with or without Longchamp's knowledge, or a fight between the two men. Which you think is the weakest scenario." She closed the notebook. "Sounds solid to me."

Duncan started to stand. "Anything else I can help you with?"

She motioned him down. "Sit."

He dropped into the chair.

She clasped her hands on the table. "Can I be blunt and go off the record?"

Duncan lifted an eyebrow. "Sure."

"You're as smart as Greaves told me." She paused. "I need your help. More than that, I want it. Would you be willing to ride shotgun with me on this?

"I'm flattered, but why? I'm in a different troop area and you've already got Travers to do any grunt work."

"I'll talk to your l-t, smooth it over. I think I can persuade him to loan you out. You're local, you know the people around here. You've already made contacts. Me, I got here six months ago. As for Travers…" She paused, then said, "Close the door."

Duncan complied.

Foster leaned back in her chair. "Travers is a decent trooper, good with the basics. But this kind of work is not his strong suit. Hell, you've given me more actionable information in the last fifteen minutes than I've gotten all week. You've got drive and you don't stop until you're satisfied. Least that's what Greaves said, cleaned up a bit."

"I've been told that's not always a positive trait."

"It is for investigation. I spoke to a friend of yours at the Stewart scene earlier. Sally Castle."

Duncan didn't say anything. He should have known Sally wouldn't be able to stay away from the Stewart situation.

"Ms. Castle said you'd be willing to help." Foster waited a beat. "What do you say? Technically you'd be working under my direction, but I'm open to any suggestions you may have. And I'd be willing to put in a good word for you when you apply to CI."

Duncan laughed. "Who said I was going to do that?"

She grinned. "Call it intuition. So?"

Duncan thought over the offer. He knew himself well enough that he'd continue to pick away at the problem until he had an answer. And he was petty enough to be satisfied that if Travers decided to be a pain in the ass, accepting Foster's offer meant he would have to suck it up. "Okay, why not? I'll play."

"Good." She handed him a business card. "This is my contact information. First task. Take another crack at Caroline Longchamp. See what shakes loose."

Duncan took the card. "She's already thrown me off her property once."

"Get creative. I'm sure you can do that." Foster put her notebook away and stood. "I think it's going to be a pleasure to work with you, Duncan. And mutually beneficial. I close my case, you get your career move." She opened the door and left the room.

Duncan followed her. "Who said I wanted a career move?"

She turned around. "What's your favorite drink?"

"Dark beer or aged whiskey."

She stuck out her hand. "If by the end of this you decide to apply to CI, the first round's on me. Deal?"

Duncan took the proffered hand. "Deal."

* * *

Duncan stood in the parking lot next to a patrol car, watched Foster pull away, and spun the keyring on his finger. Nicols had hesitated, but only for a fraction of a moment before agreeing to loan out Duncan's services. In fact, the look on Nicols's face was resigned, as if he'd expected the request.

Full-time investigator. An intriguing concept. And more than a little appealing. At least working with Foster would give Duncan a good indication if a move to Criminal Investigation was truly what he wanted to do.

Talk to Caroline Longchamp. Except the CEO had already shut him down. He needed something before he took another crack at an interview.

He needed that environmental report. The assumption everyone seemed to be working under was that CWPS found dust pollution, traced it to Laurel Mountain, reported it, made the quarrying company clean up its act, and the pollution abated.

Assumptions were not always true.

As he stood there, McAllister came out, headed toward her personal vehicle. "Hey, Boss. Looks like you're doing some heavy thinking."

"I am. Where are you off to?"

"Home. Tommy-boy and I are going to see some heavy-metal cover band in Uniontown. I'm not sure why I let him talk me into it." She rolled her eyes.

McAllister might know where to find the information he wanted. "Question for you," Duncan said. "If I want to find an environmental report, not necessarily one done by the DEP, where would I look?"

"You aren't talking about the study on the Casselman by CWPS, are you?"

"Maybe."

She tsked. "You're so transparent. Anyway, let me think." She pursed her lips. "CWPS isn't a government agency, so their stuff may or may not be posted online. You check their website?"

"Only for background information. I didn't see anything like this."

"Look again. Then Google for any combination of the organization name, dust, Casselman, pollution, Laurel Mountain, fish, bass…you know, words associated with the topic. But if they forwarded their information to the DEP and the state took action, there would also be an official finding posted."

Duncan opened the car door. "Public?"

"Oh yeah. Those in charge like to show the taxpayers their money is going to good use."

Duncan reached in, started the car, and set the A/C on high. "Now all I need is thirty minutes with a computer. Maybe I'll head to the library. It'll be quieter than working here."

McAllister sighed. "I keep telling you, you've got one in your pocket. Might not be the easiest thing to read, but at least you can find the reports and make a note of them to look at later. In fact, if I get a chance, maybe I'll take a stab at it myself. You've got me interested."

"You said you and Burns have plans." His protest sounded half-hearted.

She waved him off. "Don't worry. I'm not fond of heavy metal. Besides, if I put a puzzle in front of him, Tommy-boy might abandon the noise machine for a quieter night at home." She lifted an eyebrow and grinned.

Duncan got in the patrol car. He was pretty sure McAllister's quiet night would only partly be spent on computer work.

Chapter Thirty-One

Sally and Tanelsa returned to the courthouse. Tanelsa pled an upset stomach and headache as a reason to clock out early. "And it's the truth," she muttered as she gathered her things from her office. "I don't know how you're still standing." This last was addressed to Sally before she left.

Honestly, Sally did feel a little queasy. Her matter-of-fact demeanor was mostly a façade. She hadn't known Ryan Stewart the way she'd known Colin, but seeing a man with his head bashed in, lying in a pool of his own blood, was not such a commonplace event for her that it had zero effect, either.

Stewart had fought with Mike Brower. Stewart was dead. He abused his wife, who was also missing. The only certainty was Brower had not resurrected himself to finish the fight. As she twirled a pen, Sally replayed the scene in her head. The body, the blood. Stewart had been beaten with an object, not merely fists.

Could Angela have done it? Had she snapped and struck out at her husband? Possible. She had a job that required her to lift and carry heavy boxes. She could swing an object capable of doing violence. An adrenaline rush would add to her strength in the short term, too. People in crazed states, or those who were terrified, had been known to do some pretty unlikely things. Angela could also have been hopped up on drugs, but Sally found that scenario unlikely. Angela had not presented as a drug addict and had no tell-tale track marks, at least not anywhere visible.

Another possibility occurred to her. Stewart might have been involved in the Ritchie and Brower deaths with someone and had a falling out with his partner. That was as likely as anything else.

On a hunch, Sally looked up the number for Mulligan's and dialed. "Yes, I'm trying to get in touch with Angela Stewart," she said when a man answered.

"Good luck. When you do, tell her she's fired. I've got no use for employees who can't show up as scheduled."

"She's not at work?"

"Didn't I say that? I don't have time to jabber with a restaurant full of hungry people. Especially not with a dumbass who can't listen." He slammed down the phone.

Sally ignored the insult and placed the handset back in the cradle. Angela hadn't gone to her job. Did Trooper Foster know that? She had to.

Bryan stuck his head through her door. "What was wrong with Tanelsa? And don't give me the upset stomach bullshit."

"I'm quite sure she was not bullshitting you. We did a wellness check on a woman I met over the weekend. I believe her husband is abusing her."

"Let me guess, you found her dead."

"Not quite. We found her husband dead. Quite messily. Tanelsa was shaken, to say the least."

Bryan's face sobered. "What about the wife?"

"Missing."

He paused. "You okay?"

"I'm good. Or at least more so than Tanelsa. I don't think she's ever seen a dead body up close and personal. Whereas I…" She trailed off.

"Right." Bryan drummed his fingers on the door frame. "Do you have anything else to do today?"

"Not really." Sally rubbed her face and straightened in her chair. "I planned to put some stuff together for tomorrow, that's it."

"Go home. Have a glass of wine. Call your boyfriend." Bryan winked. "I'm sure he'll know some way to take your mind off things."

"Get your mind out of the gutter." She tried to sound offended, but based on his answering grin she failed. "Thanks, Bry. See you tomorrow." He left and she gathered up her keys and briefcase.

Out in the employee parking lot, she unlocked the door to her Camry and tossed her things inside. She was about to get in when a hissing sound stopped her.

"You. Ms. Castle, over here."

Sally turned in the direction of the frantic half-whisper. Crouched behind another vehicle was Angela Stewart. Despite the July heat, she clutched a trench coat around her. Her hair resembled a bird's nest, the formerly sleek bob in disarray as though she'd just gotten out of bed. Or fled a murder scene. A suspicious dark smear stood out on her chin. "Angela? People are looking for you."

"I know. You…you said you were a lawyer, didn't you? I need help."

"I am. Whether or not I can help depends on what you tell me." Sally paused. "That's blood on your face, isn't it?"

Tears welled in Angela's eyes and she nodded. She let go of the trench coat and it fell open. Her shirt and pants were covered with blood. "I need help," she repeated, voice strangled. Similar reddish-brown marks stained her cuticles.

Sally sucked in her breath. "Let's go over here," she nodded to the edge of the parking lot where they were less likely to be picked up by the security cameras. When they got there, she confronted Angela. "What happened?"

"I got home from work last night, around the regular time."

"What time is that? And how'd you get home? You don't have a car."

"It was almost five-thirty, a friend drove me. Anyway, Nate's truck was there, and all the lights were on. It was odd. He's not usually home until later, closer to six or six-thirty."

"He's employed at Laurel Mountain Quarrying."

"Yeah."

"What does he do there?"

Angela swiped a hand across her runny nose. "He runs one of the machines that hauls away the stone once it's been dug out of the quarry."

Sally filed that fact away. "Go on."

"I went inside. Ryan was lying in the kitchen. Somebody'd beat him up, bad. His head…" she gulped, "one of his hunting trophies was next to him. I think whoever it was used it to beat him 'cause the base was all bloody."

"What was the base made of?"

"Marble or something. I don't think it was real marble, though. Heavy, but nobody'd use real stuff for a cheap trophy. Ryan won it a few years ago for bringing in the biggest buck at his hunting club." Again, she rubbed her nose. This time, the mucous mixed with dried blood and left a dirty streak.

Sally opened her purse, removed a tissue, and handed it to Angela. "Continue your story."

"I figured people would think it was me. That I'd finally had it with him hitting me. 'Cause of the trophy and he was in our kitchen and everything. I threw the trophy in the garbage, tied it up, and put it out for trash day. That's how I got like this. I slipped in the blood and fell." She waved at her clothes. "Then I grabbed this coat, closed the door, took his truck, and beat it."

"You shouldn't have touched anything, just called 911."

"And had the cops find me standing over Ryan? They'd arrest me for sure."

"Running away and throwing out the trophy makes you look guilty." Sally shook her head. "He did hit you, then?"

In response, Angela let the trench coat fall off her shoulders and lifted her shirt. Her torso was a mess of fresh and half-healed bruises. "Never where anyone could see it and never anywhere it couldn't be explained by an accident. He used his belt sometimes. These," she pointed at the newest marks, "were from when he found out about Mike." She let the shirt drop. "Help me, please."

Sally pursed her lips. "You have a job. Ryan had a job. What about money in the bank?"

"Some, not much though."

Sally thought it over. "Is your name on the truck registration?"

"It is."

Sally shook her head. "I doubt you'll qualify for representation from the public defender. That's where I work."

Angela sobbed, a defeated look in her eyes. "I'm screwed, is that what you're saying? I don't know any other lawyers."

Sally thought a moment. "I do."

* * *

Sally and Angela sat in the Nemacolin Woodlands Courtyard, a small, tree-filled corner directly across from the courthouse. With the bench tucked back in the trees and the decrease in people after business hours, Sally was confident they wouldn't be noticed.

Angela fidgeted on her seat. "On second thought, I don't think this is a good idea. I should go."

"Sit tight. She'll be here shortly." Sally strolled to the edge of the courtyard, looked up and down East Main Street, and glanced at the towering gray stone building on the other side of the street. No sign of Kim's flaming red hair. "At least that's what she said."

"What did you say?"

"Nothing." Sally turned back to the trembling figure still wrapped in the trench coat. That was the one thing people might remember seeing. A woman in a long coat in July. *Come on, Kim.*

As if summoned by thought, the click-clack of heels sounded from the walk. "What's so damn important and secretive we couldn't have held this meeting at a civilized location, like Dex's?" Kim asked. She sauntered over to Sally. "Come to your senses and decided to accept my offer? I don't see any libations if that's the case."

"Not yet." Sally nodded toward Angela. "I have a business proposition of my own."

Angela gave a half-hearted wave. "Hi. You must be Ms. Castle's friend."

Kim took in Angela's haggard face, messy hair, and the suffocating coat. "Wrong weather for that thing," she said as she faced Sally again. "What gives?"

"Kim Dunphy, meet Angela Stewart." Sally waited as the two women murmured greetings. "Angela is in need of legal help."

Kim lifted an eyebrow. "You can't help her? I mean, you called me, so I assume this is criminal legal help. Isn't your specialty helping lost waifs?"

"I'm qualified to help, but under the circumstances I have strong doubts that Angela would be approved for representation from my office. Or more accurately, the public defender in Somerset County. We don't handle all the waifs, unfortunately."

Kim's other eyebrow rose to meet the first. "And I do? What the hell?"

Sally inhaled. She'd known Kim would have to be convinced. Sally had only one card and she played it for all it was worth. "Here's the proposition. You hear Angela out, represent her, and I'll accept your offer."

Kim snorted. "Since I doubt this woman can afford my fee, I don't see much upside for me here. No offense."

Angela gripped her coat. "None taken. It doesn't take a genius to see you're used to a better class of client. I'd better go." She half rose from the bench.

"Angela, sit down, please," Sally said. She took Kim by the arm and pulled her a few steps away. "You get me, that's your upside. Hear her story. If you want to walk away, fine."

Kim studied Sally's face. Apparently deciding things were serious, she turned back to Angela. "You've got five minutes. Go."

Angela's gaze flicked from lawyer to lawyer. "I don't know where to start."

Kim huffed and Sally jumped in. "Angela's husband Ryan was murdered last night, beaten to death with one of his hunting trophies. The trophy has a heavy marble base. She came home from work and found him in the kitchen. Unfortunately, she did what most people do, which is become agitated and examined the body. Show Ms. Dunphy your clothes, Angela."

Angela pulled open the trench.

Kim sucked in her breath.

"Ryan has been abusing her for some time. Lift your shirt, Angela, show Ms. Dunphy the bruises." Sally nodded.

Angela hesitated but complied.

Kim let out a breath in a long hiss. "I see where this story goes. You freaked, left the scene, and have been hiding out, yes?"

Angela nodded.

Kim glanced at Sally and continued the questioning. "Ms. Castle said the murder weapon was one of your husband's trophies. Where was it?"

Angela shot a look at Sally, who nodded to encourage her. "It was on the floor next to him, all sticky-like and covered with his blood."

"What did you do with it?" Kim asked.

"I…I put it in a plastic bag and threw it in the trash."

"Did you call 911?"

"Nuh-uh. I beat it out of there. I could tell he was dead. If I called the cops, they'd probably arrest me. Nobody ever believes me."

"Did you talk to anyone else today? Or have you been hiding out?"

"After I left last night, I went to Ryan's hunting camp. I've been driving around today, waiting for Ms. Castle to get off work. I knew she most likely'd be at the courthouse until five." Angela swallowed hard. "If anyone was going to know I was telling the truth, I figured it'd be her."

"Let me get this straight." Kim raised her fingers one by one as she spoke. "You got home last night and found your husband dead. You threw away what was most likely the murder weapon. You did not call for help. You drove away in his truck, then you hid for the night and all day today. Is that about it?"

Angela stared, mute, but gave a small nod.

Kim threw up her hands and turned to Sally. "You want me to take this? It's impossible. She'll be convicted based on the circumstantial evidence alone. Everything she's done screams guilty, even if her husband was beating her. And she probably can't pay a tenth of my fee."

Angela whimpered.

Sally grabbed Kim's arm and dragged her to the edge of the courtyard. "Listen. Did she say anything, *anything*, that indicates she's actually guilty?"

"No, but—"

"Okay. She might be snowing us. Maybe she's guilty as sin. Then again, she could be exactly what she looks like. A scared woman who came home to find her abusive husband dead on the floor. Any way you slice it, she needs help. You're right. The easiest conclusion is that she snapped and killed her husband. Left on her own, that's what a lot of people, maybe including the

DA, would assume and they'd count this as a slam dunk. She needs someone on her side to make the prosecution work for their conviction. This is what we do."

Kim yanked her arm away. "This is what *you* do."

"This is what defense attorneys do. We make sure our client's rights are protected. We make sure the prosecution does their damn job and proves, beyond a reasonable doubt, to twelve members of the public, that our client is guilty."

Kim glared.

Sally crossed her arms. "You want me in your firm? First step, you defend this woman. Yes, pro-bono or at least at a reduced fee."

"And if I don't win, you walk?"

"I didn't say that. You give it your best shot. Show me you're serious about the principles of our profession, not simply making money. You do that… yes, I'll accept your offer. That's my proposal, take it or leave it."

Kim studied Sally's face, maybe searching for a sign she could be bartered down or a weakness. Apparently finding none, she closed her eyes, exhaled, and held out her hand. "Deal." She and Sally shook. Then she went back to Angela. "Okay, Mrs. Stewart. Let's go through it again."

Chapter Thirty-Two

It was shortly after six on Tuesday evening when Duncan pulled into Caroline Longchamp's driveway. He'd considered the merits of postponing the visit until he could do it in civvies, as well as calling ahead. Ultimately, he decided on neither. She hadn't been particularly welcoming the last time he visited. Dressing in jeans wouldn't change that and if she explicitly told him to stay away, he'd get into trouble if he showed up anyway.

Longchamp stood in her front yard wearing gardening clothes and holding a hose with a yellow bottle attached to the nozzle. As soon as she saw the PSP Ford she turned away. "I thought I made it plain I didn't want to talk to the police again."

Duncan got out of the car. "Ms. Longchamp, I understand you're not happy. But I really wish you'd talk to me."

She swung around, an arc of water flashing in front of her. "I've seen you before. Didn't I tell you to get off my property?"

Duncan stepped out of range of the hose. "You did."

"You came back anyway."

"Yes, ma'am. I'm stubborn that way." He paused. "Weren't you watering the flowers the last time I was here? Seems we've had enough rain lately that wouldn't be necessary."

Her mouth thinned. "I'm feeding them. Doing it in the evening means the water evaporates more slowly, gives the fertilizer time to sink in."

"Must be why you have such beautiful flowers."

"You're not here to admire my garden, Trooper."

"No ma'am. I'm here to talk about Mike Brower."

"I didn't want to discuss that man before. What makes you think I want to talk about him now?"

Duncan removed his hat. "I know CWPS, and Mike Brower in particular, was a thorn in your side. But the fact is someone killed him and dumped him in the river."

She tossed her head. "And you think it was me."

"I don't know what to think. I'm looking for information. I knew Brower. He was an environmentalist. Wanted to preserve the local landscape. I understand where that could bring him into conflict with a business like yours."

"He was a fraud."

The statement made Duncan pause. "Why would you say that?"

"Hold on a moment." She dropped the fertilizer and walked around the back of the house. When she came back, it was through the front door and she was holding a thin folder. She must have gone into the house through a back entrance after she turned off the water, because the hose now lay flat and limp, like a deflated balloon.

"Quite a trick with the hose."

"It's one of those ones that goes flat when there's no water. Makes it easier to roll up. Are you going to talk garden tools or about Mike Brower?"

Duncan cursed himself for getting distracted by trivialities. "Sorry. You called him a fraud. Why?"

"If you've read up on my company, and I'm sure you have, you know my grandfather founded Laurel Mountain Quarrying. When the government started implementing environmental regulations, it nearly bankrupted him, what with the cleanup and new controls."

"You think the government should have left you alone."

"Not at all." She turned the folder over. "I was a young girl, but I remember the mess. It was awful. When I took the helm, I resolved two things. I'd rebuild my grandfather's investment and I'd do it in a way that protected the natural environment. I've been proud of what we've done. If you look at our record with the Pennsylvania environmental agency, as well as the

EPA, we've never failed an inspection. Our particulate levels have steadily decreased, and we've returned to profitability."

"Sounds like quite an accomplishment."

"Thank you. Which is why I was stunned when a representative from the DEP turned up at our offices with this." She removed two sheets of paper stapled together from the folder and handed them to Duncan.

He read. It was a report from CWPS. In it were tables of figures and charts. He skimmed the data, looking for the conclusion. The last paragraph summed up the findings. Increasing levels of dust pollution that was having a negative effect on local wildlife, particularly the fish population. The report was signed by Mike Brower. "Somebody screwed up. Or something broke. It should be easy to fix, right?"

"If something were indeed broken, yes." She removed another paper from the folder. "This is a report, from last May, conducted by our in-house environmental control department."

Again, Duncan skimmed. The first thing he noticed was the charts and tables of figures, very similar to the ones in the CWPS report, but also very different. "Your in-house audit shows vastly lower particulate and dust levels."

"Indeed." She removed another set of papers. "This is our latest inspection from the DEP, dated this past June, less than four weeks ago."

For the third time, Duncan studied the data. "This matches your in-house findings. Everything well within limits. Even slightly lower than the study conducted a year ago." He looked up. "I don't understand how things go so bad so quickly."

"They didn't." Longchamp removed a final set of paper. "When the DEP received that report from CWPS, they sent someone out to take measurements. Acting on data provided by the public, they said. That is their finding. Let me save you the trouble." She recited from memory. "Levels of particulate matter are within federal guidelines. The DEP finds no evidence of pollution at this time."

"I don't understand."

Longchamp shook her head. "Come on Trooper, don't be dense. The

CWPS report shows data to support their claim that dust pollution was rising and that it was attributable to my company. LMQ's in-house environmental department as well as the state DEP found the exact opposite. Do the math."

The calculation was easy. "CWPS falsified their data. Did they hate you that much, even if you were within the guidelines?"

"It would seem so."

Duncan chewed over that fact. Mike's devotion to the environment was well known. So devoted he'd make up accusations to try and get LMQ shut down, just because they were industrial? Duncan didn't want to consider it, but people had done worse in the pursuit of a cause. "I appreciate your time, Ms. Longchamp. May I borrow these papers? I'd like to show them to the trooper in charge of the investigation."

She handed them over. "I would like them back when this is all over. Those are official company reports."

"Understood." He paused, then said, "One more question. Do you know a man named Ryan Stewart?"

Her forehead wrinkled in thought. "Stewart? The name sounds familiar, like I should know it."

"He works for your company. Hauls away the rock after it's removed from the quarry."

"That explains it." Her expression cleared. "I don't know everyone who works for me of course, but if the name is familiar then it is possible, probable even, that we crossed paths at some point. Do you need to speak with him?"

"That would be difficult. He's dead. Someone bashed in his head last night after he got home from work." He watched her face.

She didn't blink. "That's awful. Who found him?"

"His wife."

"I'll have someone follow up with her about death benefits," she said. "Unless she's a suspect in his murder? You did say someone hit him."

"I'm not at liberty to say."

Still not a flicker of emotion. "Is there anything else you need from me right now?"

"Not at the moment. Thank you again, Ms. Longchamp. You have a good evening." Duncan touched the brim of his hat and left.

* * *

Sally slid a tray of enchiladas into her oven, shut the door, and set the timer. She knew Jim worked until at least eleven tonight, maybe later if a call came in. She considered texting him to let him know about Ryan Stewart and Angela. Except there was nothing he could do about it. And information like that shouldn't be communicated in a text anyway.

She set the table and thought about Angela. Only a fool wouldn't consider her a suspect in her husband's death and Sally wasn't so naive as to believe the story without question. She'd listened as Kim grilled Angela. She stayed firm on the details, which was good. It didn't sound like a rehearsed narrative, either. Both were positive signs. Kim had also been able, after some cajoling, to convince Angela to contact the police and make herself available for questioning.

"You'll be with me?" Angela asked in a quavery voice.

"Absolutely," Kim said. "But it's imperative you end the 'on the run' act and turn yourself in."

"That makes it sound like you think I did it."

"The longer you stay in hiding, the more the police are going to wonder why. It hurts your case." Kim handed Angela her cell phone. "Call them now. That way I'm here when they show up and can advise you."

Two Uniontown officers responded to the call and Kim accompanied her client to the station. She'd texted Sally later. "Angela released for the time being. You find anything out, lmk."

There was still fifteen minutes on the enchiladas, so Sally went into the living room, picked up a magazine, and sat down to read. She turned the pages, but didn't absorb a word. Stewart worked for Laurel Mountain Quarrying. Mike Brower, and maybe Carl Ritchie, had issues with LMQ. Stewart had a history of assault. It was easy to draw the line that Stewart had beaten up and killed, maybe inadvertently, both CWPS men.

But then who killed Stewart?

A knock on her door interrupted her thoughts. Who'd be visiting on a Tuesday evening? She went to the door and peered through the peephole. "Jim?" she asked, as she opened the door. "What are you doing here in uniform? Aren't you working?"

"I am." He took off his hat and gave her a quick kiss. "I need to look at the contents of that camera card. Do you have it?"

"In here." She closed the door and headed to her office in the spare bedroom, Jim trailing. "Did Travers ask for it?"

"Travers has nothing to do with this. I'm working with the trooper out of Somerset CI. Nate Greaves told her to find me."

Sally turned. "Really?"

"Yep. It's all on the up and up. Nicols okayed it. Oh, and get this." He told her about his meeting with Caroline Longchamp and the data discrepancy.

"You think that's what Mike and Carl argued about? Mike was going to file a falsified report and Carl tried to talk him out of it?"

"Maybe. Longchamp also told me she's heard of Stewart, but doesn't really know him. Wish I could talk to him. Too late for that. Speaking of Stewart, Trooper Foster tells me she spoke with you at the scene of the murder. What the hell were you doing there?"

She filled him in on her day's activities, including being approached by Angela Stewart and handing the case off to Kim.

"Damn it, Sally, didn't I say I'd take care of this?" He pinched the bridge of his nose, his tell for when he was frustrated.

"You did, I know."

"I realize Angela Stewart's situation is important to you. Even before her husband was killed. But don't you understand that when you act like this, do exactly the opposite of what you say, you send the signal that you don't trust me?"

Crap. After last spring, that was the last message she wanted to send. "You're right, I should have stayed away. I do trust you, I wanted…" She looked at his face and his expression cut her self-justification off at the knees. "I was impatient. I can dress it up however I want, but the bottom line is I didn't want to wait. I'm sorry."

He stared at her for a long moment, letting the tension hang between them. "Apology accepted. I'd ask you not to do it again, but that would be making a promise you can't keep."

She kissed him. "I will think twice next time."

"Yeah, yeah." He blew out a breath. "You think the wife could have done it?"

"I don't know. I don't want to think she did it. But I'm not stupid. I know it's the first thing the cops will look at."

Jim drummed his fingers on the desk. "Hmm. Or was he involved with the fraudulent environmental report? That is, was he helping Mike and Carl or acting to take care of a problem?"

"On his own or at someone's orders? I mean, the guy wasn't too bright. I could tell that from what we saw of him. And what about Whitney? I suppose it's still possible he bumped off Mike and Carl, and Stewart is a completely different situation."

"I don't know." Jim shook his head. "The card?"

She retrieved the card from her top drawer and the reader from another. Then she opened her laptop and plugged in the peripheral cables. "Here they are." She clicked through the images. "Close-ups. That doesn't help."

"No. Wait, here we go. That's definitely the Casselman. I recognize it, that's maybe twenty-five yards upstream from where we found Mike's body. Keep going."

More close-ups. Lindy Hunter had an artistic eye, that was for sure. The subjects varied. Flowers, leaves and twigs floating on the water, even some garbage. The images switched to more panoramic shots. "I don't recognize this area. Is it still the Casselman?" Sally asked.

Jim frowned. "I think so. But this would be way upstream, nothing near Confluence looks like this. Wait, hold on. That one." He removed his phone, swiped to a picture and held it up to the computer screen. "Same plant, you think?"

Sally considered a moment then nodded. "I do. I mean, comparing from your phone to the computer isn't perfect and we should print it out to be sure, but it looks similar. See? The flowers are the same. What did your friend call it?"

"Northeastern bulrush."

"Then we're looking for an area with both sandstone, the commonality between the victims, and the bulrush?"

"Exactly. Keep going."

The pictures continued, but nothing jumped out at Sally. Pretty shots, but a bust.

Suddenly, Jim pointed at the screen. "That one, right there. Can you zoom in on that?"

"Yes, but it won't be anything wildly precise." She zoomed in on the picture. "What do you see?"

"More bulrush, a ton of it. Is that a creek through there? And that shadow, see it? Wonder if that's a depression in the land."

"Like a sinkhole? Maybe." She considered the image. "You think that's your murder scene?"

"Or the dumping spot. At least a good candidate." Jim straightened. "Can you print that picture for me? In color, if possible. Actually, email me the images."

"All of them?"

"Yes. I'll have them printed off and take them to Lindy." He paused. "Don't suppose there'd be geo-location data on them, huh?"

Sally create a zip file of the pictures and emailed them to Jim. "If the camera had GPS, sure. But I doubt it. It looked like a pretty basic model to me. But you'll have date and timestamp. That should help."

He rubbed his chin. "It will if Lindy remembers where she was when she took them."

Chapter Thirty-Three

Wednesday morning, Duncan double-timed it over to the Hunter residence. He had stopped at a drugstore last night to get Lindy's pictures printed, but he wanted to talk to the girl and see if she could give him a more precise location where she'd taken them. If he arrived first thing in the morning, he'd increase his chances of catching the family at home.

Karen Hunter answered the door. "Jim, what's up? You need something else?"

"Actually, I do." He glanced into the house. "Is Lindy at home?"

"She's even out of bed, if you can imagine that. A pre-teen getting up before ten in the morning. But she's going on a day trip with some of her photography club friends from school, so that explains it." Karen opened the door. "Come on in. What do you want to talk to her about?"

Duncan removed the stack of photographs from his pocket. "I need to know where she was when she took these."

Karen took the pile and rifled through the photos. "Based on the date stamp, these are from a club trip earlier this month. It was along the Casselman, I remember that. She'll know." She handed back the pictures. "She's having breakfast. I made pancakes if you want some. This way."

Duncan followed her back to the cheerful kitchen. "I'd love some, thanks."

Karen went to the stove, where a portable griddle held three perfect golden circles. "Lindy, Mr. Duncan has something to ask you. Put that camera away and eat."

Lindy sat at a round wooden table set for four, a stack of steaming pancakes in front of her. She was ignoring the food while she fussed with her camera. Dozens of photos adorned the plain white refrigerator, many of nature, some of the Hunter family. Lindy's work, Duncan guessed. "Hey, Lindy."

"Hi, Mr. Duncan." The girl set aside the camera. "Are you here to return my card? I'm going on a trip today and I'd like to have it. I've got a spare, but the one you have has more storage."

"No, sorry. I need to keep it for a while longer. I have some questions about the pictures on it, if you can spare a few minutes."

"Sure." She put aside the camera and cleared some space.

Duncan laid out the photographs. "I'm particularly interested in these. I can tell this is along the Casselman. Correct?"

"Yep." She studied the shots. "My photo club took a trip a couple weeks ago, we went up the river." She tapped the date on one of the pictures, "We were all over the Casselman that day."

"Do you remember where?"

"Oh gosh." The girl bit her lip. "We started outside Confluence, but went miles up the river. Mr. Tate, our advisor, drove us."

"Up near Rockwood?"

"I think so. Maybe even past that. We didn't go into any towns." She rearranged them in chronological order. "This is from the first part of the morning and we worked our way upriver."

"I'm particularly interested in this one." Duncan pulled out the shot with the swath of bulrush.

She took the print. "I don't take a lot of wide shots. I like extreme close-ups, but the clouds were casting some really cool shadows on the water."

"Do you remember where you were when you took this?"

"No, sorry Mr. Duncan. We were out there for hours."

Damn. "Your camera doesn't have GPS, does it?"

Lindy laughed. "I can't afford one of those. They're super expensive."

Well, it had been worth a shot. "Thanks anyway, Lindy."

Karen set down a plate of pancakes dotted with butter and with syrup dripping off the edges. "Lindy, what about your phone? That has GPS."

"I didn't take these with my phone," Lindy said.

Duncan snapped his fingers. "But you might have taken another shot, maybe to document your trip on social media? Can you check?"

"Sure, but I don't think I'd have been able to upload from out there." Lindy pushed away from the table. "Can I go get my phone, Mom?"

"Yes, since Mr. Duncan needs it. No phones allowed at the table," Karen said in response to Duncan's raised eyebrow. The girl dashed away and Karen turned to him. "You're thinking even if the picture didn't make it to whatever social media app, it'll still be on her phone with the information you need."

"How'd you guess?" Duncan spread the butter around, cut the flapjacks, and took a bite. Might as well eat while he waited.

Karen giggled. "I watch *CSI*. Sorry, I know those shows are ridiculous, but there it is."

A minute later, Lindy returned, phone in hand. "I was looking through the pictures. Here, this one. I took it right about the time I took the one you asked about. I liked the way a flower was reflected in the water."

Duncan wiped his fingers and took the phone. "Very pretty." He looked at the picture. No location was attached to it, but Lindy was right, the date and timestamp were the same as the one he'd printed. "Would you please send that to me, Lindy?"

"Sure, I'll text it if you give me your phone number." Her thumbs flew as he recited the digits.

Moments later, Duncan's phone pinged. "Thank you. No prank texts now, you hear me?" He winked.

The girl smiled. "Promise."

Karen pushed a plate back in front of her daughter. "Now eat. You're going to be roaming all over the place, you need a full stomach." She turned to Duncan. "I suppose you'll be running off as soon as you finish?"

Duncan attacked his pancakes. "I think I'll have time for seconds."

* * *

Sally arrived at work with her mind on two things, Angela Stewart and Lindy's photograph. No question the latter could be a lead in the investigation into Carl's and Mike's deaths. But what about the former? Sally would never condone murder, but in her innermost heart, she thought it couldn't happen to a nicer guy than Stewart. She'd seen a tagline on a book recently, "Some people just need killing." She wouldn't go that far, but men like Ryan Stewart definitely deserved punishment. When the law couldn't deliver, maybe it wasn't so bad that someone else could. At least he wouldn't be beating his wife anymore.

"Morning, Doris," she said to the office secretary as she entered.

"Good morning." Doris rustled the newspaper on her desk. "Did you hear about that murder in Markleton?"

"Uh, a bit." The press must have kept her and Tanelsa out of the story.

"This morning, the paper says the wife turned herself in. The police questioned her, but she was released. There's a statement from her attorney, Kim Dunphy." Doris looked up. "Isn't that the woman you know?" She handed over a stack of messages.

"Yes." Sally sorted through the slips of paper. "In fact, I was the one Angela first approached. I could tell she wouldn't qualify for public defense, never mind that the murder happened in a different county. So I called Kim."

"She took the case? From what you said, she was all about the high rollers."

"She is." Sally avoided looking at Doris, hoping the older woman would let it go.

"You sweetened the pot for her, somehow." Doris's voice was shrewd. "Look at me."

Grudgingly, Sally lifted her gaze from the messages. "Okay, yes. I did. Angela may or may not have done it. But she needs help. I helped her."

"What'd you offer your friend? Not money." Doris's gaze was keen. "You said you'd join her, didn't you? In that practice she's building."

Distracted from Angela, Sally stared at the secretary. "How'd you know?" Sally hadn't told Doris about her agreement with Kim.

"Tanelsa," Doris said simply.

Of course. "Here's where you try and convince me to stay, right?" Sally stuffed the papers, most of them unread, in her pocket.

"No."

"You don't?" That was a little unbelievable. Doris adored her lawyers. She wouldn't want to see any of them leave the office.

"Nope. Obviously, I'd miss you. But Sally, this could be a big opportunity for you, one that doesn't come along very often." Doris folded the newspaper and leaned on her desk. "The chance to be your own boss. Build a successful firm and fight for the people you want to protect. A successful female firm, I might add. How many big-name woman defense partnerships are out there?"

"None that I can think of."

"That's my point." Doris stood, came around her desk, and grasped Sally's hands. "You are, without a doubt, one of the best attorneys we have. You and Tanelsa. She'd be devastated if you left, I could see that in her eyes when we talked. Bryan would be lost. But honey, you gotta think of yourself. You're what, thirty-four?"

"I'll be thirty-five next month."

"Still lots of time in your career. Public defense has been good for you. What does Jim say?"

"He said it's my choice and he'll support me whatever I decide. I honestly don't think it matters to him one way or the other. He wants me to be happy."

"Smart man. He's a keeper, that one." Doris squeezed. "I'm not going to push you one way or the other. Promise me you'll think it through from both sides though."

The older woman's obvious concern touched Sally. "I will."

"Good. Oh, and one more thing."

"What's that?"

"If you and Kim need a secretary, give me a call."

* * *

Sally left Doris in the outer office, went to her desk, and shot off a text to

Kim. *Meet at lunch, talk about Angela?*

The reply came a few minutes later. *You're buying. Dex's.*

Determined to arrive before her friend this time, Sally arrived at the restaurant fifteen minutes before noon and got a table for two. She ordered a water and the summer strawberry-chicken salad for herself, but didn't feel confident choosing for Kim, who arrived ten minutes later.

"Here I thought I'd beat you," she said and took her seat. The waitress returned and Kim skimmed the menu. "Turkey club with fries and a sparkling water." She handed the menu over.

The waitress nodded. "I'll put in the order for your salad now, Ms. Castle."

"Thanks, Lynn."

The waitress left and Kim picked up her napkin. "You're on a first name-basis with the staff?"

Sally shrugged. "Jim and I eat here a lot when he comes to Uniontown."

Kim spread her napkin on her lap. "First order of business. Angela Stewart. She came to you first and she wants you involved. I had her sign a waiver to make that happen. While you may not yet be my partner, you're officially part of the Team Angela defense."

"Good to know." The waiver would allow Kim and Sally to talk freely. Talking to Tanelsa would be a different matter, but Sally would cross that bridge when she came to it.

"Now for her story," Kim said.

"You think she's telling the truth?"

Kim made a see-saw motion with her hand while she took a sip of water. "Yes and no. On the one hand, the story she told the cops when they questioned her pretty much mimicked what she told me, and she told it not once but twice."

"Which matched what she said to me before I called you. Word for word?"

"No. But the details are consistent. You and I both know that's a plus for honesty."

Sally took a drink. "Something's bothering you."

"The story itself." Kim steepled her fingers. "She told us she arrived home from work the previous night around five-thirty, that would be last Monday, and got a ride from a friend."

"What's the problem?"

Kim took a sip of water. "Angela got a ride from a friend all right, but according to her employer, Angela said she had a migraine and needed to leave. They let her go at one."

Sally did the math. "If she didn't get home until five-thirty, where was she the rest of the time? It's not a four-and-a-half-hour drive from Ohiopyle to Markleton."

"I did talk to the friend, who confirmed she took Angela home and they left Ohiopyle sometime around five. The friend assumed Angela had worked her normal shift."

"This friend doesn't work at Mulligan's?"

Kim shook her head. "No, another restaurant in town."

"What did Angela say to this? I'm sure you asked."

"She said she had to wait for her friend to get off work, so she sat in the shade near the river and tried to take a nap. She neither saw nor talked to anyone. I can't talk to everyone in the park that day to ask if they saw a sleeping woman."

Sally swirled the ice cubes in her glass. All the details were explainable and sounded possible, but it was one of those alibis that she hated, one that was completely unable to be corroborated. Of course, those often turned out to be legitimate. Innocent people rarely made sure they had an ironclad alibi during the commission of a crime.

Kim continued. "Angela also claims her husband's truck was in the driveway when she arrived at home, indicating he'd got there before she did."

"What's the problem?"

"That's it. I'm not sure." Kim paused to drink. "I interviewed the neighbor who, by the way, I'm pretty sure wasn't wearing pants when we talked. What kind of people live down here?"

Sally grinned. "Same when I was there. I'm hoping she had on really short shorts."

"Whatever. This woman, Debbie, said she was home all day and didn't hear the truck at all after that morning. Now who doesn't hear a Ford F150? At the same time, the TV was at an unholy volume when I arrived so I suppose it's possible. But she did say she heard shouting in the afternoon around four. A man and a woman, she told me. The woman said Ryan's name. At the time, she assumed the speaker was Angela."

"But she was at Mulligan's."

"Not after one o'clock that afternoon she wasn't."

Sally leaned back as the waitress arrived with both orders, deposited the plates, and walked away. "Debbie didn't mention the arguing to me." She picked up her fork. "What was Stewart doing at home that early? Shouldn't he still have been at work?"

"I wondered the same thing. I called LMQ and am waiting on an answer. Angela told me he left that morning, same as usual, and didn't say anything that led her to believe he wouldn't be gone until that evening." Kim took a bite of her sandwich, chewed, and swallowed. "Then there's the fact the coroner said Stewart was still in full rigor when you found him and had been dead for at least twelve hours, but no more than thirty."

"What the hell does that mean?"

"You know coroners. Basically, Stewart died some time Monday, during the day."

"When Angela was at work."

"Except it's possible he was killed in those four hours we can't account for." Kim passed on ketchup, but ground pepper over her fries.

"You're saying Angela went home before she said she did and killed Ryan, instead of finding his body as she claims."

"That's one option."

"She would have had to know he was home, exactly the opposite of what she expected," Sally said.

Kim shrugged. "Of what she says she expected. Maybe he *didn't* go to work that day and she's lying."

"What about all the blood? She didn't meet her friend looking like that."

"Could be that's part of her cover. She went back to the house, messed herself up to match her story, then went to find you."

Whose side are you on? Sally took a deep breath. Kim was only playing devil's advocate. "What about her cell phone? It would track her movements."

"She forgot it in her rush to get out of the house that morning."

Damn it. "Here's an idea." Sally speared a strawberry with her fork and pointed it at Kim. "Stewart worked for Laurel Mountain Quarrying. Jim recently learned the Casselman Water Protection Society falsified water pollution claims to get LMQ in trouble with environmental authorities. The two guys who headed CWPS are dead. Stewart could have been involved."

"He killed them, and then what? They came back from the dead to get revenge?" Kim picked up a piece of bacon that fell from her sandwich and ate it.

"Don't be absurd. Maybe he had an accomplice and they had a falling out. Or," Sally paused as an idea struck her, "Stewart worked with the other two victims to implicate LMQ, someone found out, and got rid of him, too."

"Now you're reaching. What motive could Stewart have to shut down his employer?"

"We're brainstorming. No idea gets thrown out at this stage. The idea is to look at other people who had a motive to kill him."

"If you say so." Kim polished off the first half of her sandwich, washed it down with some water, and wiped her hands. "Back to Angela. The thing that really bothers me is the fact she had the presence of mind to ditch the murder weapon and run for it. I asked for the police report, no prints on the trophy. Just smears of blood."

"Angela admits she tossed it."

"Okay, but after wiping it down?" Kim snorted. "If a woman snaps and attacks her abuser, she doesn't clean up the scene. Same if she stumbles on a body, she's usually too freaked out. Except that's exactly what Angela did. Then she bolted, which is fine, but she hid."

Sally played with the last strawberry in her salad. "She had enough presence of mind to cover herself."

"And that raises the possibility she's not only an abused wife, but a stone-cold killer."

Chapter Thirty-Four

After Duncan left roll-call Wednesday afternoon, he drove to the tech office. He didn't have the equipment or know-how to pull the GPS location from the picture file, but the guys there did.

When he entered, he saw Andy, one of his favorite staffers, in the office. A bit of luck. Andy would hand over the information with minimum fuss. "What's up?" Duncan asked.

Andy looked up from the computer he was disassembling. "Not too much. You?"

"Not much more. I need a favor." Duncan held his phone, which displayed Lindy's picture. "I need the geo-data from this image."

"Holy shit, Jim. I think that's the most tech speak I've heard out of you, like, ever." Andy took the phone. "This for a case?"

"Could lead us to the murder scene in a double homicide. Well, at least one of them."

"Got a warrant?"

"I don't need one. The image was surrendered voluntarily."

Andy handed back the phone. "Email it to me."

"It's in a text message. How do I send an email from that?"

"Oh for God's sake." Andy tapped away on the phone, it made a *whoosh* noise, and he handed it back. "Why don't you ask the person who took the picture where he was?"

"Because the photographer is a pre-teen girl. She can tell me she was on the Casselman, but I need more specific information than that."

"A pre-teen girl? You sure about this?"

Duncan held back a sigh. "Her mom was there during the conversation. What's with the third degree? You're never this picky."

Andy's fingers tapped on the computer keyboard. "Making sure everything's on the up and up."

"When have you ever known me to be otherwise?"

"You got a point." Screens popped open and disappeared. Finally, Andy pointed to one. "There you go. Longitude and latitude for the location where the picture was taken."

"Perfect." Duncan took out his notepad and copied the numbers. "I can look this up for myself, but can you save me some time and tell me where that is on a map?"

"Ask and ye shall receive." Andy tapped out another set of commands. A map appeared on his screen. "There." He touched a point. "Want me to print it out?"

"Please." While Andy waited at the printer, Duncan peered at the screen. He didn't know the scale, but the place indicated didn't look that far from Rockwood. Upstream, maybe less than a quarter of a mile.

The tech returned with the paper, which he presented with a flourish. "Here you go."

"Thanks." Duncan took it and checked the map's scale. He'd been right. The GPS coordinates were upstream from Rockwood, maybe even as little as a tenth of a mile away. Which made sense, since Carl had been alive when they'd rescued him. He didn't have time to drown.

He folded the map and put it in his pocket. Time to call Foster.

* * *

After lunch, Sally had enough time to sketch out the events she and Kim had discussed earlier before her "work work" as she called it took her attention. It wasn't until two hours later she was able to ponder the question of Angela Stewart's whereabouts the day of her husband's death.

The first thing Sally did was confirm via Google Maps that the trip from Ohiopyle to Markleton didn't take longer than she remembered. Nope. The drive could be made in a little more than half an hour, forty minutes at the outside. Why had Angela not asked a second friend for help if the migraine had been bad? Kim had passed all the names and phone numbers to Sally, who'd followed up with all of Angela's friends. Both suspected Ryan Stewart beat his wife. "What gave it away?" Sally asked.

"Lots of little things," one of the women said. "Things Angie would say. One day, she was wearing a long-sleeve shirt and it was ninety-five degrees. When she bent over to pick up something she'd dropped, I saw the bruising."

"You never called the police?"

"Angie said she fell. Bull. You don't get bruises like those from a fall. But I never saw him do anything and she flatly denied there was a problem. What was I supposed to do?" The woman paused. "Although…"

Sally pounced. "Yes?"

"One day Angie started talking about how she'd like a different life. 'I fantasize about how nice it would be to get home and he's gone.' I asked her what she meant by 'gone' and she waved her hand. She never came out and said dead, but…you know."

Sally knew exactly what the woman meant. There were so many meanings to the word "gone."

Kim was right about one thing. Trying to verify Angela's alibi was almost impossible. On a whim, she called Tara Jennings to ask if she'd been working down in Ohiopyle that day, but the photographer hadn't been at the state park and didn't know of any others who might have been shooting down there. The tree wasn't all that far from the visitors' center, but no one there remembered seeing a sleeping woman, although they all said they hadn't particularly been looking and such a person would be easy to miss.

Then there was the question of how Angela would get home. She didn't have a car. She couldn't call an Uber to take her from Ohiopyle to Markleton. She couldn't take a bus, either.

What if she'd borrowed a car?

But from whom? None of her girlfriends, that was for certain. Maybe Mulligan's had a truck for deliveries. Sally phoned the restaurant.

"Look, I'm really busy. I don't have time for this," Mulligan's owner said in response to the question.

"This is for a defense in a murder case," Sally said.

"Even more reason for me to go back to work. I don't want to get involved."

Sally brushed aside a twinge of irritation. Too busy to be involved in defending someone against a felony charge? "I'll make this simple. You can talk to me now, or I can get a subpoena and force you to testify in court. Your choice."

After an extended pause, the man sighed. "Fine. I can spare five minutes. What's the question?"

Sally picked up a pen. "Do you have a truck?"

"We have a small pickup, a Ford Ranger. We use it when we have to make a produce run or send someone to get supplies."

"Did Angela Stewart ever do that? Run errands for you?" Sally asked.

"Sure."

"Do you keep the keys on you or in a desk?"

"We hang them by the back door. It's not uncommon to need something, like napkins, and this way whoever has a little free time can grab the keys and go."

"You don't track usage of the vehicle?"

"No. I'm generally busy at the grill. I'll make the runs for food supplies, me or the chef from the afternoon shift, but it's pretty common for the waitresses to take the truck."

Sally tapped her pen on her legal pad. "Would someone notice if the truck was gone?"

"Hard to say. When we get busy, there's no time to look. And a lot of times we have to park off the beaten path, especially if we go out in the middle of the day, because the tourists take up all the parking."

"Then it's possible for someone to take the truck and get it back without anybody noticing?"

"I guess."

"The day Angela left with her migraine, did anybody move the truck? That is, did you notice it was parked in a spot other than where you remember it being?"

"I really couldn't say. Look, you got any more questions? A big group walked in and I gotta get back to the grill."

Sally thanked the man and hung up.

Angela knew where the keys were. No one watched the truck. It was possible for her to take it, drive home, kill her husband, and come back to wait for her ride without anyone being wiser.

* * *

Duncan was tempted to drive right out to the photo location after leaving the tech division. But he figured Foster would want to be in on this. When he called her, he told her where to meet him and to bring boots.

He parked his cruiser in a graveled pull-off not far from the spot he wanted. Foster was already there, leaning on her unmarked Ford Interceptor, legs of her suit pants stuffed into rubber Muck boots. She pushed off the car. "You found our murder scene?"

"Maybe." Duncan glanced at her footwear, which was better suited for barn work than tramping near the river, but they'd do. "Nice boots."

"This is all I have. Where are we going?"

"Down here." He led her to the river's edge where he could see waving stems of northeastern bulrush. "I talked to a friend of mine who ID'd the plant matter from Carl Ritchie's body." He waved at the slender green leaves. Then he brought Foster up to speed on the photos, including extracting the geolocation information.

"You didn't get a warrant?"

"The girl who took the photos gave them to me voluntarily. Her mother was present throughout the whole conversation. It's not going to be a problem."

"I guess not." She followed behind him. "Nice work, by the way. Mind if I ask you a question?"

"Not at all."

"What's up between you and Travers? I got an earful, politely of course, about why it was inadvisable to work with you on this."

CHAPTER THIRTY-FOUR

"We had a difference of opinion years ago. End of story."

"He never got over it, huh?"

"Doesn't look that way." Duncan squelched through the mud, looking for signs of broken plants and checking the device he'd brought to let him know when he'd reached the correct location.

"He's no fan of mine either, so welcome to the club."

"Oh?"

"Before I moved over to Criminal Investigation, I was a trooper out of Somerset. I think Travers applied to CI at the same time I did. I'm sure he thinks I got the job because I'm a woman. He's careful not to let the resentment show too much, but I can see it."

Duncan stopped and faced her. "I don't think that's it. He'd feel the same about a man. It's not the fact you're a woman, or at least it's not only that. It's that you got the job and he didn't. Don't overcomplicate it." He pushed on. "This is it, the spot from the pictures. See anything?"

Foster pulled on a pair of nitrile gloves. "Other than a few footprints, no. Spread out and let's look."

They searched for the next hour but found nothing. Duncan stopped and wiped his forehead. This was the spot, he hadn't made a mistake reading the coordinates. He doubted Lindy could tamper with the geodata, and why would she? But neither he nor Foster had turned up anything that indicated men had been killed, or bodies had been dumped.

Foster picked her way to the shore to stand by him. "It was a good idea. But I don't see anything. Back to square one."

Duncan pulled out the picture. Held it up and studied it. "I'm a moron."

"Don't be so hard on yourself." Foster pulled off her gloves. "We all have ideas that don't pan out. Not your fault. Good thinking, actually, getting the data from the image."

"No, I'm an idiot. Look." He handed her the picture. "This is the shot that made me think this could be our crime scene. See the bulrush and the contours of the land?"

"I can't pick out the individual plants in this, but I'll take your word for it."

"Notice anything?"

She looked from the picture to the river. "This is the other side of the water."

"I got the GPS coordinates from a shot taken on this location. Look, there's the flower." He pointed. "But that picture isn't these coordinates."

"Son of a bitch. We're on the wrong side of the river." She handed back the picture. "We need to be over there, right in a straight line. I don't suppose the river is shallow enough for us to walk across."

"No. We'll have to drive to the nearest bridge, loop around, and come back." He pocketed the snapshot.

"Might as well get to it." Foster tromped toward her car.

"Wait." He took a topographic map out of the Jeep's glove compartment, spread it on the hood, and marked the location they wanted. "No sense making our job harder. That will get us close enough." He folded up the map. "Follow me. I'm not sure where we'll be able to park."

It took at least half an hour to drive to the nearest bridge, cross, park, and hike to their destination. Duncan pulled out a fresh pair of gloves. "Let's try this again." He was going to be late for his shift. Nicols would accept the excuse. He had to hope Sheffield would, too.

They were rewarded about fifteen minutes later when Duncan found an area of crushed bulrush, right next to the small stream he'd suspected was present based on the photograph. Some of the plants and grasses had recovered, but there were definite signs of disturbance. He called Foster over. "What do you think?"

"I think something big rolled through here. Look." She waved. "There's a whole swatch of broken plants leading right down to the river."

"A grown man's body could easily do this much damage. Plus the person tramping along pushing or pulling."

"I agree. And look." She bent down and picked up some rocks from the edge of the water. "Same stone as was found in both victims. Congratulations, Duncan. I think you found us a crime scene."

He took out the map he'd stashed in his belt, the one he'd picked up showing the river currents. "At least Ritchie, but maybe both. This creek is deep enough to float a body and leads right to the Casselman." He traced the river's path. "He washed up outside Rockwood. Brower went farther downstream, but here, if he'd hit this current, especially with the higher-than-average water level, it could happen." He refolded the map and put it away. "Now if only we could find something more solid than crushed plants."

"Keep looking."

They picked over the area for another twenty minutes, working in a grid pattern. In that time they found flattened beer cans, string, garbage, and bits of flotsam that had probably floated downstream, but nothing that proved at least three people, two of them near death, had been there. The mud was too soft to have preserved footprints.

Finally, Foster said, "I think I have something." She held a piece of fabric, the kind used to make work shirts. The khaki, although muddy, was too new to have been there long. "Torn from one of the victims?" Foster asked.

"No. Brower's shirt was plaid. Ritchie's was dark blue."

Foster dropped it into an evidence bag. "The killer?"

"Or a fisherman. But this doesn't look like a place I'd like to spend hours fishing. I'd go up to that bend."

He continued his examination of the ground. The crushed leaves continued for a good five yards, back to another flattened place where you could park a vehicle. It wasn't right off the road, but the sound of cars indicated it wasn't that far away. Duncan studied the ground. Tire marks crisscrossed the dirt, too many of them to identify a single set. Rocks, sandstone, and bits of broken asphalt, littered the space.

He was about to give it up as a bad job, when he saw a flash of red. *Probably more junk.* But thoroughness demanded he check it out.

It was a piece of red plastic, maybe broken from the tag of an oval keyring. Chipped gold script lettering was barely visible, the ends of two words. He blew off the dust and tilted the plastic to catch the light. The letters were in two rows, the top reading "ain" and the bottom "rying." The font looked familiar, something he'd seen in a logo. Then it hit him.

Laurel Mountain Quarrying.

Chapter Thirty-Five

Sally set aside the problem of Angela's alibi to focus on busy-work. Routine tasks that needed to be completed, but left her subconscious free to propose and set aside possibilities. Finally she decided there was nothing to do but talk to Angela again and hope that she could shake loose a detail that would either confirm the story or break it.

For the meet, Sally chose a new coffee shop in downtown Uniontown, one that roasted its own beans onsite and offered a selection of deli sandwiches. Someplace intimate and quiet where Angela would feel comfortable talking, instead of the courthouse or an office, which might make her shut down and repeat her story ad nauseam.

Sally walked to the shop reviewing the details of the story, but also pondering Mike Brower. Had Jim managed to nail down a definite time when Mike and Carl were last seen? He hadn't told her, but that didn't mean anything. Angela might be able to shed some light on that as well. It was rather unbelievable Mike would go out of town for days and not touch base with her beforehand.

Inside the shop, Sally ordered coffee and a roast beef sandwich. She selected a pair of armchairs in the corner, where they'd be less likely to be overheard.

Five minutes after she settled in, Angela arrived. Sally set her sandwich down to study the woman's body language. Angela looked around, giving off the impression of a woman looking for someone, but not nervous about the meet. She wore a drapey black t-shirt and faded blue jeans with aged, but clean, sneakers. She'd tucked her hair back her ears, and wore no jewelry aside from her wedding ring. After spending a minute or so checking around, she caught the arm of one of the staff, who turned and pointed in Sally's direction. Angela strode forward, a smile on her face. "There you are. I thought I'd gotten here before you."

Sally indicated the other chair. "Hi. You might want to get your coffee and something to eat first. If you want to, that is."

"I can eat." Angela took out her wallet and dropped her bag on the chair. "Watch my purse?"

"Of course." Sally sipped as she watched Angela approach the counter and stand in line. Every move indicated shyness, but not overt anxiety. Whatever Angela thought about the meeting, it didn't worry her. That could indicate she was confident because she was telling the truth, or because she had faith in her ability to sell her version of events.

She returned a few minutes later with a fragrant cup of tea and a scone. She moved her squashy purse to the floor, sat, and blew on the top of her cup. "I'm such a matcha fan, I don't get it often. Thanks for suggesting this place. It's cozy."

"That was the idea." Sally finished the first half of her sandwich and sipped her drink. "Are you sure that's all you want?"

"I'm good. My appetite hasn't been the same since I found Ryan."

"Understandable." Sally paused. "How are you?"

"Okay." Angela broke off the corner of the scone.

"You staying at home?"

"No, with my mother, she lives here in Uniontown. I can't sleep at home, I can't even look into the kitchen. I keep seeing his body." She nibbled the scone, crumbs dropping in her lap.

A completely normal reaction. "I'm glad you have someone to help you out."

"Mom's been great. She never liked Ryan, not really. Not even in high school, before," she took a deep breath, "he started hitting me." She blew out a sigh. "I'm working on admitting that to people. Kim said I should. She's wonderful. Thanks for introducing us."

"You should absolutely admit it. It's not shameful and it's not your fault.

I'm glad you like Kim. She's a good attorney. She'll look out for you." Sally paused. "Thanks for signing that waiver and keeping me involved. I hope you know I would've represented you myself if I could have."

"I know that."

"I've been going over your alibi for the day of your husband's death. Can you tell me again what you did that day?"

Angela offered a shy smile. "Kim said people were going to keep asking, try to get me to trip up. I had a migraine. Joy, the friend who gave me a ride, couldn't leave work until five. I went down to the park, found a relatively quiet spot under a tree, and tried to take a nap. When I got home, Ryan's truck was in the drive, so I knew he was there."

"Wasn't that unusual?"

"I guess so. He normally isn't around until after five, but I didn't think about it much. Anyway, I went in the house and called for him, but he didn't answer. I went into the kitchen and found him lying there. The trophy was nearby." She put down the scone. "I checked to see if he was dead. Then I wiped off the trophy and threw it in the garbage. I was pretty messy, so I grabbed an overcoat. Then I took the truck and went to Ryan's hunting camp for the night. Then I drove to Uniontown, found you, and you know the rest."

Different words, same story. Sally switched gears. "Tell me about Mike. What was he like?"

Angela's face transformed with happiness. "He was wonderful. He always had a joke, or a smile, or a compliment. He loved the Laurel Highlands. He and I would sometimes go out hiking and he'd point out the different plants and stuff. Mostly he made me feel good about myself. No one's done that in a long time."

"I heard he could have a temper."

"I guess. He didn't like being crossed. Mostly he hated when he saw people taking advantage of things, including other people and the land. Maybe especially nature. 'We only get one world, Angie. Just like we only get one body. We gotta take care of it.' He was never angry for the sake of being angry, like Ryan. It was Mike's love for the outdoors that made him so mad when people trashed it."

"Including Laurel Mountain Quarrying?" Sally studied the other woman over the rim of her cup.

Angela brushed crumbs from her shirt. "He didn't like companies that mined or stuff like that, but Laurel Mountain came in for a lot of abuse lately. He was so sure they were destroying the river."

"Didn't Mike realize the number of jobs that would be lost if Laurel Mountain closed? Good jobs, too."

"I don't think he did. Or if so, it wasn't as important. Mike believed people could always get another job."

"Your late husband worked for LMQ." Sally waited for a reaction.

But there really wasn't one. Angela paused a beat, then nodded. "I always thought he was a heavy machinery operator moving the broken stone that came out of the quarry. But he got drunk once and boasted about how Old Lady Longchamp relied on him to do lots of stuff and maybe he needed to ask for a raise."

"What kind of stuff?"

"He didn't say. I didn't pay much attention, I was too busy staying out of reach. Ryan always got boastful when he'd been drinking. For all I know, he emptied Mrs. Longchamp's trash once. If he was drunk, that would become a big deal in his mind."

Sally filed the fact away to tell Jim, then moved on. "Mike told people he was going out on a hike before he died and that he'd be out of cell range. You didn't see or talk to him before he left? Not even to say goodbye?"

"Well..." Angela shifted on the chair. She put down the remains of her scone and picked up her cup.

"What?"

"I did see him. Friday afternoon at the CWPS offices. I came in to do some cleaning and we, um..."

"I get it." The couple had gotten together for a quick one before Mike hit the road. "Then you were probably the last person to see him before he left. He didn't tell you where he was going?"

"No. I asked if he wanted company. I could always make up a story for

Ryan and work, but he told me not this time. He was going to be working day and night for a couple days and didn't want to be distracted."

"Working where?"

Angela shrugged. "Here and there. He had a whole bunch of test tubes so I assumed he was gonna spend at least part of the time by the water. He's been obsessed with dust pollution in the Casselman and the fish population. It's his current pet project."

Sally thought back to what Jim said, how Mike was falsifying water readings. Was the equipment for taking samples or creating them? "Were the test tubes empty?"

"I assumed so. Why would he take full tubes out on a study?"

If he was going to add pollutant to the water. Maybe he didn't want Angela's company because he didn't want anyone to see him polluting for the sake of framing LMQ. "That was the last time you spoke to him, Friday afternoon?"

"No." Angela stared at her empty cup. "He texted me late Saturday morning, right before noon. He said things were going really well, faster than he anticipated. He said he was almost done, and asked if I'd like to meet him later that afternoon when I got off work. People were already expecting him to be gone the whole weekend and it would be a good opportunity for us to get together. But he didn't show up."

"What time were you supposed to meet?"

"Five o'clock. It wasn't at a restaurant or anything, but a spot by the river. I got off work at four-thirty that day, Ryan had said that morning that he had to go into work early, and Mike said I'd have plenty of time to get home at a reasonable hour."

If Mike hadn't shown for the rendezvous, it was possible he'd met his demise sometime between noon and five the day before Lindy Hunter saw his body and two days before she and Jim found it. "Is that all?"

"Oh, I forgot. He told me before he left he was expecting Carl to join him on Saturday."

"He was?"

"Something about how what he was working on required double confir-mation."

Sally tapped a fingernail against her cup. "Did Carl show up?"

Angela shrugged. "No idea. Mike didn't mention it in his texts. Since he asked me to see him, either Carl didn't show or he was gonna be long gone by the time we met. Mike wouldn't have risked anyone catching us, not even his friend." She stared at Sally. "Does any of this help me?"

"I don't know. It might." But it would definitely help Jim.

* * *

"Thanks." Duncan tapped the end button and slipped his phone back in his pocket. "We may have our time of death window." They'd returned to their vehicles after snapping pictures of the scene.

"Oh?" Foster asked as she swapped out her boots for shoes. She threw the boots in her trunk.

"Yep." Duncan relayed all the information he'd gotten from Sally and her conversation with Angela Stewart.

"The Saturday before the victims were found, between noon and five?"

"Thereabouts."

Foster slipped on her jacket. "A lot more than we had. Stewart was Caroline Longchamp's errand boy."

"Well, maybe. According to Angela Stewart, her husband bragged about being entrusted with important tasks. But he had an ego, so the 'important task' could have been taking out the garbage." Somehow, Duncan didn't think that was the case. Although he'd seen Ryan Stewart in action. The man definitely had an overinflated sense of self-importance.

Foster pulled out her notebook and thumbed through the pages. "When did Whitney say he had the alibi?"

Duncan consulted his own records. "He didn't give a date, he said 'that day.' He said he was in a business meeting, though. How many of those are held on a weekend?"

"Whitney's alibi is crap."

"At least it's a lot weaker than he'd like us to think."

Foster pocketed her phone. "I have a request out for financial records for the Stewarts. I can add Caroline Longchamp. We also need to follow up with her and with Mr. Whitney. Got a preference?"

"I'd rather meet with Whitney. I know paperwork is important, but I'm more of a field guy. And I've talked to Longchamp twice. Maybe a new person will have more success."

"When you move to CI, you'll have to deal with a lot of paper."

"You think I don't already? You don't remember writing reports when you were on patrol?" Duncan raised an eyebrow. "You sound awfully confident you know my decision, Trooper Foster."

"I placed a bet. I'm not a gambling woman, but I like my chances on this one." Foster opened her car door. "Okay, Whitney is yours. Let me know what you find and I'll do likewise."

Chapter Thirty-Six

Thursday was normally Duncan's day off, but he called Xavier Whitney that morning. "Mr. Whitney, Trooper Duncan. Based on some new information, I'd like to speak to you again about your Casselman project."

"And my argument with Mike Brower." Whitney's tone was matter-of-fact and gave no indication about his state of mind.

Which was one of the reasons Duncan hated phone interviews. "Yes, that too. Are you in Pittsburgh? I could drive to meet you."

"Actually, I'm in Somerset County with my architect, reviewing the plans. I hope to get a little fishing in while I'm here."

"Perfect. How about I grab my gear and meet you?"

Whitney paused. "Why not. You know the spot. See you in an hour." He ended the call.

The man sounded less than enthusiastic, but that didn't mean anything. Could be he didn't want to talk to the police, or maybe he had been looking forward to some solitude. People who fished rarely wanted to conduct long conversations at the same time. They definitely didn't want the company of a state police trooper who was a relative stranger.

A little more than an hour later, Duncan parked his Jeep at the spot where he'd previously interviewed the fishermen, Frank and Don. They weren't present today, but a Land Rover gleamed in the sunlight and took up much of the space. Duncan followed the sound of the water down to where he expected to find his target.

Whitney, dressed in high-end fishing gear, stood at the edge of the river and barely glanced up. "I see you made it."

"I said I would. A little out of my normal range, but the locals like this spot." Duncan set down a small cooler and baited his hook. "Nice pole. Graphite?"

"Keen eye." Whitney twitched the rod. "You fish for bass often?"

"I usually go down to the Youghiogheny Reservoir Dam, which is good for trout. Sometimes the Middle Yough Gorge. Don't often fish the Casselman, even though it flows right by my house." He cast into the river.

"Why not?"

"Personal preference, I guess." They stood in silence for a few moments. Whitney broke it. "You said you have new information and questions."

"I do." Duncan reeled in his line and cast again. "We now believe Mike Brower was killed the Saturday before his body was found. While we still aren't sure about Carl Ritchie, it's reasonable to assume he entered the water about the same time as Brower."

"Oh?" Xavier's expression was unconcerned. "I don't see where you'd have questions for me based on that."

"Your alibi."

"What about it?"

"You said you were at a meeting. Did that meeting occur on a Saturday?"

Whitney reeled in his line and cast again. "Of course not. Who works on a weekend? You do, of course. I used to, but not now I'm semi-retired. Why does it matter?"

Duncan glanced at the other man out of the corner of his eye. "The last time we talked about this, you said you had an alibi for 'that day.' I assumed you meant the day Brower was killed. Where were you that Saturday between nine in the morning and six in the evening?"

Whitney licked his lips. "That would be two weeks ago?"

"Correct."

"That's a long time ago to remember, Trooper."

"If you need to check your phone calendar or a day planner, I'll wait." Again, Duncan glanced at his companion. Whitney looked grouchy and maybe a touch resigned. As though he didn't want to admit something?

"I don't have an alibi for that day," he muttered.

"I'm sorry?"

"I don't have one, an alibi, okay? I was on the river, by myself." Whitney's voice was defiant.

Duncan faced him. "When was the last time you saw or talked to Mike Brower or Carl Ritchie?"

Whitney wound up his line. "I talked to Brower on the phone Thursday, no, Wednesday before the day you're talking about."

"What was the topic of conversation?"

"What else? My project. Brower was dead set against it. Wouldn't listen to a damn word I had to say. He was convinced I meant to bulldoze the entire riverbank." Xavier threw out his free arm in a sweeping motion. "I tell you, that's not my intention at all. I want more people to be able to enjoy the beauty of this area. I don't frigging understand why all the locals seem dead set against it. Don't you want more people to come to the Laurel Highlands? Wouldn't it be a good thing to see this entire stretch of river filled with happy fishermen?"

Duncan chuckled as he reeled in his bait. "You're a fisherman, Mr. Whitney, but not a *fisherman* I see."

"What the hell does that mean?" Whitney's expression had lost its resignation. Now he fumed with indignation.

"We don't like to share." Duncan removed the bait from his hook and put away his gear. "We like to keep our spots to ourselves. I admit to feeling this way myself. More people mean less fish for us. City folk come in with their picnic baskets and radios and kids. Make a lot of noise, maybe scare the fish away. Then we have to find a new place."

"Or it could mean the Game Commission releases more trout and bass into the rivers and there's plenty for all. Those city folk get to like nature and fight for conservation, get on your side. Is that such a bad thing?"

"No, but natural prejudice runs deep." Duncan finished packing up. "No one saw you. Did you have your phone?"

"Of course, I'm never without it."

"Then we can verify your story through the GPS location data. I either get a warrant for it, or you agree to surrender it. Be faster with your cooperation."

Whitney scowled. "I don't see how that helps me."

"We also know, or very strongly suspect, where the crime was committed. Our phones track our movements. If your GPS data backs up your story and puts you in a location that isn't anywhere near where Mike Brower was murdered, you're cleared. Or at least you become a less-likely suspect."

"You're assuming I kept my phone with me."

Duncan didn't know if Whitney was being stubborn in order to get a rise out of him or because the man was naturally combative. He maintained his calm. "You just said you did. Are you changing your story?"

"No." Whitney paused. "You're not going to tell me the location, are you?"

"No, sir." Duncan held out his hand. "Your choice. I can get the information. Personally, I believe you have the best of intentions for the area. Mike Brower and I weren't best buddies or anything, and I've learned he could be prickly when it came to confronting people with other ideas. Doesn't mean you killed him. But that data from your phone will go a long way toward moving that from my belief, which isn't worth a damn, to solid fact."

"When will I get it back? I need it, you know."

"When we're done with it."

Whitney didn't say anything for a long moment, annoyance stamped on his face. Then he dug out his phone and dropped it in Duncan's waiting hand.

* * *

Sally arrived at work Thursday deep in thought. There had to be a way of confirming, or breaking, Angela's alibi. On the one hand, it was a pretty weak story. Wouldn't she have come up with a better one if she murdered her husband? On the other, maybe she was a fan of crime fiction and knew such alibis were generally used by innocent people who didn't think they needed an ironclad cover for a crime. She could be counting on Sally and the police thinking that way.

Sally paged through her messages without really seeing them. If Angela was her client, and hers alone, how would she proceed? The snapping of fingers broke into her thoughts.

"Earth to Sally, are you in there?" Tanelsa stood beside her. "Good lord, I've been trying to get your attention for at least two minutes."

"Sorry. I spaced out."

"Obviously. What's got you so focused elsewhere?"

"Angela Stewart." Sally took the message slips and headed for her office.

Tanelsa followed. "What about her? She's not your client."

"I referred her to a friend of mine. That doesn't keep me from thinking about her."

"True." Tanelsa leaned on the doorway. "What is it about this one that won't leave you alone?"

"Let me see. Abused woman kills husband out of revenge or out of fear. I can't see why I'd be interested in that." Sally let the sarcasm color her words as she spoke. She sat and powered on her computer.

Tanelsa held up her hands. "Okay, okay. Point taken." She sat in the guest chair. "It's a pretty weak alibi. There's no way of confirming it?"

Sally had reached the point where she couldn't say anything sooner than she expected. She should have. "Tanelsa, I'm sorry. Not only did Angela come to me with the intent of obtaining representation, she signed a waiver to keep me on her defense team. I can't talk about this."

"Ah, privilege. I get it." Tanelsa tapped her finger on the chair. "Mind if I chatter on? You don't have to say anything."

Which meant Sally could listen and reap the benefit of anything Tanelsa said. "Be my guest. It's a free country and all that."

Tanelsa's answering grin was sly. "Okay, so you can't confirm the alibi. Not without talking to everybody who happened to be in Ohiopyle that afternoon and that's impossible. What about her cell phone?"

"What about it?"

"Those damn things know everywhere we've gone. You pull the GPS data and bam, you know where she's been."

Sally stayed silent.

Tanelsa tilted her head. "Of course, you're smart. You would have thought of that, asked Angela. I'm guessing the phone's a non-starter. She could have left it at home for some reason."

"Mmmm."

Tanelsa continued. "But that begs the question. How did she arrange a ride home without a phone?" Tanelsa thought a moment, then snapped her fingers. "She walked. Lisa talked me into going to the park over the holiday. That town is tiny. You can walk the entire area in ten minutes. Angela probably strolled over to her friend's job during a break and asked for a ride. Besides, we know she did. That's not the point."

So far, Tanelsa hadn't said anything earth-shattering and certainly nothing Kim and Sally hadn't discussed. She drummed her fingers on the desk. There had to be a way.

"Oh." Tanelsa leaned back in the chair. "You know, maybe you're going about this from the wrong direction."

Sally looked up. "What do you mean?"

"Instead of proving Angela *was* in Ohiopyle, prove she *wasn't* at home when her husband was killed."

"We talked to the neighbor, Debbie, when we were there, remember? She wasn't any help."

Tanelsa rolled her eyes. "There are more people around than Debbie No-Pants. What time of day was Ryan killed? What about the mail man? Other neighbors? People walking their dogs?"

Sally typed a text to Kim. *You follow up with Stewart neighbors?*

I took a little while for Kim to answer. *Duh. Nobody saw her. But several admitted they weren't looking 100% of time. She cld have come & gone without notice.*

Tanelsa watched Sally carefully. "What's the verdict?"

Sally bit her lip. "I can't say."

"I'm going to guess no one saw her. Which won't help you. You'll argue she wasn't seen, prosecution will say that's not ironclad. It's a wash."

Sally made another noncommittal sound in her throat. Damn, but keeping her mouth shut was hard. Maybe she could convince Angela to extend that waiver to Tanelsa. Then again, probably not.

Tanelsa's gaze was piercing. "When did Ryan leave work anyway? You're trying to pin down Angela for an entire day. It wouldn't matter so much if he was known to be at work for a certain time period."

Sally froze. Blinked twice. "That's an interesting point."

"Of course it is." Tanelsa preened. "Wait, what'd I say?"

"Why wasn't Ryan Stewart at work?" She'd wondered the same thing when she'd had lunch with Kim, but it had slipped her mind. Tanelsa brought it sharply back into focus. Debbie said she heard a man and a woman arguing in the early afternoon, people who she assumed were the Stewarts. She shot off another text to Kim. *Did we find out why Stewart wasn't at work?*

"You don't know?"

"I haven't had time to think about it." Sally's cell phone pinged with a text alert. Kim. *LMQ HR said he left early about 1pm for personal reasons.*

"What is it?"

Sally spread her hands, a helpless gesture.

"Right. Privilege." Tanelsa stood. "If you know Ryan was home Monday afternoon, and when he left LMQ, you need to prove Angela was somewhere other than her house during those hours. It doesn't matter where. It's only important that she wasn't at home. I wish you luck." She wiggled her fingers and walked out.

Sally drummed her fingers on her desk. Ryan left work around one. She had mapped it and he would be home in thirty minutes, give or take, assuming he didn't go anywhere first. What she and Kim needed to do was determine where Angela was between two and four that afternoon.

Tanelsa was right. It was a much smaller window and should be far easier to do. Problem was, outside of finding someone who'd actually seen Angela somewhere else, Sally wasn't sure how she was going to do that.

Chapter Thirty-Seven

Duncan went directly from the meeting with Xavier Whitney to see Andy in the tech division where he'd handed over the phone. Then he'd waited until the information was downloaded. Hounded his buddy, was more like it. At least he'd hung around until Andy agreed to look at the data. For a small favor, of course. A six-pack of his favorite summer beer.

Whiskey for Burns, beer for Andy, and he'd lost track of what he owed McAllister. How had he ever done this job by himself?

He hadn't, that was how. Patrol duties might be handled by one guy, but not an investigation.

He sent a text to Foster. *Meet me in Uniontown? Got some info.*

The answer was quick. *Yep. Got a place in mind?*

He arranged to meet her at Dex's at five. It meant missing eating with Sally, but work before pleasure. He called her. "Hey, I'm gonna skip dinner tonight. I have to meet with Foster."

"Okay." She paused. "Are you going to be talking about Angela Stewart?"

Duncan knew the woman's case was important to Sally. He respected that, but at the same time, she was a defense lawyer. Maybe she wasn't Angela's primary attorney, but she talked to Kim Dunphy a lot. The same woman who was aggressively recruiting Sally to join her firm. "I expect we'll be talking about a lot of things."

"This is something you can't tell me, huh?" Her tone was resigned, but not belligerent.

Thank god. "Sorry. At least not before I talk to Foster. See you tomorrow?"

"Absolutely. Love you." She ended the call.

Duncan breathed a sigh of relief. Those conversations had gotten so much easier since spring. Back then, Sally would've gone ballistic, or at least been majorly irritated, if he'd cut her out.

He arrived at Dex's before Foster and was able to snag his favorite corner booth. "Hey, Beth," he said as he greeted the waitress.

Beth set out a coaster. "You alone or expecting someone?"

"A co-worker is joining me, she should be here shortly." He took in Beth's questioning look. "Business tonight, not pleasure, I'm afraid."

"Right. You want your usual? What about your co-worker?"

"I'll take a Laurel Highlands Yard Sale Stout. I have no idea what to order for her, so I guess I'll wait."

At that moment, Foster walked up. "You won't have to wait long. What are we discussing? Drinks?"

Duncan nodded.

"Perfect." Foster slid into the booth. "I see you have The Pursuit of Haziness on tap. I'll take that."

Beth set down a coaster for Foster and left.

Duncan unfolded his napkin. "You're an IPA woman. Well, at least you like beer and not fruity froufrou drinks."

Foster snickered. "Let me guess, you like it dark."

"Got it in one." He watched as Foster fiddled with her utensils. "What's the latest?"

"A canvas of the people in Stewart's neighborhood failed to turn up any evidence that Angela Stewart was home at the time of her husband's death."

Beth returned with the beers and took their food orders. Duncan went with his usual Reuben and Foster the blackened trout.

She took a long drink. "It doesn't help her, though."

"Oh?"

"Based on what I've learned, we're interested in the time between two and four that afternoon. She can't account for her time."

Duncan could hear Sally's retort in his mind. He proceeded with caution. "That doesn't mean she was there. I know she's gotta be your prime suspect in a situation like this. I wouldn't want to jump to conclusions, though."

Foster fixed him with a stare. "You sound like a defense lawyer."

"Just being cautious."

"I've read Travers's notes from the Brower scene. You know Sally Castle, the woman who found Stewart. Isn't she a public defender?"

Here it comes. "She is and yes, I know her. We're dating, as a matter of fact." At Foster's raised eyebrow, he hurried on. "That's not why I'm being cautious, though. I just don't think the fact Mrs. Stewart doesn't have a solid alibi is necessarily an indicator of guilt."

Foster studied her beer. "What if I told you a couple of her co-workers said she once wished her husband was dead? That she wanted to beat him the way he beat her, see how he liked it?"

Duncan sucked in his breath. "That would change things a bit."

"Thought so." Foster took a drink, then she continued. "One neighbor reported seeing a dark blue Chevy Suburban. He thinks a woman was driving it, a woman with gray hair. That's not Mrs. Stewart. But the driver was standing on the far side of the vehicle and he didn't get a good look, so he can't give a description beyond that."

Duncan lifted his glass. "Caroline Longchamp has gray hair."

"She doesn't drive a blue SUV. She has a black Land Rover."

"Company vehicle?"

"I haven't had a chance to check. But why would the CEO of a company be visiting a low-level employee?"

"Angela Stewart said her husband bragged about doing important tasks for Longchamp."

"Yeah, and he was drunk when he said it. Who knows if he was telling the truth?" The food arrived and Foster broke apart her fish. "I called LMQ. Longchamp's secretary swears she didn't leave her office that morning and although she was out in the afternoon, she was with a co-worker, who corroborated the story."

"I thought Stewart was her driver."

"He *sometimes* drove for her. Apparently not that day. He left work early for an unspecified reason."

Duncan wiped some coleslaw dressing from his fingers. "I bet LMQ has a fleet of vehicles. Be interesting to know what they are and who had one out that day."

"Sounds like a task for you." Foster grinned. "Don't be thinking Longchamp has a solid alibi, either. She and her employee definitely met. He said she received a phone call that seemed to irritate her. He had to cut the afternoon short, sick kid. Longchamp drove him back to the LMQ main office."

"When was that?" Duncan asked.

"About one-thirty, two o'clock or so. The question becomes did anyone see Longchamp after that and would she have had time to drive to Markleton."

Duncan reached for the ketchup. "When I interviewed Longchamp, she said Stewart's name was vaguely familiar, but that was all. That could contradict Stewart's claim."

Foster forked up some fish. "That or she's lying. I've requested financial records from both Stewart and Longchamp. They haven't come in yet, but those may show something. We shall see." She ate for a moment. "When you go ask about the vehicles, show that keyring, see if it's familiar."

"Will do." Duncan paused. "Are we officially throwing away the two-men-have-a-fight idea?"

"Officially? No." Foster took another bite, chewed, and swallowed. "In light of everything else, it's fallen way to the bottom of my list. In fact, I think I'll feel ripped off if we do all this work and that turns out to be the solution."

"Let's say the financials show money changed hands. I see two possibilities. Stewart knows Longchamp got rid of Mike Brower and Carl Ritchie and is blackmailing her, or Longchamp sent him to get rid of the threat." He washed down the first half of his Reuben. "We can cross one suspect off the list. Or at least demote him."

"Who?"

"Xavier Whitney. I bribed a friend of mine down in tech to expedite pulling the GPS info from Whitney's phone. It shows he was ten miles away from our suspected crime scene that day during the time we think the murders happened."

"Well, his phone was."

He took a bite and swallowed. "You're right. But that ten miles is in the middle of nowhere. Do you honestly think Whitney left his phone on the bank of the Casselman River in Somerset County to give himself an alibi?"

"He could have sent it off with an employee or deliberately left it in a company car."

"He's not the boss anymore and besides, his company does primarily urban construction. Wouldn't it make more sense for him to leave it in Pittsburgh?"

"True. I'd like to make sure we aren't acting prematurely, though. I'll check into it." Foster paused. "Between you and me, you think Longchamp did it?"

Duncan thought about the scenario. It was possible, but he'd met Caroline Longchamp. And he'd seen pictures of the Stewart crime scene. "I can see her asking Stewart to talk to Mike and Carl. She isn't the physical type to beat someone up. Shoot them, yes. Pummel them to a pulp? Not so much."

"Remember the murder weapon in the Stewart homicide was a trophy with a heavy marble base," Foster reminded him. "Longchamp is strong enough to swing something like that."

Duncan had to concede the point. But he still didn't picture Caroline Longchamp committing murder in such a physical way.

"She didn't like Mike Brower, that's for certain," Foster said.

"It's a long way from not liking someone to killing him." Duncan picked up a French fry. "I don't like a lot of people. I haven't killed any of them."

Foster inclined her head. "True. Go to LMQ tomorrow. I'll let you know if the financial stuff comes in."

"Got it." Duncan drained his glass.

"You're right, by the way," Foster said as she took another bite of her fish. "I've met Caroline Longchamp. I wouldn't see her as the physical type."

"Then again, there is the fact that Mike, and maybe Carl, was setting her grandfather's business up for fraudulent environmental charges that would get them in hot water at the least, and shut them down at the worst."

CHAPTER THIRTY-SEVEN

Foster lifted an eyebrow. "Your point?"

Duncan pointed another fry at her. "She may be an unlikely suspect. But never underestimate anyone who feels she's been put in a corner."

Chapter Thirty-Eight

Sally arrived at work Friday morning deep in thought. So far, nothing had come up to implicate Angela. Sally had had a long conversation with Kim the previous night. Nothing showed on the Stewarts' financial records. Ryan's life insurance was minimal. While Angela was his sole beneficiary, she would receive precious little, hardly enough to justify murder. "Not much of a motive," Sally said.

"The prosecution isn't going to put money forward as a motive, you know that." Kim's tone was dismissive. "They're going to argue the abuse was the prime factor. Sad, but she went too far, no excuse for murder, blah, blah, you know the drill."

"I know. But you didn't find any other accounts for Ryan?"

"No, but I'm still looking." Kim paused. "See how fun this is? Now imagine doing it everyday."

"I *do* do it every day."

"Yes, but not with me." She paused. "When do you want to start setting up your half of the office?"

Sally knew that was going to come up. "We have our agreement and we've talked about timing. I'm not going through it again. Admit it. This is more compelling than you expected, isn't it? Helping someone who honestly deserves it?"

Kim grumbled and hung up.

Sally went to get a second cup of coffee. If she dismissed Angela as a suspect, and based on the flimsy evidence she did, who else held such a grudge against Ryan it would lead to murder? The man was a drunk, a wife-beater, and a loudmouth. His beating had been brutal. That meant serious emotion behind it, or at least Sally thought so. Yes, the abused spouse getting back at him made sense from a psychological point of view. It was a good motive. Means? Yes. The trophy was right there and Sally had no problem seeing Angela wield it. Opportunity, that tripped her up. So far, they could legitimately argue Angela had not been home.

Tanelsa's voice broke through. "You've been standing there for two minutes. Get out of the way, woman. Other people need caffeine, too."

"Oops, sorry. Lost in thought." Sally stepped aside.

Tanelsa filled her mug, tasted it, made a face, and poured in some creamer. "What are you thinking about?" She headed back to her office.

Sally followed. "Angela Stewart, what else?"

"Of course. You said she waived her rights so you could stay involved. You can't do much more, not unless you leave here and join your friend on a permanent basis." Tanelsa paused. "Is that what you're doing? Thinking about where to get moving boxes?"

"No, I really was thinking about Angela." Sally hesitated. Tanelsa would ferret out the agreement with Kim soon enough. "I should let you know something. I told Kim that if she took Angela's case, I'd join her firm."

Tanelsa set down the folder she held with extreme care. "You told her what?"

Sally elaborated on her deal with Kim. "I said I need to finish up my current workload first, though."

"That's a deal with the devil."

"It is. I guess this case has me thinking. This is the kind of situation I hate, where I want to help someone and I can't because of the restrictions on my job. Being in private practice would eliminate that."

"It would. It would also bring its own slew of problems, but we'll let that go for a second." Tanelsa sighed. "Let's get theoretical for a moment. Pretend it's a client from this office. What's your main hang up?"

Sally swirled the coffee in her cup. It was dangerous ground, but if she stayed general enough, she could navigate some murky waters. "I have two. One, we've talked about. Opportunity. Was my client at home? I can't say."

"I remember the conversation. What's the other?"

"Motive. The prosecution will argue that after years of abuse, she snapped. That's possible, although as far as I know my client never admitted the abuse to anyone, so we don't know she ever thought of taking matters into her own hands. But who else would have had a motive? If we can find that, we can raise it and it might be cause for doubt."

"Got it." Tanelsa tapped a pen against her lips. "What about money? It's always a good motive. You said before the couple's shared finances were thin. Did the husband have any for himself? Separate bank account, trust, bag of cash under the mattress, anything?"

"Unknown. They didn't find any cash hidden in the house."

Tanelsa pointed the pen at Sally. "Follow the money. Always solid advice."

Sally pondered. "If the husband has a stash, and we can find it and where it came from, that might lead us to someone with another motive, someone we can offer a jury, should it get that far."

"Now you're thinking." Tanelsa returned to her work.

Sally's cell phone rang and she checked the caller ID. It was Kim. *Twice in one morning?* "Hey, what's up? Is there an emergency?"

"Your boyfriend is an asshole," Kim snapped. "Hot, but an asshole nonetheless."

"Jim?" Now there was a word Sally had never heard used to describe him. "Why, what did he do?"

"He arrested Angela Stewart for murder."

* * *

Duncan walked out of the Uniontown booking station into a wash of bright summer sun and crushing humidity. He'd endured some pretty hateful stares in his years on patrol. Nothing matched the cold look Kim Dunphy had pierced him with when she stormed into the building. She'd been the paradigm of professionalism, but the hard-eyed glare told Duncan she would have had words for him had they been alone. About how the arrest was premature and how the police were railroading a victimized wife. Words he was sure she'd tell Sally as soon as possible. He was no expert on legal ethics, but even had Sally not been helping with Angela's case, he was sure Kim would have found a way to communicate with her friend.

This was going to make for an awkward dinner.

He turned to Foster. "You didn't need me for this." She'd met him, warrant in hand, as he left morning roll call.

"It's standard procedure to have backup." She slipped on a pair of Ray-Bans. "You join CI, arresting people is part of the deal. I'm sure this isn't your first rodeo."

"It's not the concept of making an arrest I have a problem with. It's this particular one." He put on his own shades and spun the keys to his patrol car around his finger.

"Why?"

"I'm not convinced she did it."

"The evidence points that way."

"*Some* of the evidence points that way." *The very circumstantial evidence.* "There could be other information out there we haven't uncovered yet."

Foster squared her shoulders. "Judge Markham thought it was good enough." She tilted her head. "Is this about your girlfriend? The fact that she believes Angela is innocent?"

"No." Well, partially, but Duncan wasn't going to admit that. "Yes, Angela is an abused spouse. Yes, she made a statement to a co-worker, but if we arrested everybody who wished someone else was dead, the jails would be overflowing. Yes, she had access to the murder weapon."

"Then what's your problem?"

"I'd feel better if we could put her on the scene, that's all." He looked down the street at an oncoming car.

"You can't always get what you want," Foster said. "Two out of three ain't bad. You want another cliche?"

"No, I'm good." How the hell was he going to explain this to Sally? Assuming she needed an explanation. It was better to assume that she did, this way he would be prepared. "Does this mean you don't need me to go out to Laurel Mountain?"

"No." Foster opened the door to her unmarked sedan. "Angela's arrest takes care of the Stewart homicide, but not the others. We still need information about that keychain as it relates to Brower and Ritchie."

"Should I ask about fleet vehicles?"

"Wouldn't hurt. The actor had to transport those bodies somehow. Let's assume the motive is squashing or retaliating for the fake environmental evidence."

"Which we don't know Ritchie was a part of."

"For now, it doesn't matter. If our killer had access to an LMQ truck, it could mean he, or she, was employed by the company."

"Ryan Stewart?"

"Or Caroline Longchamp. Keep me posted." Foster slid into the sedan and drove off.

Duncan watched her taillights recede and turn the corner. He didn't like the Angela Stewart arrest. He wouldn't have applied for the warrant—not because he didn't think Angela could have killed her husband, but because there were still too many other possibilities, at least in his mind. But this was Foster's show. He was the guy along for the ride.

Maybe Sally would accept that.

Doubtful.

As he drove to Laurel Mountain Quarrying, he tried to push the vision of Angela Stewart's agonized face, blanketed in tears, out of his memory. Attempted to blot out the sounds of her incoherent protests, her sobs. The storm cloud expression on Kim Dunphy's face and her drill-sergeant orders that Angela be quiet and say nothing couldn't be forgotten. If this case made it to trial, he hoped Foster wouldn't ask him to testify. He didn't fancy facing down Kim from the witness stand.

He shoved all those thoughts aside as he parked in the LMQ lot. Time to focus on the task at hand. He presented himself at the main office and showed his ID. "I'd like to speak with the person who oversees your vehicles, please."

"That'd be Rich Palmer. Hold on." The secretary dialed the phone, spoke to someone, and hung up. "He'll be out in five minutes or so. You can have a seat over there while you wait."

It took Palmer closer to ten minutes to appear. He was a ruddy-faced man in his early fifties, his plaid flannel shirt and khaki work pants buttoned over a reasonably fit body. Muddy green eyes showed intelligence and his close-cut graying hair was receding, giving him a sharp widow's peak. "Trooper Duncan, sorry for the delay." He held out his hand. "What can I do for you?"

Duncan rose. "Thanks for seeing me. I need some information about your vehicle fleet. Is there someplace more private we can talk?"

Palmer looked around. "We might as well go to the office where I have all the information. This way." He led Duncan across the hot yard, air redolent of diesel and oil, and into a small office. A peg-board on the wall held a dozen or so keys, all with tags that looked similar to the broken piece.

Duncan removed it from his pocket. "Looking at your board, I think I have my answer but is this a piece of your tags?"

Palmer took it and held it up to another one for comparison. "Sure is. Trucks are red, SUVs are blue. This is off a truck key." He handed it back.

"Is there a key missing?"

Palmer scanned the board. "Doesn't look like it. No wait, number twelve." He consulted a battered three-ring binder with a ripped cover. "That's a 2015 Dodge Dakota, standard cab."

"Do you have a record of who signed it out?" Duncan took out his notebook and pen, ready to jot down the name.

"Last person was George Friedman, he's one of our foremen."

"When was that?"

Palmer ran his finger across the row. "This past Wednesday. Looks like he drove into Rockwood to pick up some sacks of sand. Here. Left at eleven-oh-six in the morning, back at two-eighteen in the afternoon."

That name meant nothing. Duncan thought. "Anybody take that truck out two weeks ago, maybe on a Saturday?"

"Two weeks ago tomorrow?" Palmer flipped back a page. "Sean Garroty took it in the morning. Ryan Stewart signed it out in the afternoon. Huh."

"What?"

"Looks like Stewart didn't sign it back in. That's odd. He was usually good about that kind of thing."

Bingo. "Is it in the yard?"

"Hold on, lemme look." Palmer left the office and came back a minute or two later. "Yeah, it's here. The key isn't though and like I said, Stewart was generally good about following procedure. A loudmouth, braggart, pain-in-the-ass, but he followed the rules."

Duncan jotted down the times. "Anything about the truck look out of the ordinary?"

Palmer shrugged. "I'd say it's a bit muddier than usual, but maybe not. Come take a look."

The two men went back into the sweltering heat and over to a dirt-streaked black truck. Mud covered the tires. Duncan pulled on a set of nitrile gloves and crouched down to look at the undercarriage. He reached up and felt along the wheel-wells. Nothing. He thought about the bodies, all the cuts and scrapes. Even if the truck had been hosed down or used afterward, there might be traces of blood that could be found with Luminol. "I'm going to have to call out a forensic team to inspect the vehicle." He peeled off the gloves. "You say the key is missing?"

"It's not hanging inside."

"Then how did Mr. Friedman take it out?"

"We have spares to all our vehicles, you know, in case one set gets locked inside. Hold on." He pulled out a radio. "Hey, George, you there? This is Rich."

The radio crackled. "Go ahead, Rich."

"You have the spare key for the 2015 Dakota?"

A pause. "I do. I need the truck later. Couldn't find the one on the board. Why?"

Palmer looked at Duncan, who nodded. "Bring it around ASAP. And you're gonna need to use a different truck." He clicked off the radio. "Is that all?"

"No." Duncan surveyed the yard, which held maybe six to eight dusty trucks and SUVs, as well as a couple of sedans. "Those belong to LMQ?"

Palmer chuckled. "Not all of them. Guys will take a company car for a trip or something, and leave their own parked here."

"How many SUVs do you have and what kind?"

Palmer thought and counted off the vehicles as he spoke. "We have two older Jeeps for when guys need to go off-road. One Chevy Trax for day trips. Oh, and the Suburban we keep for executive use. It has all the goodies. Mrs. Longchamp often takes it when she wants official wheels. It's by far our most comfortable SUV."

Foster had said one of Stewart's neighbors saw a dark blue Suburban the day of the crime. "Is it here?"

Palmer scanned the yard. "Over here."

Duncan followed him over the gravel to a midnight-blue Chevy coated in a light film of dust. He peered through the windows. "When was this one last taken out?"

"I'd have to check the book. Hold on."

While Duncan waited, he called the Somerset barracks for a team to inspect the Dakota. Might as well have a look at the Suburban while they were at it. If the killer had been Caroline Longchamp, maybe she'd brought Ryan Stewart's blood inside with her.

Palmer returned with the binder. "Gus Tully took it last Monday. I remember, he was going somewhere with Mrs. Longchamp. She loves this thing."

Duncan made a note. "Who returned it?"

"Gus. Kinda late, I was locking up. I think he had to leave, go pick up a sick kid or something, then he had to go back and get Mrs. Longchamp."

Which meant Tully would have had the Suburban. "You're sure about that?"

Palmer snapped his fingers. "No, hold on. Gus took the Suburban. He did have to take care of his kid, but Mrs. Longchamp dropped him somewhere, then came back to get him. They finished up late and he checked the Suburban back in. That was it. He said that Mrs. Longchamp must've gotten dirty somewhere. She was wearing a different shirt when she picked him up."

Oh, she got dirty all right. Dirty with Stewart's blood? From killing him or finding him? "Thanks for the info." He turned to go.

"I think Stewart drove Mrs. Longchamp around a couple times. In fact, he filled in for the scheduled driver a couple weeks ago."

The words stopped Duncan in his tracks. He faced Palmer. "Then if I asked her, Stewart should be more than a vague remembrance?"

Palmer laughed. "Hell, yeah. Mrs. Longchamp has a memory like a steel trap when it comes to things like that. Meet her once and she'll remember you forever."

Chapter Thirty-Nine

Sally didn't have a chance to dig into Ryan Stewart's finances until noon.

She couldn't believe Angela had been arrested. In her opinion, there wasn't enough evidence. Jim had to see that. Nonetheless, it was true. According to Angela's mother, two state police officers, a man in a uniform and a woman in a suit, had shown up at her house early that morning and arrested her daughter. It had to be Jim and Trooper Foster. Jim did not return any of Sally's calls or texts asking for confirmation.

She'd talk to him that evening.

In the meantime, she held a pow-wow with Kim and Angela, who was only too happy to have both attorneys on her side. Sally had a mountain of work to do for her regular cases, but if necessary, she'd work until midnight to help Angela. "Make sure all of this doesn't interfere with your regular job," Kim said. "I don't need you getting busted for sloppy work before I get a chance to put your name on the letterhead."

While Kim marshaled her defense arguments, Sally would poke around and find more ammo. And part of that was trying to come up with an alternative theory for Ryan's murder.

Kim had already run a credit and background check on Ryan, neither of which showed funds squirreled away. Sally's instinct said the money was there. The only questions were where it was and how it got there. She and Kim agreed finding out would be her first task.

Tanelsa rapped on her doorframe. "You going out to lunch?"

"No, thanks. I'm staying in."

"To do what?"

Sally hesitated. "I'm sorry, but I'm not at liberty to discuss it. Let's say I'm going fishing for information."

Tanelsa raised her eyebrows. "For Angela Stewart's defense?"

"I can't say."

"The famous non-confirmation confirmation." She turned to leave.

Sally called her back. "Hold on." Even if she couldn't talk details, Tanelsa could be useful. "General question. If you wanted to hide a bank account, how would you do it?"

Tanelsa entered and sat in the guest chair. "I'd use one of these online-only options. Although, opening the account would still raise an alert on any identity theft monitoring systems because you have to supply a social security number."

A scrap of an idea took hold. "What if you used someone else's number, someone who wasn't using one of those services?"

"What do you mean?"

"Parents often open bank savings accounts for their kids when they're little. What if you did it in reverse? Went to an online bank and opened an account in a parent's name using their SSN?"

Tanelsa frowned. "Could work, I guess. Hell, people use the numbers from the dead. As long as Mom and Dad aren't paying attention, you could do it. Online banks don't mail anything, so no one would ever know."

Sally's fingers flew as she typed. Ryan Stewart's parents were alive. Bess and Thomas. If Sally did a background check on them, she could get their SSNs. "Thanks."

Tanelsa shot her a knowing look. "Who has the hidden account, Ryan or Angela? My money's on Ryan."

Sally stopped typing. "Tanelsa, please."

"Fair enough." Tanelsa cocked her head. "You like this, don't you?"

"What?"

"You said it before. Angela Stewart is exactly the kind of case you want to handle. And she's exactly what this office can't offer you."

Sally went back to her typing. This *was* her type of case. *If only I didn't feel forced into leaving this office.* Of course, no one had twisted her arm. She'd made that deal with Kim on her own.

"Angela makes too much money to qualify for a public defender. And even if she did, she isn't a resident of Fayette County." Tanelsa stood. "Face it, Sally. You've outgrown us. You need to go private. I'm serious. Don't feel bad about the agreement you have with Kim." With that, she left.

A few minutes later, Sally hit the jackpot. "Bingo," she murmured. Bess had opened an account with an online bank a little more than a week ago. Or someone had opened an account in Bess's name. But the report only told Sally the account existed and for how long. She needed to know what the balance was and where the money came from.

She needed a subpoena. Kim could request that. Sally saved the information as a PDF and emailed it to her friend.

She sat back. Tanelsa said she should move on from public defense. Sally had agreed to join Kim, "after she cleared her current caseload." That was a nebulous timeframe. But it couldn't be put off forever.

Sally had already told herself exactly what Tanelsa had said. It had been one of those internal conversations she didn't share with anyone else. The idea of helping who she wanted, when she wanted was liberating.

But public defense was home. She'd grown as an attorney here, made wonderful friends. Bryan was the perfect boss. How could she leave?

* * *

Duncan texted Foster on his way to the Uniontown barracks from Laurel Mountain Quarrying and arranged to meet her there. He had the information on the trucks and apparently she had some financial information to share.

Foster had commandeered one of the conference rooms. Papers were spread all over the table and she was rearranging them. "Perfect timing. What did you learn at LMQ?"

He recounted the information about the key tags and what he'd learned about Caroline Longchamp.

Foster paused in her rearranging. "Never forgets a name or face, huh? I thought she told you Stewart's name was only vaguely familiar. We'll be talking to Ms. Longchamp about that."

"Everybody lies." Duncan surveyed the paper. "What the hell are you doing?"

"Trying to sort out all the facts."

"I use a whiteboard for that. Here, I'll show you." He strode to the whiteboard, grabbed a few markers, and started writing. All of the known facts went in columns headed by the names of their suspects, related facts connected with arrows. "What's the financial information you talked about?"

"You're an investigator at heart. Nice and organized." Foster came around the table and handed him a sheet of paper. "Turns out Ryan Stewart has an account with an online bank."

Duncan read. The account, opened in the name of Bess Stewart, was three weeks old. He whistled. "Opened with a deposit of ten thousand dollars? And who is Bess Stewart?"

"Ryan's mother." Foster tapped a line at the bottom.

"You're sure it's not really the mother's?"

"I talked to her. She's well into her eighties and doesn't even own a computer. When I mentioned the account, she and her husband, who is almost ninety, were genuinely confused."

Duncan looked up. "Where does a blue-collar guy like Ryan Stewart come up with ten grand, in cash no less?"

"Come on, you know the answer to that." Foster took one of the markers and wrote down the information. "He was paid off."

"Okay." Duncan paced. "Longchamp lied about knowing Stewart. She paid him to take care of Mike before he released the false environmental report to the appropriate agencies."

"I'm surprised she wouldn't talk to Brower first."

"Maybe she did." Duncan returned to the whiteboard and wrote. "Could be she tried to talk him out of it. He refused so she sent her attack dog after CWPS."

"I like it." Foster came up beside him. "But why kill Ritchie? Was he in on the fake data plan?"

"I don't know. I've been going over it and I don't think so. Especially if that was why the two men argued, as we've learned." Duncan tapped the marker on his palm. "I can talk to Tara Jennings again. She's the freelance photographer who worked for CWPS. Maybe she'll remember more this time. And we can go back to Longchamp. But it could be that Ritchie was simply collateral damage. Maybe he saw Stewart, or Longchamp, kill Brower so he had to go, too."

"Fortunate for Longchamp that Angela bumped off her husband," Foster said.

"Do you really think that? Isn't it more likely Longchamp tied up her own loose end?"

"It's possible, but aren't you the one who said you didn't figure Longchamp would beat someone to death?" Foster retorted.

He had said that. But he disliked the coincidence that Angela Stewart happened to kill Ryan at the exact moment he could prove to be a liability to Caroline Longchamp.

Foster laid down her marker. "I may have jumped the gun on Angela, though."

Duncan shot her a look. "I'll refrain from saying it."

"Yes, I know. You told me so. Given this new idea, you may have been right." Foster twisted up her face. "Hey, what about the LMQ truck? Any word from forensics?"

Duncan tossed his marker from hand to hand. "I stayed while they combed over the truck that belongs to the missing key. They pulled out the usual crap-ton of debris, don't know how useful any of it will be. But they did find blood traces using Luminol. No word on test results from that."

"And the key tag could definitely have belonged to that vehicle?"

"Like I told you. Color's right and the key is missing."

Foster took out her phone and snapped a picture of the whiteboard. "Nice tactic, by the way. The board. I'm more of a 'Post-it on the wall' person, but they tend to fall off after a while." She put the phone away. "Blood, huh?"

"Don't get too excited. For all we know it's from someone who cut himself while working. But yes, it's there."

"We didn't find a key in the Stewart house. Well, not one we didn't match to something." Foster walked out of the room. "I'm going to go search again. Meanwhile, lean on the forensic guys. See if they can get us a lead."

Duncan followed her. "You think that will work for you? I've never found it particularly useful. The leaning, I mean."

Foster chuckled. "It usually doesn't work for me, either. But you can try."

* * *

Sally was in the kitchen when she heard her apartment door open and close, followed immediately by Jim's voice.

"Hey, where are you? I brought dinner."

She went to the entry way. Jim stood there, balancing a pizza box and a plastic clamshell of salad while he kicked off his shoes. "What is that, a peace offering?" she asked.

He went into the dining room and set the boxes on the table. Then he faced her. "A peace offering for what? It's Friday. I always bring food."

She crossed her arms. "Arresting Angela Stewart." Was it her imagination, or did he wilt a little?

"I have no apologies for that." He went to the cupboard for plates, returned, and set the table.

"Why not? She's innocent, Jim. You know it."

"No, I don't." He didn't stop working as he talked. "As far as I'm concerned, she remains a suspect in her husband's murder."

"Not a very good one." Sally rounded the table to force him to meet her gaze. "She's a victim. First of her husband, now the police. As a man, I'm sure you find that hard to understand."

"Time out." Jim looked up. There was a glint of anger in his eyes. "First of all, I didn't write the arrest warrant. It was written by Ilene Foster, a woman, and signed by Judge Markham, another woman. Don't play the 'you men don't understand' card with me. Second, did Angela tell you she threatened her husband?"

Sally froze, his words hitting her like a two-by-four. This was every defense attorney's nightmare. A client withholding information, and it coming out to bite them in the ass.

"I didn't think so." Jim took a deep breath. "This stays between you and me, although I'm sure Kim will find out from Angela. Turns out she made a comment about wanting to beat on Ryan for once, so he could see how it felt."

"I…I didn't know that." Sally's voice was small, quiet.

His expression softened. "I knew you were going to be upset over this. Hell, Kim didn't look happy when she showed up at the booking center in Uniontown. But you need to understand. I didn't make this decision. Foster called me for backup since Angela was in Fayette County."

Sally fidgeted. "You didn't have to go. She's not your boss."

"No, but Lieutenant Nicols is and he ordered me to." He nodded at the pizza. "Please. Let's sit down, the food's getting cold." He went into the kitchen and returned moments later holding a bottle of Edmund Fitzgerald porter and a can of Coke.

They ate for a few moments in silence. Sally broke it. "I know this is another one of those situations where we can't tell each other everything. But answer me this. Would you have written that warrant?"

He didn't respond immediately, his expression letting her know he was wrestling with how much to say. "Probably not. I might have done it eventually, but not yet."

"Because she might not have been there, and nobody can prove she was." Sally took a drink. "You didn't hear that from me."

"I didn't have to, I know." Jim lifted another slice of pizza from the box. "That and we have other information I'm not at liberty to divulge right now."

Sally thought. What information? What would hold Jim back? She knew he wouldn't like the ambiguity surrounding Angela's alibi. That might be enough for him to put on the brakes, but she sensed he knew something else. Like what? The idea came to her like lightning. "Someone else was at the Stewart house at the time of the murder. Someone else who is a viable suspect."

He focused on his food. "No comment."

"I'm right, aren't I? The main reason you'd hold back is there's another person in the picture, someone you can't rule out. Tell me I'm right."

He took a long pull from his beer and looked her straight in the eye. "Since you know so much, you don't need me to tell you, do you?"

They were her words from Memorial Day, her way of confirming a statement he'd made without breaking her ethics. He was throwing it back at her.

Which meant she was right. Someone else had been at the Stewart house. But who?

Chapter Forty

Duncan met Foster at the barracks mid-morning Saturday. "Where do we stand?"

She rubbed her temple. "Until I know Angela Stewart wasn't at home when Ryan was killed, I can't rule her out."

"She still in lockup?"

"No, she made bail. As I understand it, her mother used her home as collateral for a bail bond." Foster didn't look at him as she talked. "There are witness statements about this dark-blue Suburban and the gray-haired woman who may or may not have been Caroline Longchamp. I very much doubt she'll admit to being on the scene when Stewart was killed. And why would she have been there, anyway?"

"Reasonable. Maybe we should—"

Duncan was interrupted by the desk trooper. "Excuse me, but there are two people out front holding a box. They say they need to talk to you, Duncan."

He frowned. "Who are they?"

"Gave their names as Harold and Gladys Brower. You want to see them?"

Duncan shared a look with Foster, who nodded. "Yes," he said. "Put them in conference three and we'll be right there."

The trooper nodded and left. Foster took out her notebook. "Mike Brower's parents. What do they want? It's a long drive from Altoona."

"Let's find out, shall we?"

The Browers were sitting at the table when Duncan and Foster entered. A medium-sized cardboard box, the flaps folded shut, rested in front of

Harold. Both of them looked nervous, maybe a bit scared. Duncan crossed to shake their hands. "Mr. and Mrs. Brower, it's good to see you again, even under unpleasant circumstances." He waved. "This is Trooper Ilene Foster. She's investigating your son's death."

"We've spoken on the phone," Harold said, voice gruff. Gladys murmured something that might have been a hello.

Foster pointed at the box. "Trooper Duncan and I were saying how it's quite the trip from Altoona to Uniontown. What's in the box?"

Harold glanced at his wife, who merely sniffed and nodded. "We were cleaning out Mike's things. Most of it was stuff he never got around to taking from home. Old clothes, outdoor equipment, things like that." He stopped, looking uncertain.

Gladys continued. "Mike brought us this box a few weeks ago. He said it was some material he didn't have room for at the moment and could we store it? Of course, we said yes." Tears leaked out of her eyes.

Duncan handed her his handkerchief. "What's in it?"

"I think maybe you should see for yourself," Harold replied.

Both troopers automatically pulled on nitrile gloves. Duncan opened the flaps of the box. Inside were tightly stoppered tubes full of a whitish substance, not quite powder but thicker than pure liquid. Each was labeled with a letter of the alphabet. He passed them to Foster. Underneath was a map. Duncan spread it on the table. Several spots were labeled to correspond with the test tubes. "This is Somerset County. There's the Casselman." He traced the river.

Foster studied the map from the other side. "All the marked spots correspond to the tubes. Maybe they're the spots where he decided to dump the contents? Or where he collected samples? But why would he hold on to them instead of sending them out for analysis? I can't tell for certain what's in them, but I'll get everything over to the guys who can. Any ideas, Duncan?"

He ran his finger over the map. "Like you, I'm not positive. We know Mike was falsifying environmental data."

Beside him, Gladys gave a little cry. Harold said, "But Mike loved nature.

Why would he do that?"

"We have some ideas," Duncan said, meeting Harold's eyes. "Let me ask you a question. Did Mike talk to you about a company called Laurel Mountain Quarrying?"

"Once. Aren't they a mining company?"

"Quarrying, not quite the same," Foster said. She indicated the tubes. "Our analysts will be able to tell us if what is in those is a pollutant."

"You think Mike planned to pollute on purpose? I don't understand why he'd do that," Harold said.

Duncan hedged. "We aren't sure."

Harold squeezed his wife's hand. "Then Carl found out and they argued? Is that how they wound up dead?"

The troopers exchanged a long look. Duncan knew Foster was debating the same thing he was. How much should they say? "While it's a possible scenario, we aren't inclined to pursue it. We think there are other people who may have had more to lose."

"People like Laurel Mountain Quarrying," Harold said.

"That's yet to be determined," Foster replied, voice gentle. "Thank you for bringing this to us, Mr. Brower. You could have turned it in to your local state police barracks."

Harold shook his head. "Trooper Duncan came all the way to us. We figured we'd return the favor." He put his arm around his wife. "We knew you'd see this as evidence, so after we opened the box and saw what it was, we didn't touch it."

"Thank you." Foster folded up the box flaps. "I'm very sorry. Knowing your son was killed is hard. Finding out he may not have been as truthful as you'd like has to be salt in the wound, as they say."

Gladys hiccuped and wiped her eyes.

Duncan noticed and followed up. "Tell me, was this normal behavior for him, Mike? Did he have a habit of being untruthful, ever bend the rules a little to get his way?"

Harold's face tightened and Gladys murmured. She refused to lift her gaze from the floor.

"Mrs. Brower." Duncan kept his tone calm, inviting confidence. "It's hard for any parent to admit their child may not be as perfect as they hoped. If you know something, tell us. It can only help find out who killed him."

Gladys shot a furtive look at her husband, who shook his head. *Up to you,* the gesture seemed to say. Gladys swallowed and spoke. "Mike always was too passionate. It wasn't only who he was as a man, but as a boy. There were a couple of times I caught him cooking up a scheme to get someone in trouble. Someone who he said had broken the rules but wouldn't get caught. 'They deserve it, Ma,' he'd tell me. I never could get him to understand that if someone's crossed the line, it would catch up to them in the end. That faking things, doing something wrong in the name of right, wasn't the way to go." She passed Duncan his handkerchief and looked in his face. She blinked tears from her eyes. "Of course, the same goes for whoever killed him."

Duncan folded the square of fabric. "Yes, ma'am. It does."

* * *

Around ten o'clock, Sally entered the temporary office of Dunphy & Associates in downtown Uniontown. *Associates,* Sally thought. *There's a pleasant title.* As far as Sally knew, Kim hadn't brought on any staff. Planning for the future or clever marketing? Sally couldn't decide and it didn't really matter.

Kim and Angela were waiting for her in a small room, a table big enough for six wedged into the space. Steaming to-go cups were in front of both women and a third waited for Sally. "I seem to recall you like a touch of cream and sugar," Kim said, nodding at the cup.

Sally sat. "Thanks. How much do I owe you?"

Kim waved it off. "For today's agenda, I want to focus on our rebuttal argument. I've spoken to the prosecution and I have an offer from them. It's as I expected. The argument is that you, Angela, finally lashed out after years of abuse and things went too far."

"An offer of what?" Angela asked, cup halfway to her lips.

"A plea bargain agreement," Sally said, by way of clarification. "What is it?"

Kim pushed over a sheet of paper. "Voluntary manslaughter, fifteen years, with the possibility of parole."

Angela's hand trembled and coffee sloshed out of the cup. "Fifteen years?"

Sally snorted. "I hope you didn't tell them yes."

Kim laughed and took a sip of coffee. "I said I'd present the offer to my client."

"The answer is no," Sally said. She paused. "That was a bit presumptive on my part. Let me rephrase. My advice is the answer should be no."

Angela blotted up the brown spill in front of her. "What other choice do I have?"

"Well, that's what we're here to talk about." Kim opened her laptop, a word-processing program, and created a new file. "You, Angela, have a few options. We can take the deal as offered."

"I don't want to go to jail." Angela bit her lip. "I didn't do anything."

Sally covered the woman's hand with hers. "This is the opening salvo. We can make a counter-offer."

"Or we can go to trial," Kim said. She set aside her cup. "If we decide to do that, we have the problem that we can't verify your alibi. Think. Did you speak to *anyone* while you were in the park?"

"No. I was trying to rest."

Kim blew out a breath. "Not good, but it also means the prosecution can't prove you *weren't* there. So. We need to present options. Who else could have murdered Ryan?"

"Do we have to show it's true?" Angela asked.

Kim typed. "No. The burden of proof is on the prosecution. But if we can introduce a different narrative, it may create reasonable doubt in the minds of the jury members. Reasonable doubt is good."

Angela continued to look perplexed, so Sally elaborated. "The prosecution has to make the case you are the guilty party and the jury can only convict if they believe, beyond a reasonable doubt, that you did in fact commit the crime. If they have any doubt at all, they must acquit. What Kim is saying is that if we can show that it's possible someone else killed your husband, we introduce that doubt."

Angela wadded up the damp napkin. "They'd find me innocent?"

Kim kept typing. "They'd find you not guilty. It's not the same as innocent. It means the prosecution didn't do their job well enough." She looked up. "First task. Who else had a motive to kill Ryan? Did he have enemies?"

Both attorneys looked at Angela, who flushed. "Ryan was, well, he was a jerk. I don't know of anybody who liked him. Debbie, our neighbor, argued with him all the time."

"The woman without pants?" Kim asked as she resumed typing.

"She lives on the other side of our duplex," Angela replied. "I don't know what you mean about her not having pants."

"Never mind, it's not important." Sally shot a stern glance at Kim. "What did they argue about?"

"You name it," Angela said. "He said she left her trash on our side of the porch. She said he threw snow on her walkway during the winter. He said she parked on our side of the lawn. The list was endless."

"Domestic squabbles," Kim said. She didn't look up. "Not the greatest suspect because she'd have to get into the house, but it establishes the fact Ryan wasn't agreeable. Who else?"

"I don't know." Angela picked at her cup. "He didn't talk much about work. I mean, he'd complain about things, but he didn't tell me details. From his stories, I can't imagine he was any more popular there than he was in the neighborhood."

Angela's words dragged up a memory for Sally. "You said Ryan often bragged about doing favors for Caroline Longchamp. What kind of favors?"

Angela shrugged. "He didn't say, at least not that I heard. I didn't pay much attention."

Kim had not stopped her work. "And because they talked at the company you'll never know."

"There was that time she came to the house, but I didn't ask him about it."

"Still, you—" Kim stopped. "Wait, Caroline came to your house?"

"Yes, at least twice and maybe more."

Kim groaned and buried her face in her hands.

Angela chewed her lip. "Did I say something wrong?"

Kim's words were muffled by her hands. Sally was grateful because whatever Kim was saying couldn't be polite. She hadn't been keen to take this case in the first place and now Angela was making things more difficult than they needed to be and in more ways than one.

Sally patted Angela's arm. "No, not exactly. But Angela, you have to stop hiding information. Or if not hiding it, exactly, failing to disclose it. Like with the threat you made against Ryan. These are the kinds of things that drive defense attorneys to drink and make it difficult to construct an argument."

"Well, I'm telling you now, isn't that okay?" Angela looked from Sally to Kim and back.

Kim's muttering continued.

"Better late than never." Sally reached for pen and legal pad. "Caroline Longchamp came to your home. When?"

"Let me see." Angela's forehead creased as she thought. "The first time I remember seeing her was three weeks ago, maybe four. She and Ryan were standing in the front yard, talking. Caroline said something like, 'Get him off our backs.' I'm not entirely sure because Ryan cut off the conversation when he saw me."

Three weeks would have been right before Mike Brower and Carl Ritchie ended up in the river. Sally jotted some notes. "When was the second time?"

"Geez, a week ago? Give or take a couple days."

"How many days before Ryan was killed?"

There was a beat of silence as Angela thought. "Two or three, I suppose."

Kim had finally lifted her head, but she motioned Sally to continue.

"Did you hear what they talked about that time?"

Angela's hair swung as she shook her head. "No, but Ryan was angry. I could tell. He gets this expression when he's pissed, real mean. Mrs. Longchamp yelled at him. 'We had a deal!' Then Ryan grinned and said, 'You know the movie line. I'm altering the deal.'"

Kim spoke. "What did Mrs. Longchamp say?"

Angela looked at her. "Nothing, she stomped away. She slammed her car door, though, so I guess she wasn't happy."

"What kind of car?" Sally asked.

"It was big and blue, that's all I could tell," Angela replied.

Sally shared a look with Kim. Both visits were significant. The first made it look like Caroline had asked Ryan to at least talk to the men from the Casselman Water Protection Society, if not more. The second intimated that something had happened between Caroline and her employee, some kind of deal, and Ryan reneged. If the deal involved killing Brower and Ritchie, it gave Caroline Longchamp motive.

Again, Angela's gaze darted between the two lawyers. "Is that all?"

"It's enough to get us started," Kim said. "But you've got to promise us something."

"Anything. What?"

Kim resumed typing. "Stop keeping information from us, please." She shot a pointed look at Sally. "I really don't need my job to be any harder than it already is."

Chapter Forty-One

Duncan showed the Browers out of the barracks, then returned to the conference room. "That was an illuminating visit."

Foster taped up the box and affixed an evidence sheet to it. "Brower didn't stop at dummying up some data, he went all in. Or was going to, if this stuff proves to be what we think it is." She noted the time and date on the sheet.

"That kind of passion never came through when I talked to him," Duncan said, hooking his thumbs in his belt. "I mean, I could tell he was gung-ho about the area. But not that he would stoop to environmental sabotage."

"Just like PETA, going a little too far in pursuit of a worthy cause." Foster peeled off her gloves.

Before Duncan could respond, another trooper entered and handed him a sheet of paper then left.

Duncan read it, then went over to the whiteboard, which held the columns of information from his last brainstorming session with Foster. "Report from forensics," he said and handed her the sheet.

She scanned the text. "What does it say?"

He wrote at the bottom of Ryan Stewart's column in all caps. "The blood in the truck is human." He put down the marker and faced Foster.

"Stewart met up with our victims. They may or may not have talked, but it ended with two bodies in the back of that truck. Do you think they were alive?"

"Doesn't matter. They both ended up dead in the end."

"True." Foster stared at the board. "I don't see Stewart doing this on his own. Everything we've learned about him points to a 'what's in it for me?' kind of guy."

"He'd lose his job if Laurel Mountain shut down," Duncan said.

"Who cares? I mean, not like he was the CFO or on the board. He was a grunt. He could get another job at another company doing pretty much the same thing."

Duncan reviewed her words. It made sense. Losing employment was never nothing, but was working as a low-level manual laborer worth killing over? It didn't make sense. As Foster pointed out, it wasn't like he was a company director or even a manager. An idea struck. "Caroline Longchamp."

"What about her?"

"Wouldn't you say she had a lot to lose? CEO of the company, one her grandfather founded and she rescued. That means money, as well as personal pride. That would be worth killing over in my book."

Foster nibbled an already short fingernail. "Except she wasn't at the scene the day Stewart died. Not positively. All we have is a nebulous description of a gray-haired woman in a blue Suburban."

Duncan picked up his hat and headed for the door. "Then let's make it a little more concrete."

* * *

Duncan and Foster were halfway to Markleton when his phone rang. "Duncan," he said.

"It's Andy from tech. Mike Brower's computer was a cesspit of random information, but we finally broke through."

"Hold on, let me put you on speaker." Duncan tapped the icon. "Cesspit how? Porn?"

"Nah, nothing like that. Tons of spam, emails from environmental activist groups, adverts from outdoor equipment companies. So much garbage to sift through."

Foster identified herself. "What kind of activist groups?"

"Some benign, some not so much," said Andy. "A couple that are right on the border of enviro-terrorists. You know the ones, 'do anything to save the trees,' that kind of crap. Anyway, I found an email exchange between the two victims."

"Brower and Ritchie?" Duncan asked. "Not surprising. They worked together."

"Yeah, but Brower tried real hard to get rid of this chain," said Andy. "Good ol' internet, though."

"Once it's out there, it never goes away," Duncan said. "What did the exchange say?"

"Brower was hot on Laurel Mountain Quarrying. Specifically, determined to make them close up shop at all costs."

"We know he dummied up data, and Brower's parents turned in a box of what looks like polluted water. We aren't sure what he intended to do with it, though," said Foster.

"I can clarify that. He told his partner," added Andy. "That's what the email exchange is about. Brower said he was going to do a 'controlled dispersal' of some chemical. That way he could collect samples elsewhere to show the pollution. Ritchie objected, said it wasn't ethical, and whatever the feeling on Laurel Mountain, it didn't make deliberate pollution right. Brower accused Ritchie of going soft, Ritchie said he'd go to the authorities, the whole thing devolved into swearing and threats pretty quickly."

"Thanks, Andy. Send paper copies of those emails to the barracks, will you?" Duncan asked.

"You got it." Andy ended the call.

Duncan tapped the steering wheel. "That seals it. Was that why Ritchie and Brower were together? Trying to resolve this argument?"

"And that might be why Longchamp went after both men," said Foster, as she stared out the window at the fields zipping past. "Ten to one she only knew about the pollution plan, not that Brower was solely responsible and Ritchie wanted no part of it. I still don't get Brower's hang-up on LMQ. They weren't polluting."

"We've been wondering why Ritchie would have been targeted." Duncan glanced at her. "Brower didn't like industry, period. If there wasn't a legitimate reason for the government to shut them down, seems like he was willing to manufacture one."

Foster looked at her notes. "Makes sense. We still need to find out whether Longchamp knew anything about the murders." She glanced at Duncan. "Can't you drive any faster?"

Duncan pressed down on the accelerator. "Are you always this much of an armchair driver?"

Foster grinned. "Only when I can get away with it."

But they might as well have saved themselves the drive. Of the people at home in Stewart's neighborhood, no one remembered seeing anything beyond the SUV. A couple thought they'd seen a woman. They were going to have to verify Caroline Longchamp's presence some other way.

Chapter Forty-Two

Sunday afternoon, the sun beat down on Sally and Jim as they wandered hand-in-hand along the walkway next to the Yough River near Ohiopyle Falls. The torrential rains of three weeks ago were a memory and the river levels had returned to normal. Down the river, safely past the falls, kayakers navigated the water. Above the rumble of the cascades were the cries and yells of the summer adventure seekers who thronged Ohiopyle. Sally felt the sweat trickle down between her shoulder blades and fantasized about jumping into the river, rapids be damned.

She glanced at Jim. He'd come home last night in a foul mood and hadn't been disposed to talk about it. Sally could guess why. The case against Angela Stewart was crumbling, and she could only surmise he and Foster were unable to put it back together, which meant they once again had three murders and no viable suspects. It was enough to make any cop cranky. She wondered if they'd discovered the connection between Ryan Stewart and Caroline Longchamp, but that subject was taboo.

He was a little more forthcoming about Mike Brower and his plot against Laurel Mountain Quarrying. Sally shaded her eyes as she surveyed the crowds in the state park. "I can't believe Mike would endanger all this to get rid of one mining company. Was he that much of a fanatic?"

Jim leaned on the railing above the river. "He wouldn't have hurt the Yough or anything in Ohiopyle. I'm not even sure how much real damage he would have done to the Casselman. I don't think his plans were that big. The lab guys haven't gotten back to us about what's in those test tubes. My best guess is he planned on some kind of limited action, something that would temporarily raise the dust levels in the Casselman area where the EPA and DEP would focus their attention. The source of the pollutant would be traced back to LMQ and the company would either face stiff fines or legal action. Or so he hoped. I'm not sure it even would have worked."

"Which would shut them down?"

"Maybe he hoped it would."

"Did Caroline know?"

He turned from the railing. "Not sure. Brower definitely sent her a report from CWPS and that was almost certainly faked. I can't say anything else."

Sally recognized the dodge. He knew more, but he wasn't going to tell her. She let it pass. "And Carl knew?"

"That's what the email said." Jim took her hand. "Are you going to tell me your ulterior motive for today's little jaunt?"

The question didn't really surprise her. She'd never been able to pull the wool over his eyes. But she gave it a shot. "What ulterior motive? You seemed down in the dumps last night. I figured a day out in the park by the river, maybe a nice dinner with me would cheer you up."

His mouth twitched. "I can see you planning a romantic dinner. But a day at Ohiopyle? Sally, you've come a long way since we've been together, but you still aren't my definition of an outdoors person. A trip to Fallingwater, yes. A day spent roaming Ohiopyle State Park? Please. What's your angle?"

"Being outdoors makes you happy. I prefer having you in a good mood, so I'm willing to make the sacrifice. Can't you leave it at that?"

"Uh huh." He surveyed the crowd. "You're still trying to find someone who saw Angela Stewart the day her husband was murdered."

"No comment." She looked away. Damn. He was simply too perceptive for games.

"Don't worry, I'm not going to push on you over that." He nodded toward a tree in the middle of the park. "It's hot as hell out here. Let's grab a seat in the shade and rest a bit."

They wandered over to the tree, circling a pair of young men playing Frisbee. The plastic disc sailed over them and landed on a man lying face down on a blanket. The man sat up and threw the Frisbee, along with a selection of epithets unfit for the ears of the children running through the grass.

The Frisbee landed at Jim's feet and he bent to pick it up.

The young man closest to them approached. "God, what is with people? What moron expects to take a nap in a crowded outdoor park?"

Jim cracked a smile and sent the Frisbee sailing back to the man's waiting friend with an expert flick of his wrist. "No expectation of privacy in a public space."

"I know, right?" The young man brushed hair off his forehead. "Yet that's the second time it's happened lately."

Sally's ears perked up. "Second time?"

"Yeah, the last time it was a woman. She said she had a migraine and was trying to rest. Good luck with that." The man waved at the people. "Between the heat, the noise, and the crowds, this is a sucktastic spot to try and sleep off a headache."

Beside her, Jim tensed. Sally knew he'd understood the importance of the young man's words and how it related to Angela, but she continued. "When was this?"

The young man turned wary. "Uh, no offense, but I gotta go." He took a step.

"Wait, please." Sally glanced at the other player. "This is important. My name is Sally Castle. I'm with the Fayette County public defender's office."

The young man raised his eyebrows. "Public defender, like lawyer? Oh no. Now I'm really outta here."

Desperation rose in Sally's chest. "Yes, I'm a defense attorney. You could really help me out and keep an innocent woman out of jail."

"No can do, lady. Sorry. Last thing I need on top of summer college classes is to get mixed up in a legal mess."

Sally fired her last shot. "I could subpoena you."

"You can try, but you don't know my name. Don't ask. I'm not giving you that, either. Bye." He jogged off to join his friend. They hightailed it out of the park without a backwards glance.

Sally watched them go, her hopes for Angela's defense trailing behind them. "Damn it!"

Jim put his arm around her shoulders. "Ah, today's youth. What fine, upstanding young men. More concerned about the impact on him than a woman's freedom."

"It's a big deal. He could have corroborated…" She wiped her forehead. "Never mind. You know." She flopped down on the grass and Jim settled in next to her. "You gonna tell Foster about that?"

"Relax, Counselor." He gave her a lopsided grin. "I will let Trooper Foster know what I heard, which, admittedly, is not much. What she does with it is her business." The grin faded. "Caroline Longchamp and Ryan Stewart. I've already found out enough that I want to question her again. Does Angela know anything about her? Have you considered a deal where she testifies to her late husband's involvement with the deaths of Mike Brower and Carl Ritchie in exchange for…something?" He waited. "Let me guess, no comment."

Sally's laugh was half-hearted. "I'll take the information to Kim and we'll discuss it." She leaned against Jim's shoulder. "Sometimes I hate our jobs."

He kissed her head. "I know."

Chapter Forty-Three

When Duncan left roll call Monday morning, he saw Foster waiting. She held two to-go cups from Starbucks and a sheet of paper. She handed him a coffee. "Good morning. I hope you like it strong and black. The desk trooper said the paper is for you."

"Perfect." He took the cup. "You didn't come here to give me coffee."

"No, I didn't." She went into the conference room, where the whiteboard of notes was exactly as they'd left it. "Our canvassing finally paid off. I have a witness who not only saw the Suburban but got a plate number. LMQ-15. I've already confirmed that every Laurel Mountain vehicle's plate number starts with 'LMQ.' This plate belongs to the fifteenth vehicle registered in the Laurel Mountain fleet."

"And the woman?"

"Same witness was able to provide a better description and it's a dead-on match for Caroline Longchamp." Foster added the information to the whiteboard and circled it. "Also, the request for Laurel Mountain's finances came through. Caroline Longchamp withdrew five thousand dollars cash a few days after Ritchie and Brower were found and another five the day before Stewart was killed."

Duncan gave a low whistle.

"Did we get the analysis results of that blood found in the truck?"

He glanced at the paper. "Funny you should ask. The full battery of tests isn't complete, but there are two distinct blood types. Just so happens they are a match for both our victims."

Foster tossed the marker on the table. "I think we need another visit with

Ms. Longchamp."

On the way to Laurel Mountain, Duncan filled Foster in on what he'd learned yesterday at Ohiopyle.

"But he didn't identify Angela Stewart?"

"No. But if I were the prosecution, I wouldn't want to hear him talk about any woman with a headache in the park on the witness stand. Even if he couldn't make a positive ID."

"You know what lawyers say. Don't ask a question if you don't know the answer."

Duncan shrugged. "Pretty sure this defense team would get their answer beforehand. And it would blow the case against Angela Stewart right out of the water. In front of a jury."

"Or not. However…"

"Yes?" Duncan prompted.

"It does raise that pesky reasonable doubt."

"Yes, it does." He studied her. "Are you going to talk to the DA?"

"Right after we visit with Longchamp." She flipped on the turn signal and shot him a sideways look. "What were you doing looking into Angela's alibi?"

"I wasn't. I was hoodwinked." He deliberately focused on the road ahead.

"By?"

"Ms. Castle. I gather she's working with Kim Dunphy, Angela's lawyer. She suggested a trip to Ohiopyle 'to relax and unwind.' Except she was also looking for someone to corroborate Angela's statement. She's been trying to do that for a while. I should have seen it coming."

"Ms. Castle, huh? A cop dating a defense lawyer." Foster clicked her tongue. "How do you even make that work?"

Duncan could hear the curtness in his voice when he answered. "We have rules."

Foster must have heard it, too, and dropped the topic.

They spoke very little about the case until they pulled into the parking lot at Laurel Mountain Quarrying. After Foster turned the car off, she stared at the main building. "All right, how are we going to play this?"

"I'm never a fan of the full-frontal assault. It makes suspects clam up. I suggest a more sideways approach."

Foster tapped the steering wheel. "Let her know we have more information and invite her to explain it?"

"That's my advice."

"I like it. Let's go."

* * *

Monday morning, Sally met Kim and Angela in the Somerset County courthouse lobby. Kim looked unflappable, her red hair swept back into a stylish chignon, her dark blue jacket and skirt so expertly pressed it must have come straight from the cleaners. Angela had the anxious, ruffled look of most defendants. She'd clearly tried her best. Her shirt and skirt were clean, but a couple years out of style. She'd brushed her hair back and applied some makeup, but either she'd not used lipstick or she'd already chewed it off.

Chewed it off, Sally thought as she saw Angela worrying her lower lip. Her hand came up to pick at the peeled skin and Sally gently brushed it away. "Don't do that. I know this is hard and you have to be a bundle of nerves."

"You can say that again," Angela said in a wavery voice.

"I won't tell you to relax, because that's impossible. I will tell you to *act* relaxed. Confident. You have a damn fine attorney on your side—"

"Two damn fine attorneys," Kim cut in.

Sally permitted herself a smile. "Kim and I have done this a dozen times. The prosecutor is going to try and make you think he has all the answers. He'll hit you hard. Kim and I are going to hit right back. Your job is to be quiet and not be goaded into saying anything. We've got this." She looked at Kim. "Nice suit. I thought red was the power color, though."

Kim winked. "Check out the shoes."

Sally looked down. Deep red Louboutins with three-inch heels. "Nice. You ready?"

Kim looked at Angela. "You sure you don't want the deal?"

A little of Angela's nervousness fled and her face calmed. "Yes."

Kim squared her shoulders. "Then let's do this."

***

The troopers made their way to the lobby, where they presented themselves to the receptionist. After producing their IDs, Foster said, "We're here to talk to Caroline Longchamp."

The receptionist consulted her computer. "I don't see an appointment on her calendar."

"We don't have one," Duncan said. "But I'm sure she'll make time for us. Tell her it's about the murders of Mike Brower and Carl Ritchie."

The young woman paled. "Um, okay. She's in a meeting, but…hold on a moment." She picked up the phone and dialed an extension. "Uh, Frank? Sorry to interrupt, but, um, there are two state troopers here to see Ms. Longchamp. They don't have an appointment, but they tell me it's about those two murdered men from CWPS. Yeah. Yeah. Okay, I'll tell them." She replaced the receiver. "Ms. Longchamp says she'll be out in a minute. If you'd have a seat over there." She indicated two chairs and a small couch grouped around a low table cluttered with magazines.

The troopers sat. Around them, the lobby was eerily quiet, enough that Duncan could hear the faint clacking of the computer keyboard as the receptionist typed. The scent of mountain laurel from a drooping bouquet on the table lingered in the air. It wasn't too long before a staccato beat of high heels broke the silence. Both troopers stood.

Caroline Longchamp appeared from an adjacent hallway. "Trooper Foster and Trooper Duncan, correct? Why don't we talk in my office. Follow me." Her words were as brisk as her footsteps as she led them down another hallway to a mid-sized executive office. The room only held a modest wood desk, a leather executive chair, and two armchairs, but the view out of the windows that made up much of one wall was stunning. Mountainsides covered with lush green trees dappled with shade from the clouds overhead stretched for as far as Duncan could see. A pair of hawks glided overhead, cruising on the thermals. It was a vista the people who built homes in the Laurel Highlands would pay a million dollars for.

"Nice view," Foster said as she took a seat.

"Thank you." Longchamp seated herself behind her desk. "I find it incredibly soothing in all seasons. It also reminds me of the importance of conducting my business in a responsible fashion."

Foster glanced at Duncan. "Which is why Mike Brower's claims upset you so much, I'm sure."

"Indeed." Longchamp waved her hand at the second chair. "Please, Trooper Duncan. Have a seat."

"As someone who enjoys being outdoors, I'm incredibly jealous," he said as he sat. "People pay a lot of money to look at that."

"Yes, they do." Longchamp folded her hands. "Enough about the scenery. My time is valuable, and I'm certain yours is as well. What can I do for you?"

Foster removed her notebook from her pocket and made a show of flipping pages. "We've gathered some additional information and it's raised a few more questions. We hoped you could answer them."

"I'd be glad to try."

Foster read. "It has come to our attention that Mike Brower was doubling down on his allegations of dust pollution. The ones in that report you shared with Trooper Duncan. All indications are that he was going to release pollutant into the water that would have resulted in higher readings that could be used to force the EPA and DEP to investigate."

Longchamp frowned. "I find that hard to believe. What kind of pollutant?"

Duncan answered. "We aren't sure yet. The materials are with our lab for analysis. Why don't you believe it?"

Longchamp spread her hands. "I argued with Mr. Brower on several occasions, but I never doubted his commitment to the environment. I can't believe he would risk causing damage simply to bring down Laurel Mountain Quarrying. He hated industry and wanted to close every company he could. He made that clear. But I thought he loved the environment more than he disliked us."

Duncan studied her face for signs of dissembling. "We have email communication between Mr. Brower and Mr. Ritchie that confirms the plan."

"I'm, well, I'm shocked, to be blunt."

"You didn't know about this?"

"Absolutely not." Longchamp's voice was indignant, and two spots of color appeared on her cheeks. "If I'd known I would have notified the proper authorities immediately."

Foster consulted her notebook. "Had the plan gone ahead, and if the resulting governmental audits found increased levels of dust or whatever, what would have been the consequences to Laurel Mountain?"

The red in Longchamp's face receded. "It depends. It may have meant nothing more than time for remediation followed by another inspection. I suppose LMQ could have been fined if the agencies felt it was appropriate."

"Would it have shut down your company?" Foster asked.

"That's extremely unlikely." Longchamp rose, went to a sideboard, and removed a bottle of water from the mini-fridge. "Would you like some water?" Both troopers demurred and she returned to her seat. "It has been many years since this company failed an environmental inspection. I don't think one black mark would close our doors."

Foster remained quiet, and Duncan took over. "At one point, we asked you if you knew Ryan Stewart and you said his name was vaguely familiar."

Longchamp raised her bottle. "Yes, that's correct."

"Since then we've learned he drove you around in the company Suburban, your preferred vehicle, a couple of times. Other employees have spoken of your ability to remember names and faces. In fact, one of them said once you met someone, you never forgot them again. That doesn't quite sync with your statement."

For the first time, Longchamp's poise faltered. She took a drink of water. "Come to think of it, you're right. I do remember Ryan. I'm sorry. Yes, he'd been my driver on a couple of occasions. A little rough around the edges, but a good man."

"His wife said he boasted on a regular basis of doing favors for you," Duncan added.

"Well, yes." Another pause, another sip. "I did ask him to do things once or twice."

"Like talk to Mike Brower? Smooth this whole incident over and get him to retract his allegations?"

"Of course, not, I'd…well, I'd never do that…delegate a task like…I'd prefer to talk to Mr. Brower personally." Longchamp stuttered as she spoke, now clearly flustered. The blush returned to her cheeks.

Duncan exchanged a look with Foster. *Not time to spring the witness statement,* she seemed to telegraph. He continued. "What about Carl Ritchie?"

"I never spoke to him," Longchamp said, now eyeing Foster and then the door.

* * *

Sally and Kim flanked their client as they entered the DA's office. After they were shown to a conference room, they took seats on one side of the table. The receptionist offered them beverages, which they declined, then left.

"What's taking so long?" Angela asked, gaze darting around the room.

"They're making us wait," Kim said. She opened her briefcase and removed a pad and pen. She laid them on the table in front of her, next to her phone.

"Why?"

Sally patted Angela's shoulder. "They're trying to throw us off our game. It's a simple trick and one we aren't going to fall for."

"Are they going to make us wait all morning? It's been ages."

Kim consulted her phone. "It's been five minutes. It only seems longer." She turned to Angela. "The assistant DA we're going to be seeing is Michael Bonarotti."

"Do you know him?" Sally asked, taking out her own pad and pen.

"By reputation. My old firm handled a case down here last year. He's not the worst assistant DA we could have pulled, that's for sure. He's smart and can play hardball with the best of them. But he's not so full of himself he treats opposing counsel like lesser beings. He'll keep us on our toes, but he'll be fair." The door cracked open. "Here he is." She stood and so did Sally, who tugged Angela into a standing position.

The minute Michael Bonarotti entered the room, Sally knew he was an opponent to be respected. His charcoal gray suit, with subtle pinstripes, white shirt, and red power tie broadcast an unmistakable message of being in charge and confident. The creases on his pants were so sharp they could have cut butter. "Ladies, sorry to keep you waiting." Even his voice—a strong, mellifluous bass—added to his image. "Please, sit down."

They sat.

Bonarotti took his own seat, clicked open his briefcase, and nodded to Kim and Sally. "Ms. Dunphy. Ms. Castle, I've seen your picture in stories out of Fayette County. You do good work. But I'm surprised to see you here. The defendant hasn't engaged a public defender for representation and this is Somerset County."

"Thank you for the compliment. I've heard good things about you as well." He didn't have to know she'd heard them from Kim two minutes ago. She folded her hands. "I'm assisting Ms. Dunphy with Mrs. Stewart's defense, especially since Mrs. Stewart first came to me for advice."

"I see." Bonarotti uncapped an ebony fountain pen. "On to business. I assume we are here to discuss the plea agreement offered by this office."

"It's going to be a short discussion." Kim inclined her head toward Angela. "Mrs. Stewart doesn't want the deal."

Bonarotti tapped his pen on the table. "What if I offered man two, probation after eighteen months?"

"What, saying that after suffering years of abuse, her actions were understandable?"

He nodded.

Kim shot a look at Angela, who gave her head a small shake. "The answer is still no, sorry," Kim replied.

He laid down the pen. "You're determined to go to trial? You must like your chances."

"We do," said Sally. "Mrs. Stewart has an alibi."

He offered a slight smile. "Which cannot be corroborated."

"We think it can." Sally watched as his face sobered. "In addition, we are prepared to offer additional information, including witnesses, to show that another person is responsible for Ryan Stewart's death."

"What kind of information? Who's the witness?"

Kim wagged a finger. "You know the way it works, Mr. Bonarotti. You'll find out in due time."

This time, the smile was fully-fledged. "I've heard about you, Ms. Dunphy. I have to say, the stories don't do you justice."

Kim gave him an exaggerated wink. "Wait until you see me in action in the courtroom."

This time, he laughed. "I half wish I could." He sat forward. "Let me be blunt. My boss doesn't want this going to trial. The optics, as they say, are horrendous. Prosecuting a battered wife? You've got to be kidding me. So let's get down to it. What do you want?"

Sally glanced at Kim. "We want the charges dropped. Angela Stewart did not kill her husband. You're barking up the wrong tree. If we have to go to trial to prove that, so be it."

At that moment, the door opened and another man stuck his head in. "Michael?"

A shadow of annoyance crossed Bonarotti's face. "Not now, Jeff. I'm busy."

"Uh, it's important and related to what you're working on here."

"Can't it wait?"

"No. You're gonna want to hear this."

Bonarotti stood and tugged his suit coat down. "Excuse me, ladies. This won't take long." He left and shut the door.

"What are they talking about?" Angela asked, her voice about an octave higher and charged with tension.

"It's a tactic. Nothing more." Kim sat back and crossed her arms.

Sally wasn't so sure. Bonarotti's annoyance was genuine. She had no doubt the Somerset County DA wanted a swift, quiet end to the Stewart case. As Bonarotti had pointed out, the political consequences of going to trial were high. No politician, and a district attorney had to be a politician to succeed, wanted to be known as the man who tried a battered wife for murder. "I think it might be more than a ploy, Kim," she said. "I'm sure Bonarotti can play games, but not this time.

Kim tapped her fingers on her arm. Then she leaned forward. "This is a mistake. You should take the deal."

Emotions played across Angela's face—shock, surprise, fear. "But I didn't do it."

"Look, Sally's statement was a bluff. We don't have someone to corroborate your alibi." Kim waved off Sally's attempt to speak and continued. "Yeah, the guy said he saw a woman sleeping. But he refused to say it was you. That means Bonarotti will argue it could have been anyone."

"But—"

"No 'buts.' Angela, listen to me. If we go to trial and you're convicted, it'll be a lot longer sentence. Maybe the rest of your life. Is that really what you want to do?

Angela turned a pleading look at Sally. "What do you think?"

Sally paused. She knew what she wanted to say, but Kim had a point. They had a lot of supposition. They would present it to the jury and sell the hell out of the story, hoping twelve men and women would buy it and decide the prosecution's case wasn't strong enough, not beyond a reasonable doubt. But it would be a risk. "Angela, it's up to you. I think we could go to court. Kim thinks otherwise. You have to decide how much risk you want to take because nothing is guaranteed."

Angela's mouth worked, but no words came out. Her frantic gaze traveled between both lawyers, a rat trapped in a maze desperately seeking a way out.

Except there wasn't one.

Chapter Forty-Four

Duncan looked at Foster and gave a tiny nod. *Now.*

"Ms. Longchamp," Foster said, once again turning a page in her notebook. "A witness identified your Suburban at Ryan Stewart's home on the day he was murdered. The same witness described the driver, a description that matches you. On the day in question, you were out with an employee, but he says there was a time you were on your own. Enough time for you to drive to Markleton. Isn't that so?"

In a flash, Longchamp paled. Her hand trembled as she set down the water bottle. "Why on earth would I drive to Ryan Stewart's house?"

"You tell us."

Longchamp didn't answer.

Duncan took over again. "In addition, we found blood of the same type as Mike Brower and Carl Ritchie in the Laurel Mountain truck we took into evidence a couple days ago. The man in charge of your vehicle fleet said Ryan Stewart took that truck out and failed to return the keys." He paused. "It was the same day Mike Brower and Carl Ritchie ended up in the Casselman River, murdered."

The silence stretched out. Longchamp looked at her hands. She seemed to have aged twenty years as Duncan spoke.

"Ms. Longchamp?" he asked, keeping his voice calm.

She took a shuddering breath and wilted, all of the fire bleeding out of her. Outside the window, the hawks continued their swooping dance. "He was only supposed to talk to them," she finally said, voice almost a whisper.

"He who?" Foster asked. "Ryan Stewart?"

"Yes." Longchamp clenched her hands. "He and I were speaking one day while he was driving me, where I don't remember. Chitchat about the company and I mentioned the threats from CWPS. I said something about how tiresome the whole deal was. Ryan asked if I'd spoken to Mr. Brower and I said yes, several times, but to no productive end. He offered to give it a try. 'I'd be happy to take a shot, Ms. Longchamp. Man to man, maybe that'd make a difference,' he said. I was grateful. I said he could, but I doubted he'd get anywhere." She stopped and closed her eyes.

"What happened?" Duncan prompted.

"When I read the stories in the paper, first the John Doe in the Casselman and Mr. Ritchie's accident, then how the John Doe was Mr. Brower, I confronted Ryan. He couldn't see why I was upset. 'CWPS isn't going to bother you ever again.' Then he said I owed him for services rendered, as he called it. He demanded ten thousand dollars."

"You gave it to him," Foster said. "And then he asked for more."

Longchamp opened her eyes. "Yes," she whispered. "I told him I wasn't going to keep paying him, that I couldn't. Not without raising suspicions. He told me that was my problem to solve. After all, he'd solved one for me. I owed him."

A company executive making idle conversation, talking about an annoyance. Stewart must have seen the opportunity to make a couple bucks on the side. Considering the brutal way Stewart treated his wife, Duncan had no problems envisioning the scene. Stewart confronting Brower, who told him exactly where to stick it. The meeting turned violent and Brower ended up dead. "What about Carl Ritchie? He wasn't part of your problems with CWPS. Why would Stewart target him?"

"I asked Ryan about that," Longchamp said, and rubbed her forehead. "The way I understand it, Mr. Ritchie interrupted when Ryan was…talking to Mr. Brower. He was, how do they put it? Collateral damage."

Of course. If Carl had witnessed Mike's murder, he'd have to go. Duncan remembered Carl's words from the hospital. Ryan, Mike, water. He'd seen the fight between Stewart and Brower over the water analysis.

Foster interrupted Duncan's thoughts. "You went to Stewart's house to pay him another thousand. What happened?"

Longchamp sighed, the light illuminating the lines on her face. Outside, one of the hawks dove. "I gave him the money and said that was it. I wouldn't give him any more. And if he continued to blackmail me, I'd have no choice but to go to the authorities and tell them what I knew. Whatever the personal cost. He, he *laughed* at me. He said he knew I'd never do it, I was too weak. That's why he took care of Mr. Brower. I was a figurehead CEO, unwilling to do what was necessary like a man would be. I needed him. I'd never turn him in."

"And then?" Foster asked, disgust written on her face.

Disgust with Longchamp or Stewart? Duncan didn't know, but he guessed the latter.

"I...snapped. He was standing there, laughing at me, jeering, putting me down. There was a trophy nearby and...I hit him with it. Again and again. I wanted him to stop. When I came to my senses, he was dead. I panicked. I dropped the trophy, ran out to my car, and left. I didn't think anyone had seen me."

Duncan frowned. "Then why weren't...of course. Angela Stewart came home, found her husband's body, and wiped down the trophy. It got rid of her fingerprints, but also yours." He paused, anger rising. "She was arrested for his murder. Were you going to let her take the fall?"

Tears ran down Longchamp's face. "No, of course not. I...I would have said something. In fact, the meeting I came out of when you arrived? That was with my CFO, arranging for oversight of the company while I was away. I intended to call you, but here you are." She wiped her cheeks. "And yes, I started this conversation pretending I didn't know anything and I have no explanation for that. Maybe I'm as weak as Ryan said I was." She paused. "What happens now?"

Foster stood and straightened her jacket. "Caroline Longchamp, I'm arresting you for the murders of Mike Brower, Carl Ritchie, and Ryan Stewart." She took out her handcuffs. "Do you want to call your attorney now, have him meet you at the booking center?"

Longchamp took a deep breath and stood. "Yes, I think I will."

* * *

Sally felt like they'd been sitting there forever. That Bonarotti had walked out ages ago, leaving them in stasis. Sally imagined seeing the scene on TV. One lawyer wanting to roll the dice, one wanting to take the safe play, and the client caught in the middle.

Before Angela could answer, the door opened. Bonarotti came in, along with the man from earlier. "Mrs. Stewart, please accept our deepest apologies." He swept up his papers and looked up. "Ms. Dunphy, Ms. Castle, this office will be filing a motion with the court this morning to ask for the dismissal of all charges."

The abrupt about face had enough impact to render Kim speechless. Sally recovered enough to ask, "May we know why?"

"Another suspect has confessed to the murder not only of Ryan Stewart, but two other men. Perhaps you've followed the story. Michael Brower and Carl Ritchie. An arrest has been made and I need to refocus my attention. Jeff here will see you out." Bonarotti nodded at them and left.

Jeff stood back and motioned for them to go. Outside, the blazing July sun beat down on them. The sultry smell of wilting summer flowers, interlaced with the scent of melting asphalt, overwhelmed them.

Kim slipped on her sunglasses. "Well, I'll be a monkey's uncle. That was totally unexpected."

"What does it mean?" Angela asked. "Do I have to go back to jail?"

"No," Sally said. "They're dismissing the charges. Your mother's bail money will be returned and you're free to go home. It's over."

Angela stared, dumbstruck. "But I don't understand. Why?"

"They arrested someone else, someone who confessed."

"But who?"

Kim broke into a wide grin. "Don't know, don't care. Come on ladies. Time to celebrate. After all, it's five o'clock somewhere."

Chapter Forty-Five

After Duncan and Foster got Caroline Longchamp booked and processed, they stood outside on the sidewalk in Somerset. Duncan was still a little taken aback at how quickly the cases had come to a close. Longchamp's attorney had met them at the booking station, where Longchamp had waived her rights under Miranda and repeated her statement as given in her office. Now that he was done, he felt a little bit of a let-down. Foster would continue, through the trial or whatever came next. But his part was over. Back to patrol, writing traffic citations, responding to domestics and bar brawls.

Shit.

"Well, that was different," Foster said as she pulled a pack of gum from her pocket. She held it out. "Want a piece?"

"No, thanks." He tried to process all his emotions, but only one kept coming back to him. Disappointment. His life and routine would go back to normal, each day slightly different than the one before, but basically the same. "You talking about her confession?"

"Yup." Foster popped a piece of gum in her mouth. "I expected her to try and weasel her way out of it. I think she was going to at first."

"When she played innocent? Maybe." He hooked his thumbs in his duty belt. "But really, she's not a killer. I mean, she is. She murdered those guys, although if her attorney is any good he's going to try and get a lower charge, I'm sure. Manslaughter for Stewart, I don't know what for Brower and Ritchie."

"Not our concern, but yeah, probably. And I'm okay with that. I think you're right. Maybe she's been feeling guilty all this time and we got there at the right moment and said the right things." She cocked her head. "Hey, are you okay? You look a bit out of whack, like you aren't quite sure what to do next."

"I kinda am. Well, existentially at least. I know what I'm going to do right at this moment."

"Get some lunch?"

He laughed. "Love to, but no. I'm going to get on back to Fayette-nam and get my butt back on patrol before I get yelled at."

"By your lieutenant? I thought he was okay with all this."

"No, not him. There's a corporal at my barracks who likes to bust my balls. I'd prefer not to give him the opportunity."

Foster stuck out a hand. "Well, it's been good working with you, Duncan."

They shook. "Same here. Maybe we'll see each other again some time. If you're ever out in Confluence, say hi."

"Will do. Oh, I almost forgot. I have something for you. Wait here." She jogged over to her car, pulled a bag out of the backseat, and returned. "I was going to give you this over lunch, but since you're passing up my generosity, here. I suggest you don't let your corporal catch you with it."

"What is it?" The bag held a good-sized bottle, that he was sure of. The plain brown paper, which was folded shut at the top and stapled, gave no hint as to what was inside.

"A bottle of twelve-year-old Macallan." Foster winked.

"Wow. What's that for?"

"Winning a wager."

"That's a hell of a payout." Duncan shook his head. "This is premature. I haven't made up my mind."

Foster slipped on a pair of RayBans. "No, it's not. Take care."

* * *

When Sally arrived at Jim's that evening, she followed the scent of charcoal into the backyard. Rizzo caught sight of her and bounded over to get her attention, but after a half a minute of rubbing, he returned to his owner, who stood at the grill. Smoke blew downwind, carrying a smell of smoked wood and seasoned beef. Her stomach grumbled and she realized the salad she'd had for lunch had been a long time ago.

Jim looked up. "Hey there. Hope you're hungry." He turned over the inch-thick steaks.

She came over and pecked his cheek. "All of a sudden I'm famished. How was your day?"

"It was…interesting. You?"

"Interesting is a good word."

He kissed her. "Why don't you go inside and get things ready while I finish up out here? We can eat and we'll talk about it."

Inside, Sally set the table, tossed together a salad, poured a glass of wine for her, and opened a bottle of beer for Jim. He came in as she set the bottle down, meat still sizzling. "Dinner is served."

Over the course of the meal, they shared the details of their respective days. Jim related the confession and subsequent arrest of Caroline Longchamp, and Sally told him of the meeting at the Somerset County courthouse with Kim and Angela. "That was you," she said. "Why that guy came and pulled Bonarotti out of our meeting."

"Well, not me personally, but yeah." He took a bite of steak. "Would Kim have gone to trial?"

Sally swirled her wine. "Yes. If that's what Angela decided. After all, she's the client. And Kim would have sold the story for all it was worth. She's a good attorney."

He paused and studied her. "Would you have gone with her?"

She took a drink. "Possibly."

They finished dinner without any further work day conversation. But after the table was cleared, dishes were done, and they'd retired to the porch with refilled drinks, Sally broached the subject again. "There's a brown paper bag, stapled shut, on the countertop. What's in it?"

"A bottle of whiskey. The good stuff."

"From whom?"

"Foster. She said she won her wager."

Sally had to think back and remember. "That you'd jump to Criminal Investigation? Did she? Did you?"

"Not yet." He studied the beer bottle as though it held the answer to every question known to man.

"Are you going to?" She sipped her wine.

"I'm mulling it over." He set down the bottle. "I won't lie to you. I enjoyed the hell out of investigating. It would be a new challenge and I think I'd like that. At the same time, well, I'm damn good at my current job. If I get promoted, there will be some new things to do. Nicols likes me. I like the people at the barracks. Such as McAllister."

"I know how you feel." She stared into the ruby-red depths of her wine.

"You made the deal with Kim, right? When are you going to put in your two weeks?"

"Probably tomorrow." She drained the glass.

He raised an eyebrow. "Why do I get the sense you aren't full of enthusiasm?"

Perceptive as always. "Same as you, I guess. Yes, the thought of being able to defend people like Angela Stewart is exciting. You know, someone who needs my help, but who doesn't qualify for it in my current position. At the same time, I'd be leaving people like Tanelsa and Doris. Bryan's been a good boss, a friend. It's a little…sad is the wrong word, but you know what I mean."

"I do." He sat back and looked at his empty street. "There's nothing for it. We both need to do what we have to do and get it done. Tomorrow. Like ripping off a Band-aid."

Yes, they did. As her father would say, "And the future will take care of itself."

Chapter Forty-Six

The following morning, Sally made two phone calls. The first was to her office to tell them she would be in at noon. The second was to Kim, to arrange a meeting at Panera.

When Sally entered the bakery, she didn't see Kim at first, but then noticed her in a far back corner. Sally waved to let Kim know she'd be there in a moment, then ordered a breakfast sandwich and a latte. She waited, claimed her coffee and food, then joined her friend. "Nice cozy spot you've chosen."

"I thought it appropriate considering our conversation." Kim sipped her coffee.

"Well, you did it." Sally picked up the sandwich. "How did it feel? Helping someone who really needed you."

"To be honest, pretty damn good. Facing down Bonarotti, that was something. Even if you and Angela were giving me heartburn, wanting to go to trial with such a flimsy case." Kim laughed and immediately sobered. "I'm not taking that kind of thing all the time, though. Someone's gotta pay and keep the lights on."

"Understood." Sally took a breath. "I'm going to turn in my notice when I get into work. Two weeks. Make sure I have a desk in that spiffy new office you've leased."

Kim said nothing, just drank her coffee. Then she set down the cup, leaned back in the booth, and crossed her arms. "No."

"No, I don't get a desk? That's harsh." Sally patted her lips with a napkin.

"Of course you get a desk. I'm talking about your two weeks."

"I have to give notice, Kim. I can't walk out on Bryan."

"You misunderstand. I'm canceling the deal."

It took Sally several seconds to process the words. She set down her breakfast. "But why? I mean, you held up your end. Did working with me make you realize you didn't want me as partner?"

"Hardly." Kim shook her hair back. "I want you more than ever. But I also need *you* to want it. I don't need you to join me out of a sense of obligation, because of some *quid pro quo*. You join me because you're ready for the next step in your career. From what you've said, well, it's pretty clear your heart isn't in it. You're saying the words you think I want to hear, but it's not what you really want."

No, it wasn't. Not yet. Sally didn't need an in-depth examination of her soul to know that. She didn't feel the jump to working with Kim was the right decision, at least not at the present moment. She wouldn't have complete control because she'd be half of a partnership. Still, a deal was a deal and Sally prided herself on keeping her word. "But I—"

"No buts. I make you jump now, you'll forever be looking over your shoulder at the past. Perhaps you'll be a little resentful over time. Both will affect your work. I can't afford that." Kim stood and pushed a business card across the table. "Call me when you're ready."

Sally looked at the card. Dunphy & Associates. "I've been demoted to associate?"

"I didn't have many of these printed. Only enough to get me off the ground."

"It may take a while for me to make that call." Sally pocketed the card.

Kim's answering grin was mischievous. "Don't worry. I'm patient."

* * *

The first person Duncan ran into before morning roll-call was McAllister. "Hey, Boss. Heard you had some excitement."

He looked at Nicols's closed door. "Little bit."

"Cracked another murder. This is getting to be a habit for you."

"I suppose."

She pointed at the paper in his hands. "What's that? You putting in for promotion like I said?"

He pulled his attention back to the younger trooper. "No. I've decided that path isn't for me." He heard Nicols's office door open. "Catch you later. I have to talk to the l-t. I promise I'll tell you all about it."

McAllister shrugged and walked away, a puzzled frown on her face.

Duncan knocked on the door frame. "Got a minute?"

Inside the office, Nicols was at his desk, reading a sheaf of reports. He set down the stack. "Come on in. Have a seat."

Duncan entered and closed the door, but he didn't sit. "This won't take long, sir."

"Oh? I gather you've made a decision. Good. You'll make a good corporal, Jim."

"Sorry, sir. You misunderstand me." Duncan set his folded paper on the desk. "I've decided not to pursue promotion. Not now."

Nicols raised his eyebrows. "Oh? Then what's this?" He reached for the folded paper.

"It's a posting for a trooper position in Criminal Investigation here in Troop B." Duncan met his lieutenant's eye. "I've decided to apply."

A Note from the Author

I pulled a lot of local environmental information for this story. The Casselman River has its headwaters in Maryland and flows for over fifty miles until it meets Laurel Hill Creek in Confluence. Both of these form the Yougiogheny (prounced Yock-a-gane-y), which eventually flows into the Mississippi. The Casselman was historically used for transportation from Baltimore and Washington, D.C., to Pittsburgh as a means of crossing the Allegheny Mountains.

There isn't a real Laurel Mountain Quarrying, but dust pollution in the river did threaten many forms of wildlife in the Casselman watershed, including small-mouth bass. Fortunately, remediation efforts from various environmental organizations have resulted in an increase of the small-mouth population, as well as increased water activities, including white-water rafting, along the river.

The northeastern bulrush (*scirpus ancistrochaetus*) really is rare. A wetlands plant, it likes variable water depths, including sinkhole ponds in sandstone bedrock. Since sandstone is a major part of the geology in Somerset County, it was the perfect flora candidate for this story.

For more information about the Laurel Highlands, please visit https://www.golaurelhighlands.com/

Acknowledgements

The fourth book. Who knew? As always thank you to my critique group, Annette Dashofy, Jeff Boarts, and Peter Hayes. I couldn't do this without them.

Endless gratitude to my proofreader, Kathy Deyell, for hunting typos and helping me look good.

I had several "technical advisors" on this book. Corporal Brian Carpenter of the Pennsylvania State Police provided me with information on the promotion procedure in the PSP, as well as how one goes about joining the Criminal Investigation division. Chuck van Keuren helped with how a public defender can stay involved in a case and the privilege rules around that. Chris Herndon provided critical forensic details on water exposure and drowning. Any errors in these areas are solely my own.

Social support is important to writing and this year has made those connections even more important. Huge thanks to Sisters in Crime and Pennwriters. In a year of loneliness, you made it a little less lonely.

Thank you to the wonderful team at Level Best Books – Harriette Sackler, Verena Rose, and Shawn Reilly-Simmons – who gave Jim and Sally a chance and a place to grow. I (and they) are forever grateful.

As always, thank you and much love to my husband, Paul, who has been my partner for the last 25 years in things big and small. I love you, babe.

About the Author

Liz Milliron is the author of **The Laurel Highlands Mysteries** series, set in the scenic Laurel Highlands of Southwestern Pennsylvania, and **The Home Front Mysteries**, set in Buffalo, NY, during the early years of World War II. She is a member of Sisters in Crime, Pennwriters, and International Thriller Writers. Now an empty-nester, Liz lives outside Pittsburgh with her husband and a retired-racer greyhound.

http://lizmilliron.com

Also by Liz Milliron